Thunder Road:
The Journey Home

Stuart Nicholls

Stuart L. Nicholls
Kula, Maui, Hawaii 96790

Copyright © 2012 by Stuart L. Nicholls

Cover Design and Book Design by Cheryl J. KauhaaPo

Published in the United States of America and distributed by Amazon Books.

ISBN-13: 978-1480158153
ISBN-10: 1480158151
LCCN: 2012920401

Thunder Road: The Journey Home

Stuart Nicholls

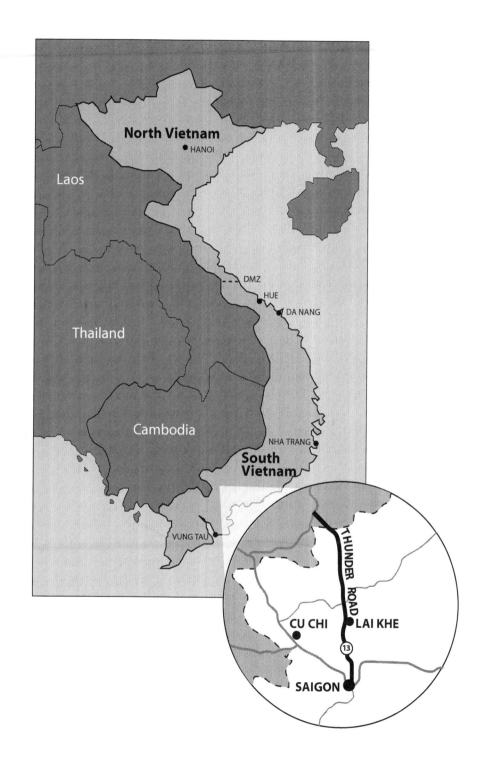

North Vietnam
• HANOI

Laos

DMZ
HUE •
• DA NANG

Thailand

Cambodia

NHA TRANG •

South
Vietnam

VUNG TAU •

THUNDER ROAD

CU CHI • • LAI KHE

13

SAIGON •

ACKNOWLEDGEMENTS

Despite swearing that I would never own a computer, I must admit that without one, this book would have remained an obscure fantasy, just as it had for the past four decades. Jennifer Nguyen's generous gift of her computer provided the vehicle to transform my dreams into reality.

A true and faithful friend, Cathe Murphy, helped get me started using the magic box and has been constantly supportive during the arduous process of creating this book.

My former Vet Center counselor, Eddie Hoklotubbe, and his wife Sara, who has published several books, have become some of my best friends and a constant source of encouragement and inspiration. Their unwavering devotion to this project has kept me at the keyboard long after I would have abandoned it.

My longtime friend, newspaper columnist and retired editor Ron Youngblood, has tirelessly read and re-read my manuscript. He edited it from a rambling, incoherent nightmare into a focused depiction of the most important time of my life. During many long nights of discussion and argument he has taught me as much about myself as about writing.

My copy editor, Jill Engledow, brought her expertise from the Maui News and added a final layer of polish to my manuscript.

Cheryl and Shaaron Kauhaa-Po have been the pillars of strength that I have often leaned on during this long process. I will always be grateful for Cheryl's wonderful job formatting this book for publication.

Arnie Kotler of Koa Books has helped with editing and advice on how to move this project forward. While attending his veterans writing retreat with Maxine Hong Kingston, I was able to focus my energy into completing this book.

My son, Kalani Nicholls, has been an invaluable ally when it came to the technical challenges of the cyber world and giving me a reason to carry on when I was tempted by the alternative.

My beautiful wife Hang not only saved my life but shared it with me 24/7 for twenty-one years. That in itself should qualify her for sainthood. She devoted herself to proofreading the manuscript and made countless insightful suggestions. Her superior grammar was vital in correcting my many mistakes.

She lived Aloha. She showed everyone by her example how to make acceptance, forgiveness, and unconditional love an integral part of everyday life. Her legacy has become the beacon that I will follow in the hope it will lead to a heavenly reunion where we can spend the rest of forever.

INTRODUCTION

It has become fashionable for TV shows, movies, and books to be advertised as "based on a true story." This leaves the audience to ponder how much of the story is "true" and how much is the product of artistic license. Memoir or novel? Over the years, many friends have encouraged me to write this book. Apparently they believe there is something worth telling which will be of interest to potential readers. They also take pleasure in reminding me that I never let the truth get in the way of a good story, and I have become famous for always embellishing. I suppose this trait was born of many hours sitting around campfires, hobo jungles, foxholes, and bars passing the time to alleviate boredom, or depression, or fear with storytelling. It is also known as the art of bullshit.

It truly seems like it was just yesterday when I was 18 and fighting for my life in the jungles of Vietnam. That is why it was such a shock to see the bald and graying face staring back at me this morning in my mirror. It is painfully obvious that if I am going to do this thing, it is now or never. Once again, I'm getting "short." At 65 years old, I know I have a lot more yesterdays than tomorrows.

There are 58,272 names on the Vietnam Memorial Wall in Washington, D.C. They didn't all die courageously. They didn't all die for freedom. But they are all dead nonetheless.

It is a little-known fact that twice as many Vietnam veterans have killed themselves as those who died in the war. This is for my wife, Le Thi Ngoc Hang, whose love has kept me from pulling the trigger. This is for all of us who went, and returned home as "the enemy." This is for all of those who never went, but tried to convict us. This is for the "VC," who welcomed us back. And here's to forgiveness which cannot tell the difference.

The Vietnam War ended on April 30, 1975. Over the last four to five decades there has been an onslaught of novels, documentaries, and memoirs published about bloody Vietnam. This is the story of a Vietnam veteran whose long and futile search for vindication in the U.S. finally leads him back to the land of his former enemy. Ironically, they give him the homecoming welcome that America denied him.

As of this writing, thousands of Vietnam veterans and other Americans have visited the Socialist Republic of Vietnam, some for as little as a week, while others have lived and worked there for years. Vietnam now has KFC, Baskin Robbins, hamburgers, bowling alleys, world-class golf courses, five-star hotels, a U.S. embassy, cell phones, and internet cafes. Little is left to remind us of a brutal war that killed millions of people; even the fabled tunnels of Cu Chi have been prostituted by arrogance and greed and reduced to a mere semblance of a Disneyland. A first-time tourist might well wonder if all the war stories were just a demented fantasy. It was not always like this.

In the mid-1980s, a few veterans driven by guilt, love, or desperation began to return. These tortured souls somehow found the courage to fight their way back to the land of the dragon. They went alone, unarmed, with no diplomatic protection, no way of communicating with the U.S. and at the mercy of a newly installed communist government which the U.S. still considered the enemy.

The infrastructure was in shambles. The cities resembled the crumbling ruins of Angkor Wat, with trees and vines growing out of the tile roofs. The streets bore potholes the size of coffins. Poverty and hunger were rampant and devastating. Opium addicts lay shriveling in doorways. Lepers died on the ruptured sidewalks. Hordes of beggars relentlessly mobbed unwary tourists. Medicine and competent physicians to treat the multitudes of war victims were scarce or non existent.

For these few veterans, coming to terms with their inner demons and finding absolution was more important than life itself.

There are approximately six billion people on this earth, each with his own story. It is humbling to know that my story is no more important or meaningful than any of theirs... except to me. There isn't enough time to teach this old dog new tricks. For me it is hard enough to learn how to use a computer, let alone stop embellishing my stories. This novel is based on a true story... mine. All the celebrities are real and have retained their actual names. The other characters are also real, but some of their names have been changed to protect their privacy.

Stuart L. Nicholls
Sgt. E-5 U.S. Army
Maui 2012

PROLOGUE
Ho Chi Minh City
August 2009

On a seventh-floor balcony he stood alone in the sunset and stared out through the twilight at the ochre shaded stucco buildings of the city. Towering mahogany and teak trees cast long shadows on teeming masses of honking, surging motorbikes far below on the noisy, smoke-filled streets. Huge new high-rises mushroomed up from ancient squalor. They dwarfed the decaying memories of a long-past colonial empire, and ruins of war that now surrendered to the prosperity of peace.

He had an ongoing forty-four-year history with this incredible country and her people. He had come in those first days of war and was ordered to win their hearts and minds. It had become quite obvious now that the opposite was true. Yet equally true was the love/hate relationship that had evolved along the way. Dripping with decades of bittersweet memories, he sipped his beer. I love it enough to keep coming back, he said to himself, but I hate it too much to stay.

He felt that Vietnam had owned his soul from the very first time he laid eyes on her. She became his friend and his enemy, his wife and his whore. She had coddled him, nearly killed him, loved him and fucked him. Then, after lulling him to sleep in a hammock strung between the realities of the past and the possibilities of the future, she destroyed him. She was an expert seductress. She had the innate talent to make him feel like a benevolent emperor who was loved, respected, and in total command of his kingdom. But once he believed it totally and became complacent, she had fallen upon him and ripped out his heart before he could even scream. Still, even after accepting this ultimate truth, he flew like a moth knowingly into the flame, in the end not giving a damn, but hoping such a glorious death would somehow give meaning to his inglorious life.

This book is dedicated to Hang:
The most beautiful woman to ever grace the earth
with her footsteps. My once-in-a-lifetime love,
true soul mate and best friend.
For the rest of forever, love always.

CHAPTER 1
Washington, D.C.
May 1965

The heel and toe cleats on their special Honor Guard dress shoes beat out a rhythm in perfect unison and echoed through the early morning tranquility as they strode down the lane through Arlington Cemetery. Both young men were eighteen years old, six feet tall and a solid 190 pounds. They wore sports shirts and slacks and whitewall haircuts. Shafts of sunlight streamed down between the lofty oaks and fell upon the neat white crosses aligned in long rows. Fragrant cherry blossoms fell upon the finely trimmed lawn like a blanket that had been pulled up over a hundred thousand graves. It was peaceful and quiet except for their footfalls on the pavement down the hill toward the Memorial Bridge to Washington, D.C.

They passed John F. Kennedy's grave. Nick remembered the times they had been assigned as guards there and had stood solemnly at parade rest as the eternal flame burned on. The robot-like regimen that they performed at the Tomb of the Unknown Soldier crossed his mind. He mentally rehearsed each finely tuned movement. In spite of the morning serenity, he felt annoyed. He wasn't reconciled to the spit and polish and never-ending harassment that they had to endure here. If it hadn't been for Big John, the supply clerk, he couldn't have handled it. Big John stood six-foot-three and weighed around 230. He had taken Nick and A.J. under his wing on the very first day.

"Don't let these pompous tin soldiers get to you," he said. "They ain't shit, but they been here longer than you, that's all. You might have to do what they tell you, but you don't have to like it. The best way to get them off you is to not show 'em you're pissed off. If they know they got to you, it's all over. *Comprendez?*" Nick and A.J. nodded.

"OK, now here's the chrome bayonets for your M-14s. We're the only outfit in the whole damned Army that can do dismounted drill with fixed bayonets. Keep 'em shiny and keep 'em sharp. You won't be getting any ammo. This here is the only weapon you got to protect all these dead soldiers." He snorted and shook his head. "But if you ever do get ammo, don't try to fire your rifles, 'cause they'll blow up in your faces. They've been intentionally loosened up so they rattle. Makes a more impressive sound when you all do the dismounted drill movements together."

The more he thought about it, the angrier Nick got. He saw no point in it all, especially when there was a war on. He felt wasted and couldn't help mentioning it to A.J.

"This place pisses me off, man! I heard on the radio this morning that them damn commies in Vietnam just killed three more American soldiers! What are we doin' HERE?" A.J. glanced over at him, then back down the road with a blasé look. Nick kept on. "We've been in the army for six months already, been through pure hell! Been trained to dig foxholes and throw grenades, shoot a rifle and live in the woods like an animal! We were taught to kill! Now what are we doin'? Guarding dead people. Marching in parades on Sunday afternoon. Shining boots and ironing a bunch of flags every night 'til midnight. Goddamn it man, I don't know how much more I can take!"

"Come on, Nick," A.J. replied. "You know what everybody says. Once you're here, that's it. Nobody leaves."

Nick waved his comment away. "Well, by God, I'M leavin'!"

"Don't be a fool! If you go AWOL…"

"No, damn it! Whatever happened to our idea about going Airborne or Special Forces? That's what we signed up for."

A.J. remained calm. "Yeah, but that would be twice as hard as this bullshit. Besides, they won't take us until we're E-5s. That'll take more than the three years we signed up for. You want to re-up already?"

Nick came to an abrupt halt and faced his friend. "Big John told me this morning that he's shipping out to Nam next week. If he can go, why can't we?" A.J. groaned and shook his head in exasperation. Nick resumed walking and fumed silently, but was soon breathing heavily as the frustration settled in.

A.J. tried to get Nick off of it. "You going to Helga's place today?"

"Yeah. I hope she didn't go to church, though. If she gets holy on me, I probably won't get laid. And I damn sure need to!"

A.J. laughed with envy. "You lucky bastard. I gotta find a broad pretty soon. What is she, Swedish or Norwegian or something?"

"Yeah, Swedish."

"What kind of work does she do?"

Nick smiled proudly. "She's the maid for that ABC news guy, Howard K. Smith."

"What? You never told me that! Where does he live?"

"Up in a huge mansion overlooking the Potomac. Helga has a penthouse apartment on the top floor."

A.J. burst out laughing. "Now I know why you wanted to volunteer for the Honor Guard!"

They reached the Memorial Bridge and focused on their destination, the Lincoln Memorial. Unconsciously marching in step the whole time, they closed quickly on the huge stone, pillared building that housed the large-than-life statue. After staring in awe for fifteen minutes, they made their exit out the east side and along the left flank of the reflecting pond that led to the Washington Monument. They saw the towering spire. It was entirely surrounded by a massive crowd of people numbering close to a hundred thousand. As they got closer to this ominous spectacle, Nick could feel a surge of adrenaline. There were parrot chants of, "Stop the war! Kill the imperialist pigs! American baby killers! Long live Ho Chi Minh!"

The two shaved-head soldiers looked at each other with mutual outrage and burgeoning hatred toward the demonstrators. Nick pursed his lips with determined fury, and A.J. stuck out his jaw and nodded in affirmation of their common mission. A.J. beckoned with a twist of his head. "Let's give these scum bags what for!" He reached under his shirt and pulled out his dog tags on their beaded chain.

Nick followed his lead and displayed his as well. He muttered, "Goddamn right! Let's show 'em who we are, by God!" And off they went, marching as to war.

By contrast, the first group they encountered consisted of a few skinny, long-haired men with linen shirts, bell-bottom pants, and love beads around their necks. As the two ferocious-looking warriors approached them, the group quieted, then withered and withdrew from their position. Nick grabbed the first man he could get his hands on, shoved him back into his co-conspirators and began yelling,

"What the fuck is wrong with you people? What do you think you're doing? We're fighting in Vietnam to stop Communism, and you are all traitors to your country!"

"Peace, brother! Please!" pleaded the man. "Make love, not war. Don't let the pigs lead you off to war based on their stupid lies! Please brothers, join us in defiance of the imperialist war mongers. Save yourselves before it's too late!"

A.J. wrestled away a cardboard sign that read, "Stop killing innocent women and children." Ripping it to shreds, he yelled, "They're the ones that started this war! They should've thought about their innocent women and children before they attacked the *USS Maddox* last year!"

Suddenly, Nick and A.J. found themselves surrounded by the mob. Attracted by the ruckus, the now-angry protesters pressed up against them. Stringy-haired women, some with wire-rimmed glasses, leaned their faces in to within inches of the men. Nick could smell marijuana on their breath as he looked into their red, glassy eyes.

"Man, you fucking commies are on another planet!" he yelled.

Then a calm and somewhat sober man made his way forward and pushed up to Nick. "No, brother. We're socialists, not communists."

"What's the difference? Same thing to me!"

"No, no. We are Marxists, not Stalinists. There's a difference."

"Bullshit! How can you stand here using your First Amendment rights to tear down our government? Do you think you could get away with this shit in Russia or China?"

The man closed his eyes and shook his head condescendingly as if speaking to a child. "You are obviously quite ignorant of the historical facts. Or else you have been brainwashed by the military."

"Fuck you! Fuck all of you commie bastards! Let's go, A.J.!" They tried to push through the wall of people but met with firm resistance. The man stood resolutely in front of them with an arrogant smile.

Nick was livid. "OK, what would you do if YOU were attacked? Would you retaliate?"

The man retained his smug smile. "No, of course not. We believe in peace, at all costs." Nick gave the man a cruel smirk and came up hard with a sucker punch right. The man's jaw went soft and ended up in a crooked grimace. A scream of anguish rose from the crowd close into them. The man fell back into the arms of his comrades, then his look of horror turned to rage as he lunged back at Nick with his hands extended towards Nick's throat. With a lightning-quick, two-handed parry, Nick deflected the attack. He brought up his knee into the man's groin and sadistically watched the face contort as he went to the ground.

"See! There's your peace and love! Lying commie, pinko faggot!"

The crowd parted as they hastily made their exit. They wouldn't wait for the protestors to form up a counter attack. A.J. was laughing, in awe of his friend's reckless assault. "Man, you're fucking nuts! You know that? What if they all come after us? You got a plan for that?"

Nick looked back over his shoulder as he led the way through the chanting masses. "Yeah! Let's get to the Capitol building! We can make a stand there!" They made their tactical retreat while pushing, shoving and arguing their way to the white concrete dome in the distance.

After climbing the front steps, to have the advantage of the high ground and the security personnel of the Capitol at their backs, the duo turned to face the huge throng. With dog tags shining in the sun, side by side, they hurled obscenities at the protestors below. Then a well-dressed man in suit, tie, and fedora stepped out of the crowd and made his way to the two men. His gray hair was trimmed short and his face was set hard with tan, leathery skin. His pale-blue eyes stared icily into them. Obviously this was not a demonstrator.

"What outfit are you men with?" he asked coldy.

Nick and A.J. looked warily at each other. A.J. stepped up proudly. "The Old Guard, sir!"

The man nodded. "Which company?"

"Bravo, sir!"

"Your company commander named Schiller?"

Nick sensed trouble. "Yes, sir. How did you know ?"

"I'm Colonel Paul Hutchinson, U.S. Army. Your battalion commander, Colonel Swagman, is a close friend."

Nick suddenly found himself standing at attention. The colonel stared the men down. "Do you men know that it is illegal for active duty personnel to participate in any political demonstration, no matter what?"

In unison they both responded, "No, sir!"

Colonel Hutchinson stepped closer and reached out to read their dog tags. "Well, it is. And you are both in violation of the Military

Code of Justice."

Nick stammered out, "Sir, we're sorry. We just couldn't stand by and let these people attack the government that we are sworn to protect."

"I see." The colonel nodded. He smiled tightly. Looking around to insure their privacy, he turned back to the men. "I'm not supposed to say this but, goddamn it, I'm proud of you men. It takes guts to take on a hundred thousand of the enemy by yourselves. If there's anything I can do to help you men, just say the word."

Nick and A.J. looked at each other and nodded. Nick managed to humbly ask, "Sir, could you help us get out of the Old Guard and over to Vietnam?"

The colonel looked up into the taller man's face. "And why the hell do you want that?" he asked.

"Because, the Old Guard sucks, sir!"

To Nick's surprise, the colonel howled with laughter and slapped Nick on the back. "Goddamn it, son! I know it does! I appreciate your candor…" He paused. "Consider it done." He smiled at them as he turned down the steps, then stopped and looked back. "And when you get there, give 'em hell!"

Standing there on the Capitol steps with jaws hanging, the two friends watched the colonel fade back into the lake of humanity. A.J. mused, "Who was that masked man?"

"I don't know, Tonto. But our work here is done!"

They began wandering aimlessly in a general direction of downtown. Nick spotted a pay phone and broke away to call Helga. "She'll be here to pick me up in about twenty minutes. Can we drop you someplace?"

A.J. looked forlorn. "No, you kids just go on home and fuck your brains out. I'll go find a peep show somewhere and release all this pent-up excitement at the prospect of going to war and getting it shot off."

Helga was five minutes late but when Nick slid into the tiny seat of her green Karmann Ghia convertible, her arms quickly shot around his neck, and her lips found his. They embraced for a long time like that, when he realized she had not been to church. "Damn! Did you miss me or something?"

She gently closed her blue eyes with her chin tilted upwards. "Yah."

She laughed at her own accent, which Nick thought was terribly sexy. "Ve go to my place?" she asked.

Nick mimicked her posture and replied, "Yah!"

Laughing, she asked him, "Vere is your friend, A.J.?"

"Oh, he's probably somewhere trying to deflower a virgin roll of toilet paper."

She looked puzzled. "I don't understand."

"Believe me, honey, neither do I." Nick laughed.

She drove them up tree-lined Massachusetts Avenue NW in the midday sun with the top down. The scents of life were on a lilting spring breeze. They turned into the long hilltop driveway, through the gardens and up to the classic colonial three-story mansion. The Potomac River flowed long and brown at the foot of a lawn that seemed to go on forever.

Helga went to open the side door to the kitchen. A man stepped out. He was dressed in civilian clothes but also had a whitewall haircut. The two hugged tightly and playfully. Nick felt the heat of jealousy behind his eyes. Helga beckoned him, smiling gaily. "Nick, come meet Jack Smith, Howard K. Smith's son."

Suddenly embarrassed, Nick walked over and shook hands. "So this is your family's place?"

"Yeah," Jack replied, "I used to live here until I flunked out of college. I see we have the same barber."

Nick grinned. "Yep. I'm with the Old Guard. And you?"

Jack gazed far away to the west. "The First Cavalry Division."

Nick looked puzzled.

"It's a brand-new outfit," Jack answered the unspoken question. "We're training to be airmobile. You know, with helicopters. A new concept."

"Really? I thought somebody in your shoes could get out of a combat unit if they wanted to."

Jack smiled ruefully. "I guess I don't want to. Time to grow up, or something like that."

"Are you guys going to Nam?"

"That's the word. But at least you're safe here in the Honor Guard. I heard that's choice duty."

Nick laughed. "You heard wrong. I can't wait to get to Nam!"

Jack shook his head, grinning. "Maybe I'll see you there."

"I doubt it. I'm trying to get into an infantry outfit. But with your connections they'll probably make you a cushy clerk typist in Saigon."

They both laughed and shook hands. The future would prove Nick wrong.

Helga led Nick upstairs to her cozy apartment. She turned on the radio. The song playing was "What the World Needs Now," by Jackie DeShannon. With French horns playing the chorus, Nick went to the bay window, lit a cigarette, and stared out over the Potomac. Far in the distance the Washington Monument pierced the blue sky. For some reason, he began thinking of Big John. Just that morning when they were listening to the war news, John announced that he had been approved to go. He wanted to make more money to support his new wife, who was already pregnant. Nick thought he was nuts to risk all that just for money. But Big John had said, "Don't worry, Nick. I'm gonna come home rich and with a lot of medals." The future would also prove Big John wrong.

Helga came behind him and turned him to her. Her eyes were worried. "Do you really vant to go over zere?"

Nick felt the softness of her heart as it broke. She had hoped they had a future. He knew different, in any event. Now, he was the selfish asshole. He stubbed out his smoke. He held her close and kissed her all over her face and neck. He laid her down on the small bed. Later, when he tried to slide into her, she was very tight and dry. He eventually succeeded, but when he came, he came alone. She pushed him gently off of her and went to light a cigarette. Six feet apart, but in two different worlds, they sat in silence for a long time.

"You told me you loved me," she sniffled.

"I do." He lied.

She gave him a sideways look. "Then vai don't you stay here?"

"I just can't, that's all. My country is at war. I'm a soldier. I have to go."

She buried her head in her pillow and began to sob. He tried consoling her, but she was too far into it. Finally, he dressed, stroked her neck for a moment, walked out and down to the river, where he knew a shortcut back to Fort Myer.

Colonel Hutchinson, true to his word, arranged for Nick and A.J. to ship out to Vietnam within six weeks.

Nick had a nine-day leave, two days with family in Illinois and the rest with another girlfriend, Tracy Sutton, in Laguna Beach, California.

Nick and Tracy went to Disneyland and immersed themselves in the magic of childhood fantasies. The next day they hit the beach and baked in the hot, dry, California sun. He was entranced by all the string bikinis, the briny taste in his mouth, and the strong aroma of Coppertone. Having learned to body surf on the small waves of Lake Michigan, he decided to show off in the eight-foot shore break. Within minutes, the icy dark-blue surf slammed him into the coarse sand and knocked the wind out of him. With abraded skin and wounded ego, Nick blushed, groaned, and stumbled as Tracy pulled him up onto the beach.

Tracy's father, who was a Marine Corps colonel, saw to it that they were never alone long enough for Nick to get anywhere with the tall, blonde beauty. He did teach Nick how to catch sand crabs, which made good bait for fishing, and Nick felt a certain rapport when they talked about the military and the fledgling war far away.

In the end, Tracy promised to wait for him and to write all the time. Then Nick kissed her goodbye at the bus station, and rode the "dog" up to Oakland, where he boarded a Flying Tiger Airlines 707 from Travis Air Force Base to Saigon, and that was that. A.J. had left a week earlier. Like Nick, he had little use for family, but no girlfriend. He promised to find Nick when he got in-country.

Nick crushed out a cigarette in the plane's arm-rest ash tray. He noticed the sky was growing lighter. His eyes strained down through darkness punctuated by scattered lights. Intermittent bright green and orange flashes flared up at them. They had arrived. Those were tracers! He imagined a beleaguered American compound being attacked by the Viet Cong. His adrenaline began to surge. Then he heard a soft feminine voice over the intercom.

"Good morning, gentlemen. We are approaching Tan Son Nhat Airport in Saigon, South Vietnam. Please extinguish all smoking materials and fasten your seat belts for landing." There was a pause. "It has truly been a pleasure and an honor to serve you on our flight." Her voice broke slightly. "Please stay safe, and we will look forward to taking you all home next year. God bless you!"

Minutes later, the stinking, hot, humid air swept through the cabin as they opened the doors. One hundred forty-two men climbed down the steps into a torrent of tropical rain. They sprinted across the tarmac to a two-story terminal building. Overhead was a sign, "Incoming Personnel Report Here." Nick felt beads of sweat forcing their way through the drops of rain on his face. On the far side of the room was a podium. Behind it stood a thick, black platoon sergeant dressed in jungle fatigues. He surveyed the milling group of sweating, rain-soaked men. With a hideous smile he said in a booming voice, "Gentlemen! Welcome to hell!"

Later, after the rain stopped, Nick and the other soldiers fell into formation and stood at parade rest on the steaming pavement. After what seemed like hours, the NCOIC, called them to attention as a big black sedan with a military police escort in two jeeps approached and parked nearby. Spilling out of the doors were several aides and ass-kissing adjutants. One of them opened the right rear door and stood at attention. Lean, graying General William Westmoreland towered over his underlings. The low morning sun gleamed off the four stars on each broad shoulder. He strode over to the sergeant in charge. Standing shoulder to shoulder Nick and a new buddy named Twig exchanged sidelong looks of awe. It was as if God himself was before them, with dark eyes and square jaw jutting out, striking terror in the hearts of all the young FNGs.

After the obligatory salutes, the general muttered to the sergeant, who did an about-face and stood before the men. "Gentlemen! You are privileged and honored to be greeted by the commanding general of all U.S. forces in the Republic of South Vietnam! General Westmoreland's policy is to meet each planeload of arriving troops and begin your orientation immediately! Stand by for inspection!" The sergeant about-faced to the general and saluted again. "Troops are ready for inspection, sir." With that, God approached the first rank of soldiers.

"Good morning, son," came the surprisingly quiet voice. An almost visible shock wave ran through the men. How could a man of such power sound so gentle and warm? "How was your flight?" he asked the next man. "Where are you from, soldier?"

A huge shadow fell over Nick and he felt the general's firm handshake. Nick looked up at the chiseled silhouette before him. The general took a deep breath and looked Nick square in the eye. With a fatherly smile he said in a voice loud enough for all to hear. "Private, I want you to win these people's hearts and minds. I want you to become Vietnamese. Learn their language, study their customs, respect their women. It's like being in the Peace Corps, but you will carry a rifle. If you can do all that, then we will win this war, and we can all go home proud of what we did here."

Nick was barely able to stammer out a "Yes, sir!" The general moved on, but those words would haunt Nick for many years to come.

STUART NICHOLLS

CHAPTER 2
First Infantry Division Headquarters
Di An – Republic of South Vietnam
January 1966

Nick stood swaying and sweating in the morning sun. He was delirious with jungle fever. He fought off the chills again, then puked up watery foam. Some of it drooled down his stubbled chin onto the front of his fatigues. The rest pooled where his bleached-out jungle boots met the red dust on the shoulder of the narrow road. He leaned on his M-14 rifle like a crutch.

Army trucks, jeeps, and Vietnamese buses roared by belching black smoke. He choked and coughed.

A red-faced sergeant marched up to the twenty-odd soldiers clustered there in a semblance of a formation. "Detail! Attention!"

There was muttering and groaning as the disheveled group straightened up half-heartedly.

The sergeant about-faced. "Sir, the men are ready." He snapped a rear-echelon salute to the major who had marched up leading a procession of other officers and a large hatless man with longish black hair, dressed in khakis. The major returned the salute and surveyed the men. He shook his head slightly.

"At ease, men! You are probably wondering why I've asked you to assemble here this morning. It is with immense pleasure that I introduce all of you to a great man and talented actor. He has come here risking his own life to be with us today and show you his support. This is none other than the famous movie star, Robert Mitchum!"

Nick peered through his pain at the broad-shouldered macho man of the silver screen. He barely felt the big man's hand in his. Mitchum paused with a look of concern as he took in Nick's demeanor. "Major, this man looks like shit. Is he OK?"

The major could not hide his revulsion at the sight and stench of the young grunt before him. "PFC Dwyer! Why do you look like shit?"

"Because I feel like shit, sir." Nick replied. "A hundred and four fever, sir."

"Well, it'll get a lot hotter before the day is done." Leaving the bewildered Nick, they moved down the ragged line until every man had shaken hands with Mitchum.

The major stood in front of them again, hands on his hips. "You have probably seen Mr. Mitchum's movie, *Thunder Road*. In the movie, the road was given that name because of all the wild hot-rod chases between the cops and the moonshine runners.

"Well, right behind you is Highway 13. As you know, it leads from Saigon right up along the edge of the Iron Triangle through some of the baddest parts of the country. It ends at Loc Ninh on the Cambodian border. Along this highway there are constant bombings by roadside mines. There have been ambushes and major battles fought on this road, which is the only supply link between Saigon and the base camps of the Big Red One and the ARVN in this part of Three Corps. Mr. Mitchum has come all the way from Hollywood, so listen up!" He turned and saluted the khaki-clad actor, who stepped up looking a little uneasy. No one had given him a script to follow.

"Men, I'm proud to be here among you. I want to thank Major Patterson here, along with his staff, for giving me the opportunity to come visit you. So now, without further ado, in honor of all you men who have fought along Highway 13, especially those who have been wounded or killed, I hereby christen this highway, "Thunder Road!"

Three days later, the olive-green Caribou plane descended over neat rows of rubber trees into the base camp of Lai Khe. Red dust whipped up behind them as they slammed down on the rough surface of PSP tarmac. The rear cargo hatch yawned open. After taxiing up to the dark wall of mature trees, the pilot shut off the engines, and they whined down in the afternoon sun.

Nick and a half dozen other replacements helped the ground crew unload crates of brand new M-16s, ammo, and other ordnance. When the plane was empty, they watched a somber group of men come out from under the trees bearing at least a dozen bloody body bags. They loaded them onto the floor of the plane for the return flight to Graves Registration in Bien Hoa.

Sergeant McClintock, one of the FNGs, watched with a blank stare. "Goddamn it, I just came from there. You know, Graves Registration? I just can't get away from dead bodies. What the fuck, over?"

Nick gave him a sideways glance, "Damn, Sarge! If you didn't want to see dead bodies, why the hell did you come here? This is the infantry, man." The sergeant gazed silently off into space. Nick shook his head. Man, this fucker's a little bit off, he said to himself.

Then McClintock turned back to him. "So, where did you transfer from?"

"Vung Tau. I was with an advisory team."

"So why'd you come up here? Get tired of the beach?"

"Fuck you! I was a grunt there too, Sarge."

The sergeant looked Nick up and down, debating whether or not to take offense, but decided against it. Curious though, he pressed Nick again. "So why DID you come here?"

Nick looked away into the trees. "Long story. Guilt, I guess."

"Huh?"

Nick waved him off. "Never mind."

An airman in a white flight suit came up to the men. "All right, form up over here, you guys. Colonel Smoke will be with you shortly."

A young hillbilly kid named Travis surveyed his companions quizzically. "Colonel Smoke?" he whispered.

Nick replied with a shrug and a "we'll see" look.

The group sauntered over to the spot in the shade and stood waiting for only a few minutes. A jeep, covered in red dust, growled up through the trees and squeaked to a stop a few meters away. Out jumped a tall black man in jungle fatigues with a silver oak leaf on each shoulder and a Big Red One patch on his left sleeve. His dark eyes darted back and forth as he sized up the replacements. He came close, his hands on his hips, and eyes wide and menacing.

"I am Colonel George Shufert, your battalion commander!" He jerked his head in the direction of the plane. "You men see those bodies? Don't let that happen to you! Welcome to Second Battalion,

Second Infantry Regiment! Also known as the *dinky dau* battalion. They call us that because we ARE *dinky dau*! We're fucking nuts and proud of it, by God!" The men chuckled. "Our battalion motto is, *noli me tangere*. It means, no one dare touch me. If they try, then God help 'em!"

He paced back and forth in front of the men, abruptly stopped and faced them. "How many of you men heard about our battalion being ambushed last November at a place called Bau Bang?"

No one raised their hand or spoke. "That's what I thought. Now, how many of you heard about the First Cavalry Division being ambushed last November at a place called the Ia Drang where the Second of the Seventh Cavalry Regiment suffered heavy casualties?"

Nick and Sergeant McClintock raised their hands. Nick recalled reading in the *Stars and Stripes* about it and wondering if Jack Smith was there. He would not find out for over three decades until a book came out called, *We Were Soldiers Once, And Young*. Jack had been seriously wounded three times in the battle but survived long enough to become an ABC news anchor like his father before him. Nick would write to him and Jack responded to offer best wishes shortly before his death from cancer in 2004.

Colonel Smoke nodded with a tight-lipped smile. "That's because the First Cav always gets news coverage over everyone else. They're under the microscope because of what happened in Korea. Well, our *dinky dau* battalion was hit at the same time, but all the correspondents were up there covering their asses.

"You have only two missions here! The first mission is to KILL VC! The second mission is to WIN MEDALS! You are all being assigned to Alpha Company because they have sustained the most casualties lately. Those brave young soldiers in the bags were from Alpha Company." He looked them up and down again then strode quickly to his jeep. "Honor their memory and KILL VC! KILL 'EM ALL, BY GOD!" He shouted as he drove off through the forest.

The men all looked at each other with raised eyebrows. Nick went off by himself and squatted down, Vietnamese style. Welcome to the REAL war, he thought.

CHAPTER 3
Lai Khe
June 1966

Nick had only two days left before he would fly down to Saigon and be shipped back to The World. He perched on the rickety wooden bench beneath a sheet of battered tin that served as a roof for the makeshift beer stand. He kicked at the grass stubble and red dirt with his worn-out jungle boots. They were bleached and scarred by months of fighting in the bush. Thunder Road lay just 20 meters away, rumbling and shaking under the heavy wheels of Army vehicles that dusted everything along the shoulder.

Across from him sat a famous tunnel rat, Pete Rejo. He was with a different battalion and also could speak some Vietnamese. He and Nick would hang out at the beer stand whenever they came in from the bush and had become friends. Pete raised his beer to Nick, "So, two and a wake up, eh? You lucky bastard!" Nick grinned and drank from his heavy, chipped glass. Pete beckoned to the girl for more beer. "So how's it feel?"

Nick looked down at the chicken skin on his arms. Then with his head still down, glanced up with his eyes. He simply shook his head. Pete nodded slightly, trying to read him.

Nick had always been in awe of the big Cuban. He and Nick were both six feet tall and at one time had been husky and strong. Months in the jungle had changed all that. But Nick was a point man. Rejo had to squeeze down into the little tunnels beneath the jungle and search out the VC. Most tunnel rats were much smaller men, but they were among the most courageous soldiers in the war. Nick had tried going into a tunnel once but got stuck only two meters in. The claustrophobia was immediate and demoralizing. He refused to ever go in again. But Pete absolutely loved it. Nick was sure that the poor son of a bitch would never survive his tour. But he would find out, decades later, that Pete had actually survived several tours before they forced him to go home.

Nick smiled at the girl as she poured them both another glass.

"You're hooked, ain't you?" Rejo asked.

Nick questioned him with his eyes.

"You love this place. I know. I can see it. But the life expectancy ain't very long." Pete nodded, grinning. "Well, as much as I'd love to stay and carry on this lopsided conversation, I gotta get back to my bunker." He chugged his beer. "Somebody's got to fight this war. Look me up in Colorado sometime."

Nick stood and reached out his hand. "OK, Pete. You take care of yourself. And thanks."

"For what?"

"The beer."

"Fuck you! Short-timers buy the beer!" He laughed, slapped Nick's shoulder and ducked out into the heat. He never looked back. Nick sat down and looked around the hootch. He was troubled by the lump in his throat each time he glanced over at Hai, a seven year old boy whose only possessions in this world were his shorts and a cardboard box which held his polish and shoe-shine rag. He made his living by shining the GI's combat boots. He was an orphan.

Nick sipped his 33 beer from the glass full of dirty ice. Hai ran his fingers over Nick's scarred and bleached out boots and looked up pleadingly. Nick nodded his OK. Hai smiled gleefully. It would take a lot of work to shine these boots. He knew he could make a little extra. Besides, *Anh Ly* was always a good tipper.

Nick gazed across the rice paddies that ran out below them to the river. There, they met the black onyx wall of jungle that stood flat and tall against a 24-carat sky. He saw a stand of areca palms that he had not noticed before. In the paddy, a small black-clad figure with a conical straw hat followed behind a water buffalo that waded belly deep in the muddy brown water, plowing through the muck. Nick could almost hear their feet making sucking sounds in the mud. As always, the afternoon tropical sun beat down mercilessly. Nick looked at his jungle fatigue shirt, soaked with sweat. He tasted salt in his mouth, but it was from tears not sweat.

Phuong, also an orphan, was the pretty sixteen-year-old girl who ran the beer stand. She sat down across the table, a slab of wood on sawhorses.

"Ly," she said, and placed her hands on his, "We are friends long time. Tell me why you sad."

Soon after arriving in-country Nick had started using his middle name, Leigh, to fit in better with the Vietnamese who spelled it "Ly."

Phuong had learned to speak English well in the six months Nick had known her. And Nick had learned Vietnamese just as well.

"Because," he answered in her language, "I know that in two days I will have to leave. Although I have watched many American and Vietnamese friends die, I want to stay. But I'm afraid, if I do, I will be killed too. I am sad because I will never again see you, whom I call sister, or the woman who sits over there, whom I call mother, or little Hai, who is like a small brother. I will never again watch the plowman down there in the paddy. Even the sun will never feel the same again, no matter where I go. So maybe by leaving, I will be dying in another way."

Ma, as Nick called her, came over to them and sat down with a weary smile. Nick had never known her real name, so he simply called her Ma, which always thrilled her. She was perhaps thirty-five years old, but her hair already revealed streaks of gray. Her eyes were gentle and kind, and her smile could warm even the coldest heart. Nick remembered how he had helped her thatch the roof of her small house in the village. Afterward they ate bowls of rice with pork steak from his C-rations. She sewed the rips in his fatigues and did his laundry while he was out on operations. He brought her soap and food. These three people were his adopted family, and he had come to love them as dearly as his own back in the U.S.

Ma smiled at him and said, in Vietnamese. "Ly, can you come to our house tomorrow morning at about ten o'clock?"

"Yes, Ma. I will come."

"Good! We have a surprise for you." And she laughed that beautiful laugh he had come to love.

The next morning, Nick walked down the shaded red-dirt road that led to Lai Khe. The morning sun slanted down through the rubber trees, and a cool breeze stirred the shadows that fell across his path. He wondered fearfully how he could bring himself to say goodbye to these wonderful people who had adopted him and worried for him each time he went out in the bush—a family of orphans who struggled through war valiantly. His family, who survived on eggs laid by one scrawny little hen, and rice when they had the five cents required to buy it, had given all of themselves to him, so he knew they appreciated the sacrifice that he made by fighting to keep them free.

Two GIs passed him in a jeep, and a radio on the seat echoed the soft music of "Michelle." Even after they had gone, the notes flowed on in his head and heightened the beauty of his Vietnam. He fantasized about coming back someday. Maybe he could find his girlfriend Lieu in Vung Tau. They could marry. They could start their own rubber plantation. They could live happily...

He came to the huge elephant-pod tree in the middle of the village. There, he turned onto a dirt path and went up to the second hut on the right. All three of them greeted him at the doorway with anticipating smiles and nervous gestures revealing their excitement at the prospect of showing him their surprise. He kissed Ma on the cheek and she laughed. Phuong took his M-16 from his shoulder while Ma tied a blindfold over his eyes. There was a sudden flash of fear. This was his trial of trust. He stopped short. They urged him on but he froze. Then he released himself from this life.

Don't mean nothin'. Give it up, Nick, he said to himself. Hai led him by the hand through the main room over the packed dirt floor and into a smaller room which he remembered as the kitchen. Slowly, Ma untied the blindfold and it dropped from his eyes. There before him lay the most inviting selection of food he had ever seen outside of Saigon. There was a bowl of lettuce-and-tomato salad, a basket of freshly baked French bread, a pot of rice, and a plate of sliced pineapple, lychee, and bananas. And in the middle of it all was a tarnished metal tray holding their one and only scrawny little chicken, roasted to a rich golden brown.

Each time Nick tried to speak, a lump caught in his throat. Tears streamed down his cheeks and silent spasms wracked his body. Ma took him by the shoulders and turned him to face her. Though his vision was blurred, he could tell she was also crying. In a trembling voice she spoke to him for the very first time in English. He was sure it must have taken her months to learn it.

"Ly, we give you this so you know we thank you for help us. We hope you come back to us someday when Vietnam no more have Viet Cong. We love you with all our heart!"

Tan Son Nhat airport was quiet. One hundred-forty two GI's were scattered in the large room. They all sat solemnly on the wooden seats in the pre-dawn darkness. Some slept while others, including Nick, sat silently in their own thoughts of the past year which they had spent in an ugly war. Rain splashed on the pavement outside. With it came a breeze that swept in through the open doors, cooling their tired, sweaty faces. The only sound in the unlit room was the hurried scuffling of the Vietnamese baggage men.

Nick let his tired mind drift back over the past year. He remembered the agonizing jungle patrols, the pain, hunger, thirst, and terror. He thought of the dead. On both sides. The torture he felt when he killed. The fear of dying. The eternal conflict between Westmoreland's "hearts and minds" and Colonel Smoke's "kill VC and win medals." The mental yin and yang was unending and bewildering. At times, when he was alone, he found solace in tears. Other times he was consumed with rage and hatred of the Vietnamese. Then he would remember Lieu and Ma, and his heart would break at the thought of never seeing them again. There were the cruel and ruthless VC who had killed his friends. Then there were comrades like his fellow interpreters Son and Xuong. He tried hard to put it all in balance, but the pendulum swung on. Though the VC were the enemy, he had not enjoyed killing them. They were fighting for what they thought was right, just like he was. They had someone or something to live for. It might not have been much by American standards, but there was something. What he felt was sometimes love, sometimes hate. Both were visceral and passionate.

He recalled the three VC he had surprised on a jungle trail one afternoon. He came face to face with them at four meters. In shock, they all froze for an eternity. Then he felt the terrible shaking in his hands and arms. Small red holes began magically appearing in the chest of the first one. He fell, face first, to the ground. Nick's M-16 chattered. There was a blood trail into the jungle. The lone remaining VC was writhing on the trail. "He's got a grenade!" Nick yelled. He fired another round into the man's back. The body lurched off the ground, then lay still. Using his rifle, Nick flipped the body over. There was no grenade. The man had been clutching at the bloody bullet wounds in his chest.

The LT came sprinting up with the rest of the platoon. "Good shooting, Nick! Now search the body!"

Nick was suddenly nauseated. He was afraid to touch the man for fear he would come back to life and become a part of him and haunt him forever. Nick's hands trembled as he reached into the man's pocket and pulled out his red, sticky wallet. Inside, was a torn and faded black-and-white photograph of a beautiful Vietnamese woman and two young girls. In the background was a grass shack like Ma's and a rice paddy beyond. This man had been a farmer, just like Nick had once been. For the very first time, with but three months left on his tour, Nick saw the enemy for what he really was, a human being. And at that moment, somewhere in the jungle east of Lai Khe, Nick and that VC family became a part of each other for all time. Their faces would appear to him randomly and without warning for the rest of his life.

But no sooner had this epiphany occurred than the immediate and inexplicable rationalization began in his mind. Deep in Nick's subconsciousness, the powerful beast of self-preservation rose up to shield him from his humanity. A montage of his dead and wounded friends' faces flashed before his eyes. You pussy! They are the enemy! They butchered your friends! This is your just revenge! Revel in the glory! Savor this moment and seek more! Make 'em pay, by God! Kill VC! Win medals!

Back on point, the darkness had returned to his eyes. If he was to survive, he could not afford to see the truth. Not yet.

In less than an hour he came to a small but well-worn path in the jungle. Leaning against a large tree was a bicycle, poorly camouflaged by weeds. He dropped to one knee and held up his clenched fist. Lieutenant Arthur and the RTO rustled quietly through the brush as they came up the file to Nick's position.

"Sir," Nick whispered, "I got a bike over there. I bet it belongs to that sniper team that we just hit. Can I booby trap it?"

Lieutenant Arthur thought for a minute. "What if it's a friendly?"

Nick reeled as his conscience lost another battle with the beast. "Come on, sir! This is a free-fire zone, right?" In his mind, Nick saw

Spec 4 Travis' face, white as a sheet, with his eyes rolled back and his severed genitals on the ground. "Let's get some, sir! Don't mean nothin'!"

The LT peered into his pointman's black eyes. They were full of blood-lust. "OK, Nick. We'll cover you."

Nick was troubled by the heat he felt in his chest. The rush of adrenaline made him feel invincible. He made his way to the bike. After a quick inspection, he placed a frag grenade against the tree trunk and secured it with trip wire. He tied one end to the pin and the other end to one of the wheel spokes, then straightened the pin on the grenade. He placed some more grass around it to conceal his trap then, satisfied, returned to the LT.

"Nick, we don't have time to hang around. Lead us out of here on the same heading. Move out."

The platoon crossed the path, one by one. When they had gone no more than 200 meters they heard the roar of the explosion behind them. Nick looked back at the LT with a wild and sickened grin on his face. Then he resumed cutting the trail, deep into hell.

— ⁓ —

Nick was jarred back into the present by Twig's elbow jabbing him in the ribs. "Here comes our plane, Tiger. Let's go."

Outside, the big silver bird came to a halt. Nick could see the Vietnamese men in raincoats pushing the loading ramp up to the door. GIs started moving toward the boarding gate with their duffel bags. Twig and Nick stared at each other as if asking, is this really happening? An old Vietnamese man in ragged work clothes stood there watching curiously as the column of men passed by. Most of the men were outwardly happy, and Nick was sure the old man knew they were going home. But he felt a strange need to tell the man of the regret that really filled his heart. When he reached the man, he spoke to him in Vietnamese.

"Goodbye, my brother. I am going home to America now but someday I will return, because I love this country, and it hurts me that I must go."

The man smiled with a look of gratitude, and amazement at Nick's fluency. Nick felt better that he had told someone. He was quite sure the other soldiers would have thought him insane. They walked out into the monsoon rain, like the downpour that had greeted them one year before, and climbed the steps to the plane. Nick hesitated at the door and turned to take one last look at Saigon in the early light. Lines from a Roger Miller song crossed his mind. *"I'll be leavin' here this morning with the comin' of the dawn. I've been a long time goin', but I'll be a long time gone."* And so it was.

The long journey home was split into three segments. The first leg took them over the South China Sea and the active Mount Pinatubo volcano, to Clark Air Base in the Philippines. Then up to Japan, where they were fed at an Air Force base mess hall with a choice of steaks, spaghetti, or fried chicken. And of course free beer. Then across the wide Pacific on the way to Travis Air Force base in Oakland, California. The men became ecstatic. The closer they got to home, the wilder their homecoming expectations. There was talk of parades, brass bands, speeches by politicians, medal and award ceremonies, sex-starved girls inviting them home. Nick became giddy at the mere thought of flying down to Laguna Beach to spend time with Tracy. She would undoubtedly seduce him before taking him out for hamburgers and milkshakes. Surely her Marine Corps colonel father would understand and be only too happy to allow the returning war hero to sleep with his daughter.

Twig had already assembled a list of all the California beauties he would fuck on his first night back in San Bernadino. Others rehearsed speeches they would deliver to the anxiously awaiting reporters. The fantasies went on and on. The fact that most of the men were only nineteen years old and still too young to legally drink alcohol, vote, or sign contracts was lost in the proliferating delusions. Most of them had been too busy out in the jungle fighting for survival to be bothered or even exposed to the realities of the political environment back home.

At long last, they felt the plane's tires touch down on American soil. This long-anticipated dream was finally coming true. There was bedlam on board. The cheering and applause was deafening. The flight crew cringed and winced, though smiling. Then they pulled up to the arrival gate and the ramp was wheeled into place. As the men literally held their breath, the front door was thrown open and the clean, crisp, sterile air of America greeted their straining nostrils for the first time in a year.

With a heavy sigh, Twig turned to Nick. "Welcome to the land of all-night generators!"

"Yeah! And nobody shooting at us! Water without iodine tabs!"

"Real beds and round-eyed women to share 'em with!" They hugged each other, laughing hysterically.

Finally the men made their way down the plane's steps in the early morning California sunshine. Their unbridled exuberation was short lived. As they entered the large plate-glass doors to the terminal they were suddenly attacked by dozens of anti-war protesters hurling rotten tomatoes, peppers, and eggs. They were shouting and cursing.

"Fucking baby killers! Cowardly running dogs! Nazi bastards! Fuck all of you! I wish you had been killed!"

Military police and airport security held back the mob and any retaliation by the shocked veterans. Nick was instantly enraged to the point that he charged the line of officers and reached through to try to grab one of the enemy. He was shoved back. Other soldiers did the same. The situation was turning ugly and dangerous. Finally the protesters, fearing the seasoned veterans, realized they had bitten off more than they could chew. They retreated under the mounting pressure from the police, but once at a safe distance, turned and resumed screaming obscenities.

Gasping for air and shaking in an uncontrollable fury, Nick and the others snarled and threatened the authorities as well as the mob. Finally a master sergeant, wearing a Combat Infantry Badge with a star, appeared in the melee and yelled, "At ease, men! At ease, goddamn it!" The wild-eyed vets began to quiet as soon as they saw his rank and position. Then, as the protesters disappeared down the corridor and order was slowly restored, the sergeant stood before them.

"Men, I'm sorry to tell you that this ain't the same country you left a year ago. What you saw here is just the tip of the iceberg. I don't know what the future holds but, goddamn it, I smell trouble! Just try to remember that one of the things you men were fighting for was the right to free speech. Even when they use it against us. Bear that in mind. I don't want any of you to survive the war and then come home to get in trouble here."

That night, Nick's taxi dropped him off at Tracy's house. Her father, Colonel Jay Sutton, greeted him, and Nick saluted as best he could remember. No one saluted in the bush. The colonel returned it, then shook his hand heartily and welcomed him inside. He thrust a cold beer at Nick, and they clinked bottles. Nick looked around anxiously. The colonel shook his head. "She's not here, Nick. She knew you were coming but, for some reason, ran off to the mountains with one of her draft-dodger boyfriends. I'm sorry."

Nick's heart sank, cold and empty. He nodded, then chugged the rest of the beer. The colonel brought more. Nick stared straight through the walls.

"Don't mean nothin', sir. Don't mean a fuckin' thing."

The colonel surveyed him curiously. "I just don't understand this country anymore, Nick. Something strange is happening. But I think it does mean something. It means a lot." He grinned. "I just don't know what it is yet." He sat back on the couch. "Tell me about the war."

Nick looked at him blankly. He saw through him and past him to a place on a different planet with a different language and different rules. In fact, there was only one rule. Survive. He opened his mouth but nothing came out. The colonel had been a fighter pilot in Korea. Nick had been a grunt in Vietnam. There was only one thing in common. Mutual respect. For that first night back, it would have to be enough.

The next day, he arrived at his family's farm outside Wheaton, Illinois, with the stench of the jungle still in his pores. There were no bands playing or banners waving. Everyone he met was untouched by the horrors that were ten thousand miles away. He felt contaminated with some fearsome disease that no one wanted to catch. They were all clean and sanitized and sterile. He was the carrier of a wretched plague. They did not want to know about it. He had wanted to tell them really, but they did not want to listen. By watching death, he had learned how to live. He was glad to be alive. He was glad to live and be able to look at things. Sometimes in the mornings, he would walk through his mother's garden and watch a spider spinning its web. He would watch until the entire web was constructed. It was a simple thing, yet filled with meaning. He enjoyed watching the ants carrying straw twice their size over hills of soil and through the jungle of grass on the garden path.

One day, sitting on the front porch, looking out past the gravel road, across the train tracks and corn fields, his childhood memories rose up out of the dust: Down in the east forty, Neighbors Unlimited, the group his parents had founded was enjoying a summer picnic. They lay on blankets beneath the fruit trees and ate potato salad, sandwiches, and ice cream covered with raspberries from the Dwyer's farm. There were his friends, Jimmy Ezaki, and the twins Mike and Shelby Steele, all from inner city Chicago, who came out for these picnics to mingle and meet people of every race, color, and religion and become friends.

The Ezakis were Japanese and had been freed from a World War II internment camp. Soon after, they met the Dwyer family who became their first white friends.

The Steele family was interracial, a marriage between a white woman and a black man. In the early 1950s they were shunned by white society, even in northern Illinois. Evelyn and Donald Dwyer welcomed them with open arms.

There were Indians, Jews, Mexicans, Arabs, and some others that young Nick could not remember, but to him they were all the same. Many years later, Mike and Shelby Steele became famous intellectual conservatives, with Mike being the National Chairman of the Republican party.

Nick got up off the porch and tossed his father's car keys onto the dining room table. Out in the mist, ghosts were calling him. He walked out the gate onto the dusty road and down the hill where the tragedy had taken place so long ago. He paused briefly at the spot where she had been pulled out from under the old man's car, crushed and mangled. He had held her tiny little body and felt the hot sticky blood soaking through his T-shirt. He had forgotten to close the gate behind him when he went down to visit his friend Diane. His little sister Kathy followed him, and the old man did not see her when he drove over the crest of the hill. She was only two years old. Nick was five.

After that, Nick's mother went temporarily insane and was sent to a mental hospital for treatment. His father began working double shifts at his factory job. Nick went alone into the woods. He was frightened at first, not knowing the dangers that awaited him there. But as the years passed the woods became as comforting as a mother's bosom.

Nick climbed the old wire fence along the road and bent over to crawl through the culvert that led under the tracks and came out in the corn field on the other side. He waded through the chest-high plants until he reached Weisbrook Road, which led to Herrick's Lake Forest Reserve. The past beckoned. This is where he had gone after Kathy's death. He turned left on Butterfield Road and walked along the shoulder of the two-lane concrete highway. When he was ten, he would deliver newspapers on horseback to a few houses on this road. He remembered the Jacklin house, there on the left in the new subdivision. He had met and become friends with the two girls, Pam, who was two years older, and Pat, who was in his class of twelve at the little Weisbrook School. In sixth grade Pat had brought a small record player to school along with some 45s such as "Green Door," "Born Too Late" and "To Know Him is to Love Him." At recess time she grabbed him and taught him how to dance, whether he liked it or not. She was the nearest thing he had to a girlfriend, but nothing serious. Still, she had helped him come out of his shell after Kathy died.

The June haze clung to the damp earth, and the air was thick with humidity. It felt like Vietnam. And just like in Vietnam, he avoided the trails and entered the Reserve through the trees. Walking stealthily, he kept to the woods until he came upon the wooden concession stand where you could buy snacks or bait or rent boats. Old Mr. Felmer sat behind the open window smoking his Camel cigarette, just as he had since Nick was a kid. Nick quietly came up and leaned on the counter. The old man jumped, startled.

"Goddamn it, Nick! You shouldn't sneak up on an old man like that! Might have the big one!" He feigned a heart attack and held his chest, chuckling now. "Don't tell me. Dr. Pepper, corn chips, and a pack of Camels, right?"

Nick grinned and nodded. "Sure. Why not?"

Mr. Felmer placed them in front of Nick but refused his money. "Where you been? Haven't seen you in a coon's age. Damn, you're skinny!"

Nick lit a cigarette behind tightly cupped hands. Then stepped away slightly. He watched the old man's eyes. "Vietnam."

Gene Felmer stared at Nick, then shook his head and walked back to his chair. He snorted scornfully. "Vietnam? Vietnam ain't shit! I was in World War II. The big one! Now that was a REAL war!"

Nick felt a dagger jabbed into his heart. He had hoped the older veterans would understand. For a fleeting moment he felt very alone, the heat of anger filling his chest.

Felmer lit another Camel. "Some friends of yours just rented some rowboats. They're down at the dock."

"Who?"

"Pat, Pam, and Judy Jacklin. Some kid named John and his brother Jim."

Nick nodded dejectedly. "OK. See ya." He quickly walked away.

As he neared the water, he could hear laughing and splashing. The two boats, side by side, were close to shore, the Jacklin girls in one, the two boys in another. Their oars were flailing water onto each other. The older boy rowed his boat very close and tried to splash the girls, but the oar skipped off the muddy water and slammed into young Judy's arm. She screamed in pain, and suddenly the fun was over.

"Oh, my God! I'm sorry!" the boy cried out, "Let's get you in to shore."

Standing on the old dock, Nick grabbed the bow of the girls' boat and held it steady with one hand and guided them out with the other. Judy held her arm, but it did not look serious. Pat was shocked to see Nick appear so suddenly. He nodded to her but reached out and gently felt Judy's arm. "Can you move your fingers?" he asked. Seeing that she could and caressing it lightly, he said, "You'll live."

Pat came up to him and shoved him playfully. "Aren't you gonna say hello? How long have you been away anyhow? "

"Couple years I guess." He added, "Just back from Vietnam."

"Vietnam? Holy shit!" It was the older boy, huddled up with the others. "What was that like?" he queried.

Nick gave him a deadpan look. The boy grew uneasy in the following silence. "Hi, I'm John. John Belushi. This is my brother, Jim." He reached out his hand. Nick took it. The boy was shorter than Nick, broad shouldered, and a little thick but not yet fat, with brown wavy hair and dark eyes, maybe fifteen. Nick thought he must be Italian.

Then it hit him. "Yeah, I remember you now. You go to Wheaton High, right?" He smiled.

Belushi nodded vigorously and shifted from one foot to the other as if waddling like a penguin. Nick's features softened as he recalled seeing this kid in the hallways at school. He was a perpetual clown and constantly made everyone around him laugh.

But now John asked again seriously. "No, really. What was the war like?"

Nick stared at him blankly. The words would not come. Then, he muttered, "Living hell." He felt the woods calling him. He turned away and began to climb the slope.

Pat threw her hands out at her sides. "Nick!" she called. "Where are you going?"

Still walking, he turned and waved back over his shoulder. "See you around!" He disappeared into the forest and set off to find his old cabin, where he used to retreat during that other painful time.

The next time he saw Belushi's face would be in the movie *Animal House*. John and Judy would marry and, following a meteoric rise to fame and fortune, John would die of a massive drug overdose in 1982. Another Wheaton High graduate, Bob Woodward, Nick's wrestling teammate at school, would write a book about Belushi called *Wired*. But first he would skyrocket into the national spotlight as a reporter for *The Washington Post*. His book, *All the President's Men*, would bring down President Nixon.

Nick bought a red 1963 Chevy Impala. It was big and powerful and better than any of the cars he had before he went away to the Army. He was glad to be alive as he raced along the open highway that led out of town through the endless fields that lay between Wheaton, Illinois, and Lake Geneva, Wisconsin. He had never been there before, but while still in Vietnam he and A.J. had agreed to meet on the steps of the police station at 12:00 noon on the Fourth of July. When Nick arrived he found A.J. sitting on the steps eyeing his watch.

"Goddamn it, troop! You're thirty-five seconds late!" They hugged and laughed. Keeping the promise reinforced their mutual trust and respect.

With a thirty-day leave to enjoy, the men were anxious to return to Washington, D.C. and reconnect with old friends. Nick had more promises to keep. His squad leader, Sergeant Davis, lived in D.C. and had come home just two months before. Nick had promised to look him up.

Then there was the foxhole promise that he had made to Carmine Genovese. Carmine was a rifleman in Nick's squad. He hailed from Rahway, New Jersey. On occasion he would take Nick's place on point. One night, as they shared a foxhole out in War Zone C, the two men promised each other that if either of them got killed, the survivor would go visit the dead one's family and tell them how much their son had loved them. Just before his tour came to an end, Nick went AWOL to try to get stateside papers for Lieu, his Vietnamese girlfriend. While he was gone, the battalion went out on an operation. Genovese had taken Nick's place on point and was killed. When Nick returned to his unit, he got the devastating news. From that moment on he was reviled by the rest of his squad. One of the men even tried to kill Nick on several occasions, the last time just days before Nick rotated back to the U.S.

Consumed with guilt and shame, Nick had considered letting Chief, a Shoshone Indian from Idaho, actually kill him as just punishment for his selfish act. But the monster inside him had grown too strong for that. Now he was destined to suffer life without parole.

As they cruised in the big car through the rolling corn fields of Ohio, Nick tried to find the courage and the words to face Carmine's parents.

When they arrived in Arlington, they checked into a cheap motel and Nick looked up Sergeant Davis in the phone book.

When the familiar voice on the other end answered, Nick felt a rush of adrenaline, like when they were back in the bush. "Hey, Sarge! How the hell are ya?"

"Nick, you son of a bitch! Where are you?"

"In town."

"Man, I got a reefer full of cold beer. Come on over."

Suddenly Nick felt fear, caught in a crossfire between excitement and dread. "OK. But I've got a buddy with me."

"That's OK. Here, let me give you directions. I'll be waiting on ya."

As Davis told Nick how to reach his house, he felt the panic getting stronger. Davis had left Vietnam just before Carmine's death. There would undoubtedly be questions about the men in the squad. How could he tell him the truth? When Nick's big Chevy was within two blocks of the house, he abruptly turned onto a side street and headed back to Arlington. A.J. was shocked.

"What happened? I thought we were going to see your buddy."

Nick stared straight ahead with tight lips. Anger burned in his eyes. He gritted his teeth and shook his head. "Let's go see Big John instead," he said solemnly.

The cemetery directory guided them to the grave that held their old friend. Nick parked on the side and they walked silently up to the marker of polished stone. Simultaneously they drew themselves up to attention.

A.J. whispered the command. "Present, arms!" Both men snapped a quivering salute to their former mentor and hero. As the afternoon sun warmed the earth, they stood quietly, each with his own memories. It had been at this very place, just one year ago, when Big John had befriended them, helped them and ultimately led them off on the biggest adventure of their lives.

Afterward, they decided to visit their old barracks and shoot the shit with their former comrades. The truth was they wanted to go rub their noses in the fact that they had gone to war while these arrogant REMFs had done nothing but played soldier. But when they got there, they found nobody they knew. Many of the men actually had gone to Vietnam.

Suddenly, Nick knew there would be no trip to Rahway, New Jersey. The guilt he carried over Carmine's death prevented him from finding the courage to face the family. Breaking his promise to Genovese only added another layer of guilt on top of others. Standing on the parade ground of Fort Myer, Virginia, Nick vowed to never again break a promise. And that vow would change his life forever.

The next day they started the long drive back. He had to report to Fort Carson, Colorado, in a few days. A.J. was being sent to Tennessee.

Nick loved the mountains. They were a symbol of strength and freedom to him, just like the new car. He would drive toward the mountains and he would feel strong and free. He would think, sometimes, about the dead. He was glad to be alive, but he thought it was unfair. Why had he been chosen to carry on? The point man slowly began cutting a trail into the darkness of an unchartered jungle. It swallowed him. There was no one to give him a heading, and there was no going back. Once again, Nick was alone in the forest.

CHAPTER 4
Wailuku, Maui
January 1989

Zach Christopher, president of the Vietnam Veterans of Maui, reached for the ringing phone on his desk.

"Hey, Zach, it's Nick."

"Nick! What's happening, brah?"

"You got a minute? I need to talk to somebody, man."

Zach's face dropped with concern. He kept the phone to his ear while he stood and closed the door to the living room where his kids were watching TV. "Any time, brother. You know that. What's up?"

"You know."

"Still?"

"Yeah, man. I just can't get it out of my head. I thought it was over when I published the story about my first trip. Shit! It was just the beginning! I just wanna farm and raise my family and be left alone, you know? But it invades my thinking all day long. It haunts me constantly."

"How about at night? Can you sleep?"

"Hell no. If I drink a bunch of beers and smoke a joint or two, then I can get a couple hours. The next day I'm so exhausted that I take it out on Malia and the boys. They don't know what the hell is happening. Neither do I, man. What do I do, brah?" There was an embarrassed pause. "Last night, I got the gun again."

"Oh no, come on, brother, please! I know it seems like the answer, but it's not! Later, when you come out of it, you're always glad you didn't, right?"

Another pause. Soul searching this time. "Yeah, I know, but…"

"Fuck it, Nick! Don't mean nothin', brah! Drive on!"

"Yeah, I know."

Zach could hear it in Nick's voice. This wasn't over. Not by a long shot. He grasped at straws.

"Nick, you mentioned your story. I've never had a chance to read it. Maybe it has a clue to something. Could you bring me a copy? I'd love to read it."

"OK. When?"

"You coming to the meeting tonight?"

"Yeah. Hey, listen Zach. I need to tell you something. I know this sounds crazy, but I've been asked to join a group that's trying to help the Amerasian kids that we fathered over there. But I'm scared. I don't know what to do. I know I need help, but I just don't know where to turn. I'm going back, but I don't even want to! Do you believe that shit?"

Zach took a deep breath. He saw a shard of hope. "OK, Nick. You bring me that article this afternoon and give me a chance to read it. We can fix this thing. Trust me, OK?"

"OK."

Nick arrived two hours before the meeting. He and Zach hugged each other tightly, then went into the house. Nick traded Zach the magazine for a cold beer and went out on the lanai where they sat in wicker chairs. Zach read while Nick gazed out at the waves breaking on the beach a mile away. Zach opened the June 1988 copy of *Honolulu* magazine and thumbed through it until he came upon the picture of the young, baby-faced soldier in his beret and jungle fatigues carrying his M-2 carbine. It had been taken just two weeks after Nick arrived in-country. He had been full of patriotic fervor and optimism as he gazed into his future of certain heroism and glory. He knew without question that, after winning the war, he would come home covered in medals, to ticker tape parades, pats on the back, and bands playing. The girls would fall all over him, while those men who had lacked the guts to go fight would look on with envy.

The article was titled, "Coming Home/Going Back." It was billed as, "The story of a Vietnam Veteran who makes peace with his past." Zach sighed deeply, leaned back in the chair with his feet up on the table, and began to read.

As fate would have it, I was in Vietnam on my wedding anniversary. On the morning of my departure, my wife—my present wife—had handed me a sealed note that I was instructed not to open until the day of the anniversary. On Sept. 22, in Ho Chi Minh City, I did. It said: 'I love you too much to hold onto you. I love you too much to let you go. So close your eyes and catch your dream, but always think of me and be happy. Happy Anniversary, Love, Malia.'

From the plane's window I gaze down between the billowing cumulous clouds. Far below, the Saigon River winds through the lush, verdant jungle. It slips silently past the twisted trunks and roots of the mangrove swamps, out into the shimmering delta. The tropical sun glints off the flooded rice paddies. It has been twenty-one years since I last saw this landscape. There has not been a single day in all that time that I have not thought about how it was. I have come to accept Vietnam as an integral part of me. It will be with me always. Here, right now, descending toward its greenness once again, remembering the many lessons I learned here, I wouldn't have it any other way.

It's September 1987. I am here on a special Philippine Airlines tour. We begin our approach into Tan Son Nhat over thatched roofs and banana groves. Below us, knee deep in the mud of the paddies, several black-clad figures bend over their work, shaded by their conical straw hats. We glide past a water buffalo plodding through the oozing gray muck, slowly pulling a plow rake carrying a young boy. As our jet roars overhead I can see the boy's face turn to watch.

Suddenly the reality of what is about to happen washes over me like a tremendous wave. I am drenched with memories. I am dripping with fear. Twenty-one years of waiting and now the climax. Now! I cannot believe it is about to happen. For a fleeting moment I am back in the past. I am lying on a muddy trail near Lai Khe. A VC .51 caliber machine gun is mowing down the jungle around our platoon. I hear the dull thuds of the rounds impacting into the bodies. I hear the screams of terror coming from my own throat and the cries of agony coming from others.

Now, as the wheels touch the tarmac and the plane rumbles over the rough surface, I am jolted back into the present, with the engines roaring in my ears. I am about to meet my former enemy.

After a brief inspection at Customs we are driven to the old Rex Hotel by an air-conditioned bus which will be our sole transportation throughout the country. We arrive in time to settle in our modest but well-maintained rooms and indulge in a few Ba Muoi Ba beers at the rooftop garden bar before dinner.

In the dining room across the hall, tables are arranged by nationality and identified by a small flag at the head of each one. It is interesting to note that the American table is composed mostly of Vietnamese who are returning to visit family, with native-born Americans in an obvious minority; at the Russian table only Soviets dine together. It is rumored that the Russian government discourages social interaction between its citizens and the Vietnamese.

After a good night's rest and a breakfast of meat, vegetable, and noodle soup, we board the bus which takes us out to Cu Chi where the Twenty-Fifth Infantry Division was stationed. It is also in the same area of operations for my old unit, the First Infantry Division.

As we drive past the lush green rice paddies and well-kept farms, I cannot help but marvel at the transformation that has occurred since I was here last. The paddies now display their fertility to their full potential— their natural cycle no longer interrupted by air strikes, artillery barrages, or companies of infantry digging them up to construct nighttime defensive perimeters.

During my tour of duty, many of us used to say that without the war Vietnam would be one of the most beautiful places on earth. I am pleased to find that we were right.

In Cu Chi we are ushered into a lecture hall where we are addressed by a young woman, an army captain dressed in civilian clothes. She speaks Vietnamese while our guide translates.

I notice that during the half-hour lecture, in spite of the presence of some twenty other tour members, Capt. Bich does not take her eyes off mine the whole time. Perhaps she senses that I am the only ex-grunt in the group.

She describes in detail how the extensive Viet Cong tunnel network around Cu Chi was constructed, how the soil from the digging was hidden and how it was designed to prevent American tunnel rats from penetrating it.

Someone asks her how long she spent underground. She answers through the interpreter that she was born there and remained there for the first seven years of her life before coming out to live on the surface at the end of the war.

We are all invited to crawl through one of the remaining tunnels, which has been enlarged slightly to accommodate Americans. It stretches about 50 meters from the jungle to the other side of the road. I am the only volunteer. My sole companion is a former Viet Cong who helped build it in 1967. He gestures for me to go first but I refuse and offer to follow him. He hesitates, eyeing me suspiciously. I then realize that each of us mistrusts and is afraid of the other. Some feelings die hard. After a moment I break the impasse by offering my hand. He shakes it and I talk to him in Vietnamese, which I still speak fairly well. "Brother, we were once enemies. Those days are gone. We should be friends and try to forget the past. Let us go through the tunnel together to show the others the way."

He looks into my eyes to see if they betray my words. Seeing that I am sincere, he smiles, bends over and disappears into the hole. While he quickly duck-walks through the narrow passage, which is approximately two and a half feet square, I am forced by my larger frame to crawl on hands and knees through water, mud, rats, and roaches. Only 50 feet in, the temperature soars to well over 100 degrees F. I am gasping for air. Suddenly I realize I cannot breathe. I begin to panic. I remember that old fear from the past. It hits me just as it did back in 1966. But I also remember how to dispel it. For the first time in twenty-one years I am forced to accept my own death once again. I realize fully its inevitability. It cannot be denied. Then, as suddenly as it came, the fear vanishes. I experience total freedom, not caring any longer. I feel I was supposed to die here long ago. Every day since then has been a bonus. I find that I can breathe again.

I grin at the guide, who is watching me with his flashlight, and motion him to lead on. We crawl straight ahead, climb up a few feet, turn left and there it is—the proverbial light at the end of the tunnel.

We emerge through a tiny opening that I squeeze past into sunlight, fresh air, and the cheers and applause of the rest of the group. We both give a huge sigh of relief and bow to each other. I offer him a pack of Marlboros which he readily accepts. We take a long look into each other's eyes and it seems he wants to tell me something but cannot. There is no need. The silent offer of friendship is unmistakable in his eyes. He pats my shoulder, which is covered with clay, as I turn and board the bus for our return to Ho Chi Minh City. On our way back, our government guide strikes up a conversation with me.

"So, Anh Ly, why do you come back to Vietnam?"

"Well," I reply, "there are many reasons. I have wanted to come back here ever since I left in 1966. This is my first chance to do so. When I was stationed here before, I was first assigned to MACV. We lived in the village with the people and trained the ARVN soldiers. I learned to speak your language, eat your food, and respect your customs. I also met and fell in love with a beautiful Vietnamese girl named Lieu."

"Were you married to her?"

"Yes, by Vietnamese law, but it was not recognized by the U.S. government. Then, halfway through my tour I was sent to an American combat unit known as the Big Red One."

The guide, whose name is Lien, smiles knowingly at this.

"Yes, the First Infantry Division. They were very notorious."

I laugh uncomfortably, then continue.

"When my tour ended, the government refused to let me bring her back home. We eventually lost contact with each other, but we were very much in love. Recently, back in America, a Vietnamese friend told me she knew Lieu before and said that soon after I left Vietnam she had given birth to a baby girl. Although I am remarried now, I just had to come back and try to find them."

"Do you know where they are now?" he asks.

"No, but I have an old address of Lieu's parents that is on the other side of the Saigon River."

"If you like, I could send someone to find them for you. Perhaps this evening."

I am overwhelmed by this offer and hastily agree to meet Lien in the lobby that evening before he can change his mind. That night I wait impatiently for him by the front door, but he doesn't show. My nervousness turns to agitation as it gets darker outside. Tomorrow we will leave for Nha Trang, so this is my only chance. To hell with him, I will do it alone. Just as I step through the door into the night, Lien suddenly appears and asks me abruptly, "Where are you going?"

"To find my family, remember?"

"It is too late now."

"Lien, I must go. I have come too far and waited too long."

"No," he commands, "You should stay here. Later I will help you."

Confronting the tunnel in Cu Chi has given me new courage. I look directly into his eyes and tell him, "Anh Lien, I am going. There is only one way you can stop me, but I know you cannot afford to murder any Americans at this point."

Lien smiles, shakes his head and simply says, "It is up to you, Ly."

I smile. "I know. See you later."

I find a man with a Honda motorbike who agrees to take me to the twenty year-old address. The Honda has no headlight, there are no street lights, there is no moon. We literally feel our way through the rivers of humanity flowing in the darkness down through the ancient smells of Ho Chi Minh City.

We encounter some difficulty. People in the street won't give us directions because they think I am a Russian, and they are leery. I explain that I am an American and why I have come. Their attitude does an about-face. They lead me to the house, laughing and chattering excitedly.

I learn from the people who now occupy the house that Lieu and her family moved away more than fifteen years ago to the village of Long Khanh, which is about 130 kilometers away. It is too far to go. The Honda driver, whose name is Mot, says that he will go there while I am on the tour, and he will bring them to Ho Chi Minh City when I return in a few days. It is a generous offer, and I thank him repeatedly for his kindness.

The next morning we board the bus for our trip over to the coast and up to Nha Trang. We drive through monsoon rains and badly flooded roads most of the day, which makes sightseeing and picture taking difficult. We spend the time chatting, dozing, or eating fresh fruits and delicious French bread sandwiches purchased along the way.

We arrive in Nha Trang that night and are served a wonderful dinner of beef, squash and carrot soup with bread, and a main dish of green beans, beef, and onions with rice.

I retire to my room and discover there is no hot water for a shower. But before I can get upset I remember that this is Vietnam, and I smile when I recall that during my first stay in this country I did not have hot water for a whole year except what was in my canteens.

The next morning we tour the beaches around Nha Trang and visit two Buddhist pagodas, one of which was built in the tenth century by the Cham minority. Both are complete with beggars, lepers, and orphaned children. I bow before the ancient statue of Buddha and pray for success in finding my ex-wife or her family. I light joss sticks to ward off evil spirits, then I give money to some of the children at the temple gate. I feel it is good luck.

The next night we lodge at the Dalat Palace, which was built by the French in the 1920s. It was obviously once a luxurious hotel during the colonial era, but is now in need of serious repair. The food, on the other hand, is a harmonious blend of French and Vietnamese and is the best we have enjoyed so far.

After dinner, many of the guests gather around the Vietronics TV set in the lobby to watch a locally produced sitcom. I decide, however, to go up to *my room. Lying in the bed under the mosquito net, I hear a Willie Nelson song blaring from a nearby recreation club. But it is not the music or the hundreds of whining mosquitoes outside the net that keep me awake. I am thinking of Lieu, of our life together in Vung Tau more than two decades ago. I wonder if, in fact, there is a daughter. If so, is she mine? Are they alive? Are they still in Vietnam? Will I ever find them? If I do, then what? Tomorrow I should have a lead, because we are returning to Ho Chi Minh City. My friend Mot should have the family and/or Lieu waiting for me, if he has kept his promise. Before closing my eyes I say a final prayer.*

The next morning is sunny and cool. After a breakfast of an omelet and French bread, we board the bus for our return. All day long I sit alone in fear of the outcome. I practice the philosophy that I learned here long ago; Hope for the best but expect the worst. The bus ride seems to take an eternity, but we finally arrive late in the afternoon in front of the Rex Hotel.

I search frantically for a sign of the family but I see only one familiar face in the crowd. It is Mot. He greets me excitedly. Yes, he has brought Lieu's mother and two brothers all the way from Long Khanh, and they are waiting at a friend's house nearby.

Minutes later, as we dismount the little Honda, my stomach is churning. As we hurry down a small alleyway between the old shacks I see a door open. Out steps Lieu's mother. (I still call her Ma.) Suddenly we are hugging and crying tears of joy. It is incredible! Inside the house I do the same with both brothers, Ysa and Liem. They immediately hand me some pictures of Lieu taken two years ago. Through my tears I fearfully ask where she is. Ma turns over one of the pictures and there is her address. I begin to laugh hysterically. It is only two miles from my brother's house in Portland, Oregon. I ask Ma if there is a daughter.

"Yes, Ly," she replies. "But I cannot remember her age."

Her answer leads me to skepticism. The Vietnamese are famous for lying to you if they think the truth will hurt. I suspect this is the case here.

We all continue our reunion over dinner that evening at a local restaurant. We try to catch up on events in each other's lives that have occurred half the world apart. Ma tells me that Lieu was placed in a re-education camp in 1975, and after she was released she ran off to live alone in the jungle for more than five years. Then in 1982 she escaped by walking across Cambodia while evading NVA and Khmer Rouge patrols until she finally made her way to Thailand. Some Red Cross people there helped her get to America.

I then tell them of the years I spent in college studying Vietnamese and tropical agriculture in order to return to Vietnam to live and work with Lieu. But when I graduated the war was over, and I found that returning was impossible.

I soon exhaust my Vietnamese vocabulary and the time comes to say goodbye. Their faces show disappointment when I tell them that I must return to America the next morning, but brighten somewhat when I say that I will go straight to Portland to find Lieu. Then the oldest brother, Ysa, says shyly, "Ly, I have never seen a man like you in real life. Only in the movies. We cannot believe that you came back to Vietnam after all these years to find us. I wish I could be your real brother."

I fight the lump forming in my throat and manage to choke out, "Ysa, Liem, Ma. No matter where we are or how long we are apart or what happens to any of us, I want you to know that I will always love you with all my heart, and you will always be my family."

At this Ysa puts his head on my shoulder and we embrace. Then, amid the inevitable tears, we all say farewell. Before they leave I remember to give them a bag full of money and medicine. Their gratitude is obvious and they thank me many times on the way outside to the waiting pedicabs. Then I am standing alone watching and waving as they disappear in the darkness.

Later, back at the Rex, feeling the greatest exhilaration of my life, I remember to thank Buddha for answering my prayer.

The next morning I awake before dawn with mixed emotions. I am excited to be on my way to Portland to complete my quest. But I also feel the heartbreaking agony of leaving the only place on this earth where I feel I really belong. I have waited more than two decades to come back here, and it is already time to leave. The funny thing is, as I watch the sun rise over the banyan trees and the decaying buildings, I remember that's exactly how I felt when I left in 1966.

Later on, as we load our baggage onto the bus, I hear someone calling my name. I look across the street where a group of Vietnamese is beckoning to me. I recognize the pedicab drivers who helped me find the man with the Honda. He is there also. There is the street vendor to whom I gave a carton of cigarettes and the young girl who needed shampoo more than I. And in the midst of them all, smiling shyly, is Ysa. The street vendor steps forward as I approach. He hands me a beautifully gift-wrapped box. He bows to me and smiles. In broken English he says, "Ly, we thank you very much for being our friend. We are poor and no have much money but have a little gift to offer you for souvenir. Today we know you go home. We wish you have a good trip and never forget us, because we will never forget you."

I fumble with the wrapping paper but soon uncover a gold ceramic ashtray cast in the shape of a water buffalo with two children sleeping on it.

I am so moved I am speechless. I bow low to all of them and when I raise my head tears are streaming down my cheeks. There is an awkward silence. I feel like Dorothy saying goodbye to her friends from Oz. Then suddenly we are all bowing and hugging. I stumble blindly to the bus. As I board I find there isn't a dry eye in the place. As the bus pulls away from the curb I look back through misty eyes at my friends who are waving, cheering, and shouting their farewells. That picture will stay with me the rest of my life.

One week later in Portland, Oregon, I rub the sleep from my eyes and knock on the door of the old wooden house. Soon I hear the familiar footsteps and the door opens slowly. It is early morning and her face is tired but yes, it is really Lieu! For a moment I cannot speak, so I just hold up a snapshot of her that I had taken in Vung Tau in 1965. I watch her eyes light up and she gasps, "Ly!" and jumps into my arms. Suddenly it all feels like yesterday again. She looks 18 and I feel 18.

Still holding me she asks excitedly, "How you find me?"

"I just returned from Vietnam last week. I saw the family there, and they told me where you are."

As she leads me into her modest home I am barraged with questions about my journey to find her. We sit together on the couch, and she asks, "Ly, after all these years why you try to find me now?"

"Because before this I couldn't come to Vietnam on account of the situation between our countries. Then recently I met a friend of yours named Mai. She said you had a daughter and it might be mine."

Lieu smiles gently and shakes her head. "Oh Ly, that's why you come?"

"That's part of it. The rest I don't understand myself."

"Sit down, Ly. Yes I have a daughter. But I adopt her. She is not yours. Now she is staying with my sister. You remember Lily?"

"Yes, of course."

"They are in Michigan now."

Seeing the relief and disappointment in my eyes, Lieu holds me and says simply, "I am sorry."

Not knowing whether to laugh or cry, I sit in numbed silence while *she explains that she is living with a Vietnamese man named Anh whom she escaped with in 1982. They are happy, but... She looks down at my left hand, and I see the resignation in her eyes when she spots the wedding ring.*

"So Ly, you have wife now, yes?"

I nod, and she looks away out the window at the gray sky.

"Is she a good woman?"

"Yes. In fact she reminds me of you. She looks like you, she has a good heart like you, and her name is Malia."

At this, Lieu looks at me and smiles. "Then I am happy for you, Ly." She pats my hand. "Would you like some café au lait?"

Over the next week we see each other daily, and up until our last goodbye the subject never comes up again.

I have always been a dreamer. Many of us are. But I follow my dreams. They have led me on many adventures over the years and I have never come away from any of them without learning at least one important lesson.

Sitting here now with Lieu, together for the first time since the war, and about to say goodbye again, part of me feels like a fool for having gone more than twenty thousand miles to find a daughter who isn't mine. But the rest of me is at peace because of having faced old fears and finding new courage. I have rekindled my love affair with an entire nation, and I realize now that Vietnam is and always has been my destiny. I resolve to go back again. For the first time, finally, the war is over.

~ ~

Zach wiped his eyes, put down the magazine, and looked over at his friend. Nick was far away now, across the sea, in a distant land where a vital part of his soul would forever be. Obviously the peace that he had found just a few months earlier when the story was published was gone. Still tortured by some unseen demons, Nick's life was spinning out of control. Zach put his hand on Nick's shoulder.

"Brother, that's a beautiful story, and you wrote it well. I gotta be honest with you though. I don't know how to advise you. You're one of a kind, man. This is uncharted territory. I never heard of anyone else who has gone back since the war. But whatever you decide, I'll support you."

Later, Zach Christopher stood and banged his fist on the long table. "All right, gentlemen!" He was met with chuckling and growling from the ragged group. "Let's move on to new business!" He paused a moment, then continued in his deep command voice. "There's only one more item on our agenda tonight, but it's a doozy. As you all know, back in 1987, Nick went back to Vietnam to find out if it was true that he had left a daughter behind at the end of his tour. And I'm proud to tell you that he was one of the very first American vets to do that. Well, he wrote a story about it for *Honolulu* magazine and this is a copy that he brought here tonight!" The applause and cheers were immediate and spontaneous. Nick grinned bashfully and looked down at the floor. A few men slapped him on the back. Nick felt his face flush and a huge lump in his throat. Zach continued, "Before the meeting started tonight Nick told me he's actually going back to Nam again!"

The simultaneous gasps swept through the room like a dry wind. Someone yelled out, "You crazy?" Another laughed derisively. Sitting next to Nick, Custer shook his head quietly.

Zach raised his hands calling for calm. "But this time he is asking us for some help. So, brother Nick, the floor is all yours."

Taking a deep breath, Nick surveyed the room with dark eyes. He took in the long unruly hair, tattered T-shirts, bristled sunburnt faces and deep-set, penetrating stares of America's rejects. The unwelcome misfits who had been vilified by an embarrassed nation sat hunched over on folding metal chairs reeking of sweat, stale beer, and marijuana. He loved them. They were him, and he was them, and there was no one else on earth who understood, or cared, or loved them the way they loved each other. In those early days, there was no VA office, no Vet Center, no veterans' clinic, no counselors, no psychologists. Nobody. All they had was each other. And that alone. Nick put his hands on the table and pushed himself up to his full height.

"Yeah, I know you all think I'm nuts."

"That's common knowledge, Nick!" someone yelled, and raucous laughter filled the room.

"So, what is it this time?" The Grizz asked. "Did you find out you had another kid over there?" He looked around conspiratorially, raising more chuckling.

Nick continued quietly. "Well, first of all, I gave my word to my ex-wife's family over there that I was coming back to give them some help, like money and supplies. It has taken me a year and a half to put it all together, and now I'm going. But something else has also come up. Did any of you guys see the news the other night about a Vietnam vet in Honolulu who is trying to help the Amerasian orphans in Ho Chi Minh City?" Tim Campbell, a tall, lanky ex-marine who had been shot in the head during the Tet Offensive and was now half paralyzed raised his good hand.

"Yeah, Nick. You mean the black dude named John Rogers?"

"That's him. He started an organization called FACES, which is an acronym for Foundation for Amerasian Children Emergency Support. I called him up, and we talked about this project that he and his Vietnamese wife started. According to him there are about twenty thousand Amerasian kids left behind in Vietnam who are the product of our liaisons with the local women."

Babaloo was an ex-Green Beret. He was short, squat, and thick. He had also been shot in the head and looked like a cross between a pit bull and a toad. He blurted out, "Is that all? Hell, I made that many by my own self!" He then leered around the room, eliciting lecherous guffaws.

Giving them a smirk, Nick went on, "When the NVA took over the south in early 1975, a lot of these women were terrified that they would be tortured and killed if they were found with half-breed children, so they abandoned them in the streets with no money, food, or anything. A lot of them died, unwanted, afraid and alone."

A hush fell over the room as this sunk in to the scores of middle-aged men in attendance. They all knew how it felt to be a pariah in their own land. Unspoken compassion was clear on many faces. A somber bitterness swept over others as a sense of guilt and helplessness overwhelmed their already-tortured minds.

"He says a group of these orphans lives in a park in Ho Chi Minh City begging, stealing, selling themselves, or whatever, just praying for someone to help them get to America."

Glenn Yamamoto, the son of a Japanese-American soldier who had fought with the famed 442nd Regiment during World War II, twisted uncomfortably in his chair. "Can't they go to our embassy for help?" he asked. Some others nodded in agreement. Nick suddenly realized how few of these vets actually understood the situation.

"Don't you remember April 30, 1975? We abandoned our

embassy when the last Huey lifted off with the U.S. Marine guards on board. Vietnam was entirely overrun. After fourteen years we are still technically at war with them. We no longer have diplomatic, trade, or relations of any kind. We can't even communicate with Vietnam. It's impossible to telephone, and written letters take a month to get there and even longer to get a reply back because of government censorship. I know, 'cause I've tried. And there are no known Americans in-country, except maybe some POWs."

This unwelcome reminder brought sullen sneers of disgust from the group, who still held their government in contempt for failing to deal with this sensitive issue, especially Zach, who leaned forward with an intensely determined glare. "Nick, you already know how we all feel about our brothers who got left behind. But what can we do to help these kids?"

"John Rogers asked me to join his organization and sit on the board of directors. He also asked me to donate money." Nick glanced over at Paul, the treasurer, who treated each expenditure as if it came out of his own pocket. Paul glowered back with one raised eyebrow. "I know our club doesn't have much money."

Paul, visibly upset, launched into a verbal tirade, "Goddamn it, Nick, you don't even know this guy! You want us to hand over our hard-earned money to a total stranger? What if he's a con man?"

"Relax, brah! I told him no." Paul sat back. "But I also decided that I'm going back, and I'm gonna check this dude out. If he's for real… then I recommend we support him with a donation."

Babaloo swilled down the last of the beer that he had half-hidden between his legs, then reached next to him and grabbed A.K.'s hand. "FOR REAL?" he bellowed. "I'll show you FOR REAL! Give me your pinkie, goddamn it!" He then jammed A.K.'s little finger up to the first knuckle into the bullet hole that still remained in Babaloo's skull. "I'M for real, by God! The bullet went in there and came out right here under my eye! But I didn't pass out. I stayed on the radio and called in some fast movers who came and saved our sorry asses. Har! Har! Har!" Then he crossed his eyes and slouched back against the metal chair, drooling from the corner of his curled lip.

The old-timers in the group howled hilariously at the look of horror that filled A.K.'s face. The poor FNG was totally unprepared for this initiation ritual for all new members. No one was allowed to join the VVM until they had stuck their finger into Babaloo's skull.

Nick shuddered as a chill went through him. He remembered the night, not long ago, when he and Babaloo had gone to a drug dealer named Dangerous Dan to score some cocaine.

They walked into the house unannounced, and Babaloo grabbed Dan's .38 revolver off the table before the stunned dealer could even blink. Babaloo strapped it on and got into Dan's terrorized face. "Give Nick that marchin' powder! I'm taking this with me." Nick put down some money and they walked out with the drugs, and the gun, leaving "Dangerous Dan" in open-mouthed shock.

Later, at Nick's house, in a coke-crazed frenzy, Nick saw Babaloo playing with the gun and put two rounds in the cylinder and snapped it shut. Nick went to get another beer, and when he returned Babaloo stuck the pistol to his own head and squeezed the trigger. Click! He walked up to Nick, put it in his hands and said, "You don't have a hair on your ass, motherfucker!"

Nick put his nose against Babaloo's and the gun to his own temple. He pulled the trigger. Click! Babaloo's eyes opened wide in shock and he grabbed Nick's head and kissed him on the lips. Then he snatched away the pistol and flung open the cylinder to expose six empty holes and demanded, "How did you know it was empty?"

Nick spit on the floor. "I didn't."

Chuckling to himself at the memory, Nick patiently continued. "What I'm saying is this. Yeah, Paul's right, we don't know this guy. But you know me, and I'm asking you to give me some money to take along when I go back in a couple of weeks. I'm going to find them and buy them clothes, supplies, and medicine or anything else they need to help tide them over until they can get processed out."

Zach scanned the rough-hewn faces. "Nick, how much do you need?"

"How much we got?"

Paul frowned at the scattered giggling. Looking down at the check register he read, "One thousand thirty two dollars and eighteen cents." Then, all eyes followed his as he stared pointedly at Nick.

Nick replied, "Five hundred would go a long way over there."

A few of the men looked at each other and nodded approvingly. Others crossed their arms and squinted at something in the distance. Zach squirmed in his chair. "Nick, that's nearly half our savings. We don't have any fund-raising plans for some time."

Nick's face softened, and he surveyed the quiet room. "The Vietnamese government won't help them. The American government is trying to help, but by the time they get off their asses there won't be any kids left alive. It's up to us. These are OUR kids. And it's the right thing to do. I'll bring back receipts for every penny I spend. I give you my word."

Zach turned to Paul, who nodded begrudgingly. Zach, with a satisfied smile said, "Nick, that's good enough for me. All those in favor of giving Nick five hundred bucks to help the Amerasian orphans raise your hand." Every man in the room, but one, gave approval. Zach stood and walked over to Nick extending his hand. "Have a good safe trip, brother!"

Later, in the parking lot, the ragged crew lit joints or popped beers and carried on with the brotherhood portion of the meeting. The six-foot-three, beer-bellied giant, known as, "the Grizz," reached into his cooler and handed Nick a cold one. He then drained his own and looked over at another FNG named Mike Murphy. For some reason, he had brought his tall, good-looking, blonde wife Cathe with him. They huddled shyly on the periphery of the group. The Grizz ran his large fingers through his long, curly red hair and beard as if to primp himself, then strode over to the newcomers and stood towering above the reticent couple. The Grizz winked quickly at Mike then reached out and grabbed Cathe around the waist. "Come here, darlin', and let me show you why they call me the Grizz!" he roared. Then, growling like a bear and laughing heartily he wrapped his powerful arms around the terrified woman and hoisted her up until her feet were kicking in the air. Whimpering, Cathe looked around in hopes of rescue, but the Grizz was not to be denied his fun. Still laughing, he finally set her back down and declared. "Don't worry, honey! I know I look kinda rough, but I'm really a perfect gentleman! I don't piss in the shower!"

The surrounding members joined in the robust laughter as Cathe straightened herself up. Then, finding new courage, and seeking acceptance, she put her hands on her hips and coyly looked the Grizz up and down. "Why not?" she said. "I do!"

The entire parking lot erupted in cheers and applause as the Grizz stood there dumbfounded and speechless. The new couple had passed their trial by fire with flying colors.

Nick's good friend Mark, an ex-marine from Texas, came up to him with a newspaper article in hand. "Nick, I forgot to give you this earlier. It's an article about a Vietnam vet that's goin' back to build a clinic in Vung Tau. He'll be there the same time as you!"

Immediately setting down his beer on the tailgate, Nick angled the paper under the street light and began to read. There was a fuzzy photo of the bearded veteran. "I'll be goddamned! No way! It can't be!" he exclaimed. Now he had everyone's attention, and they gathered around him in the dark.

Mark was obviously aroused. "What is it, brother?"

"It says here his name is Fredy Champagne, formerly Fredy Higdon. He was a machine gunner with the First Infantry Division at Lai Khe in 1966. By God, I know this guy! He was in first platoon and I was in third!"

The news drew intoxicated cheers of amazement. Custer grabbed him behind the neck and shook him.

"Well, I reckon you'll be heading down to Vung Tau too, yeah?"

Nick nodded. "Hell, I was an advisor there for the first half of my tour. Back in '87 they wouldn't let me go back down there. But this time will be different."

"So, what's this about a clinic?" asked Custer.

"It says that he organized a group of vets in northern California and, like us, they did some fund-raising, and somehow they got permission from the Vietnamese government to build and donate a medical clinic to the people in Vung Tau."

"Right on!" yelled Zach, who had scurried over to investigate the animated group. "So Nick, it looks like you'll have your hands full over there, brother! See, I told you things would change."

Nick shook his head slightly, "Yeah, and on top of all that, I have that care package ready to deliver to Lieu's family out in Long Khanh. This'll be a busy three weeks."

Mark grabbed Nick and gave him a firm hug. "You go do what you gotta do. I'll help Malia and the kids take care of your house and the dog and the farms. Don't you worry 'bout nothin', cause it don't pay to think too much on the things you leave behind."

STUART NICHOLLS

CHAPTER 5
China Airlines Flight
February 1989

Soft white clouds drifted gently over a cobalt sea seven miles below. A lilting tune caressed his soul through the headset and his third beer began to open his mind with self-discovery.

I'm truly crazy, he thought to himself, this time I don't even really want to go, but I'm doing it anyway. All because of some stupid rule I have about always keeping my word. I will make it a point, this time, not to give my word to anyone. This is the last tango in Vietnam. Maybe I'm finally learning to put the past behind me and get on with my own life. Home is where the heart is and, right now, my heart is on Maui with Malia, Keoki, and Eric. But if I hadn't taken on this adventure, then maybe I wouldn't have realized how good a life I have there. Things will have to change when, and if, I can get back home.

He took another swig of beer. He sighed and watched the lovely stewardess approaching down the aisle. On the other hand, he thought, this is truly life. There is no greater feeling than to have a mission that is beyond oneself, and is noble, honorable, and right. To be doing this is the most liberating feeling I've ever known. Once again I have purpose and meaning and importance in my life. Thank God I never squeezed the trigger all those times with the gun in my mouth, and yet I am absolutely not afraid of dying now. It is not my destiny to die now. I know it. There is so much to do, and I will do it well. I've waited for over twenty years, and now I can finally fulfill my dreams. The first trip back in '87 was just the beginning. This is what I was made for. I believe in this with all my heart and soul. This is my karma and, for the first time in my life, I know God.

A soft thigh pressed gently against his elbow on the armrest. "Sir, you like one more beer?" The smooth ivory complexion contrasted with the playful almond eyes. Red lips smiled coyly.

"Yes, thank you." Something stirred in his pants. Yes, there is a God. I'm quite sure of it now, he thought.

"So, are you from Taipei?" he asked.

With a delicate hand she sensuously poured the brew into his plastic cup. Then, looking at him from the corner of her eyes, "Yes. Will you stay there long?"

He smiled sadly. "No, just overnight."

"Are you sure?"

He nodded, taking in all of her lovely face.

"What hotel you stay?"

"The Chiang Kai Shek."

"What a shame. It is restricted hotel. You won't be allowed to leave until your next flight. Otherwise, I could show you around our beautiful island."

Her dark eyes bored into his, telling him there was something more to the invitation. He grasped her hand and held it ever so gently. She squeezed back. He looked away awkwardly now, not knowing what to do next.

"I give you my number in case you change your mind."

"You are very beautiful and kind. Thank you."

Swaying gracefully, she continued down the aisle, leaving Nick alone with his conscience and his ego. You dumb bastard, he thought. Here's another gorgeous, sexy chick that you can easily have if you want to. What's wrong with you? Asia is full of them. It's not like you're going to divorce Malia and marry one of them. It's just sex. They know that. Yeah, maybe some money gets exchanged, so what? Is that really being unfaithful? You're living every man's dream. Do it! Don't do it for yourself then, do it for the poor slob who works in a factory back in Indiana, and whose idea of a good time is bowling with the boys on Tuesday night and taking his wife and kids to McDonald's on the weekend. Do it for him! He'd do it for you, right? Better yet, do it for all those on the Wall. God knows, they won't ever have the chance again. They died for you damn it! They gave you this! Don't waste it!

CHAPTER 6
Ho Chi Minh City
September 1987

In a flash, I stood sweating in the stench of moldy Tan Son Nhat airport. Outside the mildew-streaked windows, a heavy downpour bounced off the crumbling pavement. My small group awaited the departure to Manila. Along one wall stood a petite and beautiful Vietnamese girl in a beige dress. She had curled black hair and very white skin. Mercedes, my matronly Philippine Airlines tour guide, was talking with her in broken English. I edged over closer to them, and Mercedes immediately grasped my arm.

"Nick, I want you to meet Mai Nguyen. We know each other from Manila! We just met here now by accident! Isn't that amazing?"

"It really is a small world. Especially when it comes to Vietnam. Nice to meet you." I reached out my hand. She took it gently and held on slightly longer than I expected. "So, you are Vietnamese but you live in Manila?" I asked.

"Yes. My husband is Filipino. I come back here to visit family. Where you come from?"

"I'm American, and my wife is Filipina also."

Her eyes widened in shock. "American?" She scanned my face intently. "You come here before 1975?"

I decided to show off. "*Co chu! Toi da o day tu mot ngan chin tram sau muoi lam den sau muoi sau.*"

She slapped my shoulder hard, feigning embarrassment that I spoke her language that fluently. Suddenly we both smiled and looked deeply into each other's eyes. Mercedes, seeing the obvious connection, eased away and rejoined the group. We began chatting like old friends in both languages.

Later, on the plane, we sat together. When the Philippine Airlines

Airbus lifted off from Vietnamese soil the umbilical was cut once again. A wave of emotion swept over us simultaneously. We both looked at each other with tears streaming down and clasped each other's hands, like there was no tomorrow, and no yesterday, but only here and now. Far from home, alone and yet so together, we were locked hopelessly into the moment with more intensity than we could explain.

The electricity flowed on until after we landed two hours later and found ourselves still together in my hotel room at the Intercontinental in Makati. When I came out of the shower, wrapped in a towel, my eyes fell suddenly onto her lovely, slender, naked body lying on my bed. Her legs were open wide with her left hand stroking herself. Her right hand beckoned. I took her in my arms and slid my tongue into her eager mouth. She began moaning with passion. I could feel myself hard against her and ready. A flash of light exploded in my mind. It was as if I had been in a wonderful dream when something awoke me. I had come on this trip for a noble reason. My karma had been rewarded with success and now it seemed I was being tested. I slowly let go of her writhing body and sat up.

Her mouth dropped open, and her eyes narrowed. "Nick, what is it?"

I caressed her soft cheek with my calloused hand. My voice sounded foreign to me.

"I'm so sorry, but I can't."

"But why? You no like me?"

Pointing down to my erection I said, "You know I do. But we are both married."

Shaking her head she put her arms around me again. "But we are here alone. No one will ever know."

I pulled on my pants. "I'll know."

CHAPTER 7
China Airlines Flight
February 1989

Haunted by his past once again, Nick shuddered in his seat as he watched the stewardess walking away down the aisle. Suddenly he saw Malia. She was back on Maui on her knees in the red dirt reaching under a tomato bush with work-worn hands, plucking the fruit and placing them in plastic buckets. When they were full, she carried the two 25-pound pails to the flatbed truck, dumped them into a wooden bin, then trudged back out through the choking dust under the blistering sun to squat down and do it again and again. With him gone, she worked even longer and harder. She suffered and sacrificed—all without complaining or even understanding what was driving him. How could she ever feel the torment that only vanquished warriors know? How could a simple local girl comprehend the complexities of outcasts who had been brutalized, first by the war, then by their own people when they returned "home?" Their burning yet futile search for vindication drove them by the thousands to drink, drugs, and suicide. There were few options left for the veterans. Nick had done the drinking, and the drugs and had attempted suicide. Now he was discovering a new strategy. He would go back to the source. He would give back to the ones who had taken so much from him. He would forgive the ones he had killed and who had killed him. He would discover that his forgiveness of them and their forgiveness of him were inseparable for, as one prophet said, "No one can enter heaven unless he brings his enemies with him."

"Is your name Nick?" She was back, and handing him a slip of paper.

"How did you know?"

"I'm Mei Ling. You have been upgraded to First Class. Please bring your things and follow me."

Completely baffled he pulled down his carry-on and followed her to the front of the plane, up the spiral staircase to the luxurious cabin perched high behind the cockpit of the 747. Her slim, inviting ass fueled fantasies every step of the way. She stopped and gestured demurely to the empty seat next to a clean-cut, rosy-cheeked young Caucasian man in a blue suit and red tie.

"My number." She stroked his hand that held the paper. She was very close now, and he could smell her exotic perfume. He had an overwhelming desire to kiss her full lips.

He smiled. "Thank you." She nodded and was gone.

"She's very pretty, isn't she?" said the suit. His blue eyes were confident, direct.

"Very." Nick sank into the plush leather seat, reveling in its comfort.

"Bill," said the man, extending a firm handshake.

"Nick." Suddenly, he sensed danger. There was a mine in the trail. "I just can't understand why they moved me up here from the cheap seats. I'm nobody."

"Maybe not." Bill said, almost grinning. "So what kind of work do you do, Nick?"

"I'm a farmer."

"That explains the calluses on your hands. What do you raise?"

"I raise a lot of hell, but my wife keeps praying my crops will fail."

Bill chuckled obligingly. "And where is your farm exactly?" The interrogation continued.

Nick turned to him. "Maui."

Bill nodded, almost knowingly, without surprise as was customary when people heard he was from the legendary island. "So, why are you going to Vietnam?"

Kaboom! "How'd you know that?"

"You told me when you sat down."

"No I didn't."

"A lucky guess then." Bill's cheeks grew redder.

"So, what do YOU do then?" Then it came on him. "No, let me guess. You work for the government." Bill faced him. His eyes said it all. He nodded.

"I'll bet you work with computers, right?" Bill looked away shaking his head. Nick couldn't let it go. "That's exactly what another guy told me told me two years ago on a flight to Vietnam. He was wearing the same suit and tie as you. I'm flattered that you guys think I'm so interesting." Bill squirmed. "Look, I'll tell you straight 'cause I don't give a damn what you think. Vietnam was a cluster-fuck. It was wrong from beginning to end, but those of us who fought it gave it all we had. And none of us walked away normal. We used to say, 'fuck it, don't mean nothin'. That's just how we handled it. But, Bill, you know what?"

"OK, what?"

Nick leaned close enough to let him smell the beer on Nick's breath and see his thousand-yard stare. "It meant EVERYTHING!" The confidence in Bill's eyes was replaced by fear. "When we came home the entire country shit on us. They blamed us for the whole mess. And now, technically, we're still at war with Vietnam, right?" Bill nodded. "So, we have no diplomatic relations, no communications. There's a trade embargo on, and it's illegal for Americans to travel there. Right?"

Bill nodded and mustered some composure. "So, why are you going back, Nick?"

"What if I said I'm looking for the POWs? You remember them, don't you? The two thousand missing American soldiers. The ones you and the rest of our government wrote off and refuse to acknowledge or search for. What about that, Bill?"

"Well, no, come on now..."

Nick held up his hand and took a deep breath. "Look, I'm going to help the Amerasian orphans in Ho Chi Minh City. Then I'm going to help an old war buddy build a clinic in Vung Tau. If you got a problem with that, then make your move, pal. But you're gonna need a lot of help, cause you're gonna have to kill me to stop me."

Bill shook his head and patted Nick's arm. "Nobody wants to stop you. But we're worried about something happening to you, and we won't be able to help for the very reasons you just outlined. I was too young to go to the war, so there's no way for me to understand what you guys went through. But, if you're going back to do what you say, then all I can do is wish you the best of luck." Nick stood and grabbed his carry-on again. "Where are you going? At least stay and enjoy the amenities."

"The air is clearer down in the smoking section."

Mei Ling met him in the aisle on the way back to his seat. She actually lit the cigarette dangling from Nick's mouth. "Why you come back here?" She was smiling.

"To give this back to you," he said, and handed her the note. Surprise and hurt swept over her face. Nick caressed her cheek.

"But why? You no like me?"

Silently cursing himself Nick shook his head. "I like you plenty. But I have promises to keep." He held his left hand up to her face.

Mei Ling stared hard at him, perhaps trying to discover what kind of man this was. She smiled and shook her head ever so slightly, then she turned and was gone.

＊　＊

When he finally cleared Customs and Immigration in Bangkok, he made his way through the crowds of sticky, dripping passengers outside the terminal into the sweltering stillness of the tropical sunset. It hit him again. The stench of Asia. Mold, mildew, rotting vegetation, manure, garlic, fish, and mint. Bumping and jostling, he finally reached the curb and flagged down a white taxi. A tall, burly, and beaming driver jumped out of the right-side door and took Nick's bags to the trunk. Nick settled in the rear seat on the left side. He had studied Thai nearly twenty years ago. "*Sawat dii kap.*"

The big man turned and smiled. He was amazed this *farang* could actually speak his language. "Oh! *Sawat dii kap! Khun ruujak phut pasaa Thai may?*"

"*Nitnoy tawnan. Khun chuu aray?*"

"My name is Lek," replied the gentle giant.

Nick burst out laughing. "Lek?" he repeated. "That means tiny doesn't it?"

"Yes," chuckled Lek. "It is a big joke in my family. *Khun chuu aray kap?*"

"My name is Nick." They shook hands.

"So, where to, Mr. Nick?"

"The Hotel Manhattan."

"OK!"

The ancient tradition of Chinese New Year is celebrated each January or February depending on the moon's phases. In 1989 it was in February. Everywhere throughout Asia the week-long holiday meant returning to visit family and involved much feasting and drinking and gift giving. With the influx of millions of visitors, the already teeming masses of Asia swell the cities, towns, and villages beyond capacity. Hotels are all booked and over-booked months in advance and, without confirmed reservations, prospective guests can easily end up fending for themselves on the squalid streets. This being only his second trip back since the war, Nick was about to learn firsthand about the realities of international travel.

"Here we are, Nick," said Lek as he pulled his cab into the congested driveway of the hotel. "You go check-in. I will wait here."

"It's OK," replied Nick, "I'll take my bags and pay you now."

"You better let me wait. This time of year very crowded."

Nick made his way into the lobby and, after sweating for an eternity in line, he approached the receptionist, a young Thai man whose expression told Nick that he was having a bad day.

"Good evening, sir. Do you have reservations?"

"Yes. Here is my itinerary from the Vietnam Travel Agency in Honolulu."

I'm sorry, sir. I don't see your name on our reservation list."

"It has to be there. You see here on my paper that Mr. John Rogers instructed me to come here. He said he stays here all the time. Do you know him?"

"Oh, yes sir. I know him."

"Well, he's my travel agent, and he made the reservation. What's the goddamn problem here anyway?"

"I'm so sorry, sir, perhaps you should contact him directly."

"He's back in Hawaii. If there's a problem, YOU call him. I can't afford to call. Look, never mind! Just let me have a room, OK?"

The young man's face hardened. "I'm sorry, sir, but we have no vacancies. It is New Year. Now, you will have to leave. May I help the next in line?"

Nick started to protest when two large and rough-looking men approached from the side of the desk. Nick gave them all the finger then strode out the front door to the waiting taxi with Lek napping in the front seat.

"Lek, they don't have a room for me. What can I do now?"

Rubbing his eyes, Lek shrugged. "We can try other hotels but I think everything is full."

Lek spent the next hour and a half weaving through the bustling streets and exotic smells of Bangkok. The rush of dark, humid air through the open window was a small respite for Nick, who was suffering from lack of sleep, a bad hangover, and a mounting PTSD fit. Each hotel they tried turned them away.

The futility of the exhausting search also took its toll on Lek. Finally, at a stop light, he turned back to Nick.

"Nick, I will take you to my taxi office. Maybe you can find a place to sleep on the floor. OK?"

"OK."

On concrete, under a date palm, Nick lay down, propped up by his carry-on. He made a point of touching each piece of luggage with some part of his body to alert him if someone tried a snatch and grab. He closed his eyes and lay in the saturated stillness, but sleep would not come. He fantasized about how he would kill the flaky son of a bitch, John Rogers. The only consolation was that he had not given the con man any of the club's money. But most important was finding a place to stay for two days until his flight left for Ho Chi Minh City. After hours of agony, he sat up and lit a cigarette. Lek was sitting with two other drivers on a bench under a dim outside light. Mosquitoes swarmed around it. Nick walked stiffly over to them and offered some smokes. They all accepted.

"Did you sleep?" asked Lek.

Nick looked up at him with bloodshot eyes. He shook his head. Lek exhaled heavily.

"Come on, Nick. You stay my house, but it's where the poor people live." Nick wanted to kiss him.

A half-hour later they arrived in front of a stucco house with a disintegrating tile roof, coconut trees silhouetted against the black sky, and a small short-haired dog barking and sniffing Nick's feet. Lek led him into the downstairs room which apparently served as living room and kitchen. On a wooden slab against the far wall was a young girl, who awoke and sat up groggily in the dim light of an oil lamp. Nick could see she was very attractive and perhaps half of Lek's age. Lek talked quietly to her and motioned her up some ladder steps to the second floor.

"Lek, I'm sorry for waking up your daughter."

Lek smiled. "She's my second wife, not my daughter."

"You have two wives?"

"Many men here do."

"Where's your first wife?"

"Upstairs with her parents and our kids."

"And now you're all going to sleep together?"

"Of course. Now, you sleep here." He gestured to the mat on the slab. "If you want bath, you do it in here." He reached into a small bathroom and turned on a switch for an electric light bulb hanging from a wire above a concrete tub full of murky water. A plastic bowl floated on the surface. In the corner was a round hole in the floor with a large smooth rock on each side. There was no toilet paper. The last twenty-three years fell away, and the reality was like the wind before a typhoon. Nick turned to Lek and, bringing his hands together in front of him, bowed to his generous host.

"*Khop khun maak kap!*"

"*May pen ray.*" Lek climbed the steps, leaving Nick alone and bewildered but with a strange warmth in his chest.

Three hours later he awoke, sweating in the tropical twilight. His whole body was sore from sleeping on the wooden slab. He stiffly swung his feet over and onto the concrete floor. In the tiny bathroom he tossed some water from the cistern into his face. He groggily made his way out the wrought-iron screened door and onto the red dirt road. A huge orange ball rose behind the black wall of jungle on the far side of fallow rice paddies. It burned through the rising mist. Nick saw movement. A hulking mass was traveling through the grayness. He could hear rhythmic sucking sounds in a slow, steady cadence. Finally the shape came out of the ground fog and walking nonchalantly through the paddy was a full grown elephant with its trunk swinging. Nick watched the lumbering beast make its way to a small muddy brown stream and bathe noisily in the water. Nodding, he mumbled the old cliché, "Toto, we're not on Maui anymore."

STUART NICHOLLS

CHAPTER 8
Ho Chi Minh City
February 1989

When the Air France jet touched down at Tan Son Nhat, Nick found himself trembling with excitement and fear. Once again. His stomach spasmed as they rolled to a halt far out from the dilapidated terminal building. Through the window he saw an old battered bus limping out to meet them. The steward opened the door. A hot rush of foul air swept through the cabin. Nick nearly drowned in waves of emotion. He stepped out under the afternoon's gathering clouds and came face to face with a soldier from the People's Army. All olive drab and AK-47. He stopped short. The soldier read Nick's eyes, then beamed a toothless smile under his pith helmet. "Welcome back!"

Nick searched his face for signs of insincerity but found none, then said to himself, damn, how did he know? After an eternity he nodded, returned the smile and said, "*Cam on, anh.*" He climbed down the steps to the waiting open-air bus. He wiped away the sweat as he slid down onto the tattered seat. Even while being smothered by the stench and humidity, he felt a powerful sense of belonging.

He cleared the formalities and pushed his luggage cart out to the curb. He was overwhelmed again, by masses of people that swarmed like ants over every square inch of pavement. He was immediately besieged by dozens of beggars. They poked, prodded and grabbed him. Their hands were out, palms up, and some were chanting a well-rehearsed plea for help.

"You! You! Give money! You! You!"

There were easily thousands of dark Vietnamese faces, staring and scrutinizing every move he made. Nick made his first mistake. He made eye contact. He was instantly overcome with compassion and guilt. His hand started to reach into his jeans pocket. Sensing his weakness, the crowd surged, and the volume of their pleas turned into demands. For the first time since the war he felt a twinge of fear. Just in time, two young men stepped out from the mob and began shoving their way to Nick's side. They greeted him with cautious smiles. One looked Vietnamese, but with light brown hair. The other was black with a short Afro. He spoke first.

"Is your name Nick?"

Nick grinned, "Yeah, but in Vietnam I am known as Ly. Are you Raymond Chau Van Ri ?" The young man nodded with a growing smile. Nick turned to the other, "Then you must be Charlie Brown Phuong." Another big smile.

"Charlie Brown, and I'm a clown!" he offered, laughing. "Mr. John Rogers tell us to meet you and take you to hotel." They took charge of the luggage and led Nick out through a throng of sweat soaked on-lookers to an old white Ford four-door sedan parked under a banyan tree. Standing next to the car was a tall, thin black man smiling with polished ivory teeth. He nodded and bowed to Nick as they approached.

"This is Cong. He's another Amerasian," Raymond explained. Nick shook hands, smiling. Charlie opened the rear door. Cong took the wheel.

"This is amazing!" said Nick. "Where did you get a car, let alone a big American car? There are so few in Vietnam!"

Raymond laughed. "John Rogers rented it for you to use today, but we have to give it back by 1700. Now we'll take you to the Palace Hotel on Nguyen Hue street."

"Oh yeah, I saw it on my last trip in 1987. It's right across the street from Vietnam Tourism, right?"

Charlie seemed surprised. "Yes! You come to Vietnam before?"

Nick nodded. "I was looking for a daughter that I thought I left behind during the war."

Raymond was excited. "Did you find her?"

"No. She wasn't mine, after all."

Raymond and Charlie exchanged a meaningful look and smiled appreciatively. Charlie gazed out the window with his own thousand-yard stare. "I wish my father come look for ME."

"Amen, brother," added Raymond.

Cong slid the big car through flowing throngs of bicycles and motor bikes. In a few minutes they pulled up at the hotel. Suddenly, Nick remembered everything. This was the very spot where his adventure with the secret police had begun on the night he ran off to find Lieu in 1987. He turned and looked across the street to the corner where he had met Mot in the rain. Now, his mouth dropped open in shock. Running toward him, wearing the same blue cap and checkered shirt, was his friend Mot. "*Ly! Troi dat oi! Anh Ly!* You come back, eh?" Suddenly they were hugging, laughing excitedly, and clapping each other on the back. Both fought back tears of joy. The three Amerasians stood by in shocked amazement at this unexpected reunion.

"Raymond, Charlie, Cong, I want you to meet my friend Mot, who helped me find my family on my last trip."

They all shook hands, and Raymond greeted Mot, "*Chao, chu! Chu khoe khong?*"

Mot's eyes opened wide, and in broken English he said, "You speak Vietnamee very wew!" Mot's expression of surprise turned to consternation when the others all began laughing loudly.

Nick patted his shoulder. "They are Amerasians, Mot. *Con lai.*" Now Mot joined in the laughter.

Raymond turned to Nick. "I get that all the time. I hear people saying, 'damn, that black guy speaks good Vietnamese.'"

A small, curious crowd had gathered on the sidewalk and they joined in the festive atmosphere, by giggling excitedly.

"*Anh* Mot," said Nick, "I have to check in. I will need your help getting around. Can you drive me on your Honda like before?"

"OK! No problem! I stay right here every day waiting for you!"

The boys helped Nick haul his luggage to the front desk.

"Can we meet first thing tomorrow morning?" Nick said. "There are many things to do, but tonight I must meet Miss Pham Thai Thanh at Vietnam Tourism. John said she will be expecting me."

Raymond nodded, "Of course. What time tomorrow?"

"How about 0700 right here in the lobby?"

"OK, Ly." They filed out the front door, and Nick entered the musty elevator with a familiar warmth in his chest.

An hour later, freshly showered, shaved, and sporting a new pair of jeans and a T-shirt, Nick walked out of the lobby onto the sidewalk. He waved to Mot, who sat on his Honda beaming a warm smile. "OK,

Ly! I meet you tomorrow morning! No worry!"

Nick strolled across the street past the kiosks under some spreading mimosa trees to the ground floor offices of Vietnam Tourism. To Nick's surprise there were three military jeeps with bright yellow-and-red signs saying *Canh Sat*, which meant they belonged to the police, parked on the curb immediately outside the front door. Inside, the streaky blue stucco walls were bare, except for a portrait of Ho Chi Minh hanging over three simple hardwood desks on the marble-tiled floor. Behind one of them, against the far wall, sat a young, attractive girl, who looked like a Vietnamese Julie Andrews with short black hair. She greeted him with a wide smile. Then in a heavy British accent she said, "Yes, sir. May I help you?"

Nick returned the smile and approached her desk. "Yes, I'm looking for Miss Pham Thai Thanh."

"And you have found her. Are you Mr. Nick, by any chance?" He nodded, still in awe of her accent and fluent English.

"Yes, but you can call me Ly."

"Your passport says Nick, and that is what I'm required to call you." She said with an officious smile. "Mr. John Rogers wrote to me recently that you would be coming in to meet with us. Something about his project to help with the Amerasian orphans?"

"That's right," he said and trailed off. She hasn't even seen my passport yet, he thought suspiciously.

"You really should close your mouth you know. Some flies may fly in there."

Fully embarrassed now, Nick laughed loudly. "I'm sorry but I've never heard a Vietnamese speak English so fluently. Where did you learn?"

"In Hanoi. And thank you. You're quite kind. Won't you sit down?" Her eyes smiled. Interest? Curiosity? Suspicion? He mirrored her smile and took a seat.

Well, at least now we have each other's attention, he thought. "Back to the Amerasian orphans."

"Do you work for John Rogers?" she interrupted.

"Not yet. He asked me to join his organization and perhaps represent him here in Vietnam. For now I represent only the Vietnam Veterans of Maui."

The smile faded. "So are you a Vietnam war veteran?"

Nick sensed that his reaction here would dictate how much cooperation he would receive. He looked down at the floor and nodded humbly. Thanh's eyes registered only suspicion.

She asked sternly, "What did you do here during the war?"

"At first I was an advisor, then I went to the First Infantry Division and became a point man."

"What is a point man?"

"I was the one who went first and cut the trail through the jungle."

Nodding, Thanh's eyes went blank. Tapping the sensitivity that had saved his ass in the war, he took in her face and posture and read pain and hatred toward him and all Americans. She was from Hanoi. American warplanes had bombed the city again and again. Thanh sat silently with her hands clasped in front of her on the desk. Nick leaned forward in his chair and reached out and placed his hands on top of hers, which made her start and quickly pull away with a reprimanding frown.

"Can I please tell you something?" he asked in a soft voice. She looked at him and nodded. "I first learned about war from a foxhole. Then I went back and learned about it in the classroom where I studied Vietnamese language, history, and culture. I studied tropical agriculture so I could come back here after the war and help rebuild the country. This is my first chance to do that, and I really need your help. To be honest, if I knew in 1965 what I know now, I never would have come here in the first place. But that's water under the bridge, as we say. This is the only way I know how to make up for what I did." He reached out again and gently squeezed her hands. "Will you help me?"

Pham Thai Thanh pulled her hands from his grasp. "Have you eaten?"

"I'm sorry, what?" he asked, surprised.

"Are you hungry?"

"Yeah, actually I'm real hungry. Would you allow me the privilege of inviting you to dinner?"

With a genuine smile back on her lovely face she stood up, slung her purse on her shoulder and led him out the front door. "Do you know the Rex Hotel?" she asked.

"Oh yeah. That's where I stayed back in 1987."

"They have a lovely restaurant. Shall we go there?"

"Yes, ma'am."

Nick stepped out onto the broken sidewalk. Memories and yellow mimosa flowers drifted down onto his shoulders in the heavy evening air. Nick knew the Rex was to their left, but his head turned involuntarily to the right and his eyes scanned to the Saigon river. His heart stopped when he saw it. He froze stiffly and tried to brace against the cold chill that swept over him. There it was, with a new sign, and slightly upriver from before, but the ghostly words "My Canh" stared resolutely back at him in defiance of the twenty-four years that had passed since that evening when he and A.J. had witnessed its fiery demise.

CHAPTER 9
Saigon
June 1965

I had arrived in Vietnam just the day before. I was driven by a fortified gray Navy bus to MACV headquarters the next morning and, once past the sandbagged bunkers, MPs, and Vietnamese *Quan Khanh*, I was surprised to see a smiling A.J. running toward me.

"Hey, troop! Welcome to the war! It's about time you showed up! I've been here waiting on you for a week already." We grabbed each other, laughing.

"Yeah, and I'll bet you got all the whorehouses staked out too, by God!"

"Hell yeah, and I know a great restaurant where we can go for dinner tonight."

"Forget dinner, let's just go straight to the whorehouse, man!"

"There's plenty time for that. Let's eat first and get our energy up, then we'll go get a short time."

"What's a short time?" I asked.

"A quick fuck, dumb ass! I'll meet you right here at 1700 when you're through with your classes."

"What classes?"

"We all have to go through classes. History, culture, language, dos and don'ts, all that bullshit. Get your ass in gear, troop, you'll be late."

Later that afternoon I emerged from the Quonset-hut classroom into a drenching monsoon downpour. I spotted a lone, dark figure leaning against a building under a corrugated-tin awning. A.J. plodded slowly through the mud, sopping wet. I knew immediately there was something wrong. A.J.'s normally happy-go-lucky face was set hard and distant. I tried to grin but got no response. A.J. simply beckoned me with a jerk of his head. He led me out through the front gate, hailed a tiny blue-and-yellow Renault taxi and told the driver, "My Canh Restaurant. *Biet khong?*"

The diminutive cabbie nodded vigorously and gave us the thumbs up. "OK! My Canh numbah one!" He drove expertly through the narrow streets lined on both sides with towering teak and mahogany trees, past French colonial villas, street vendors, and thousands of beautiful Asian faces.

I elbowed my friend. "What? I owe you money?"

A.J.'s eyes were red and watery. He just looked away and shook his head. His mouth quivered.

Minutes later, we pulled up in front of the Majestic Hotel. A.J. told the driver to stop, handed him some strange-looking currency, and ushered me into a sidewalk café. We sat at an outdoor table in the rain and ordered beer. I had had enough.

"What the hell's wrong with you, man?"

A.J. emptied his beer in seconds. He waved an impatient hand for more. He began slowly.

"While you were in class, I went and visited a buddy at headquarters. He always gets the fresh scoop. Drink your beer, goddamn it! Out east of here is an American advisory team compound at Xuan Loc. A few klicks down the road from there is an ARVN post called Gia Ray. The other night the VC attacked it, and it was going to be overrun, so they radioed Xuan Loc for reinforcements. At first light, a convoy of deuce-and-a-halfs full of ARVN troops headed out. They got ambushed. Big time. VC killed 'em all."

We drained our beers and A.J. looked me in the eye. "When more American troops came to the rescue, they found the bodies. One was a big, tall American. He had been sliced open and molasses poured into his gut. The ants were still feeding on him when they found him." A.J.'s hands were trembling. "It was Big John."

I felt the life drain out of me. In a flash, I was 120 klicks out east alongside the road. I saw the smoking wreckage, blood soaked ground, I heard the screams of the dead hanging in a ghoulish mist. Our friend, mutilated and staked down on an ant hill, crying out in agony for his wife or his mother or his god. And no one to answer.

"Fuck those slimy little bastards!" I yelled. "Fuck 'em in the ass! Fuck their mothers and their wives and their daughters! Then blow 'em all to hell! Kill 'em A.J.! Kill 'em all, by God!"

My venomous hatred and fury were contagious. A.J. began nodding and snorting like a bull. He stood and grabbed the table with both hands and flung it far out into the boulevard where it crashed and was immediately crushed under the tires of a large truck. The Vietnamese waiter came scurrying over to us with his arms open wide. He jabbered frantically and looked helplessly around in protest. Others came running, but soon retreated when they saw the raw blood-lust in our eyes. A.J. threw down a wad of money on the wet concrete and we stormed out. We walked fast, and in step, as we quickly put distance between us and the Majestic Hotel. The rain suddenly stopped and the evening sun broke through the towering cumulous clouds. Unconsciously we walked clockwise around the city block, and a short time later we found ourselves standing in the same place. But now we were calm. A.J. looked at me and shrugged benignly.

"So where's this restaurant?" I asked. "I'm fucking hungry, man."

A.J. pointed across the wide, bustling street toward the muddy, rolling Saigon river. There was the sign "My Canh," and just past it was a gangplank leading from the shore out to a wide, open-air floating barge. It was filled with white-linen-covered tables occupied by men in various types of military uniforms, a few civilians, and some exotic Vietnamese women in long traditional *ao dai's* or the more western Suzie Wong-type short dresses. I caught the scents of garlic, fish, ham, and beefsteak on the evening breeze. I needed more beer.

Finally grinning at each other, we had just stepped off the curb to cross the street when the restaurant suddenly disappeared in an orange flash followed by an enormous roar that shook the pavement. A huge black cloud and flying debris erupted above the fringe of trees on the bank and rained down on us. The concussion knocked bystanders to the ground like so many dominos. A.J. and I were deaf for several minutes and in a bewildered state of shock. When I came to my senses I could hear terrified screaming and yelling. Some people were running away in a shameless panic. Others sprinted toward the disaster to offer help. A.J. and I stared at each other in utter shock and confusion for a moment, then A.J. blurted out, "Let's go!" Not knowing what was happening, I stood wobbling and started to follow my friend toward the plumes of billowing smoke and blood-chilling screams. Mangled survivors were stumbling toward us on the gangplank when the second explosion ripped from the riverbank and swept the wounded away.

This time, when we were able to stand up, I grabbed A.J.'s shoulder firmly. "Come on, hero, let's get the fuck outta here! Let's get back to my quarters and get some weapons for Christ's sake! We don't know what the hell is goin' on!"

When we arrived back at my BEQ the French ambulance sirens were already shrieking through the city. We scrambled to the makeshift arms room and drew M-2 carbines with two banana clips each. We raced back out to the outer walls of the compound and took up defensive positions and stayed far into the night until we were relieved.

Somewhere in the early morning Hans, my Australian MP roommate, staggered through the front gate past the guards and up to our room. He was covered from head to toe in fresh and not-so-fresh blood. He stared at that faraway place where we all go when we can no longer handle where we are—a lonely place without consolation or understanding or compassion. It is a place with many questions and illusive answers. It is numb and cold and barren but, once you know the way, it is easy to find again if you need to.

Hans kicked open the door, threw down his rifle, bent down and reached under his bunk for a quart bottle of whiskey. He unscrewed the cap and tossed it away, then sucked down at least a third of the booze before coming up for air.

"Goddamn, Hans! You were there too, weren't you?" I said.

Hans stared through me, through the walls, past the compound to that place. He nodded.

A.J. was still in shock. "We were across the street when it blew up. A second explosion went off, and we ran back here. What the fuck happened?"

Hans didn't even blink. "The VC set off a bomb in the restaurant, mate, then when the survivors tried to escape they set off claymores on the shore. Our commander sent us in to do what we could."

I searched the man's eyes. "You OK?"

Hans was far away now. "I found my best friend's head, floating in the river. But, oh yes, mate. I'm quite all right, you know." He up-ended the bottle again. "Yes, I'm quite all right actually. I mean, I'm still alive. Right?"

Just before dawn, A.J. and I could hear sobbing coming from the room as we left him alone and sprawled in the dark, sweltering hallway.

CHAPTER 10
Ho Chi Minh City
February 1989

"Nick?" She came around between him and the river and pointed behind him. "The Rex is that way." Twenty-four years and 200 yards had fallen away in an orange flash, leaving him trembling in the heat of the evening in a place once called Saigon.

"Are you OK? You look a little strange."

"Oh yes, I'm quite all right, actually." He turned with her, but looked briefly back over his shoulder at the mist rising off the river. Ghosts were gathering in the twilight. "For a moment, I thought I saw some old friends."

The fifth-floor dining room at the Rex Hotel had changed little in two years. It was touted as being the best in Ho Chi Minh City, but for Nick it was all too reminiscent of a summer-camp dining hall, complete with a piano in the corner where a middle-aged man in a dark suit played a competent rendition of Barry Manilow's "Feelings." The notes echoed off the barren tile floor as Miss Thanh ordered steamed fish with rice and tea. Nick went for his old favorite, water buffalo steak, well done, with a glob of rich local butter on top, French fries and bread. He washed it all down with *Ba Muoi Ba* beer. The steak had all the texture of an old rubber slipper, but the flavor was entirely there. As he swilled down the last of his third beer, it hit him. He had stayed here on his last trip. There were memories of that, but other ghosts lurked in the shadows. He shuddered.

Thanh studied his sunburned face. "So, please tell me how I can help you with your Amerasian project."

Nick motioned the waiter for another beer. "Would you join me?" he asked.

"I think you're doing enough for both of us."

"How well do you know John Rogers?"

"Not well, but he came here a couple of times in the last year and wanted to help the *con lai*. He asked me to introduce him to the government officials concerned with their plight."

"But you work for Vietnam Tourism as a tour guide. How can you get involved with these other kinds of projects?"

Thanh sipped her tea, deep in thought, then she looked up at him sheepishly, "Well, I know people in the government."

"Yes, I noticed your office is in the same building with the secret police."

Pham Thai Thanh blushed. "If you like, I could set up a meeting with the director of the People's Social Services Department. She can tell you the situation with these children."

"That would be great. Thank you."

"What exactly do you wish to accomplish? According to our files, you will only be here three weeks."

"I brought some money from our veteran's organization. I want to buy these kids whatever I can to help them until they can get to America where they belong. Also, I want to go down to Vung Tau and meet up with some other veterans who are building a medical clinic there."

"Oh yes. Do you mean the Veteran's Vietnam Restoration Project?"

Nick nodded. He thought, this chick sure knows a hell of a lot for being just a tour guide.

"I believe the leader is a man named Fredy Champagne, formerly Fredy Higdon, is that right?"

Nick smiled. "He's an old friend of mine."

Thanh chewed the corner of her lower lip. "Would you like me to arrange the trip for you? There's a bus load of Russian farmers leaving for Vung Tau in a few days. You could join them if you like."

"That would be absolutely perfect!" He raised his glass, and they toasted each other. Nick drained the brew quickly. Euphoria briefly swept over him before he spotted the familiar doorway and he heard them calling his name from behind the mist.

CHAPTER 11
Saigon
September 1965

"Private First Class Dwyer, come this way!" commanded the MP sergeant who stood over me. He grasped my arm, lifting me from my chair outside the large double doors. The Rex Hotel served primarily as a BOQ but also housed the military-justice department where court martials were conducted for those who chose to disobey the rules of war. It was 1030 on September 9, 1965. My Special Court Martial was about to convene.

Flanked by two MPs who wore new starched and pressed fatigues with spit-shined combat boots and white-wall haircuts, I stepped into the large high-ceiling room and faced a broad linen-covered table. Behind it were seated six crisply dressed officers who ranged in rank from captain to lieutenant colonel. They grimly took in this trembling young soldier. I was followed by my defense counsel, Captain Snyder, and my platoon sergeant, named Morris, who would be my character witness. The MPs stepped aside, and the three of us simultaneously saluted the court martial panel. Lieutenant Colonel Strohecker gave me the once-over and seemed impressed by my strack appearance and bearing. "You may all be seated." They did, but I remained standing.

After some paper shuffling, the colonel looked up and read the charges. "PFC Dwyer, you have been charged with sleeping on guard duty at Vung Tau airfield, Republic of South Vietnam, on July 20th, 1965, at approximately 0350 hours. Do you understand the seriousness of these charges?"

"Yes, sir."

"How do you plead, guilty or not guilty?"

I swallowed with difficulty, my jaw tightened, and I squinted hard, trying to hold my fear. "Guilty, sir."

The officers of the tribunal exchanged solemn looks.

The colonel continued. "I see. Is there anything you would like to say before we decide sentencing?"

"Yes, sir," I stammered. "I would like to say that I am 18 years old and I've only been in the Army a short time. I realize the seriousness of the offense I have committed and deserve any punishment you deem necessary. I am truly ashamed that I could not stay awake that night, and I promise that if you give me a chance I will make up for this mistake and be a better soldier in the future."

The colonel read some papers in front of him, then looked directly into my eyes. "It says here you served in the Honor Guard in Washington, D.C. at Fort Myer in Arlington Cemetery. You volunteered for duty here in Vietnam. Is that right?"

"Yes, sir."

"The Honor Guard has the reputation of taking only the best of the best soldiers in the Army. Can you explain how it is that you fell from that prestigious position to where you are at this moment?"

I stared at the floor then stood tall and fixed my eyes on those of the officer. They needed to understand what was happening at Vung Tau.

"Sir, we were ordered to pull twelve hours of straight guard every single night, alone and without relief, for three nights in a row before getting one night off and then repeating it all over again. During daylight hours we were not allowed to sleep because we had to dig bunkers, fill sand bags, run patrols, and help train the local ARVN. Everyone in my platoon resorted to taking the Dexedrine pills in our survival kits in order to stay awake on guard. The night I fell asleep, I had taken my last pill nine hours earlier. I guess it just wore off. I tried my best but I passed out on my feet. I know that sounds like an excuse, but I hope policy can be changed in the future to avoid any more problems of this nature. In any event, I am truly sorry for what happened, and all I want is the chance to make up for what I did."

The expressions on the officers' faces changed to shock and outrage. They turned to each other and a heated discussion ensued. Then Colonel Strohecker directed his attention to Captain Snyder.

"Captain, do you have any more witnesses for the defense?"

"Yes, sir. Platoon Sergeant Morris would like to speak on behalf of the accused."

"Sergeant Morris, please stand. What do you have to say?"

Sergeant Morris had blond hair, soft features, and a gentle manner that contradicted the normal image of the tough, hard-nosed platoon sergeant. He rose slowly and looked directly into the faces of his superiors.

"Sir, I have been in the Army for seven years and I have been in Vietnam for only five months, but I can tell all of you, without reservation, that there are forty-five men in my platoon and every single man has fallen asleep on guard at least once. Out of those forty-five men, twenty-nine of them, including PFC Dwyer, have been court martialed for this same offense. I am here to tell you that there is not a man in this room, including myself, who could possibly do what these men have been ordered to do. And I suggest that you either change policy at Vung Tau immediately or else go ahead and court martial the rest of us and be done with it." By now Morris' face was red, and his voice had risen sharply. His words bordered on insubordination. But Colonel Strohecker's face had softened along with those of the other judges, into what I perceived as at least understanding, if not compassion.

"Captain Snyder, I think we have heard enough. Will you and your party please wait outside while we deliberate?"

Fifteen minutes later the MPs called the three of us back into the room. I knew that the other twenty-eight men who had gone before me had been busted down two grades in rank, fined $480 and sentenced to six months hard labor in the stockade on Okinawa. I also knew enough, by now, to always hope for the best, but expect the worst.

"Will the accused please rise?"

My knees were about to betray me, but I managed to stand and face the brass.

"PFC Dwyer. You have been found guilty of the charges made against you, and we have no choice but to impose the following sentence. You are to be demoted one grade in rank to Private E-2 and fined $70 per month for three months. This court is adjourned."

STUART NICHOLLS

CHAPTER 12
Ho Chi Minh City
February 1989

"Are you listening?" Thanh's lovely face was bent sideways, peering intently up at Nick, who found himself gripping his glass with a trembling hand that made a tapping sound on the table. He looked over at her as if seeing her for the first time. His face paled. His eyelids fell to cover the growing redness of the thousand-yard stare.

"Why do you keep doing that?" she asked. "Are you tired? Would you like to go your hotel and sleep?"

Nick straightened up. Why am I always on the verge of losing it? he asked himself. Get a grip, damn it! "I'm really sorry, Thanh. Please don't think it's the company. But, yeah, it has been a long day. Can we meet again tomorrow?"

Thanh flashed her brilliant smile. "You know where to find me."

"And I think you know where to find me," he joked with a quick wink.

She immediately returned his wink, "Yes, probably in the nearest bar."

Later, back in a room reeking of mildew, Nick turned on the rattling air con, brushed his teeth, and changed into a pair of khaki shorts. Exhausted, he threw himself down onto a thin foam mattress on a wooden slab. Sleep would not come easily. In spite of the foreignness, or perhaps because of it, his mind was reeling in ecstasy at finally being back in the one place on earth where he really belonged. He fully sensed a pending miracle. Something was coming, and it would change his life forever. Yet he was confused and somewhat frightened by the intrusion of the past coming uninvited and without warning.

And now, here, alone in the darkness, his body and his soul tingled with electricity. He had never felt so alive, except in the war and during his last trip in 1987. Life on Maui was beautiful and easy, comfortable and... boring. Vietnam was the antithesis, a drug. The more he did it, the more addicted he became. Now there was a new fear. What if I can't go back to my other life? What about Malia, the kids, and the farms? How do I handle that? Jesus Christ, Nick! What are you thinking? You have a mission to accomplish! Forget the romantic shit! Get to sleep! But Nick knew that sleep would never come until he went through his daily ritual.

It was a gossamer morning. Mist lay thick and heavy against the red laterite trail, which led through an open field between the rubber trees. He could hear the shuffling feet and faint clunking of shoulder-borne equipment long before the first dark figure emerged. It was followed by others who either crawled or limped out in a ragged single file. Their steel helmets, baggy fatigues and weapons at port arms, or held in the crook of their elbows, were silhouetted against his tortured past. They trudged on, bloody and mangled and dismembered, covered in mud and slime. Their gaunt faces and hollow eyes peered at him from the darkness.

He recognized the haggard face of their leader, the tall, broad-shouldered point man from first platoon. His sandy hair stuck out above heavy-lidded blue eyes and a toothy grin. Staring directly at Nick, he beckoned silently with his jaw and a twist of his head. Nick immediately felt the rush of fear. His guts quivered uncontrollably as he pushed himself up out of the red dust and fell in with the ghosts. Silently, sadly, the dead looked deep into Nick's soul. In all of it was an unspoken acceptance. Nick felt compelled by some mysterious force to join them on their journey to an unknown destination. And later, somewhere in the night, he would dream—the first time in two years—and it would be followed by other dreams until he could leave. Vietnam had become the only place where he could dream. It seemed there were more and more mysteries, bricks being laid on top of each other and creating a wall between him and the other world. Now he asked himself. Which side is fantasy, and which side is real?

The next morning rose cool and fresh on a light breeze from the north. Nick went down to the lobby and found Raymond and Charlie waiting out on the sidewalk. Their expressions told him there was something wrong.

"*Chao cac con*," he greeted them warmly. "Why didn't you wait in the lobby where it's more comfortable?"

The two Amerasians glanced at each other with embarrassment. Charlie sneered. "They no let us inside hotel! They tell us, *con lai*, get out of here or we call police!"

Nick felt his face reddening from a burning rage. "Who told you that?"

Charlie pointed with his chin at the uniformed doorman standing guard behind Nick. When Nick spun around to confront him, the doorman's eyes widened in fear as he saw the unbridled fury on Nick's face. Nick knew it was socially incorrect to make a Vietnamese lose face in public but he could not contain his anger. He got directly into the man's face and said in loud, cutting Vietnamese. "Why didn't you let my friends into the hotel?"

The man squirmed and looked down at the pavement, then replied in a whisper with wringing hands, "I am so sorry, sir. They are *con lai*. They are *bui doi*, children of the dust. I did not know they were your friends. Please forgive me, sir."

Nick poked his finger sharply into the man's chest and with wild, murderous eyes he yelled, "I am a guest at this hotel and these are my friends. You make sure they are treated with courtesy and respect from now on! Do you understand me?"

Bowing very low repeatedly, the terrified doorman did all but kiss Nick's hand in repentance. "Yes, sir! Yes, sir! I am so sorry, sir!"

Nick turned to his friends who grinned triumphantly at each other and followed him past the mortified guard with their noses markedly pointing into the air which was alive with the aroma of the street vendors' breakfast offerings. They went by elevator to the rooftop restaurant, where Nick ordered omelettes, juice, Vietnamese bread with butter, dragon fruit, papayas, and lots of thick black coffee.

Raymond was beaming. "Man, you sure scared the shit out of that guy! Nobody has ever done anything like that for us before! Thank you, Ly!"

"Yeah, thank you, Ly." Charlie echoed, with teary eyes.

"Nobody's gonna fuck with you while I'm around! But if they try, you just let me know, and I'll kill their sorry asses!" Nick roared. Then he held up his glass of juice, and the trio drank a toast to their new-found sense of worth and self-respect. And in that moment a bond was formed. Nick hoped he had earned their trust and that would be the basis upon which the success of his mission would rest. He had heard many stories of how badly the Amerasians were treated. They had been threatened, abused, raped, and murdered for years, with no one to support or protect them. Until now.

They spent the morning briefing Nick on the situation with the Amerasian orphans, what their needs were and what Nick could realistically do to help ease their suffering with a mere $500.

Nick determined that, at any given time, there were about eighty homeless orphans living in a park near the UN's Orderly Departure Program Office which was staffed on a part-time basis by personnel from the U.S. embassy in Bangkok, Thailand. They flew into Vietnam every three weeks to process applications of Vietnamese and Amerasians to emigrate to the U.S. Then they would return to Thailand to make further investigations and travel arrangements then go back to Ho Chi Minh City and repeat the process.

The main problems facing the orphans, aside from discrimination, exploitation, and other abuses by the Vietnamese, were a lack of shelter, clothing, medicine, and personal hygiene materials. Nick made up a list of supplies that could be purchased at a local market with the Maui veterans' money. It included shirts, pants, slippers, blankets, mats, pillows, toothbrushes, toothpaste, soap, aspirin, bandages, antiseptics, quinine, pots, pans, water bottles, plates, chopsticks, and a huge plastic tarp to provide cover from the rain.

They agreed to meet again the next morning, and Nick gave the young men money to rent the big Ford which they would use to transport the supplies to the park. The meeting ended with hugs and huge smiles. Nick felt a tremendous sense of accomplishment. He went back to his room with that strange warm feeling in his chest once more. He decided to celebrate by asking Miss Thanh to dinner again. After several failed attempts at calling her, he decided to walk across the street and do it in person.

Right in the middle of Nguyen Hue Street, amidst the heavy noontime traffic, Nick heard a man screaming loudly in Vietnamese. As he wove through the gathering crowd of on-lookers he came upon a wild, bearded, long-haired vagabond, clothed only in a ragged burlap bag. The man was crying out in tortured agony and lifting up the bag to expose only dirty black pubic hair where his genitals once had been. The Vietnamese crowd was gasping in horror and running frantically away from the poor wretch, who seemed to be challenging them to look and see one of the many horrors of war. From what little Nick could gather, the man had been an ARVN soldier and had been terribly wounded by a Viet Cong mine.

STUART NICHOLLS

CHAPTER 13
Lai Khe
January 1966

After arriving in Lai Khe and receiving my "Kill VC and Win Medals!" speech from Colonel Smoke, I was flown out the next evening to our battalion's NDP on a Huey with two other replacements.

The following morning we climbed out of our foxholes in a rice paddy a short way from Thunder Road. Our squad leader, Sergeant Davis, kept yelling to watch out for mines and booby traps.

Our mission was to flank each side of Thunder Road and walk abreast to look for wires that could "command detonate" bombs buried in the dirt-and-gravel road to destroy the vehicles in a resupply convoy. As we spaced ourselves out at five-meter intervals I found myself on a well-traveled trail that went through the jungle parallel with the road. The other two FNGs were on each side of me and forced by their position to crawl through the thick brush.

One was Sergeant McClintock from Bien Hoa, and the other was a skinny hillbilly kid who had arrived in-country just days before. I started down the trail at an easy pace while the other two pushed through the foliage, stumbling and cursing. I had gone only ten meters when suddenly my feet came to a halt and refused to budge. I could not believe that they would not obey my brain's order to move, but they remained stubbornly in place. Frozen on the trail, I paused and tried to explain this phenomenon to myself. There must be some danger here, I thought. Maybe I saw something that did not register in my conscious mind. Following my instincts and intuition, I figured if there were a booby trap around, it would have been placed on the trail where American soldiers would be more likely to walk than in the jungle.

I immediately stepped off into the tangled brush and told the kid to move over, away from the trail, but seeing that wide-open path was too tempting for him and the new sergeant as well as two other squad members. They quickly filled the slot that I left and stepped briskly down the path just as I yelled out, "Sarge! Don't go down that trail!"

Too late. The explosion ripped through the trees, and the concussion knocked me to my knees. I heard the shrapnel whizzing by my head and glancing off my helmet. I heard the terrified screams. I instinctively made my way to the four men, who were moaning and crying and writhing in agony on the trail. Blood was everywhere. I bent over and grabbed the kid, whose groin area was saturated with blood, and lifted him onto my right shoulder. I fought through the bushes until I came out onto the road. One by one the wounded were laid in the dirt, and the medic came to treat them. The sergeant's right leg was blown off at the knee and hanging by a bloody tendon. Chief, a Shoshone Indian, was also hit in the groin. Billy Standridge, a tall, lanky kid from California, had a piece of shrapnel sticking out of his thigh. But the hillbilly kid was rolling on the ground screaming. Doc pulled down his fatigue pants. The boy's genitals fell out onto the dirt. Doc gasped, and in a hoarse voice filled with horror said, "Oh my God, your cock and balls are gone!" With that, the boy's face turned pure white and his eyes rolled back up in shock and stared wide into the eternal sky. He died in the red dust on the side of Thunder Road long before the medevac chopper came to take them out.

CHAPTER 14
Ho Chi Minh City
February 1989

The wild-eyed Vietnamese veteran moved in a circle, confronting each person he met with a tortured glare, shouts and insults. Clearly, his mind was gone, and he had nowhere to turn for help. He came to a halt in front of Nick and pulled up the bag even higher to expose his mutilated groin with one hand, the other outstretched with his filthy, calloused palm up. He stared intently into Nick's soul, and Nick unflinchingly stared back into his. Without hesitation, Nick pulled a wad of Vietnamese dong from his pocket and handed it to the man with a firm handshake. Not knowing what to say, or how to say it, Nick simply let the man see the compassion with his eyes. Suddenly the man became calm, bowed to Nick and whispered, "*Cam on, anh!*"

They went their separate ways, with each looking back over his shoulder at a tormented place from their mutual past. In that moment, Nick could easily see himself stumbling away in that greasy burlap bag. The chicken skin did not fade until he walked through the door of Thanh's office and was greeted by that warm smile once again.

"Well, I must say, you don't look any more rested than you did last night," she teased.

"It's hard to feel rested when you're being constantly ambushed by the past," he said.

"Ambushed? I don't understand."

"It means, being attacked when you least expect it."

She squinted her eyes and studied his face. "Bad memories?"

He nodded solemnly and tried to swallow away the lump in his throat. Her face softened, and he thought he saw a quick flash of concern in her eyes. Or was it something else?

"Please sit down, Nick." She reached behind her for a thermos bottle and placed two tea cups on the desk and poured the golden steamy brew into each cup. She slid one toward Nick. Their hands touched when he reached for it. For reasons he did not understand, he stroked the back of hers. This time she did not pull away immediately. When she did, he detected a slight smile.

"Nick, I have made an appointment for us to meet Mrs. Nguyen Thi Quynh at the Department of Social Services. She is in charge of the Amerasians in Ho Chi Minh City. We can go to her office as soon as you like."

"That's wonderful! How can I ever thank you?"

"You could take me to dinner again."

He leaned back in his chair and, for the first time since he arrived, let loose a real belly laugh.

"Actually, that's why I came here to see you today."

"I know." She smiled happily.

"Oh really? How did you know?"

She replied with a sly grin, "We have your room, how do you say? Bugged?"

Mirroring her expression, he raised one eyebrow. "So, you do work for the secret police!"

Her smile vanished. "Finish your tea."

They arrived at the beige colonial-style building with a red curved tile roof, went up a flight of stairs and into a room with tall French windows at the far end. A short wiry-haired woman was sitting at the head of a long polished table. She had sunken cheeks and beady deep-set eyes, reminding Nick of the wicked witch of the west. Her face had the texture of a prune, and her thin lips were set in a frown. Nick tried to appear affable as he smiled and bowed to her respectfully. Thanh introduced him in Vietnamese. Her face was immobile as she gestured for them to sit. A woman of similar disposition appeared with the obligatory tea tray, and then Mrs. Quynh asked Nick, "*Anh biet noi tieng Viet khong?*"

"*Da co,*" he replied. "*Mot it thoi.*" Then he thought he detected a slight smile.

"Where did you learn our language?"

"Here, during the war."

The beady eyes narrowed, and she nodded accusingly. "So, you are a veteran. Why do you come back to Vietnam?"

"To help the Amerasian orphans. The *con lai*."

Her face suddenly twisted into a cruel grimace. "The *con lai*?" she sneered. "How can you help them?"

Nick desperately tried to keep from jumping over the table and ripping her throat out. He forced a sympathetic smile. "I have brought some money to buy them the things they need until they can leave for America."

The witch turned to Thanh for translation. Nick realized his Vietnamese was not getting through. Thanh nodded humbly to the witch and calmly explained. Then the shrew turned disdainfully back to Nick.

"You give me the money, and I will help them for you," she ordered. Nick glanced over to Thanh who shrugged ever so slightly. He was on his own now.

"No, I'm sorry but I must do this myself. I am responsible for the money being spent directly to help them."

Mrs. Quynh shook her head and turned again to Thanh and lectured her sternly for a minute. Nick could understand nothing until Thanh finally turned with her hands clasped and an apologetic look.

"She says that it is illegal for anyone but the government of Vietnam to give aid to the people. You must give her the money. I'm sorry, Nick."

Nick's eyes burned a hole through the skull of this wretched disgrace of a human being. He knew all too well that if he handed over the money it would go directly into her purse, and the kids would never see a single dong. He tried to smile at Thanh. "Please thank Mrs. Quynh for her time and the tea. I will consider her request and get back to her."

Nick and Thanh both bowed to the greedy old bitch and made their exit. Once out on the street, Nick faced Thanh with a reproachful glare. "What the hell was that? She doesn't care a bit about the Amerasians! She just wants to stuff her pockets! Why did you waste my time like that? I thought you were going to help me!"

"Are you quite finished?"

"Hell no! I'm just getting started! I didn't come here for this shit! I'm going to do it my way, and nobody is going to stop me. Understand?"

Pham Thai Thanh stepped closer to him looked up into his

reddening face. She patted his arm calmly. The empathy was obvious and appeared genuine. "Listen, Nick. This is Vietnam, not Maui. Please try to accept us as we are. We tried. Now it is up to you. I cannot advise you, but… what she doesn't know won't hurt her, right?" The corners of her lips curled upward slightly. Nick took a deep breath and looked past her to a cluster of small tables and stools on the sidewalk under a tree. A sign said "beer." He gestured with his hand invitingly. When she followed his gaze she turned back laughing and shaking her head. Before she walked away, they agreed to meet at the rooftop restaurant of Nick's hotel at seven.

Nick went to find his old friend Mot and climbed on the back of the familiar, dilapidated Honda for a short trip to the place known as Amerasian Park across from Notre Dame Cathedral. The group of outcasts was easy to find. They were clustered under the shade of the giant teak trees, sitting and lying in the parched grass. Their hair and skin color were a dead giveaway. The minute that Mot and Nick drove up, the orphans were quickly on their feet and smiling a warm, hopeful greeting. Nick returned their smile and greeted them in Vietnamese, which drew an appreciative gasp of awe and excitement. They all began talking at once and patting him, tugging at his arms and hands. As they pressed close to him Nick could smell their sweat and the stench of feces and urine and bad breath. Their clothes were stained, of course, and many had holes and tattered edges. Their hair was matted and covered with grass from living on the bare ground. This was even more evident with the children of black Americans, whose Afros were a magnet for the park's litter and debris.

Nick introduced himself and Mot to the children, who appeared to range in age from 15 to over 25. There were several girls carrying babies on their hips. A stark reality hit Nick hard as he realized that there was now a second generation of Amerasians on the way.

The ones closest to Nick kept jabbering and pulling at him and asking him questions such as, "Are you my father?" "Can I go to America with you?" Some just said, "Hello!" in English. Some asked for money. But every one of them was smiling and laughing and cheering because they had heard about this American veteran who could speak their language and who had come back to help them. Nick could feel that his presence was energizing and that they considered him their savior. This was very disconcerting, because he came humbly and with few resources to help them. He wondered how he could possibly live up to their wild expectations.

Shortly after, Charlie and Raymond appeared and embraced Nick, then they all sat on the ground to talk. Nick related the outcome of his meeting with Mrs. Quynh. Nick decided now was the time to set the record straight and be honest with them so as not to raise false hopes. He gestured for quiet and then began in halting Vietnamese.

"Children, I am very happy to finally meet all of you." More laughing and cheering. "I am a Vietnam veteran who represents a group of other vets from a place called Maui in Hawaii. I think you already know John Rogers." They nodded. "He has asked me to help him with the organization called FACES. I want very much to do that and I want to help all of you." There was more cheering and nodding and they exchanged looks with each other as though this was the second coming of Jesus. "But please understand this. We are a small group and don't have much money." As this sank in, their expressions went from joy to despair. The look said that they knew this was too good to be true. "But this much is also true." He continued. "You might not be my children, but right now, I FEEL like you are!"

The smiles returned. "The Vietnam Veterans of Maui have given me enough money to buy each one of you some things to help you get by until you can get to America. Tomorrow, Charlie, Raymond, and I are going to the market to buy these things for you. When we come back here to the park I will give each of you these gifts, but I want something from you first. I want to write down all of your names and the names of your parents, and your birthdays, if you know them. And I would like to take your pictures so that I can show people back home about you and maybe get more people to help us."

A young blonde girl and a thin boy with blue eyes each grasped Nick's arms and laid their heads on his shoulders. Fighting back the waves of tears that he knew were coming, he paused and put his arms around the two and looked at something far away in the mist until he found the strength to carry on.

Nick spent the afternoon with the children learning much about their plight. Story after story revealed all the horrors that these poor kids had endured over the many years since the last Huey lifted off from the embassy roof on April 30, 1975. When he finally got back onto Mot's Honda he felt as if they all had become a family.

That evening, Nick sat alone at a window table in the restaurant on top of his hotel and watched the bats flying erratically above the rooftops and those magnificent trees. The sun was setting over the Cambodian plains far away. He sipped his beer and reflected on his productive and educational day. It had been very enjoyable with Thanh and the Amerasian kids and Mot, but Mrs. Quynh had left him feeling disillusioned and helpless. Her surly attitude and obvious hatred of the kids enraged him to the point that he was fantasizing about all the ways he could torture and kill her when he saw that pearly white smile above a red T-shirt and black slacks entering the dining room through the open French doors by the elevator. He returned Thanh's smile and stood to greet her.

"What were you thinking of just now?" she asked. "Your expression was quite frightening."

Nick blushed and called over *Anh* Chau, the waiter who had kept Nick company before Thanh arrived. "What would you like to drink?"

"I think I will get crazy tonight and have a cold soda." She winked.

"I'll have another beer." He handed the empty to Chau who bowed, smiling, and withdrew.

"What a surprise!" she exclaimed tauntingly.

"Shhh, don't tell anyone. It's our secret."

"There are no secrets in Vietnam, Nick."

He smiled and raised one eyebrow. "On the contrary, I think there are many, but not about me."

"Are you sure? You say you want to help our country, but maybe you have another reason."

"Like what?"

"Like maybe searching for American POWs." Her smile vanished and she studied his eyes. Nick felt a prickly feeling all over his body as Chau set down the drinks.

"Here's to the *con lai*," he raised his bottle and they toasted. "I want to thank you for trying to help me today, but that bitch Quynh…"

"Forget about it, Nick. Let's enjoy tonight. By the way, I have made your travel arrangements to Vung Tau for the day after tomorrow. You will leave by bus from this hotel and accompany a group of Russian farmers. I hope you will make an effort to get along with them. After all, their country and yours are not exactly friends. Right?"

Nick grinned broadly. "Actually, their president Mikhail Gorbachev has opened up his country with a concept called *perestroika*. He and our President Reagan are on the verge of making peace after decades of the Cold War. If there is any way I can make friends with the Russian people then I will be only too glad to help."

"Did you know that Vietnam is also making similar gestures to the U.S.? We are going through what we call *doi moi*. It is a change in policy away from the hard-line communist traditions of the past."

Nick felt the euphoria of the beer working up from his gut to his heart. He flushed in the fading sunset and suddenly felt so honored and privileged to be here at this moment and a part of an exciting time in history. Who knows? Maybe I can really make a difference here! he thought. The idea began energizing him and grew in intensity with the fantasy unfolding in his mind.

"There you go again," she said.

"What?"

"You were looking right through me."

"I'm sorry. Again." He smiled bashfully. "I was just looking down the trail and saw my destiny. I want to come back here again, soon. I want to be part of this. I want to help. Is that possible?"

Thanh looked at him quietly but intently. "Yes, I hope you will come back again." They sat and stared at each other while the sun disappeared behind the trees and the piano player in this hotel also broke into "Feelings." Nick downed his beer and called Chau over to order dinner.

They laughed and lingered through the evening, sometimes joking and teasing, sometimes serious and profound. But when they parted company that night in the hallway by the elevator, Nick felt that they had really become friends.

As the elevator door closed, Nick checked his Timex. Only 9:20. What the hell, one more beer. Just then he heard a man's voice, tainted with an unmistakable American arrogance, booming from just inside the restaurant.

"So I have to go and meet with the local People's Committee because Fredy is all PTSD'd out! I just signed on to help, but now I have to do everything! I don't know what's going on, but he and Sherry are down in Vung Tau and claim to be sick while I do all the work to get this clinic built!"

Nick stepped through the open doors and peered around to his right and saw a long table with two Vietnamese men and a woman, along with three Westerners, one of whom was a woman. Overall, it was an attractive group with an average age of perhaps forty. The loud-mouthed American was a bearded fellow with long curly brown hair, wearing dark sunglasses in spite of the late hour. He was addressing the Caucasian couple, while the expressions on the Vietnamese appeared somewhat lost. As Nick approached the table he nodded first to the Vietnamese then to the Westerners. He was shocked to hear the thick British accent as the woman greeted him, smiling. "I say, Gordon, is this one of your veteran friends?" The bearded man rose quickly to his feet and extended his hand to Nick

"Hi, I'm Gordon Smith. Are you American?"

Nick put on his diplomatic face. "Yeah. I'm sorry to interrupt, but are you with Fredy Champagne's group of vets ?"

"It's more like they are with me, but yeah. What's your name?"

"Nick. And I'm really glad to run into you folks because I would like to help out, if I can."

"Nick, this is Leon Bartlett and his Vietnamese wife Mai. They are from England. And this is Lady Elizabeth, who is also not only from England, but is actually Queen Elizabeth's first cousin! And last, but not least, is Mr. Le Van Huy and Mr. Pham Ngoc Hien from the People's Committee here in Saigon. I mean Ho Chi Minh City," he added apologetically. Mr. Le nodded politely, seemingly oblivious to the common error of referring to the city by its former name. Nick bowed slightly to the three Vietnamese and greeted them respectfully.

"*Da, chao cac ban. Toi rat han hanh duoc gap cac ban!*" The surprise swept over them simultaneously as they heard Nick address them in their own language. Mr. Le stood up appreciatively and stuck out his hand to Nick, who grasped it firmly and blushed while the trio complimented his linguistic ability. Mr. Bartlett also stood to meet Nick and then gestured to the empty chair at the head of the table.

"Nick, I'm sure we would all be quite honored if you would join us for a bit. Would you care for a drink of some sort?"

Nick turned to *Anh* Chau, who had been standing by, and waving his hand around the table, ordered another round for everyone and a beer for himself. As they sat down, Gordon leaned forward into Nick's space.

"Goddamn, Nick, where did you learn to speak Vietnamese like that?"

Nick smiled with false modesty. "It's a long story."

"OK then, how did you know about the clinic project?"

"A friend of mine back on Maui showed me a newspaper clipping. Actually, I knew Fredy during the war."

"That's incredible!" Gordon cried. "So, you are a vet?"

"Absolutely. I was a point man in third platoon and Fredy carried the M-60 machine gun in first platoon. Alpha company, Second Battalion, Second Infantry Regiment, First Infantry Division." Nick paused for effect. "What did you do in the war?"

Gordon Smith shifted in his chair, looked down at the table a moment, then shrugged. "I was an assistant air traffic controller in the Air Force out at Bien Hoa."

Nick studied him silently. "You mentioned Fredy's PTSD earlier. You said it in a very insulting manner."

"Oh look, I didn't mean anything by it. It's just that he uses it like an excuse, you know?"

"Well, to be honest, I haven't been in contact with Fredy since the war, but I can tell you that he has problems for a very good reason. We were grunts, brother. And it is very common for those of us who did the actual fighting, so give us a break, huh? What do you say?"

Gordon Smith began looking for the door. With a stupid smile on his face he blushed and finally said, "Will you be joining us in Vung Tau then?"

"You can count on it!" Nick lifted the newly arrived beer. They toasted each other with nervous laughter. Gordon was relieved to change the subject by giving Nick directions to the construction site in Vung Tau and promising to meet him there in a few days.

The queen's cousin asked Nick, "So did you come to Vietnam to work solely on the clinic or do you have other projects as well?"

"Yes, I'm also here to help the Amerasian orphans by representing the Vietnam Veterans of Maui and also contemplating working with an organization called FACES."

"Oh, my word!" she exclaimed. "We are also! In fact we heard about this chap named John Rogers recently and we were hoping to meet him here to offer our support. Do you know where he is?"

Nick revisited the torture chamber in which he had fantasized about locking up John Rogers, then smiled innocently. "No, but I wish I did. I think he lives in Honolulu."

For the next hour the group drank and exchanged ideas about the best way to help Vietnam re-enter the global community and what they, as individuals, could contribute to the effort. Subjects ranged from lifting the trade embargo, normalizing relations and resolving the POW issue to help the country with humanitarian projects such as the proposed medical clinics. Finally Nick said goodnight after promising Gordon to meet the veterans in Vung Tau in two days.

The next morning, he had Mot drive him to the Amerasian park, where the group had grown considerably in size as the word spread about his mission to help the *con lai*. Parked on the curb was the big Ford once again. Then he and Cong, Charlie, and Raymond drove to a market that was slightly away from the city center. The prices here would be cheaper. Charlie cautioned Nick, "Ly, I think better you give us the money. If people know you are paying, then the price will go up."

Nick's natural sense of mistrust raised its ugly head, but he knew Charlie was right, and besides, he would still accompany them. He nodded and pulled out the five-hundred U.S. dollars and handed them to Charlie. The three of them roamed the market while Cong stayed with the car.

Three hours later they began loading the supplies. It was a tight squeeze, but they managed to fit everything in the car and rode back to the park. On the way, Charlie handed Nick the change and many receipts so that he could show the vets back home how much he had spent.

At the park they were besieged by the kids, who were cheering and climbing all over each other, trying to grab whatever they could. Nick yelled out in Vietnamese for quiet and order. They immediately obeyed while still jostling each other. He told Raymond, "Tell them they must wait until we can assemble a package for each person. They will all receive the same thing as everyone else. Once you have done that, I will photograph each one and gather information before we begin handing out the packages. Understand?"

Raymond smiled heartily and, basking in his position of authority, spoke loudly to the group.

By the end of the afternoon a huge crowd had gathered beneath the trees to witness the spectacle of an American veteran documenting each child and giving them a care package along with a warm embrace. Nick asked Mot to take a photo with Nick's camera of him sitting on the ground surrounded by the kids. Nick noticed that many of the children hugged their new gifts as if they were the only possessions they had ever owned. Cold reality swept over him. That's exactly what these gifts were. Standing nearby was Mot who, like many others, smiled and shook his head at the strange sight. In the middle of the Vietnamese onlookers, Nick thought he saw the angry face of Mrs. Quynh. But he had won this battle, and she was helpless to interfere. He smiled contentedly as the orange ball behind the trees began its descent.

Finally, Mot grasped Nick's arm and led him to his Honda. The ragged group of urchins cheered and waved farewell. Mot turned back over his shoulder. "Ly, today you do numbah one! I never forget this!"

Nick's struggle to hold back his tears was futile. In front of the hotel, he hugged Mot and went up to his room. Once the door was closed behind him, he wept for so long that he feared he would never stop. Indeed, he did not want to stop. Something inside him had been lying dormant for over two decades, and now unabashedly it erupted with such force and intensity that he feared it would kill him. And once again, just as in the war, he accepted totally his own death. It seemed so appropriate to die here and now after having done such a meaningful thing. He had made a difference. He had made a small payment on his debt of guilt. He had built some good karma, and he could feel something strange and marvelous happening in his heart. He began to see the world through a new set of eyes, a different filter. In that small dark room, somewhere in the night, in a place called Ho Chi Minh City, the old Nick died.

At dawn, he emerged from the womb of unconditional love and greeted the first day of his new life as it rose up out of the mist. Today he would return to Vung Tau for the first time since the war. He would carry on with the mission, tingling with excitement and anticipation at the prospect of meeting Fredy and lending a hand to build the clinic. He felt like screaming with unbridled joy. This is how life is meant to be lived! he thought.

The hotel manager showed him a musty, vacant storage room where he could leave the crate of supplies for Lieu's family. Nick checked out and confirmed he would return in a week.

The old, badly dented bus coughed up clouds of diesel smoke as it waited by the curb outside the Palace Hotel. Mot ran over to Nick and carried his hard-sided suitcase to the Vietnamese driver to stow in the undercarriage. At the door was a rotund Vietnamese man in slacks and checkered shirt offering a warm smile.

"*Anh* Nick, *phai khong?*" he asked.

They shook hands. "*Da phai.*" Nick returned his smile.

"*Ten toi la Hung. Toi se huong dan anh di Vung Tau.*"

Nick hesitated before nodding that he understood. "I'm sorry, Hung. Do you speak English?" The man smiled apologetically and shrugged. Nick turned to the driver and asked him the same. The driver shook his head. Perplexed now, Nick stuck his head into the bus and scanned the pale, angular, faces of the Russian tour group. "Does anyone speak English?"

One middle-aged man with thinning hair and bulging biceps under a threadbare sports shirt nodded to Nick and said "*Draswtichtya!*"

"Hi!" he replied, and sat in the seat right behind the driver, who closed the door and pulled away into the bicycle traffic with Mot waving farewell from the sidewalk. Mr. Hung sat opposite Nick, still smiling. This is gonna be an interesting day, Nick thought.

The friendly muscle man spoke in Russian to Hung and gestured to Nick curiously. Hung replied "American," then turned to Nick and said in Vietnamese, "Excuse me Mr. Nick, this man is called Koda. He wanted to know where you come from."

Nick nodded. He then asked Hung in Vietnamese, "What part of Russia do they come from?"

"Ukraine," Hung replied.

Koda then asked Hung something else and Hung translated. "He wonders if you were here during the war."

Nick hesitated, then nodded to Koda and Hung. Koda immediately searched Nick's face intently. Then he jumped slightly as if he had remembered something. He stood up and brought down a bag from the overhead rack. Nick prepared himself for the worst. I hope he doesn't have a gun, he thought. He braced for action until Koda finally produced a small paperback book. He came and sat next to Nick and handed it to him. Nick breathed a sigh of relief. It took a moment for Nick to realize it was a Russian-Vietnamese-English dictionary. Grinning broadly, Nick showed the man a sentence. "What is your name?" Nick read, then pointed at the Russian letters.

"*Kak vas zovut,* "Koda replied smiling.

"*Kak vas zovut?*" Nick repeated.

"*Da, da!*" Koda exclaimed excitedly. He gripped Nick's hand and pointed at Nick. "*Kak vas zovut?*"

"Nick." Then he pointed at Koda. "*Kak vas zovut?*"

"Koda! *Da, da!*"

Nick thumbed through the book and pointed to a word and read it, "Friendship." Then he looked at Hung and said in Vietnamese, "*Huu nghi.*" Hung nodded and smiled.

Then Koda read it in Russian. "*Drujbah.*"

"*Drujbah?*" Nick asked.

"*Da.*"

Nick reached out for Hung's hand while still grasping Koda's. With a wide grin he looked at both men."Vietnam, Russia, America. *Drujbah!*" Suddenly, a man Nick would come to know as Vova appeared with an open bottle of vodka and thrust it at Nick.

"*Drujbah!*" he yelled. Nick was shocked to hear cheers and applause erupt from the group. Even the driver turned and shared in the laughter of the new-found camaraderie as they put the bottle to Nick's lips and up-ended it until Nick sputtered for air. With eyes watering, he did the same to Koda who in turn did it to Hung. Then the driver teased Hung by beckoning him to bring him the bottle. And suddenly, not only the language barrier, but political and national barriers were breached and overrun as the peoples from three different warring countries enjoyed that moment in time on a highway through the jungle with a dictionary, laughter, and a bottle of vodka.

By the time an hour had passed, Nick had drunkenly scribbled down over a dozen words and phrases in Russian. There had been much hugging, laughing, and story-telling in all three languages. At one point, Hung asked Nick why he had come back to Vietnam. The Russian farmers were also extremely curious. Nick closed the dictionary and handed it back to Koda. He took a deep breath and began speaking to Hung in Vietnamese.

"During the war, in Vung Tau, I met a beautiful Vietnamese girl named Lieu. We were in love and I wanted to take her back to America and marry her. But the U.S. government said no. So I was forced to leave her behind. Twenty years later I met another Vietnamese woman, in the U.S., who had known Lieu and said she had a daughter who was born six months after I had gone home. So I came back here two years ago to find out if the daughter was mine."

Hung leaned forward in his seat. "Did you find her?"

Nick smiled and nodded. "Yes, but not in Vietnam. By then, Lieu had moved to the U.S. and was living two miles from my brother in Portland, Oregon. So I went there and found her and it was our first reunion after twenty-one years."

Hung translated this for the group and then anxiously motioned for Nick to continue. "Was the daughter there? Was she yours?"

Nick's eyes began flooding. He simply shook his head. Hung studied Nick with quiet empathy.

"I'm sorry, Nick. Did you marry Lieu then?"

Nick shook his head again. "I was already married to another woman. I still am."

In 1989, Americans in Vietnam were virtually unheard of, and their presence was very rare in the Soviet Union as well. The ten-year Vietnam War was over and the cold war between the Soviet Union and the U.S. was on the verge of ending because of mutual diplomatic efforts between Presidents Mikhail Gorbachev, the architect of the new *perestroika* (openness), and Ronald Reagan. Everyone on the bus recognized this unique opportunity to get acquainted with each other on a personal level and for a little while there was no talk of politics. But somewhere along the road, Vova asked Nick, through Hung, which American president he liked better, Reagan or Bush. Nick shrugged. "I don't know yet, but we'll soon see. Who do you like better, Breznev the old hard-liner, or the new President Gorbachev?"

The answer was an emphatic, "*Perestroika!*"

Soon the bus pulled off the road and parked under some trees at an orphanage. The group of newly found friends dismounted and were immediately swarmed by dozens of laughing, jabbering children of all ages. A middle-aged woman appeared and quieted them down. She told them to greet the foreigners in their own language and all were quite surprised to hear the children yell out in unison, "*Draswiktya!*"

A cute little girl grasped Nick's hand and many of the other children did the same with the Russians. Nick then spoke to her in Vietnamese. "*Chao con.* What is your name?" The surprise of hearing this swept through the throng of kids and they were suddenly mobbing Nick and trying to speak Russian with him. Nick threw up his hands, laughing. "Wait, wait I'm not Russian! I'm American!" Surprise turned to shock as this sunk in.

One of the older ones came up in front of Nick and with a puzzled look asked, "American and Russian not enemies?"

Nick looked around at the crowd and, smiling at the farmers, simply said "*Drujbah!*"

Then the farmers, in turn, shouted, "Friendship!"

Later, as the old bus lumbered into the outskirts of Vung Tau, Nick grew quiet and withdrew from the others to a seat by himself and began searching through dirty windows for familiar landmarks. By now, the others understood his situation and left him alone with his demons.

There's the old airfield, Nick said to himself. As they passed the brick walls crowned with concertina wire, he was suddenly overcome with a montage of clips projected onto the mist.

CHAPTER 15
Vung Tau
October 1965

I saw a Viet Cong sapper crawling through the wire that lonely night when I was on perimeter guard. I captured and disarmed him without firing a single shot. When I radioed into the CP the sergeant of the guard drove out in a jeep to take the prisoner in for interrogation. I immediately recognized the sergeant as the man named Dieter from West Chicago who had come with a large truck to buy my cow so I could finance my trip to Hollywood when I was fourteen.

In the distance was the tarmac runway, now overgrown with weeds. I was in a single file to board the rear cargo hatch of the Caribou. A South Korean ROK soldier was in front of me. The prop blast blew his hat off and the ROK went sprinting after it, directly into the roaring propeller of another plane which was also waiting in line. Right before my eyes, the top half of the man disappeared in a huge, red cloud spitting out behind the engine as the remainder of the body crumpled in a tangled heap. I could feel the spasms in my stomach, the tingling all over my body, and the tears brimming.

The mountain in the distance was still adorned with the old red and white light house, perched in the jungle at the summit. That's where the Special Forces team was stationed, overlooking our advisory team compound next to the big swamp.

CHAPTER 16
Vung Tau
February 1989

As the bus entered Vung Tau, headed toward Front Beach, it all swelled up over Nick like a huge wave. He squinted hard, eyes piercing the pain and sadness, searching desperately into the past for something or someone to help him deal with this overwhelming onslaught of memories. I should have prepared for this, he thought.

He could feel his hands trembling, his lips quivering, and it struck him suddenly that no matter what he was feeling, he had to put it back inside quickly. He could feel eyes on him. He was a man. He was an American war veteran. He was the only representative of his country that the others had ever seen.

Straighten up, chin out, he ordered himself. Fuck it! Don't mean nothin'! Show 'em who you are, by God! That's right! Don't mean nothin'!

They arrived at the Hoa Binh (peace) Hotel on Front Beach. He shook hands and smiled with all of the Russians and bid them farewell, along with Hung and the driver, who seemed genuinely sad to see him go. With a final wave he entered the elevator and went up to his seventh-floor room where he showered, shaved, and opened a warm beer from the tiny, non-functioning refrigerator next to the bed.

In the sunset, Nick pulled on his beer and gazed wistfully from his balcony down through the ironwoods and coconuts to the ships anchored out in the bay. He began to remember again, perhaps a little too much, now that he was alone. There was a strong current running in from the east, and a warm breeze rustled the leaves of the trees stretched out along the boulevard. With his eyes, he followed the street out to his left, past the rocky headland that reached into the sea. There, it turned into a narrow, winding road leading out to French Beach. He saw a scrawny little pony struggling to pull a black two-wheeled buggy. The mist began gathering against the shoreline.

CHAPTER 17
Vung Tau
1965

The driver stung the pony's rump with a long switch. We snuggled together in the back. I had my arm around a long-haired girl with very dark skin and breasts bulging against a tight white blouse. In my free hand I clutched my M-2 carbine. I stared briefly into her smiling brown eyes between long periods of scanning the jungle along the road.

CHAPTER 18
Vung Tau
February 1989

With the memories awakening inside him, Nick had to ask himself. Why did I come back here again? To hurt some more? What is it with me anyway? Am I really such an insatiable glutton for punishment? Or is this how I get it out of my way so that I can go on unhindered by the past? I hope so. I have been haunted for twenty-four years now. It is long enough. I will take a shit, go out, and be done with it.

Strolling along the beach under the trees, he passed many small huts with thatched roofs. Vietnamese music blared from each one. There were signs offering everything from beer to seafood to massages. He had gone only a short way when a young boy with light skin and light brown hair and round eyes ran up to him. "*Draswiktya*," came the familiar greeting.

Nick shook his head and replied, "*Chao con. Toi la nguoi My. Khong phai nguoi Lien Xo.*"

The boy beamed. "You American? Oh, my God!" He pointed to himself. "My father American! What your name please?"

"Ly. What's yours?"

"Hai."

"*Con Hai, may tuoi?*"

"I'm eighteen. You take me to America?"

"I wish I could, but I already have a family. I'm sorry. But some of us American veterans are trying to help the *con lai*. If you give me your address then later maybe we can help you."

The boy's face registered his disappointment briefly, then he brightened somewhat. "Where you go now? I guide you, OK? You give me money, OK?"

Nick nodded, "You take me to 9-A Duy Tan Street and I'll give you two dollars, OK?"

"Four dollah."

Nick laughed, "Three dollars, OK!" The boy nodded laughing too. They both knew it was way too much for the short walk. Besides, Nick remembered the way. He hadn't been a point man for nothing.

The two chatted comfortably, like old friends, with the boy clinging tightly to Nick's hand. It was an old Vietnamese custom for men to hold hands. There was no stigma attached to it, but Nick still felt uneasy. Soon, he recognized the small open-air market that he had walked through more than two decades ago. It still reeked of rotting fruits, fish and vegetables. Rats scurried over the heaps of rubbish. And there on the right was the old Duy Tan Theatre.

Another memory wave swept over him. Again he stood in the void between here and now, there and then. There she was, smiling, giggling, and bouncing toward him in her flowered silk pajamas, with several ears of corn in her hand. She wrapped her arms around him and gazed dreamily into his eyes. Through the prism of love he looked down at her dark round face but did not see the smallpox scars covering her cheeks. And with her love, she would look past the cold emptiness behind his eyes. But no matter how hard he tried to never let her see what they had seen, there would be times when the beast would break out of his cage, and then…

"Ly, we here now." Hai pointed to a small alley that led back to a one-story stucco building covered by bougainvillea vines.

Nick went down, turned left and there it was. The same door with the same number.

The coconut tree that Nick had planted in 1965 was now 30 feet tall. The past came crashing down on him.

CHAPTER 19
Vung Tau
1966

I held Lieu's baby brother, Ysa, in my arms on a chair in the doorway. I hoped for a cool breeze while I sang him to sleep in the still of the evening. My M-16 leaned against the door within reach.

I still reeked of a month in the jungle and had flown down from Lai Khe on a Huey that morning. Technically I was AWOL, but I didn't give a fuck. I didn't give a fuck about anything. Today I'd have to tell her the bad news…

CHAPTER 20
Vung Tau
February 1989

Soon a small crowd of curious onlookers began stirring about in the tiny courtyard. Nick looked for familiar faces. He asked if any of them had lived here back in 1965. Everyone shook his head. He chatted briefly with a couple of the women and told them he used to live here. One had a northern accent. She had moved down from Haiphong after they won the war. Her husband had been a soldier.

They obligingly took Nick's picture in front of his door, then he was on his way. *Hoa Binh.*

Hai led him down Duy Tan until they reached Le Loi Street. They turned left toward his hotel. Hai began chattering excitedly and pointing way down the street at a woman approaching them on a rickety bicycle. "My mother is coming. Right there!"

Nick was stunned as he stared at the face in the distance. Even at 100 yards he recognized those eyes. How can it be possible? "*Con Hai!* That's your mother?" Hai nodded emphatically.

The woman's eyes locked on his as she pulled up and dismounted the bike. Nick's mouth was hanging open. "Hello," she greeted him.

"Hello, Hoa! It has been a long time!"

Her face first registered shock and then fear. She backed away. "You know me?"

Nick nodded. "You used to live up on the side of the mountain in a blue house, right?"

Now her mouth dropped open, and she nodded, dumbfounded. "Yes, but I no remember you. There were so many, you know?"

"Yeah, I know. I was your boyfriend for a week or so, then I met

Lieu. Do you remember her?"

Hoa's deeply wrinkled face broke into a toothless smile. Embarrassed, she nodded. "You please come our house. It is very close."

"OK."

Two blocks away, she leaned the old bike against a building next to a tattered tarp that was nailed to the wall and hung down over the dirt floor of her "house." Underneath was a hammock, and a small table. Six members of her family sat on a makeshift mat. An open sewer flowed just eight feet away. Several men used it, squatting, naked and unashamed. Other people scooped water with metal buckets and poured it over themselves to shower.

"Ly. You please help us? We no have money." He looked into her pleading eyes that he remembered so well. He also remembered how he had arrived at her house unexpectedly one day and found her in bed with another soldier named Spitz, who was in his platoon. But then, all is fair…

Nick reached into his pocket and paid Hai his three dollars. He handed Hoa a ten. She hugged him and then began crying. He could still smell the stench of the sewer as he stepped out onto Le Loi Street and headed back to his hotel.

Later, sitting alone at a table in the second-floor open-air restaurant, he nursed a beer. He heard a familiar voice call his name. Turning, he was pleased to see Hung and the bus driver approaching from the stairs. They were followed by another man who was smiling broadly. Nick recognized him instantly. He stood and reached out to shake his hand. "*Troi oi, Anh Lien*! Long time no see!" The two laughed and patted each other's shoulders.

Hung was surprised. "*Troi oi*, you two know each other?"

"Oh yes," said Nick. "Lien was my tour guide back in 1987. We had a very interesting time together, didn't we, Lien?"

Lien rolled his eyes, "Oh yes, VERY interesting!"

Nick gestured to the chairs. "Please join me, and be my guests." The three were all smiles. Nick ordered beer for everyone.

Lien leaned forward anxiously. "So, Ly. First, I want to know if you ever found your Vietnamese wife when you returned to America."

Nick smiled and nodded. "But the daughter I thought was mine turned out to be an orphan who Lien took in when they escaped to Thailand with some other people."

Lien shook his head and smirked. "So, all that trouble you caused me was for nothing."

"*Au contraire*! It was the greatest thing I have ever done!" He leaned over and shook Lien's shoulder.

CHAPTER 21
Ho Chi Minh City
September 1987

I sprinted away from the Rex Hotel through the pounding monsoon, down the slippery streets in the night. Behind me I could hear the running footsteps of Lien's appointed pursuers. This would be my only chance to find Lieu. There appeared a man on a little Honda motorbike. I thrust some money into his hand. "You take me to Pham The Hien quickly, OK?"

The man spotted the police chasing me, stuck the money in his pocket and with a sly smile said, "OK!" We sped off into the rain, laughing at the shouts and threats fading behind in the blackness.

The man's name was Mot, and he would soon become my best friend in Vietnam.

CHAPTER 22
Vung Tau
February 1989

Hung was still curious about how they had met two years before. After the beer arrived, and a quick toast to *huu nghi*, Nick turned to Lien and asked him to help translate his story for Hung's benefit, because his Vietnamese was still shaky. Lien protested, saying Nick was quite fluent. After some coaxing, Lien agreed.

Nick began. "Well, it was September 1987. When I came out of Customs at the airport there were hundreds of people standing around outside the terminal and every one of them was watching me. They had not seen an American in many years." He paused while Lien translated. "I saw this handsome guy coming through the crowd with a very mean expression on his face. From far away he never took his eyes off of me, and I suspected he was secret police. I was beginning to worry that maybe he wanted to kill this lone American who was stupid enough to come back to Vietnam." He paused again while the others howled at Lien's blushing translation. "I prepared myself to die at that moment. When he finally got to me, he smiled, shook my hand and said. 'I think you have been here before.' I nodded. He said, 'Welcome back!' So, I immediately bent over and kissed his ass and we have been friends ever since!"

At this, the entire group broke out in raucous laughter and toasted each other again.

"So, *Anh* Lien, what are you doing in Vung Tau?" Nick asked.

"I am the guide for a group of Australians who were also stationed here during the war. Would you like to meet them?"

"Hell yes! Aussies are a lot of fun, and they love to drink."

Lien pointed, with a grin, to several white men at the bar. "Exactly what they are doing now. I will ask them to join us. If that is OK?"

"Of course!"

Lien brought the men over and made the introductions.

"Nick this is Sam, Graham, and Billy."

"Good day, mate! Pleased to make your acquaintance!" The tall and lean one named Graham pulled up a chair next to Nick. "Lien says you're a Yank and a vet to boot."

"Guilty on both counts." Nick grinned. "And you?"

Graham nodded solemnly. "I was in the First Battalion Royal Australian Regiment. We landed right out at Back Beach. Do you know it at all?"

"Yeah. Too well. I was also infantry. First as an advisor here, then after you guys showed up, I transferred up to the Big Red One in Lai Khe on the edge of the Iron Triangle."

"I know it too, mate." He hoisted a bottle of vodka. "Here's to the grunts, boys! May we never have to do it again!"

"Aye! Damn right!" they all growled. The three Vietnamese raised their glasses though they barely understood.

Nick ordered beer for everyone in Vietnamese. Sam was impressed. "Damn, Nick! You speak good Vietnamese!"

"Not really. I only know how to get a beer, a bed, and a blowjob. But hey, I figure that's enough!" The Aussies roared, slapped Nick on the back and pounded the table.

Billy was a white-haired, heavy-set man with rosy cheeks and thick mustache. He placed a half-empty bottle of rum on the table then leaned toward Nick and slurred, "Were you here when the First Infantry got ambushed up the road by Baria?"

Sam winced. "Take it easy, Billy, we just got here." He turned to Nick, "Sorry, mate. We need to get you caught up before we start with the war stories. Here, have a swig of this, it'll put some color in your cheeks, like Billy here." He passed over his bottle of vodka. Nick grinned and took a short pull. Graham motioned to the waiter for shot glasses. Soon the entire table was roaring drunk.

Lien ordered a feast of fresh fish, shrimp, soup, rice, noodles, vegetables, and more beer. As the evening wore on, there was a series of toasts to everyone from General Vo Nguyen Giap and General Westmoreland to the bevy of whores who once worked at a house known as the "Villa," and to the doctor who discovered penicillin.

Nick noticed Graham had fallen quiet and was staring off into the darkness. "Well, Graham, it's good to know I'm not the only one having flashbacks."

The Aussie's gaunt face was red and tight around the eyes. "You know mate, lots of people think Vung Tau was nothing more than an R&R center." He gritted his teeth. "I can tell you, they're full of shit. Do you know how many men we lost just north of here?"

Nick felt numb. He scanned Graham's eyes, which were beginning to water. His eyelids sank low. Nick could see the death staring back at him. He listened intently as Graham continued, more to himself and his own ghosts than to anyone else.

"Our battalion was on a sweep around Long Tan. The bastards ambushed us with .51-caliber machine guns and RPGs. We were outnumbered three to one. We had no artillery support, and by the time we could call in air strikes, mates were dropping. In the end, we gave them a bloody whipping, but..." He lifted his shirt, exposing two bullet scars. He turned and showed Nick his back. There was only one exit wound. "Still carrying a souvenir next to my spine. Can't operate. Fuck it, mate! That's all, just fuck it!"

Nick's numbness spread. "To answer Billy's earlier question. Yeah, I asked to come down here with the Second of the Sixteenth even though I was with another battalion. It was April 1966. I knew the AO, could speak the lingo, and it would give me a chance to try to sponsor my girlfriend back to the U.S. But they denied my request. They came down here thinking it was just a pussy sector, and Charlie ambushed them too. Eighty percent casualties. Yeah, fuck it! Just fuck it!" He and Graham touched glasses. Nick sighed heavily and shook his head.

Billy raised his index finger and tried to lean forward but missed the table with his elbow. The thud of his chin crashing down onto his plate sent chopsticks and left-overs flying in all directions. Sputtering and embarrassed, he pushed upright with soy sauce dripping from his mustache and noodles hanging from one ear.

Nick looked helplessly around the table at the somber faces, not knowing quite how to respond. His consternation was short-lived, however, as the Aussies suddenly erupted in wild, unrestrained laughter. Tears flowed freely down their ruddy cheeks at the same time. Billy scowled at them and wiped his face with his T-shirt sleeve.

Nick noticed two older Vietnamese men dressed in button-down shirts and slacks approaching the table. They were well groomed, confident and exuded authority. One grasped Hung and the driver by the shoulder and motioned them out of their chairs. The two looked pointedly around the table and stared directly at Nick. Their expression was bland yet somehow menacing. Nick knew they had some position of power. They sat down uninvited. The older one asked Nick. *"Anh biet noi tieng Viet khong?"*

"Yes," he replied politely.

The man switched to English. "I hear you speak our language. Where you learn?"

"Here, during the war."

The old man nodded with a quiet smile and asked in Vietnamese, "Which division were you in?"

"The First Infantry."

The two newcomers eyed each other. Nick glanced at Lien and raised one questioning eyebrow. Lien shook his head slightly and frowned, as if cautioning Nick to beware.

The old man nodded and reached over the table and shook Nick's hand first, then the others. "I am Colonel Tran Van Minh. This is Major Le Vinh Tho of the People's Army of Vietnam. I think before you called us *Viet Cong*." He smiled at Nick and the Aussies, awaiting a reaction.

Graham set his jaw and narrowed his eyes, but before he could say a word, Nick reached under the table and patted his knee reassuringly.

The colonel folded his arms across his chest and announced, "We served in the D800 Regiment which fought against all of you in this province."

Billy's eyes widened with outrage and shock, but Sam kept a poker face and watched intently as Nick smiled broadly and bowed forward in his chair respectfully.

"My name is Nick. This is Graham and Billy and Sam, from Australia. We are very honored to meet both of you. Would you please allow me to offer you some beer?"

The two men quickly laughed and growled their assent. Nick wondered where the world would be without beer.

The two army officers spoke to Lien in a rapid northern accent which Nick had difficulty understanding. They all obviously knew each other and as they spoke they would direct suspicious glances at Nick. When the beer arrived they stopped talking and looked to Nick who raised his glass in yet another toast to *huu nghi* and *hoa binh*. There was a silent appraisal of Nick's sincerity. The verdict seemed favorable. They set down their empty glasses, smiling.

Colonel Minh asked Nick why he had come back to Vietnam. Nick retold his story. As he talked, the two Vietnamese soldiers looked at each other with what appeared to be an honest appreciation of a former enemy. Soon Nick felt there was mutual respect.

"I have waited a long time to come back here." Nick told them. "The longer I stay, the more I love Vietnam."

Colonel Minh's face grew contorted. He leaned over the table at Nick. "You say you love Vietnam?" He pounded his chest. "Vietnam is MY country! Why YOU love Vietnam?"

The alcohol surged through Nick's veins and opened the floodgates of emotion that had been building every day since his arrival. He leaned forward and thrust his face into the colonel's, but at the same time he grasped the man's hands and held them tightly. "When we went back to the U.S., after fighting here in the war, we expected to be greeted as heroes with respect and admiration by our people." Sadness and anger burned in Nick's eyes. "But do you know what they did?" The colonel stared back unflinching. "They threw rotten vegetables and fruits at us! They spit on us! They called us cowards and baby killers! They said they wished we had been killed!"

The colonel's face reflected shock, disbelief, and even sympathy. Without taking his eyes off of Nick, he spoke loudly, for the whole table. "The American and Australian soldiers that I fought were never cowards or baby killers. Although you were our enemy, we had great respect for you then, and even more now because you come back to Vietnam. I think this takes much courage."

Nick's voice became soft and calm. "Thank you, Colonel. But now, when I come back to Vietnam, I am greeted everywhere, even by my former enemy, with open arms and acceptance. You have treated me better than my own people. THAT is why I love Vietnam, and I can tell you honestly and sincerely that I feel Vietnam is MY country, too."

With jutting jaws and pursed lips, they grabbed each other by the shoulder. Nick could feel that an unseen gap had just been bridged and a bond had been forged. He knew that something beautiful and mysterious was awakening inside of him. After this journey was completed, he would never be the same again. For whatever reasons, he and the Aussie grunts had come thousands of miles to meet their former enemy at this table. Somewhere in the time that lay between sobriety and the sunrise, this group of strangers became brothers in the darkness of a Vung Tau night.

CHAPTER 23
Vung Tau
1989

When Nick awoke, the sun was already peeking over the lighthouse on the mountain. His head throbbed and his stomach was queasy. He fumbled in his bag for Alka-Seltzer. Heat steamed off the tin roof tops. He began sweating as he pulled on his gray shorts and blue T-shirt. He slipped on his socks and sneakers, then went to the bathroom and threw some tepid water onto his face. He opened a plastic water bottle and fizzed two tablets.

After his usual breakfast of eggs, bread, juice and lots of thick black coffee, Nick went down onto the vendor-clogged street and hailed a *xe-om*. This meant that you sat on the back of a Honda motorbike and held onto the driver, who would wind you through the crowds of milling people, dodging coconut husks, stiff-legged dogs, and foraging chickens. Nick gave the driver Gordon Smith's directions and the man excitedly asked Nick if he was one of the famous Americans who had come to build them a clinic.

Nick blushed and laughed, amazed that the project was already common knowledge. "I only came to help."

The man gave Nick a thumbs up and said, "Numbah one!"

Nick's head whirled as they swerved around bicycles, motorbikes, and ox carts. The driver took him along Front Beach, past the curb-side soup kitchens with tiny stools and tables, and turned right, just before reaching the mountain that they used to call VC Hill.

Heading north with the mountain on their left, Nick recalled the time the VC hanged the district chief from a tree on the crest of the hill in an attempt to terrorize the citizens into submission.

They passed Viet-So Petro, headquarters for the Vietnamese/Russian joint-venture oil drilling company off-shore in the gulf. Next to a small elementary school, they turned down a narrow dirt road under some poinciana trees and pulled up to an open field. Conspicuously white-skinned men were toiling under the brutal tropical sun. Nick dismounted, paid the driver and looked around for Fredy or Gordon. He saw neither, but a jovial fellow in a red plaid shirt, jeans and a head bandana came up and stuck out his hand. "Mike Anderson," he said, and cocked his head as if asking if they had already met.

"Nick Dwyer. I'm looking for Fredy or Gordon."

Mike shook his head. "Fredy and Sherry are back at the hotel, sick. I don't know where Gordon is. Probably at the nearest whorehouse," he said laughing. "Are you part of the team?"

Nick shook his head. "No, but I'd really like to be. Back on Maui I heard about you guys. Besides that, Fredy and I served together."

Mike's mouth dropped open, and his eyes bugged out. "Holy shit! Hey you guys! Get over here! You're not gonna believe this!"

More than a dozen sweating, dirt-streaked men dropped their shovels and picks and ambled over to shake hands with the FNG. Nick blushed at his instant celebrity status but revelled in the immediate acceptance of the other veterans. He fell easily into the group, as if he had just been assigned to a new squad in the war. A large, rough-hewn character named Tex stepped forward. He had long curly hair, mustache and horn-rimmed glasses. His hand was huge and strong.

"So, did you come all the way over here just to see us, or what?"

"No. Actually I came to help the Amerasian orphans in Saigon. I've been working with Charlie Brown and Raymond..." The roar of recognition that arose from the group cut Nick off.

"You know Charlie Brown? Oh my God! He hit us up for some money as soon as we got into Saigon. How much did you give him?"

Nick was embarrassed. "Actually, my veterans group back on Maui gave me some money to buy them supplies and clothes, so that's what I did. But I came down to Vung Tau to give you guys a hand, if you'll let me. I've got a weak mind but a strong back."

Tex slapped him on the back and roared with laughter. "Boy, you're just what we're looking for! Grab a shovel and help Hernando here dig that footing for the north wall." Within five minutes Nick was just as sweaty and filthy as any man there.

Hernando Sanchez was a Mexican-American from Santa Cruz, California. He and Nick fell into a familiar, easy rhythm, picking and shoveling gray sandy soil along the string line for the footings. Buried in the soil were hundreds of broken brick fragments from an earlier era. They made the digging difficult. Nick grunted as he pried loose the chunks. It seemed to remind Hernando of something.

"Hey, Nick. Be careful, brother. Yesterday we found some live ammo buried along here."

Nick stopped digging and straightened up. "Are you serious?" Hernando nodded ruefully. "Then why the hell did they give us this site to build the clinic?"

Hernando shrugged. "It was our ammo. I guess they want us to clean up our old mess." He laughed. "Wouldn't that be the shits, to survive the war, then get killed coming back here to make peace?"

They kept digging.

Nick began sweating out last night's beer in buckets and was soon drenched. Farming on Maui had taught him how to pace manual labor, but after he got into it, he started to work like a machine. Instead of slowing down as the morning wore on, he actually accelerated and was driven to work until the job was done. No matter how long it took.

Suddenly his shovel hit something that felt weird. He knelt down and pulled dirt and rocks away from the object with calloused fingers. Hernando bent over next to him and started cleaning from the other end. Soon, they pulled out a live 40-millimeter M-79 high-explosive round. They shook their heads, smiling and simultaneously looked skyward with a nod of thanks.

Hernando took it gently from Nick, "Well guys, here's another one!"

The sun rose in the tropical sky. The heat began taking its toll on the team. One by one, they dropped their tools and retreated under the trees to guzzle bottled mineral water. Nick kept digging as if he were possessed. A mission of life or death. He had built up some incredible momentum and did not want to stop even if he was dizzy and faint. Soon, he was alone in the field, whipping up clouds of choking gray dust as he kept digging furiously.

From the shade of the cashew trees, Tex called out, "Goddamn, boys! Look at ol' Nick over yonder! Looks like a cat tryin' to cover up a pile of shit!" The men roared with laughter as Nick played along and bent over to start clawing at the dirt with his hands and throwing it back between his legs.

John Cahill chimed in, "Nick, you look hotter than a depot stove! Come on in here and get some water, brother!"

Nick stood for a moment and shook his head. "Can't stop now! Besides, I can only help you guys for a day or two. You'll all be here for the duration. Let me do all I can before I go."

The group nodded their heads in admiration and then headed back out to work. Two Vietnamese soldiers went over to Nick and grabbed pick and shovel to help. Nick greeted them in their language and enjoyed watching their faces register their shock and appreciation. Immediately, a lively conversation ensued which was not lost on the other team members.

Mike Anderson trudged over with his mouth agape. "Damn, Nick! You speak the language too? Who the hell are you anyway?" Nick just grinned and kept working. "No, really! You don't work for the government now, do you? I'd hate to think the CIA sent a spy in here to keep an eye on us."

Nick threw down his shovel and walked up to face Mike. With his T-shirt wrapped around his head and his muscular torso dripping with sweat and grime, Nick presented a formidable figure. The ex-Marine edged back slightly, but stared Nick straight in the eye. Nick shook his head and opened his arms, palms up. "Mike, I give you my word. I'm a vet, just like you guys, and I think we're all here for the same reasons. We're searching for the peace that we couldn't find back in the states. This is a chance to prove to the world, and ourselves, who we really are. I share your paranoia about the government sticking their nose into this thing and either trying to stop it or sabotage it somehow. But I am not part of that. I'm part of you, and you're part of me. I swear to you on every name on the wall."

Anderson studied Nick's bloodshot eyes for a moment, then stepped forward. With everyone watching closely, he stuck out his hand and said in a shaky voice, "Welcome home, brother!"

Nick looked around them at the jungle-covered mountains and the fishing boats resting gently on the shimmering sea and the beautiful little people passing by in their conical straw hats and said, "Yeah, you're right. We are home, aren't we?" He pushed Mike's hand away and grasped him in a bear hug while the team laughed and cheered with relief.

They turned and went back to work. As the afternoon heat

intensified, the team worked on, choking, coughing and sometimes vomiting. Nick stopped for fifteen minutes at lunchtime, for several bottles of water, then went back out. By the time the shadows grew long again, not only had he become a member of the team, but he had made friends with the two Vietnamese soldiers and had learned about twenty new words. As they went in under the trees to hose off the dirt, Nick met Mike Oricchio, from the San Jose Mercury News. He was writing a documentary about the undertaking.

Nick gave an interview, when asked, but stepped out of the photo shoots to let the regular team members have their due. The high point of the day was watching Anderson dance and sing to a group of kids from the school. They shrieked with wild laughter at his unabashed antics while the cameras rolled.

When Nick boarded the bus back into town, he felt that now familiar warmth in his chest. The team invited Nick to their hotel that evening, then dropped him off at the Hoa Binh, where he went up for a shower and a change of clothes.

Later, he ran into Sam, who insisted Nick join them for a quick beer with him and the other Aussies. He said the two VC officers were coming as well. By now, Nick knew that with them there was no such thing as a quick beer, so he told Sam of his prior commitment.

Sam was astonished, "You mean you Yanks came here to build a medical clinic? That's phenomenal, mate! Why didn't you tell us last night? We'd love to pitch in and give you a hand!"

"I guess we were preoccupied with getting plastered. By the end of the night I couldn't scratch my ass with a pair of deerhorns!" Sam roared with laughter. Nick shook his hand and said, "Thanks, brah. I'll mention it to the team when I get there."

Nick strolled past the beggars, charcoal fires, and street vendors on Front Beach. Several poverty-stricken waifs, people with deformities and missing limbs, clung to him, chanting their begging songs. As usual, Nick handed them all some money. The gesture soon escalated into a near riot as others came scurrying over to get their share from the naïve American with a guilty conscience. Nick yelled at them to back off and actually starting pushing and shoving them back as they tried to climb onto him and pull him down. When they saw his rage erupting and heard him snarling at them in their own language, they finally backed off and slunk away.

Slightly shaken, he moved on to the dimly lit compound, set back off the street behind a brick wall. He instantly knew it was the team's hotel when he heard their voices. He stepped into the small courtyard, under some fragrant plumeria trees that reminded him of Maui, and was greeted enthusiastically by Mike Anderson, Steve Rivers, and Tex. Seated at the tiny table, on one of the typical kindergarten stools, was a heavy-set, bearded man with long, brown, curly hair and very red eyes. He looked exhausted.

Tex dug out a beer from a bucket of ice and handed it to Nick. "Fredy, this here's Nick, the other vet that we were telling you about. Man, he just showed up and worked his fucking ass off digging those footings! Brother Nick, we want to give you beaucoup thanks for helping us out today!" There was a growl of assent from the others. Fredy extended his hand to Nick. It felt cold and clammy to Nick. This man was obviously sick. Nick peered at him intently in the darkness and took a swig of beer.

"Are you Fredy Champagne?"

The man nodded.

"Was your name Fredy Higdon before?" Now the man looked somewhat wary and uncomfortable.

"Yeah, how did you know?"

"Were you in Alpha company, Second of the Second in the Big Red One?"

Fredy nodded. "Yeah, I think I was."

Nick was suddenly apprehensive. Everybody knows what unit they were with in the war, he thought. "You carried the M-60 in first platoon, right?"

There was a hesitant, "Yeah."

"I'm Nick Dwyer. I was the point man in third platoon. Do you remember me? 'Cause I sure remember you." Fredy leaned forward and scrutinized Nick carefully, then nodded. "Yeah, by God, you do look familiar."

Nick watched him closely, "How's the foot?"

Now Fredy began squirming. He looked down. "It's OK. Why?"

"Remember that day we did a combat assault out in War Zone C? It was a hot LZ and the incoming fire was so heavy they were kicking us out of the choppers at about fifteen feet up. We were all wearing hundred pound packs and we hit the fucking rice paddies so hard that we sank up to our knees in the mud. I heard a bunch of shouting coming from the squad that came out of the next chopper to me. You were limping back and waving the chopper back down. They landed and yanked you aboard and I saw your foot bleeding as they took off with the door gunners laying down cover fire."

Fredy looked humbly over at Nick. "Yeah, I remember you now." He reached out with his beer and they clinked bottles. "Small world, yeah?"

Nick nodded, grinning. "Welcome home, brother!" Then the others took up the new battle cry and raised their beers. "I really want to thank you guys for letting me help out. I didn't know what to expect just showing up out of the blue."

Fredy shook off a fever chill, "We always said that if any other vet showed up and wanted to help, then it was OK. But we're the ones who want to thank you. So tell me your story. What brought you here? What are your plans and all that bullshit?"

Nick downed some beer and told them about how he was mistreated when he went back after his combat tour, felt rejected, and abused, and began to hate his own country. But there was always this voice calling him back to help the people they had wronged. While he talked, the others kept nodding and grinning and shaking their heads in agreement. The feeling was obviously universal.

Shortly, Tex cut in with his drawl. "Same thing happened to me, Nick. I come home thinkin' somebody might like to at least buy me a beer. Shit! Them motherfuckers like to not even talk to me, bro! I walk in the room and it all gets quiet. I see their faces. I know what they're thinkin'! Fuck 'em, bro! Fuck 'em all! You know?" Nick nodded and snorted with disgust. Then Tex added, in a subdued voice, "So, next thing I know, I'm spending all my time with a needle in my arm and a gun in my mouth."

Mike pretended to unzip his fly and elbowed Pat's ribs. "Put this gun in your mouth, you toothless old bastard!" Then he leaped up and out of reach as the big man made a fist and swung at the air, but grinned good-naturedly.

Tex lit a joint, pulled on it before handing it to Nick. "There ain't been a day I didn't think about this place and now, thanks to Fredy, I'm doin' something good with my life. Thank you, brother!"

"That's right," Steve said. "Fredy, I don't know what got you started on this. But I believe it will be a good thing. I was part of destroying this country. Now maybe I can help put it back together."

Nick passed the joint to Mike and after blowing the smoke out his nose asked, "Have you guys noticed how forgiving the Vietnamese are? I mean, yeah, we destroyed their country and killed millions of them. But still, they somehow smile and treat us like family. What kind of people can do that?"

Fredy smiled in the darkness behind the candle on the table. "Well, Nick. Basically, they whupped us. And it's easy to forgive when you're the whupp-ers. But not so much when you're the whupp-ees." Tex slapped his knee and joined the others, who growled with laughter.

Nick turned to Fredy. "So, do you have plans beyond this project? Will there be other clinics?"

Fredy coughed up some phlegm and spit on the ground. "The first objective is to get this one built. If it goes well, then hell yeah! We'll build others. I'm getting Oliver Stone interested and a lady named Le Ly Hayslip. The hard part is raising money to fund the projects. There ain't none of us getting paid. And, just like you, what we're doing here we do from the heart! But this is the first time that American vets have come back to Vietnam to do humanitarian aid. And now there's another group called Vets With A Mission that's here too. Would you guys on Maui like to get involved? We could sure use some help. Maybe we could join forces. Use Hawaii as a logistics center. I hear you speak good Vietnamese. Man, if this goes well, it could be the driving force behind our two countries' mutual conciliation. It could mean lifting the U.S. trade embargo and normalizing relations between us. I believe in this with all my heart. I believe it is all beginning right here, right now, with all of us. We are taking the point and cutting a new trail. Let's just hope that others will choose to follow it!"

Nick stood and raised his bottle, "Amen, brother! Right on!" Then they were all standing and cheering and toasting. Some curious, giggling Vietnamese passers-by stopped and peered through the gate. There was something exciting and rare going on, and they could feel the energy.

As they sank down on the little stools, Nick could feel inspiration surging up from his gut. "You know, there's an old saying that if you give a man a fish, you feed him for a day…"

Mike interrupted, "But if you teach a man to fish, you feed him forever."

"That's right, brother. So here's what I'm thinking. There're beggars on every street in Vietnam. The economy here makes our Great Depression pale in comparison. I just realized that if I had $70 million dollars, I could give each person in Vietnam a dollar and feed them for one day. But then I would be broke too. And the next day it would take another $70 million to feed them again. So obviously standing around handing out money to everybody is not the answer to this country's problem. But if we can get the embargo lifted, then we have opened the door to let them fend for themselves. And I believe they can do it."

Fredy was beaming with vitality, having forgotten his sickness. "Goddamn it, Nick! You're absolutely right!" Then he quickly deflated. He added quietly, "I know I've done some things that I'm not proud of." He looked directly at Nick and nodded to emphasize the point. "But just maybe, if we can do this thing, maybe we can still have our parade."

The evening turned to night. The beers and joints flowed on; fueled by the energy that came with each glimmer of hope for redemption. Nick stood up and gave each man a firm hug. They exchanged phone numbers and addresses and promised to stay in touch. Fredy stumbled along with him out the gate onto the street in the night. Turning to ensure that nobody had followed them, Fredy offered his hand to Nick. "Thanks, brother, I owe you one."

"For what?"

Fredy shook his head. "You know. For not telling them how I got shot in the foot that day."

Nick patted Fredy's shoulder. "There ain't nobody knows the truth but you. It don't mean nothin'. Besides, everybody knows how fickle a Colt .45 can be." They hugged tightly, and then Nick turned down the street and listened to the waves caressing Front Beach as he made his way through the memories and, of course, with that warm feeling...

CHAPTER 24
Vung Tau
1965

John, West, Twig, Killgallon and I sat in a circle on cots and foot lockers on the concrete slab that was the foundation for our new wooden hootches at Vung Tau airfield. A half-empty bottle of Johnny Walker Red lay next to John on his cot. We had been up for three days and nights, pulling nonstop guard and patrols around the perimeter. John's eyes were deep red, vacant, and droopy. He slowly pulled out his pistol and scanned his friends. He mumbled something incoherently. I sat on John's wooden locker, at the foot of his cot. "Whadidya say?" I asked.

John tried to enunciate, "I'm gonna clean my gun." He began to fiddle with the .45. The explosion of the gun going off shocked all of us. I felt something hit the locker right beneath me. Immediately everyone was yelling and cursing.

West, a black man from Ohio who had been a semi-pro boxer, was on his feet in a flash. "Goddamn, mothafuckah! What the hell you doin', man?"

John was clearly in as much shock as anyone. He shrugged and looked around at his friends helplessly, and the pistol went off again. Everyone was up and gone in less than a heartbeat, except me. John and I locked eyes. I'd been up just as long as him, and I remained calm, not from courage, but sheer exhaustion. Then I said, slowly and without emotion. "John, don't move a muscle, brother. Just freeze right there. I'm gonna reach out and take the gun, OK?" John nodded, trance-like. I very slowly and calmly got my right hand on the barrel, then with my left, pulled John's finger away from the trigger and extracted the pistol from the man's trembling grip. I pushed my thumb down on the magazine release. It slid out into my hand. I pulled back the slide and ejected the live round from the chamber. I slipped the bullet back into the magazine and handed both back to John. "Here, man. Let's try to sleep. We can clean our weapons some other time, OK?" Down between my legs I saw the hole in the wood. It was two inches below where I was sitting…

CHAPTER 25
Vung Tau
February 1989

Nick waded through the thick, still humidity and fended off several more beggars until he reached the Hoa Binh Hotel. From the street, he could hear the rowdy voices of the Aussies up on the terrace. He slipped by them unseen, and up to his sweltering room. There was no electricity. The air-con was useless. He opened every window and door, pulled a warm beer from the fridge and stepped out onto his balcony in a vain search for relief. He swatted some mosquitoes as they landed on his dripping forearms. Out in the bay shone the lights of the freighters. He counted thirteen before the tears began to mix with his sweat.

CHAPTER 26
May, 1966

We met for the last time in Saigon when my tour was nearing its end. We'd planned to meet in front of the Dong Khanh theatre in Cholon at three in the afternoon. We had planned it one week earlier when I flew down to Vung Tau by helicopter. I was supposed to be in Saigon awaiting an R&R flight to Bangkok. It was just luck that changed my plans. There I was, standing at the Lai Khe airstrip, in khakis now several sizes too large. They had been tailored when I was still 190 pounds. That was long before reaching the blazing tropical sun and steaming jungles. Sweat and labor quickly melted off 45 pounds. It would not have been that bad if there had been enough to eat, but it was war, after all. And being the point man for my squad, and even for the platoon, meant that besides the stress of watching out for mines, booby traps, pungi pits, snipers, ambushes, and snakes, there was the constant swinging of my machete as I slashed through the saturated stillness of the jungle.

The sun was already high that morning and could be clearly seen rising above the giant rubber trees. The wall of shadow that they cast grew shorter as it fell across the parked choppers on the east side. A Huey's turbine whined. The rotor blades swooshed as they began to spin faster and faster. They beat the thick air and blasted a mixture of heat, dust, and the unique smell of aviation fuel. I turned away to face the hootch where the dispatchers sat. They wore white flight suits and earphones and were in conversation with an unseen pilot. One of the men looked up and covered his microphone with one hand. "You going to Vung Tau?"

There was a moment of indecision. It had not occurred to me. Vung Tau… the words had a more homelike ring than did Wheaton, Illinois. It was where my war had started. It was where I'd become

Vietnamese. An occasional feast of fresh crab, French bread, and buffalo steak, but usually fish heads and rice. Sometimes an afternoon at the beach drinking *Ba Muoi Ba* beer but usually on patrol in the swamps and sand dunes looking for Charlie.

And it was in Vung Tau where I'd met and fallen desperately in love with a girl named Lieu. I had been in the water facing out to sea awaiting the next wave to ride in when I heard the laughter behind me. She ran toward me, stepping high out of the water to keep from falling. A bikini showed she was short, brown, muscular and had large, beautifully formed breasts. Above them, set in the dark exotic face, were the brilliant white teeth and smiling black eyes in which there was no mistaking the gaiety of one who enjoyed every minute of being alive.

"Going to Vung Tau?" The man shouted above the deafening roar of the chopper blades. I had one day to kill anyway. Why sit in a Saigon hotel room when I could just as easily spend it with her? I'd have to do some bullshitting when I returned to Saigon tomorrow, but I'd become a good bullshitter.

"Yeah!" I answered. "Is he going?"

"Hurry up! He's leaving!"

Sprint to the bird, leap aboard and strap in next to the gunner with the butt of my M-16 on the floor between my legs. Nod to the co-pilot. The gunner gave the pilot a thumbs up. I felt the vibration of the craft increase as the weightlessness settled over me. In seconds, the rush of the green forest was below and past as the Huey leaned forward and upward simultaneously. A refreshing coolness swept over me. I leaned out the door a little and smiled with relief and satisfaction at the wild, tangled jungle which threatened the neat rows of rubber trees that stretched for miles in all directions. Beyond, there were shimmering silver reflections of the sun off streams and flooded rice paddies. They glinted up between the gathering cumulus clouds that would surely bring the afternoon rain.

The Lambretta driver dropped me off in front of the house on Duy Tan Street, named after a famous Vietnamese general. My small coconut tree stood listless in the still air. The tin roof creaked and groaned under the heat as it expanded against the nails that held it to the rough-hewn beams. A familiar face appeared. It was Huong, a young bar girl who was a friend of Lieu's. My smile was met with horror. It left me immobile and stunned.

"Huong. What's wrong?" I asked in Vietnamese. No answer. The girl side-stepped around me in a wide detour but still facing me. "Don't you remember me?" She broke into a run and disappeared into the crowded street market.

Puzzled and even a little frightened I made my way to the louvered door of my house. It was fastened with a new padlock. Knocked hard. Nothing. Knocked again. Knuckles smarting against the hard wood. A rustle of movement from inside.

Then her familiar voice. "Who is it?" I waited. She opened the door. The sleepy black eyes opened wide. Her mouth dropped open. I suddenly realized that she was looking at me with the same horror as Huong.

"Ly!"

"*Chao, em!*"

"You not dead?"

"What?"

Through tears now. "Everybody say you die!" Now I knew. She fell into my arms. For a long time we held on like that, clutching each other, trying to breach the span of the five-month separation. We were still in love. That and the certainty of death were the only things I knew for sure.

Afterward, lying naked and sweating on the bed in the heat of the afternoon, I drank thirstily from the iced beer that she had bought from one of the street vendors. Her baby brother, Ysa, somehow slept on his small cot in the sweltering room. I took a long pull on a Salem, experienced the sweet coolness of the menthol hit and asked her. "Lieu, who say I die?"

"Everybody say it, Ly." She named some of my friends from my former platoon.

"When did they tell you?"

"Maybe three weeks after you go."

"Who told you first?"

She paused. "Danny." That figures! I thought. Some friend! All he wanted was to get in her pants, just like everybody else in this place.

"And you believed him?"

"Not at first. But then Bill tell me too."

"Who asked you to be their girlfriend, Lieu?" She looked down, ashamed. She was only half Vietnamese, but that was enough to keep from telling you the truth if she thought it would hurt. She knew if she told me I'd make big trouble. She had seen my temper and my rage. She had seen it and felt it.

"It was Danny, right?"

Her normally happy, care-free, dreamy eyes were tortured. She glanced at me, tears forming. She grabbed my broad but bony shoulders and squeezed, sobbing. I knew the rest. No point putting us through any more of it. All is fair…

I crushed the Salem on the concrete floor. Lit another. This is as good a time as any, I thought.

"Lieu. I have bad news."

She pushed away slightly, trying to read my eyes through her tears. Another puff. Heart breaking. Pain gripped my chest. I looked down, and also broke. Body shaking, I wiped the wet hair off of her scarred cheeks and caressed her lightly.

"Our request to let you go back to America with me." Holding her head in my hands. I kissed her cheeks, forehead, and lips. "It was denied."

Our eyes burned into each other. Tears brimmed and slid down my cheeks. It was her turn to be strong. We often traded like that.

"How long you know that, Ly?" She was calm. It was setting in now—numbness replacing the pain. I remember hanging my head and wiping my face, embarrassed. "How long, Ly?"

"A few weeks."

"And you no tell me 'til now?"

"We were out in the bush. I couldn't get a letter off to you. I'm sorry."

She sat up in the bed with a fatalistic smile and lit her own cigarette. "You want me to meet you in Saigon when you come back from Bangkok?"

"Would you?"

She nodded slowly. "But tonight you take me go French Beach, OK? There are many ships to count."

Six days later I stood in front of the crowded Dong Khanh theatre. She was late, of course. I had expected that. Like most of her countrymen, punctuality was not one of her virtues. At 3:25 she finally emerged from the crowd. We walked down Tran Hung Dao for a ways hand in hand, before surrendering to the crush of civilization overflowing the streets and sidewalks. We found an upscale French/Vietnamese restaurant. After I ordered drinks, Lieu leaned forward.

"Ly, what you do in Bangkok?" She pretended to be jealous. "You find new girlfriend, yes?"

"Yes. I have beaucoup girlfriends in Bangkok now. Same like you have beaucoup boyfriends in Vung Tau." She slapped my scrawny arm and hid a smile.

"Ly, I think you are very skinny now. Not big and strong like before. What happened to you? Is American army so poor it cannot feed you?"

Chuckling, I said, "Yeah, maybe I should join the VC. I think they eat better than we do. But in Bangkok I ate good food. They even had hamburgers and milkshakes, but the milk made me sick because I haven't had it in almost one year."

She stared vacantly out the window at the street. "I don't know milk. I never have it all my life." Which made me feel like an ass for bringing it up. "Ly, how is Bangkok now? I have not seen it since I was small girl. When I lived there with my parents it was a beautiful city. Not dirty like Saigon. Is it still like that?"

"Yes. It is still like that. Very clean. You can walk around at night with no fear. There are American movies and good restaurants and every hotel has air conditioning. There are beautiful temples and pagodas. I visited about a dozen. I saw the reclining Buddha and went to the bridge on the River Kwai. How long did you live there, anyway?"

A faraway look came into her eyes then. I knew she loved to reminisce and talk of times gone by or to dream of some future thing that was impossible, but still worth dreaming about because anything was better than here and now in Vietnam. Even Lieu knew this, but somehow she had come to accept it, as she must, for her tour of duty would never end. Mine would be over in less than six weeks.

We both knew this would be the last time. A man on death row, knowing it was coming soon but powerless to change it.

"We live there about twelve years and we were VERY happy." She smiled as she said the word very. "But then my father and mother fight very much and I don't know why. So my mother, my sister, and two brothers and me go to Cambodia. We stay there for two years, and my mother find new husband. Then we come Vietnam."

"Yes, I remember now." I took her hand and felt her strong yet feminine grip. Our eyes met, and the tears welled up in both of them at the same time. A weight fell on our shoulders. It became too much to bear.

"Ly, when you go?"

"Tomorrow."

"Then I never see you again, right? Tell me, Ly. Don't lie. You have to tell me!"

"Not now, Lieu."

"What you mean, not now? There is only yesterday and today! We no have tomorrow! We have to do it now!"

I pulled her face to meet my eyes. "All right then, Lieu. Listen to me now. It is true that we only have today. That's all we ever have. But we will live it and live it together so that no matter what else happens, we will have done it all together and nothing can ever change that. We will have dinner now and afterwards, if you like, we can go to the Dai Nam theatre and watch the cinema. Then we can go to the hotel where I have a room. OK?"

"OK, Ly." She wiped her face with the linen napkin. "I will always remember when we live Vung Tau and we go in horse and buggy to French Beach for dinner and we watch the sunset. Then when we come back and watch the moon come up over the mountain." She smiled dreamily. "I make you happy, Ly?"

"Couldn't make it without you, baby."

"Hey! No call me that, Ly! You know I no like!"

"*Xin loi, em.* Yes, you have made me very happy. And in return, I have always hurt you and made you cry. How can you love a bastard like me?"

"I don't know too," she said smiling. "Maybe I never know until I am old woman. When I find out I will tell you. I will write a letter to the address you give me in Illinois and I will tell you why. But then it will be too late." It was her favorite fatalistic expression. "It will be too late, Ly. You will have American wife and American babysan and you will tear up the letter so your wife no get mad, right?"

"Wrong! You are my wife now. In America it is illegal to have more than one wife. But I will take another wife if it makes you happy."

She took up her table knife and pretended to threaten me with it.

"You!" she said mocking hostility in her voice. "I *cat cai dau* you!"

We laughed as the waiter arrived with the drinks, looking on with disdain at our uncouth behavior. It was, after all, a high-class restaurant. So, as he walked away, we rolled our eyes at each other and laughed again.

Later that night, back in my hotel room, I made love with her, not to her, for what seemed like hours. Again and again, as if the world would end at dawn. And it did. My eyes opened and I was instantly wide awake with the same anxiety that I awoke to each day in my foxhole, sensing the impending danger. I was immediately aware of the emptiness in the room. The note lay next to my head on the moldy pillow. I ran to the balcony and searched frantically through the chain link screen for a sign of her on the quiet street below. Cholon was not yet awake. The sullen, damp mugginess was smothering. Spasmodic sobs welled up in my throat. She was gone forever. Her words echoed in my ears and would ring through the chasms of my mind for the rest of my life. They would come back to haunt me nine years later on a quiet night while I sat and watched TV with my American wife and American babysan. And, just as she said, it was too late.

On April 30, 1975, Vietnam fell to the communists. And all the years of preparation for my return—the courses in Vietnamese language, history, culture and geography, my degree in tropical agriculture (my new weapon to fight the oppressive hunger of the Vietnamese) were all suddenly in vain as the news came over the screen.

The note was short. A reflection of her wonderfully innate simplicity.

My Darling Ly,
I no can say good-bye. It hurts too much, Ly. Remember, I will love you forever, with all my heart.
Yours Always,
Lieu

Before I touched a match to the paper, I burned the words into my memory. I dressed, picked up my bag, slung my rifle, and walked out into the street and caught a taxi to Tan Son Nhat airport. I didn't see the tear-filled eyes that watched me go.

CHAPTER 27
Long Khanh
February 1989

Nick reluctantly boarded the bus with the Russian farmers for the return trip to Ho Chi Minh City. He wanted to stay and work more on the clinic but he had another mission to accomplish—picking up the crate of goods that he had brought for Lieu's family and asking Mot to get him a car to deliver it. The family lived outside the town of Long Khanh, which lay about 120 kilometers east of the big city.

The following morning, Nick walked out of the hotel lobby into the sunlit street where Mot was waiting anxiously beside an old Renault Dauphine sedan. The hotel bellmen struggled under the weight of the box. After much discussion and adjustment, the box was crammed into the small trunk. The lid was secured by a piece of rope. Nick and Mot squeezed into the tiny car. Mot introduced Nick to the driver, *Anh* Lai.

Mot was beaming his perpetual smile and asked Nick, "*Anh* Ly, you eat breakfast yet?"

"Yes. Did you?" Mot shook his head and waited. Lai looked back at Nick in the mirror. Nick smiled back. "OK, OK. We go eat first, then we leave for Long Khanh." Mot and Lai laughed, relieved. The little car groaned away coughing black smoke.

Once outside the city, they stopped at a roadside hootch made of bamboo poles with a thatched roof. The greasy wooden tables and one-foot-tall rickety stools sat unevenly on the red dirt floor. A pleasant woman dressed in *ao ba ba*, or black silk pajamas, brought them three bowls of *pho bo*, beef noodle soup with a variety of condiments. Nick recalled eating this delicious breakfast item many times before, but still managed to spill broth and noodles onto the table and the ground. Curious onlookers were delighted at his clumsiness with chopsticks as well as his fluency in Vietnamese. It was quite common for people to crowd up to Nick wherever he went. They would hang onto him, rub his hairy arms, feel his bulging muscles and make clucking sounds as if impressed by his superior size and strength.

At first, Nick felt a smug satisfaction at all the attention, but soon it became overbearing and obtrusive. He finally broke away from their grasping hands and paid the woman. At once, there was a near riot as people began scrutinizing his roll of money and begging for a share. Nick, once again, forcefully pushed them aside and made a quick run for the car.

They chugged back onto the potholed highway and left the yelling mob behind, with outstretched hands.

They rolled down the windows and tried to summon up a draft of hot air. Mot always had a way of keeping them entertained with his funny stories or dirty jokes. They laughed their way through the vast countryside for over an hour. Just past the town of Long Khanh they met a smaller road. On both sides were grass shacks, rice paddies, water buffaloes, and fields of cassava. Nick grew melancholy.

"*Anh* Mot. Two years ago, you drove all the way out here on your Honda to find Lieu for me, right?" Mot nodded, smiling. Nick reached out and took Mot's hand. "You only asked me for two thousand dong to pay for your gas. Remember?"

Mot laughed and bashfully grasped Nick's hand in both of his. "Don't worry, Ly. It was enough."

"It was only like 50 cents. Why didn't you ask for more? I would have paid you anything you wanted."

Mot looked warmly into Nick's eyes. "Because, somehow I knew you had a good heart. What you were doing was right. You came all the way back to Vietnam to find your daughter and wife from before. I just wanted to help you do that." He shrugged, smiling. "Ly numbah one."

"No. Ly number ten. YOU number one!" He pressed something into Mot's palm and they laughed some more. Then Nick saw the sign. Xuan Loc 5 km, Gia Ray 20 km. He stopped laughing. This is where it had happened. Big John had been tortured and killed on this very road in June 1965. Soon they passed a cluster of old barracks under some trees. There was a sign that said "The People's Army of Vietnam" and above it on a pole, a red flag with the gold star stirred listlessly in the midday heat. He could see Big John's face and hear his words like it was yesterday. "I'm gonna come home rich and with lots of medals!"

He had come home in a plastic bag to be buried in Arlington Cemetery by the same company in which he had served so honorably. About three million Vietnamese and sixty thousand Americans had died in that long and bloody war. Now, there was still poverty, corruption, and farmers in the paddies.

The people were no more and no less free than they had been. Different soldiers occupied the same forts. In the end, the only thing that changed was the color of the flag. Twenty-four years ago, at the age of eighteen, Nick and the other GIs had known all that they needed to know: It don't mean nothin', don't mean a fuckin' thing!

Mot stuck his head out the window, searching for a familiar landmark. A young girl carrying a basket of peanuts walked beside the road. Lai stopped. Mot asked her if she knew the dark skinned, Malay- Vietnamese family. She smiled cheerfully and pointed far down the road in the same direction she was taking. Mot invited her to ride along and guide them. She slid into the front seat and was surprised to see Nick's face. She asked what country he came from.

When Nick answered in Vietnamese that he was American, her eyes bulged out and she gasped in shock. There was fear in her face. Nick tried to explain why he was there. She relaxed. When they arrived and pulled off the road, she jumped out and began shouting to the neighbors that a rich American had come with gifts. Suddenly, people of all ages appeared from behind every tree and house and a near-riot ensued. Standing in the gathering crowd was the shy and humble Ysa.

Nick walked up to him with open arms. Both men smiled broadly as they embraced each other. Out came the other brother, Liem, and waddling with some difficulty was Ma. They all hugged and laughed for a minute, and then they recognized Mot. They playfully slapped his shoulders, and the reunion headed into the stucco-walled shack with a grass roof and dirt floor.

They led Nick into the bedroom and sat on the wooden slat bed. Within one minute the entire house was filled with fifty people. Standing room only. They even spilled out of the house and climbed up to completely block every doorway and window opening with excited, curious faces. The effect on Nick was immediate and devastating. The body heat generated by the pressing crowd, on top of the normal tropical heat was sapping his energy and concentration. There was no oxygen. He could not breathe. Sweat literally gushed out of his body and soaked his clothes. He looked around pleadingly to Mot and Ma and Ysa.

"Please! I need air! Please tell these people to leave!" Ma merely shrugged and laughed helplessly. Nick began to panic. Fight or flight! He was outraged and appalled at the lack of respect for someone else's house or privacy. Why don't they just leave us alone? he thought. There are more people in this room now than I see in a month back home.

There were at least five children poking, prodding, and wiping his dripping arms. They kept marveling at his body hair and how much he sweat. Then they started yelling, "Hello! Hello!" or "You! You! Give money!"

Nick snapped. He stood, wheeled around and shoved as many of them as he could. He snarled and roared like a mad dog. "Get the fuck outta here, goddamn it! You leave us alone! I came here to see only them! Understand? Get out, now!" A shock wave swept through the room and Nick could see the look of embarrassment on his family's faces. But slowly and somberly the throng ambled out of the house, muttering to each other.

Nick knew he had not made any friends here. He didn't care. He had come to bring Lieu's family some gifts, not the whole village. Now he had made them lose face. After he left there would be trouble. Liem appeared with a glass of iced lemonade. Nick held it to his forehead momentarily while he waited for Mot and Lai to get theirs. But none came. He offered them to drink from his glass. They curtly refused. Nick realized that Ma had only enough money to buy one and he was about to commit another social sin so he put it down on the bed and pretended it wasn't there.

The silence was deafening. Nick tried to smile and suggested they bring in the crate from the car. When he and Mot and Lai finally placed it on the floor he felt the mood lighten. They gathered around as he cut open the thick cardboard with his survival knife. The first items that he pulled out were the *Honolulu* magazine with all their pictures in it, and some other photos from Oregon after he and Lieu had reunited. There were gasps, oohs and aahs and laughter. The appreciation was heartwarming as Nick watched their faces light up. This is what he came for. Then he related the contents of the article that he had written and they all seemed very impressed, especially when he went through and showed them all their names in print.

Then he brought out dozens of cans of meat, sardines, beef stew, and spaghetti. There were bags of rice, boxes of various medicines and clothes and of course toilet paper. This got a big laugh as they probably had never used it all their lives. Then when he had emptied the box of its contents and it was heaped on the bed, Nick reached in his pocket and handed an envelope to Ma with $50 cash inside. Nick knew it wasn't much by American standards, but in Vietnam it could go a long way. The average wage then was $ 10 a month, if you could find a job. Mission accomplished. Nick nodded to Mot and Lai.

Ma thanked Nick for everything. Then she asked, "Ly, when will you marry Lieu?"

"I'm sorry Ma, but I'm already married to someone else."

Ma shook her head. "No, you marry Lieu."

Nick blushed. Reality hit him right between the eyes. It just wasn't meant to be. His destiny was still unfolding, yet somehow he knew that he would never see them again.

Ysa appeared with a handwritten letter that he had just finished. "Ly can you mail this to Lieu when you go back to the U.S.?"

"Of course."

Ysa stuck out his hand. "Ly, you give us more money, OK? We need a lot of money."

Nick's heart sank. He had spent hundreds of dollars to buy the supplies in the box. He had spent hundreds more to ship and deliver it to them out in the boonies of Vietnam. He had given Ma some cash, and now Ysa has the balls to ask for more? He folded the letter and put it in his pocket. He took a long look at their life. He tried to empathize. He asked himself what he would do in their shoes. His answer was to be thankful for what they did have. "Ysa, if you want more money from me, then first you must give me an AK-47."

Ysa's eyes darted around, confused. "Why, Ly?"

"So I can go rob a bank to give you all the money you want." Then he squeezed into the little Renault. They drove out onto the road and turned into the setting sun. Nick never looked back.

CHAPTER 28
Ho Chi Minh City
February 1989

Over the next several days, Nick was busy meeting with a Mr. Nhiem from the Department of Social Services. Mr. Nhiem was a wounded war veteran with a pronounced limp. But instead of resentment or hostility, he exuded a quiet, warm acceptance. Nick soon felt a real friendship blossoming. Even Mrs. Quynh began to receive him with some respect. With a growing sense of cooperation, Nick felt they were on the verge of great things. Together, they searched for a permanent building to house the Amerasian orphans until they could leave for the U.S. Mr. Nhiem and Ba Quynh requested a long-range plan from FACES to deal with new incoming orphans. Mrs. Quynh also persisted in requesting money for the housing project. The amount came down to $150,000, $30,000 less than her previous demand. Nick promised to talk with John Rogers about it.

He visited Amerasian Park daily. He conducted English language and American cultural classes to help the Amerasians adjust once they got to the U.S. As new orphans arrived from the countryside, he bought them the same supplies as the others. He gathered their information, took their photos, and placed them all in a book which served as the first Amerasian Registry ever assembled.

He met with Bob McMillan from the Orderly Departure Program out of the U.S. Embassy in Bangkok. McMillan told Nick to lobby Washington for an extension of the Amerasian Homecoming Act sponsored by Senator John McCain of Arizona.

In the evenings he met Thanh and her girlfriend Phuong, who also worked at Vietnam Tourism, for dinner and drinks at the piano bar. They discussed his progress with the Amerasians and how important the project was to the long-range reconciliation between Vietnam and the U.S. Nick always reminded them that the whole world was watching to see if their two countries could resolve this issue. The more he got to know these wonderful people, the more he became convinced that if Thanh was the president of Vietnam and he was the president of the U.S., then they could quickly bring an end to the trade embargo as well as normalize relations. The days passed quickly. Each one brought Nick a growing sense of fulfillment. Common goals were closer to fruition.

The morning sun streamed in through the large plate glass windows that looked out onto Dong Khoi Street. Brodard's Restaurant was bustling with mostly foreign customers. There were Japanese, Korean, Taiwanese, Singaporeans, Australians and even Canadians. Nick was the only American. He liked that. It made him feel somewhat special. He was often mistaken for a European, usually French, but he did not mind.

He watched impatiently while the rich Vietnamese coffee dripped at an agonizingly slow pace down from the French press into the thimble-sized cup. He went through four Marlboros by the time it was finished. And in one quick swallow, it was gone. Finally, Charlie Brown pushed in through the front door and spotted Nick sitting with his back to the far wall by the kitchen. Charlie flashed a smile. "Good morning, Ly! *Anh co ngu ngon khong?*"

"Yes, I slept very well, thank you. And you?"

Charlie shook his head of tousled hair. "I sleep on the ground in park. Not in soft bed like you."

Nick felt a flush of resentment and gave Charlie stink eye. He was uncertain if it was an insult or just teasing. He let it go. "Charlie, you like coffee?"

"Yes. Thank you, Ly. When you go back to America?"

Nick signaled for more coffee. "Tomorrow." They locked eyes. For a full minute not a word was spoken. The tension between them was tangible. "How long do you think, before you go?"

Charlie shrugged. "Maybe a month, maybe six. I don't know. Don't worry, Ly. I be OK." Charlie paused. "Why you want to see me today?"

"I've been thinking. Maybe I could sponsor you to come to Maui and live with me and my family. It is a lot like Vietnam. I could build you a house and you could work on our farms. It's not an easy life, but I think it is better than living on the streets of Ho Chi Minh City."

Charlie chuckled. "Thank you, Ly, but I already have a sponsor. Do you know of Rosemary Battisti?" Nick shook his head. "She has a place in New York called the Mohawk Valley Resource Center. Amerasian children can go there to begin new life in America. I think many of us will go there. But first we must go to a camp in the Philippines. On Palawan island. I think we stay there six months, then we go U.S."

Nick watched the torturously slow dripping of the coffee into their tiny cups. "Where is Raymond today?"

Charlie looked around suspiciously. "I don't care about Raymond! Ly, I tell you now. Raymond and other black Amerasians are no good! They act nice to your face but behind you back they talk bad. John Rogers too. He no good, Ly. He tell us, 'You give me one ounce of gold. Then I take you to America. But no gold, then you cannot go.' Raymond take away any money we have and buy drugs. They are very violent. I can't wait to get out of here!"

Shocked, Nick leaned forward into Charlie's face. "Are you serious? Why you never tell me this before?"

"No worry Ly, it is my problem."

"No, it is OUR problem! John wants me to work for FACES. How can I be part of that? Now I only have one day left. There is nothing I can do." Nick felt betrayed and helpless. Just when he was feeling good about everything, now this revelation. An insidious thought crept into Nick's mind. Do I really believe this? What if this is a ploy to involve me in some internal power struggle? Why do I feel like I'm being manipulated? Nick's natural mistrust of people and propensity to always believe the worst were in direct conflict with the fantasy created by three weeks of living his dream, making a difference. Blossoming illusions of grandeur had led him to believe that the fairy-tale would actually come true. He could still be the hero and have his long-overdue parade.

Stunned and dejected, Nick handed Charlie a card with his phone and address on Maui. He threw down some money and shook Charlie's hand. "If things don't work out. If you ever need me." He pointed at the card. "Goodbye, Charlie."

Nick circled the block and came back to Nguyen Hue St. and the

Palace Hotel. At the corner, perched atop his little black Honda, Mot waved enthusiastically. "*Anh* Ly! Ly!" He jumped off and ran up to Nick with his ever-present smile. "Ly, tonight we take you to dinner, OK?"

"Who is 'we'?"

"Me, my sister Lan, and her daughter, Dao and Lai. OK?"

"OK, but I would like to take YOU to dinner." Laughing and pounding Nick's shoulder, Mot readily gave in. "OK, OK! We meet here at six o'clock, OK?"

Nick joined his laughter. "OK, Mot. *Cam on!*"

Nick went shopping for some Russian vodka but could only find a Vietnamese brand. It would have to do. At exactly six, Nick stepped out of the lobby doors onto the sidewalk and was shocked to find Mot already waiting for him on his motorbike. As they swerved and wound their way at suicidal speeds through the flowing throngs of two-wheeled traffic, interlaced with milling pedestrians, Nick felt the exhilarating rush once more. He knew it was all coming to an end. He would revel in every moment of this adventure and burn it into his heart for all time.

They whisked up to a Chinese outdoor garden restaurant. Mot left his Honda with the parking attendant. They found their way to the table where the others were waiting. There was much giggling and flattery with each telling the others how young and good looking they were. Nick ordered beer and soda. Mot and his sister Lan ordered the food.

When the drinks arrived, Nick stood up and held out his beer. He recited some lines from a Guy Clark song. "*To old friends, they shine like diamonds. Old friends, you can always call. Old friends, Lord you can't buy 'em. You know it's old friends, after all.*" They laughed, cheered, and touched glasses. Mot and Nick emptied their beers and poured another. When the food arrived Nick inspected it carefully but in the growing darkness could not identify a single dish, except the rice. Lan quickly began loading up his bowl with a wide variety of strange looking items. As they all dug in with chopsticks flying, Nick looked around at his guests who were eating ravenously. They were obviously quite hungry and he probably would have been also, except that the food was all a mystery. But his rule had always been: Don't ask, you really don't want to know.

He chewed his first bite and thought there were some onions involved, no problem. He felt something crunchy in his mouth, like fingernails. He pulled out something hard and brown. It was a cockroach. He fought down a gag reflex and tossed it into a nearby bush. Another bite revealed the same thing. This time he took it out with his chopsticks and sent it flying as well.

Mot saw it. "Ly, what are you doing?"

"Oh, it's just a cockroach that must have fallen into the dish. Don't worry. It's OK."

Lan was shocked and glanced around at the others. "No! No! Don't throw them away! It's part of the dish!"

Nick ordered another round of beers. It was going to be a long night. He tried small, beige quail eggs in a rich sauce. No sooner had he swallowed them than a wave of nausea swept over him. This was followed by a plate of meat that Mot proudly announced was dog. Nick's head began swimming when the tray of sauteed field rat arrived. Afraid his queasy stomach would betray him he ordered a basket of bread. He wolfed it down, followed by more beer.

Finally finished, Nick asked for the bill. Four adults, and one ten-year-old child had shared a four-course dinner with two sodas and fifteen beers. Thirteen dollars. Nick fumbled with the strange currency.

Mot said, "*Anh* Ly, now we want to go shopping for a souvenir to give you to take home tomorrow." Nick managed a weak smile. His stomach swelled and churned. "No, Mot. Please. I already have my souvenir. In my heart and mind I will carry the memories of our trip to Long Khanh, our friendship, and a lovely dinner that we shared in happiness. Trust me, I will never forget this dinner as long as I live."

His guests thanked him profusely. The normally quiet *Anh* Lai spoke out for the first time. "*Anh* Ly, not only do you speak Vietnamese very well but you also speak fluently from your heart. I am proud to be your friend."

Little Dao, looked shyly down at the ground and twisted her tiny shoe in the dirt. She received a prod from her plump mother. "Ong Ly." She glanced up coyly. "Here." With both hands, she gave Nick a miniature ceramic glazed pagoda.

Nick squatted down and took her lovely face in his hands. He kissed her gently on her forehead and the bile surged in his gut. He turned away just in time. The vomit erupted from his mouth, covering a nearby hibiscus bush with several half-eaten cockroaches.

Back in his room, Nick sat naked on the tiled floor of his shower. He left the water running to wash away two hours of vomit and diarrhea. When he finally felt it was over, he cleaned up and gulped Pepto-Bismol, then brushed his teeth. He dressed, stuck a half-roll of toilet paper into his pocket and made his way to the twelfth floor restaurant where he knew Thanh and Phuong would be waiting to say goodbye. He found them at a window table near the piano. Their new-found friend Hung was playing "Yesterday." Nick sat down. Thanh and Phuong looked at each other with obvious concern.

"I say, Nick, are you quite all right?" Thanh asked with a frown. "You look so pale." Phuong nodded in agreement. She placed her hand on his forehead to feel for a fever.

Nick shuddered. "I'd rather not discuss it if you don't mind. Have you eaten?"

"Yes." Thanh replied.

"Why?"

She smiled at Phuong. "Because we were hungry."

"Just as well. How about a beer?"

Phuong collected her purse. Her rosy round cheeks broke into a smile. Extending her hand, she said sincerely, "Nick, I have another appointment. I hope to see you the next time you come back to Vietnam. I really enjoyed your company. Thank you."

Nick held her warm hand in both of his cold and clammy ones. "Actually, I don't think I'll be coming back. But thanks. I have also really enjoyed you. I wish you the best of luck and a happy new year. *Chuc mung nam muoi!*"

Phuong gave him a knowing smile, looked at Thanh, then back at him. She winked. "I think you'll be back."

Nick blushed and saw something sad in Thanh's eyes—a silent resignation, something beneath the surface but left unspoken. Then a sudden twinkle. "You're not really going to have another beer are you?" she asked.

He shook his head and reached into his shirt pocket. "I know you like poetry. Here's something I think you might like. It's called 'Solitude.' A souvenir, I guess."

She opened the folded note and began to read while Hung replayed

'Feelings' once again.

S- ilence falls softly a moment
O- n the crest of a hill
L- ost in the gathering shadows
I- pause in the evening still
T- he last slanting rays fall about me
U- nder spreading arms of trees
D- reams softly stir within me
E- ven as my hair is stirred by the breeze.

When those normally staid brown eyes looked back up, they were brimming. Shaking her head she folded up the paper and placed it in her purse. "Who wrote this? It's beautiful."

"My mother. Shortly before she died."

Pham Thai Thanh tilted her head and looked back at him while she reached out her hand. He took it and gently massaged it. Then she stood abruptly and smiled. "Please have a safe trip back to your farm and family on Maui. I hope someday I could come to visit you there, or if…" She shrugged.

"You'll be welcome anytime. Could I at least write to you? It only takes a month to get here." He laughed.

She smiled, nodded, and turned away. "Goodbye, Nick."

CHAPTER 29
Ho Chi Minh City
March 1989

After a night of sweating and more nausea, Nick felt weak, but was able to keep down his usual breakfast. He finished packing and checked out at the front desk.

He left his bags with the porters, and made his way up the street to the Thang Loi Hotel to say goodbye to the Russian farmers. But the petite young girl at the reception desk informed him that they had already checked out.

Nick looked down at the case of vodka under his arm. "Are there any other Russian guests at the hotel?" he asked.

The girl smiled slyly and nodded. "Yes, I am Russian," she teased. They both laughed. "Which guest would you like to meet?"

"I don't care, as long as they're Russian," he replied.

She got on the house phone, and shortly a husky white man in a beige suit exited the elevator and approached Nick with a puzzled look. Nick grinned and said "*Draswitchya!*"

The big man nodded and grinned in return. "*Dras!*"

Nick handed him the box. Realizing his Russian vocabulary was too limited to explain, he turned to the Vietnamese girl. "*Co biet noi tieng Lien Xo khong?*" She nodded. "Please tell him I am an American who went with a group of Russians to Vung Tau. We became friends and I just wanted to give them a souvenir to remember that our countries may be enemies, but we are not."

After she translated, the man smiled broadly and, gesturing at the vodka, said "*Plysibe.*"

Nick shook his hand firmly. "*Drujbah!*"

A taxi ride later, Nick was stunned, once again, to see a huge crowd at the front entrance of Tan Son Nhat Airport. Many had luggage and papers in hand, but it was utter chaos. No lines. Literally every man for himself. Thousands of people were shoving and yelling. They were on the verge of becoming an unruly mob. Their panic and fear was contagious. He felt like it was April 30, 1975, all over again, with terrorized masses of Vietnamese storming the barbed concertina wire, walls, and gates of the U.S. embassy in those final desperate moments before the last Huey lifted off.

Nick fought through the surging hysteria to hear something familiar being shouted at him from close by. Then he heard it clearly.

"Ly! Ly! Wait, Ly!"

He spun around, and his wild eyes focused on the smiling face. "Mot! What are you doing here?" he yelled above the bedlam.

From under the flailing passports and tickets, Mot squeezed up to him. "*Anh* Ly! I have souvenir for you!" Mot thrust a small box, wrapped in brown paper, into Nick's hand. As they were jostled and bumped, their eyes met. Nick returned Mot's infectious smile and suddenly felt a strange, calm acceptance. "I hope see you again!" Mot called as the crowd swept him away.

With his hands and arms full, Nick couldn't wave back. He watched the small, round, beaming face as it disappeared in the pandemonium. Sweating rivers, Nick pressed on through the stench and dripping heat to the ticket counter. Fighting in close now, he spotted Bob McMillan, an American ODP official that he knew. Shaking his head in exasperation, Nick fumed. "This is total insanity!"

Bob's face was dry and calm. "Is it?" he replied with a sarcastic grin.

Nick stood at the ticket window. People ducked beneath his armpits and popped up in front of him to toss their papers on the counter in a growing pile. The bemused airline agent looked hypnotized by the chaos around her. Nick, once again, hit the wall. He could take no more.

He roared like a wounded bull and grabbed the nearest Vietnamese interloper. His eyes bugged out over teeth bared like a mad dog. He was shocked by the fury and contempt that swept over him. He felt pushed to murder. He seized the throat of another man who tried to squeeze in front of him. When Nick's powerful grasp left the man choking and purple faced, the others surrounding him immediately began backing away.

Nick released his death grip and wiped the pile of passports and tickets onto the filthy floor. While the mob quickly bent down to scavenge for their papers, Nick placed his own on the counter and ordered the girl to give him his ticket. The fear in her eyes was obvious, and she processed him swiftly.

Finally through the gate and into a long, gritty, corridor reeking of mold and mildew, Nick found a quiet corner. He set down his bag and opened the box. He lifted out the beautifully ornate black lacquer-ware ashtray with gold lettered engraving. "Dear *Anh* Ly. Souvenir from Mot, Lai, Lan, and Dao. March 3, 1989. Ho Chi Minh City, Vietnam."

Later, Nick gazed out the plane's window at the dismal world that he was leaving behind. A swirling rush of scenes from his past flashed in his eyes. The war, then returning in 1987, and now. And once more, his emotions swung like a huge pendulum, from one extreme to the other. He felt the wheels come up. He leaned over and watched the shimmering rice paddies and the brown, slow-winding Saigon River fade away below. He broke out his note pad...

"This time there were no tears, no sad farewells, no mission with which to carry on. Just to make it home to the ones I love. To the place where I really belong. I hope and pray that what I have learned on this trip will be of value to me in the time to come... for however much longer I will have to live. Just as my last night in Vung Tau enabled me to see Ly and Lieu riding off in the moonlight for the last time, I needed to do what I have done today. Say goodbye with a smile and no regrets. Knowing I will probably never return here, but also knowing that I don't need to. That was all yesterday, and yesterday is gone. I will not forget what it has taught me but neither will I linger on it. I will try to grow and use my experience to make the life I have left with my beautiful family the best it has ever been. For now I can concentrate on what is really important. The future."

STUART NICHOLLS

CHAPTER 30
Maui
March, 1989

Two days later, his Aloha Airlines flight touched down on the 'aina that lay between West Maui and Haleakala. Nick let go a huge sigh. The midday sun greeted him while soft trade winds cooled his walk across the tarmac to the small terminal. The ocean air was clean and fresh.

On the other side of the large plate-glass doors, he spotted her beautiful Filipina face in the crowd. Her brilliant white teeth shone against her tan skin in a loving smile, tinged with relief.

"Malia!" he called. She made her way through the placid throng of onlookers, who parted politely for the impending reunion. They threw their arms around each other and kissed warmly.

"So, how was it?" she asked.

Nodding, he stroked her cheek. "It's over now. It's finally over."

She smiled thoughtfully and led him out towards the baggage claim. "Are you sure this time?"

Nick glanced around at Maui's gentle, smiling people surrounding them with warm aloha. He smiled contentedly. "Yeah, I'm sure."

But...

A few days later, Nick pored over his notes from the trip. Bill McMahon, from ODP, had suggested he contact his local Catholic Charities about how to help place incoming Amerasian orphans and integrate them into American society. Though Nick had promised himself no further involvement, he found himself thinking, just one more thing, then I'll be done.

He called the Honolulu office. A lady named Dahlia Corpus was extremely excited and appreciative of the fact that he had just returned from Vietnam and had done so much to help the children there.

"Oh, Nick! You really should come to Honolulu next week! We are forming an organization called the Amerasian Task Force. It will be composed of a broad spectrum of agencies in the public and private sectors. Your input would be invaluable in helping us formulate policies and directives to accomplish our common goals of helping these kids. Won't you please come?"

Before he knew it, his ego had made a promise that he would now have to keep. When he hung up the phone he was startled to look up and see Malia standing in the doorway.

"Well, you lasted only three days. And now you're leaving again? When is this going to stop? We have two farms to run, Nick. Me and the kids need a break. We worked our asses off while you were gone. You can't do both these things. You have to choose. Us or the Vietnamese?"

Nick was crestfallen. Holding her with both arms he said, "I already gave my word. You know how I am. Now I have to keep it, no matter what. "

"Really, Nick? What about the promises you made to us? Do you remember them? It seems you have a selective memory." She broke free and stormed out of the house.

Nick heard the van start up and drive away. For the first time, he felt the seeds of resentment germinating in his mind. He had never been a fan of ultimatums, unless he was delivering one. The problem was that he knew she was right. Carmine Genovese's eyes bore into him. The guilt was overwhelming.

"What the hell's wrong with me?" he asked aloud. "I want to be done with this thing, but it's like I'm addicted to it. Just like the coke. I love it, but I hate it too. OK. I'll go to Honolulu and try to end it there. But I'm in a unique position to help out with this project. Why can't Malia understand? I've been carrying this pack for twenty-three years. I can't just lay it down now. Ah, fuck it! I'll talk to her later. Get back to work, damn it!"

He climbed into his flatbed truck and drove down Kimo Drive. He arrived at their 16-acre vegetable farm at the Kula Ag Park as the sun began its ascent over Haleakala. During the return flight home he had already made up a long list of jobs and goals that he would begin so he could hit the ground running.

In his absence, Malia and their two boys—Eric, 22 his son from his first marriage, and 14-year-old Keoki, Malia's son from a previous relationship—had been forced to harvest, plant, spray, and weed the fields of cabbage, lettuce, and onions. Several of his friends who owned neighboring farms had come over to help with the tractor work and heavy labor.

The farm looked to him as if he had been sorely needed to keep everything going on schedule, but he knew they had all tried their best. He climbed on top of his big Ford tractor and eased down into the seat. He turned the key, but the engine only made the weak clicking sound of a dead battery. He sighed. "Welcome home, Nick!" he said to himself.

He swapped the battery in his truck for the one in the tractor. After it coughed to life, Nick hooked it up to the forklift attachment and loaded a pallet with knives, twine and cabbage bags. Straddling three rows of cabbage he drove the tractor into the field.

For the next four hours he bent over and cut the heads of cabbage by hand and rolled them over for packing into the bags. There were twenty heads per bag and he needed to cut, pack, load, and deliver 100 bags by the end of the day. He bent over stiffly and felt the pain immediately in his lower back as he started to cut the heads. He marveled at how quickly his body had gotten soft while on the trip.

The sun blazed down. A light breeze did little to ease the heat and humidity. He was drenched in sweat within five minutes. He suffered miserably, but by 6 p.m. he had delivered the cabbage to the cooperative downtown in Wailuku. While coiling up his ropes in the fading sunlight he heard another truck pull in. It was his good friend, Benito Galolo, who had helped Nick's family with the farm while he was gone.

"Hey, Nick! Welcome back, man! How was it?"

"Hard to explain. I'm still kinda numb. I guess it was one of the best things I've ever done, but I'm really glad it's over, you know?"

Benito shook his full head of black hair. "No, I don't. So wait 'til I'm done unloading and we can go next door to that Vietnamese bar for a cold one. You can tell me all about it." He laughed conspiratorially.

Nick really wanted to go home for dinner with his family, but he owed Benito for his help. "OK." He reluctantly agreed. "But I gotta get home early."

Benito just laughed and gave him an OK sign. "We'll see about that, brah!"

As soon as they entered the bar, Nick was hit by the familiar reeking of urine, cigarette smoke and stale beer. It was as if he was still in Saigon. Somewhere in the recesses of his mind he missed the stench of Asia. Not because the odor was appealing but because it was real. At least you knew where you stood against it. It was tall and staunch, as opposed to its resilient people, who were as flexible and versatile as bamboo. Outside the bar, Maui was clean and sterile, sanitized and pasteurized. Disinfected of life's harsh realities, paradise was oblivious to the everyday suffering so far away, although island roots were anchored in it.

"*Anh* Ly! When you get back?" called Michelle, the owner. She ran up to him as he put down the bag of cabbage and they hugged tightly. He brought her a bag each time he came to the bar. She was a pudgy middle aged woman of French/Vietnamese ancestry who was very interested in Nick. But he thought of her only as his sister.

"Couple of days ago." He grinned shyly.

"You come sit down. I buy you both first round, OK?" She ushered them into their usual booth which was always sticky and foul. Nick looked back and saw the clumps of mud that they had both tracked in on their rubber boots.

Benito followed his gaze and shrugged, laughing. "Hey man, how come all the Vietnamese call you *Anh* Ly, anyway?"

Michelle handed them both their open beers. Nick glanced up and thanked her. "*Cam on, em.*" He toasted Benito, and they chugged the cold panacea to a long day in the fields. "It's my middle name. I used it in Vietnam because I figured it would help them identify with me more." Nick paused. "Hey bruddah. Thanks for helping out while I was gone."

Benito waved it away. "Anytime brah, you know that. So what happened over there?"

Nick took a deep breath. "I met an old friend from the war and helped him and some other vets build a clinic for the people in a place where I was stationed. I also met some Australian vets, a bunch of Russian farmers, and even a few of our former enemy. The weird thing was that, as soon as I met them, I felt like we were all long-time best friends. I helped out a group of Amerasian orphans, and I brought some presents and supplies to my ex-wife's family. I made new friends in the government, and I think I made a difference. But in the end, I couldn't wait to get the hell out of there. Does that make sense?"

With a blank stare, Benito just said "No. But let's have another. We'll figure this out."

Nick waved Michelle over and said, *"Xin em cho chung toi hai cai nua di."*

Michelle's mouth dropped open. "My God, *Anh* Ly! Your Vietnamese is much better now. I never hear any American speak good like you." She smiled as she walked away. Nick's ego swelled and he blushed with pride. Benito gave Nick a high five.

"Nick, I gotta give you credit, man. You're something else. You know, I've always been against that war but..." He hung his head, looked up, gestured broadly with his hands and looked about the room as if searching for the words. When their beers arrived he toasted Nick and chugged his down without taking a breath. Nick was confused. He watched his friend's face intently. Benito picked up his thought again. "OK, look. This is really hard to admit but... I never went into the military during the war. I didn't believe in it. I was going to college in San Francisco and..." Another painful pause. "Man, I protested against the war. Then I burned my draft card and moved to Canada." He sighed with relief and looked Nick in the eye. "I'm sorry, brother. I know you probably hate me for that."

Nick shook his head. "At the time, I would have, yeah. But since then I learned the truth about the war. We were totally wrong to go over there. That's why it's so important for me to go back and try to make up for what we did. There's a lot of guilt inside me, brah."

Benito's eyes watered. "What about me? You don't think I have guilt, for NOT going? You guys went through hell and then when you came home... well, you know. That's been eating at me ever since."

Nick nodded, "That's the worst part of it, our whole country has some kind of guilt over that fuckin' war. It affected almost everybody. But the ones who really suffered were the Vietnamese."

Benito extended his hand. "Thanks for going back and trying to make things right. You're all right, brah."

By the time they finished their fifth beer, Nick could feel the pain in his lower back subside. A kind of euphoria set in. Thoughts of home, family and responsibility faded far away. Michelle's newest girl, seeing Nick's condition, slipped into the booth next to him and began rubbing his thigh. She spoke to him in Vietnamese. "*Anh* Ly. My name is Linh. I hear you just go to Vietnam. You buy me drink, OK? I want to hear about it."

Nick took in her natural beauty and leered at her drunkenly. "OK honey, but only ten-dollar kind. I don't have much money." As she left, Nick and Benito grinned at each other with raised eyebrows.

"Man, I bet she knows how to get the wrinkles out of your dick!" he teased Benito, who laughed loudly.

"Hey Nick, our friend Paco says he has the goods, man. Whatdya say, brah? Let's go pick up a gram."

"No, man. I gotta go."

But as soon as Linh returned with her drink, she sat down and stroked his penis under the table. Three drinks later she ran her sensuous tongue around his ear and whispered. "*Anh* Ly, you take me home tonight, OK?" Nick's self-control crashed like a tree in the forest.

But when midnight came, Nick found himself tweaking in the parking lot, alone, broke, and with twenty-five miles between him and the justifiable wrath that he must face when he arrived home. Benito had split earlier with his share of the stash and while Nick was in the filthy restroom, Linh had made her escape and never returned.

"Goddamn it, Nick! When will you ever learn?" he said to himself. And guilt, his faithful companion, tortured him all the way home.

The next Wednesday was the monthly meeting of the Vietnam Veterans of Maui. Nick pulled up in the parking lot outside the Wailuku Community Center and was greeted with shouts and laughter from his best friends Tim, Custer, the Grizz, Mike, and Mark.

"Oh shit! Look who's here," called Custer. He had been given the moniker because he physically resembled the legendary cavalry commander and, like Nick's friend Jack Smith, had actually served in the Seventh Cavalry.

Nick was met with firm hugs from all, especially the Grizz, who growled and picked him up in his famous bear hug.

"Welcome home, brother!" Mark said as he gave Nick a warm embrace.

Mike grabbed his hand. "So how was it this time?"

Nick shook his head. "I'm glad it's over. Let's go inside and I'll tell you all about it."

Inside, Zach Christopher stood at the head table and saluted Nick as the ragged band began cheering and waving beer bottles at the conquering hero. Nick laughed humbly and took a seat close to the front. They shook his hand and patted his back. This really felt like home.

Zach banged his fist on the table. "Gentlemen! This meeting is now in disorder!" Scattered laughter. "I move that we dispense with any of the normal bullshit and get right to the matter that we all want to hear about."

"Aye! Aye!" yelled the unruly membership.

"Yeah, fuck all that other shit! Come on, Nick! What happened, brother?" shouted Custer.

"I brought a few pictures so you can see what the Nam looks like now." Nick said, spreading select shots on the table. "It's really changed since there's no one shooting at us. Bumbye you can come up and look at 'em, but first I want to tell you about the $500 that the club gave me to help the Amerasian orphans."

There was scattered muttering and expressions of skepticism on several faces. A few men rolled their eyes at one another as if expecting to hear some feeble excuses about how the money got lost or stolen. Nick read from his notebook.

"I was able to locate and help about eighty-five of our kids. I bought them all clothes, shoes, blankets, cooking utensils, pillows, medicine etc., and here are the pictures of the supplies all piled up in the park where they stay." He handed Paul, the treasurer, an envelope full of paper slips, written in Vietnamese, but the numbers were self-explanatory. "The exchange rate was 4400 Dong per U.S. dollar. I spent 1,305,480 Dong which comes to about 310 U.S. that leaves a balance of 190 U.S. Here it is along with the receipts. Nick counted out the money for Paul and Zach. The skepticism instantly turned to a kind of awe.

Alan Decoite, a former Marine Recon, raised his hand. "Nick, I'm impressed that you actually went over there and did all this, but I'm even more shocked that you brought money back. Why didn't you spend the rest or give them the cash?"

Nick expected the question. "It's a very complex situation over there. There are a lot of nasty rumors and accusations. There are different factions competing for control of the group, and I heard all kinds of things."

Zach leaned forward, "Like what, brah?"

"Like John Rogers is a crook, and that he charges them money to get them out of Vietnam. And that he charges the American sponsors money to get them an Amerasian orphan who might end up like a slave to some rich pervert. I don't believe it really, but there is racial tension, and they are split into gangs according to the color of their fathers. There is rampant drug use, and my fear was that if I gave them money it would only lead to more conflict. It was a tough call, but I decided to bring it back with me. Besides, if it's gonna get spent on drugs, then I figure it should be on OUR drugs!"

The room erupted in wild laughter. During the next half-hour Nick fielded questions and told them his stories. By the end of the evening, the men could feel a certain connection with Vietnam that they had formerly rejected. Especially when they heard about the friendship and camaraderie between the American, Australian, and Vietnamese veterans while getting drunk together.

Yes, Nick thought, There's no place like home! And the best part is that I kept my word. This time.

The following week, with Malia's protests still fresh in his ears, Nick arrived at Honolulu International Airport and took a cab to the local Catholic Charities Office on School Street. He found his way into the large complex and entered the conference room where a group of about twenty people had already gathered.

"Excuse me. I'm Nick Dwyer from Maui. A Ms. Corpus invited me to attend today's meeting."

A middle-aged Filipina with glasses rose from her chair. "Oh yes! Nick, thank you so much for coming! Everyone, this is the man I was telling you about. He just returned from Vietnam where he was helping the Amerasians." She turned to Nick. "Won't you sit down?" The members nodded with appreciative oohs and aahs, and Nick felt like a celebrity as he shook Dahlia's hand. She proceeded to make introductions.

"This is Ron Scott with the Department of Social Services, Dr. Irv Cohen from Diamond Head Mental Health Center, Lieutenant Tony Sitachitta from HPD, Dwight Ovitt who is our director here at Catholic Charities, and David Morata, who is also from Kula, Maui, and Cecilia Motus with the State Employment Service."

Nick sat next to the round-faced Morata, a Japanese man with gray hair, and shook hands with his fellow Mauian. All eyes seemed to be on Nick as David asked him, "So Nick, are you a Vietnam vet?"

Nick nodded shyly. "And you?"

David shook his head. "You are the only vet here today. I'm amazed that you actually were able to go back to Vietnam. I bet it took a lot of courage to face your former enemy again."

"Not really." Nick said, trying to be humble. "I think I made peace with that the last time I went back, in 1987."

Dahlia leaned forward in her chair, "That's incredible! Why did you go back that time?"

"To look for my Vietnamese wife from the war. I had heard she might have had my baby. But she didn't." There was an audible sigh of disappointment in the room.

Cecilia Motus spoke, "So you have a personal interest in the Amerasian situation. That's quite unique. All of us here are merely trying to help them acclimate once they arrive from Vietnam, but we have no experience there. We are honored and grateful for your participation and hope you will become a permanent member of this task force."

Everyone nodded their approval. Nick blushed slightly and held up both hands. "Well, wait a minute. I must tell you that, as much as I want to help you, I'm a full-time farmer. I really can't afford to donate much time. But I will sure do whatever I can. Is there some way I could help those kids coming to Maui? Maybe I could talk to some of the other farmers about hiring them to work in the fields. There's a huge labor shortage on Maui."

Cecilia nodded emphatically. "Nick, that would be a great help. Could you look into that when you return home and maybe coordinate with David there, since you are neighbors?"

They nodded in agreement. "There's one other thing that I would like to bring up," said Nick, looking at Dwight.

The chairman gestured with his hands. "You have the floor."

"Thank you. While I was in Saigon…"

Dahlia interrupted, "Excuse me, Nick. Don't they call it Ho Chi Minh City now?"

"Yeah, they do. But old habits die hard. Anyway, I met some people from the Orderly Departure Program, and a Mr. Bob McMillan asked me to initiate a drive to petition Congress about extending the Amerasian Homecoming Act, which is due to expire soon. As you know, it was introduced by the former POW, Senator John McCain from Arizona. I brought a petition with me today that I would like to leave with you for signatures. It has already been signed by virtually every member of the Vietnam Veterans of Maui, and others. When it is completed could you please send it back to me so I can forward it to our Senator Dan Inouye?"

Dwight nodded, "Absolutely, I think we will all be happy to add our support." There was unanimous nodding in agreement from the others.

Dr. Cohen took the floor. "Excuse me Nick. I'm very interested in anything you can tell us about the Amerasians' mental condition. Are they excited about coming here or is it merely an escape from Vietnam? Do they have drug or alcohol problems? Do they suffer from PTSD? Are they violent?"

Nick paused, reflecting on his interactions with the kids. These were good questions and he quite honestly realized that he had never considered them. His mission was only to help them until someone else could get them out. Now he was becoming a part of that as well.

"My impression is that they are very street smart, because that's where they live. Believe me, Vietnam is a tough place to be homeless, and they all stand out like sore thumbs because of their different racial features. They are targets for every seedy, sleazy character there is. They are forced into prostitution and used to commit crimes for others' benefit, but they take the blame. They are systematically abused, beaten, raped, and even murdered, with no one to protect them. I don't know too much about PTSD yet, so I can't really answer that."

"PTSD means post-traumatic stress disorder," explained Dr. Cohen. "In fact, many Vietnam war veterans like yourself suffer from it. Have you ever been examined for it?"

Nick dismissed the question with a shake of his head. "Nah, I'm OK."

The doctor seemed concerned. "Symptoms typically are guilt, anger, rage, flashbacks, drug and alcohol abuse, violence, and the like. Did you observe anything like that while you were with them?"

Nick felt his face flushing as the reality swept over him. That description fit him like a tailor-made suit. "Well, yeah. I guess that's a pretty accurate description."

It seemed the doctor was about to continue but then thought better of it. He smiled at Nick, then around the room. "It appears we are going to have our hands full, dealing with some very complex psychological conditions."

Dwight Ovitt nodded in agreement. "Irv, please make up a list of suggestions about how we should address these issues when these people arrive. Thank you Nick, for your insights. And during the course of the meeting please feel free to come forward with any other pertinent information that you think would help." Nick nodded and smiled back.

But, once again, Nick realized he had made another commitment without thinking of the consequences. Silently cursing himself, he sat quietly through the rest of the meeting, but revelled in the glory of being a member of this organization that he truly believed would make a difference. At the end of the day he exchanged phone numbers and business cards with those in attendance and promised to keep in touch. The family and the farm would have to be patient a little longer.

STUART NICHOLLS

CHAPTER 31
Maui 1989

Much to Malia's dismay, Nick continued to be active with the Task Force for the next several months. He made enquiries with the Farmer's Cooperative, to which he belonged, as well as the Maui Pineapple Company, about hiring Amerasians when they arrived on the island.

He made two more trips to Honolulu to attend conferences. Malia was infuriated. They were struggling financially. She couldn't see spending money on this cause, no matter how noble it was. The tension grew. When the stress level increased, so did Nick's drug and alcohol abuse. Soon, he was drinking every day, smoking marijuana and snorting cocaine several times a week. His temper would flare more frequently. Flashbacks began to plague him when he tried to sleep.

As time passed he began reacting to current situations and arising problems the way he had in the war—with extreme violence. When he felt lonely and misunderstood by his family and friends on Maui, he would go to his office and write to the two people who he felt would understand—Fredy Champagne and Pham Thai Thanh.

In late June he received a *Par Avion* envelope post marked Ho Chi Minh City.

"Dear Nick, It's a pleasure to hear from you. I never expected you would send me those delicious dried apples and T-shirts. Thank you very much, Nick, for your friendship, openness, honesty, and especially keeping your promise.

"I really appreciate the short but very nice time we all had together. Phuong sends you her best regards. She is now practicing Carpenters' songs on her guitar so she can play them for you when you return.

"Do you think of coming back one day? Well, I don't ask you for a firm promise, but don't you think it's nice to come back again to a place where you think you belong to and have friends? I myself think it would be very fantastic if we will have a chance for seeing each other again, sharing our thoughts, listening to the music in the dining hall, joking and laughing, enjoying and appreciating the friendship that we have together built up. I am glad and touched when you say in your letter that you have finally found peace and that the war is over. Well Nick, may peace be always with you and may our friendship grow in the years ahead.

"A couple of days ago, I learned that John Rogers has gotten into some trouble with local authority and was deported last week. I don't know exactly what the reason is. Hopefully what he has done won't damage the good will of healing and conciliation that so many people have put up much effort to do. John came to see me a few times but I was too busy to talk to him.

"Best wishes to you and your family. Please stay in touch with us, your friends here. Bye for now, Your friend Thanh."

Just days later, he received a letter from Fredy Champagne thanking him for his help with the Vung Tau clinic. He also described being overthrown as the leader of the VVRP while he was in Vietnam. Gordon Smith had been in the middle of it and had tried to steal Fredy's thunder as well as the organization. But Fredy had rolled with the punch and was on a new mission to Vietnam, working with a lady named Le Ly Hayslip as project director for her East Meets West foundation.

They had enlisted support from Vietnam combat veteran Oliver Stone, producer of *Platoon,* to build two more clinics in Da Nang. Fredy invited Nick to come join them and lay some bricks. He also wanted more information about FACES. Fredy had gotten a letter from Charlie Brown Phuong saying that John Rogers was a fake and asking Fredy to help the Amerasian orphans again. Fredy also wanted to organize a conference for all the different aid groups who were now working in Vietnam, to coordinate efforts there and cooperate with each other for a stronger impact.

When Nick put down the letters, his stomach fluttered excitedly at the prospect of going back and being a part of this important movement. He felt honored and flattered that his abilities and expertise were finally being recognized. This is what he had been waiting for.

But reality cast a long dark shadow over his enthusiasm. The farms and the family stood in the way. The glory that he sought would have to be forgotten. He still had promises to keep.

Then the letter arrived from Utica, New York. The return address was the Mohawk Valley Resource Center. Even before Nick opened the handwritten letter, he knew who it was from.

"My Dear Friend Ly, I am writing you from this hell that I cannot escape. They treat me very bad here. Why do they want to hurt me, Ly? I do nothing wrong, but they lie to Amerasian orphans. They say they give us jobs, but there are no workings here. They promise money but we no have. I beg to you please help me out of this place, Ly.

"I want come Maui and live with you. I will work hard. I will be good, I promise. Please write to me here very soon Ly, before I die. You can call this phone number and leave message. I will call you back. Please help! Love, Charlie Brown Phuong"

That evening, with the family finally gathered together at the same table for dinner, Nick poked at his spaghetti and took a deep breath. "OK, look. I know things have been kinda crazy around here lately. I'm sorry for all the yelling and screaming. I'm sorry if I hurt anybody." He forced himself to glance over at Malia's swollen cheek and bruised eye. She kept her head down, focusing on her food. The two boys, Eric and Keoki, looked sullenly at each other as if to say, "Yeah right, Dad. We've heard this bullshit before."

Nick tried to sound jovial. "Look, I got a letter today from one of the Amerasian orphans that I met in Vietnam last February." He placed it in the middle of the table and watched disheartened as it was met with unanimous scowls. "He's in New York, but the refugee center there has been mistreating him. He's begging me to let him come here and live with us."

Immediately, Malia belched a sarcastic laugh. "Oh yeah, Nick. That should help us solve our problems. Bring in another mouth to feed. We don't have enough problems already. A few more will really help."

Eric faced his father. His curly, sun-bleached hair contrasted with tan sinewy arms from working on the farm. Nick could see the tortured look of hopelessness in his blue eyes. "So what, Dad. Are you bringing him here?"

Nick shrugged. "Yeah. He could help us on the farm, and we can build him an employee house on our other lot. Meanwhile you two guys can share one bedroom and he can have the other. Besides, I think it would do everybody good to see what kind of life he's had to suffer. It would make us all appreciate how much we have."

An exasperated Eric could take no more. "Look, Dad! You know what? I've had enough! I'm sick of you always wanting to help everybody else but ignoring us. You divorce Mom, then you marry Malia and adopt Keoki, but now you care more about these Vietnamese than us. I want my final paycheck. I'm moving out and going to live with Ricky Mau and his family." With that, he threw down his fork and slammed his chair into the table and stormed off cursing, on the verge of tears with desperation.

"Fine! You do that, you fucking punk! We don't need you and your fucking attitude around here! Maybe you go off on your own and you'll see what the world is really like! Charlie Brown has seen more suffering than all of us put together and I'm going to help him! It's the least we can do and that's that! If anybody else wants to leave, there's the door!"

Malia left the table in tears. Nick could hear her sobbing up in their bedroom as he and the young, bewildered Keoki tried to eat their supper in tormented silence. Before getting up from the table, Nick reached over and patted the small, round shoulders. Keoki looked up at him with soft, sensitive brown eyes that began to brim with helplessness. He was hurt and confused yet grateful. He had never known his biological father, but his features revealed the beauty of his Filipina mother and his Caucasian father, who was also a Vietnam veteran. To Keoki, Nick would always be his father, no matter what.

CHAPTER 32
Maui 1990

Strong October trade winds buffeted Nick as he made his way into the terminal. The evening air was chilly, but Nick could feel the warmth in his chest again. He was about to do something good for someone else. That always made him feel the happiest. Checking the TV monitor for Charlie's incoming flight, he lit a cigarette and made his way up to the gate. Shortly the United flight arrived, docked, and Nick began craning his neck, searching for the young Amerasian vagabond. After the plane was nearly empty, Nick became anxious and worried. Then, there he was, stepping out the door carefully and timidly. His white Levi's were new, and he wore a leather jacket that appeared quite expensive. He carried an oversized nylon backpack. Charlie's eyes widened with excitement and joy as he spotted the balding, broad-shouldered Nick making his way through the crowd.

"Ly! Ly!" he shouted, waving frantically.

"Charlie Brown! You're a clown!" Nick called back and they were hugging tightly—like a reunited father and son. "Aloha! Welcome to Maui!" Nick draped a lei of red carnations from his farm around Charlie's thin neck. Charlie hugged him again and began to cry. Nick led him down the escalator to get his bags, but Charlie stopped him.

"No, no, Ly. This is all I have right here." And he held up a medium-sized carry on bag. Charlie had only been in the U.S. for two months. Not long enough to acquire much.

During the half-hour drive home Nick tried to sound positive and make Charlie feel secure and welcome. "OK now, you'll have your own bedroom in my house. It is where my oldest son used to stay. I'm taking out a loan to build you your own house, but you can stay with us until it's ready. When you're rested up in a few days you can start working around the farm and I'll pay you minimum wage until you learn the ropes, but room and board and clothes and everything else I will take care of, OK?"

Charlie smiled and said emphatically, "That's fine Ly, but I can start work tomorrow. I will work hard. Don't worry."

"OK, but I think you should call me Nick. We're not in Vietnam anymore."

"OK, Nick."

At the house Nick led him into the living room where Malia and Keoki were watching TV. "OK, Charlie, I want you to meet my wife, Malia, and our son Keoki."

Malia turned her head briefly and muttered, "Hello." Keoki sat and waved his hand from his chair. The cold reception was not lost on Charlie. He looked at Nick with a questioning gaze.

"Come on in here, Charlie. This is your bedroom. The bathroom is right there. Keoki sleeps in that room, and Malia and I have a room upstairs. You get cleaned up and have a good night's rest. I'll call you for breakfast. OK? Understand?"

Charlie nodded frowning. He gestured towards the others. "Why don't they like me, Nick?"

"Don't worry. They like you all right, but they are afraid of having a stranger living in the house. Once you show them what a good guy you are, they'll change." He smiled and hugged Charlie good night.

But the climate in the house would never grow warm.

The next day, Nick took Charlie down to the ag park and showed him how to plant zucchini. "Hold the tray with your left hand like this. There are seventy-two plants in each tray. You take one out with your right hand and stick it in the ground. Then you take one step, this long and plant the next one. Two-and-a-half feet apart. OK? You keep going until you empty the tray, then you come back, get another one and pick up where you left off. Understand?"

Charlie pushed his long brown hair off his face, nodded and stepped off with his new tennis shoes and slowly began to plant. Nick picked up his own tray and joined him planting. He quickly passed Charlie who watched Nick work like a machine. His tray was finished in three minutes. Charlie stood and watched with his mouth agape as Nick went briskly back for his second tray. He looked down at his own tray which had only seven empty holes. When Nick passed him the second time, he saw the discouraged look on Charlie's face. "Don't worry Charlie. You'll get faster as time goes on. The main thing now is to learn the movements correctly." He patted Charlie's shoulder. But as Charlie resumed planting he picked up the pace, trying to compete with Nick. When Nick passed him the third time Charlie yelled out in frustration and tossed the half empty tray as far as he could.

"Fuck this! I cannot do this work! I will never be as fast as you!" and he sat down in the dust and began to cry like a baby.

Nick was shocked and confused at Charlie's childish behavior. He came back to him and tried to put his hand on the boy's shoulder, but Charlie pulled away and lay down and rolled around in the dirt.

"Come on now, Charlie! I told you. Don't try to go fast just yet. It takes time to learn, that's all."

Charlie jumped up and clung to Nick tightly. "Please, Nick! No make me go away! I want stay with you! Please! Please!"

Perplexed and even a little frightened by this volatile display, Nick began wondering what he had gotten them all into. It didn't get any better. As the days turned into weeks, Charlie seemed to become more obnoxious and alienated, even from Nick. Malia and Keoki felt estranged as well, since Nick and Charlie often spoke in Vietnamese.

One afternoon, Nick took Charlie with him to deliver cabbage to the co-op and visit Michelle at her bar. Nick introduced him to the Vietnamese girls in hopes that he would feel more at home with them, but Charlie acted sullen and resentful. When Nick ordered them both a beer, Charlie said something to Michelle in a very insulting manner. Nick did not understand what was said but saw Michelle's face flush with anger. Her eyes shone with hatred and Nick knew he had made a mistake bringing Charlie there. "Charlie, what's wrong with you anyway? Why did you insult my friend?"

"Because I hate all Vietnamese! I remember what they do to me! You no be friends with her, Nick. She is no good. I know."

"Now you listen to me, Charlie! Michelle is my friend! Don't ever tell me what to do! Never! Do you understand? Don't make me hurt you!"

Charlie began crying furiously. He picked up his beer bottle and threw it against the wall, just missing the large plate glass window. Nick snapped. He grabbed up Charlie by the shirt collar and literally dragged him out choking and gagging to the truck where he picked him up and threw him into the cab like a bag of cabbage. Nick got behind the wheel and squealed out onto Lower Main Street. Charlie sobbed even louder. He opened his door and tried to leap out as they sped away. Nick caught him by the sleeve just in time to drag him back inside while swerving onto the shoulder to stop. He slapped Charlie hard across his face.

"Now you get back in here and close that door!" Charlie struggled and twisted but Nick held him firm. "Charlie! You stop right now or I'll kick your fucking ass right here! You understand me goddamn it?"

"No! No! Somebody help me! Please!" he screamed.

Suddenly Nick saw the situation clearly. He had brought Charlie here to help him not hurt him, but somehow Charlie's behavior seemed to taunt and provoke him. "OK, Charlie. OK. Please just calm down. I'm sorry I hurt you. You know I love you like a son. Please. Let's just not talk until we get home or even tomorrow, OK?"

Sobbing, Charlie covered his head defensively with his arms. The sobs subsided to sniffles. Charlie nodded weakly. "OK, Nick. We go home."

Nick pulled a long roach out of the ashtray. He lit it expertly behind cupped hands with his elbows on the wheel. He pulled long then passed it to Charlie who took it and drew in a drag. He passed it back. Within minutes the weed calmed and relaxed them. They drove the long winding road up through the cane fields in a peaceful silence.

A week later Nick called Eric and invited him home for Thanksgiving. He hoped to take advantage of this opportunity to make peace as well. "Yeah, OK, Dad. That sounds cool. But can I bring my new girlfriend? I think you'll like her. She's an Amerasian orphan from Saigon."

Nick was shocked. "Really? How the hell did you meet her?"

"At Michelle's bar. She just started working there the other day."

Nick just had to laugh. "Yeah! Of course! Maybe I even know her. Charlie probably does too. Wouldn't that be something?"

"How's he working out, anyway?"

"Not so good, but we're all trying. See you at noon."

Eric arrived, to find the family watching football despite Charlie's accusation that this wasn't really football. He insisted that soccer was football, not this. Nick had to agree. When Eric walked in and introduced his girlfriend, Bich, Charlie and the girl locked eyes immediately. Nick knew by their expressions that they had a long history. And it was not a good one. They all but sneered at each other, and looked away with clenched teeth. But Nick didn't recognize her.

After bringing everyone drinks, Nick tried making light conversation with her in Vietnamese, which annoyed Malia, Eric, and Keoki. Charlie jumped in with a visceral caterwaul. Bich responded in like fashion. They were on the edge of their chairs exchanging insults and threats that Nick did not really understand.

Eric was alarmed. "Dad, what are they saying? What's going on?"

Nick shook his head. "Goddamn! I don't know! But they obviously know each other!"

Charlie turned to Eric and yelled. "In Vietnam she is a whore! No good! No good for you, Eric!"

Bich returned fire but her English was seriously lacking. "Charlie Brown lie! He is sell drug! He steal money me! He bad! Number ten!"

Nick held up both his hands pleading for calm. "Look, you two. This is Thanksgiving here in America. I don't care about your past in Saigon. This is here, now, OK?" They relaxed a little and both nodded. "OK, now. This is a day for everybody to stop and look around at their life and be thankful for what they have. Instead of fighting and arguing you should remember where you came from and be grateful that you're not there anymore. I think nobody here has more to be thankful for than both of you. Right?"

Bich nodded bashfully. "I sorry, *Anh* Nick. Sorry, Eric. Everybody."

Malia forced a weak smile and went to the kitchen. Eric took Bich by the arm to Keoki's room, and Nick nodded for Charlie to meet him on the deck outside. Keoki was left alone petting the cat on the sofa.

The midday sun spilled down over the roof of the two-story cedar home. They were met by a breathtaking view of the central valley, four thousand feet below. Nick sipped his beer. "Look, Charlie. I don't know what your problem is. Why do you seem to hate everybody? Everywhere you go, you hate the people. It seems to me there is something wrong with YOU, not them."

Charlie looked away briefly. "Yeah, sometimes I look at all your son's rifles and guns that are locked up in my room. And I think, how can I get those locks off? Maybe I like kill somebody."

Nick studied Charlie carefully. He could see that this was no joke. "Man, what the fuck are you talking about? Are you threatening us?"

"Nick, why don't you understand? You just like me. I see you the same way. You hate everybody too. But you try to hide it. I am tired of hiding. I just be me. Fuck them!"

Nick gazed out over the valley to the blue sea beyond and shook his head. There was an uneasy feeling in his guts. It was fear. Fear that Charlie, for all his faults, might have just given him a peek through a different window into his soul. Or maybe fear that Nick had taken on more than he could handle. Maybe more than anyone could handle. Had he put all of them in danger? Bringing harmony into this family now began to appear impossible. The first smell of defeat assaulted his consciousness, and he felt more misgivings than thanksgiving.

Ironically, the day the land was cleared for his new cottage was the last time that they ever saw Charlie Brown Phuong. They had all been down at the ag park farm, harvesting tomatoes. The morning sun was unusually hot. There was not a breath of wind. Charlie kept complaining about his sore back, blistered hands, the sweat, the heat and anything else that came to mind.

Nick bit his tongue for more than an hour before he stood up from picking the fruit and yelled directly into Charlie's face. "Listen to me, you chicken-shit little pussy! Look there at Malia! A small woman. Look at Keoki. A little boy. And now look at me, a man twice your age. Do you see us working? Do you see that we are suffering too? Do you hear us complaining? Now shut up and work! When we finish this row, we will stop to eat lunch."

Charlie kicked his plastic bucket over and stood defiantly against Nick. It was a big mistake. "No, I eat now!" He declared and started to walk off towards the shed where the food was waiting in the shade.

"You get your lazy fucking ass back here, boy, or so help me I'll kill your sorry ass!" Nick was infuriated beyond control. Even Malia could sense the abnormal tone in his voice. She stopped working and watched him carefully.

Charlie kept walking away. He yelled back over his shoulder, "No! I eat now! I'm hungry!"

Nick leaped over the tomato plants and was on Charlie's back before he could even blink. Charlie collapsed screaming in fear with the big man on top of him pounding his fists into Charlie's face and body mercilessly. Malia and Keoki grabbed Nick from behind, holding his arms.

"Nick! Stop! You'll kill him! Please stop!"

In the middle of a ferocious overhand right, and panting heavily through clenched teeth, Nick froze and took a deep breath. The Amerasian orphan was screaming, crying, and bleeding. Nick stood slowly and quietly. He picked Charlie up by the scruff of his neck. "Let's go, boy. This is over, right now."

Charlie huddled in a mangled mess on the floor of the truck. Nick took him home, collected all of his things, let him clean up, then drove him straight to the homeless shelter down in the valley next to the HC&S sugar mill. He pulled up in front, reached over and opened the door, and pointed to the dusty brown building.

They reluctantly eyed each other for the last time, silently asking themselves what the hell had happened. Charlie got out and closed the door. Nick was overcome, swaying between murder and suicide, anger and tears, forgiveness and damnation. In the end, he pulled away and never looked back.

When Malia and Keoki came home that afternoon, Malia called out to him. No response. But the truck was parked askew outside. She ran fearfully upstairs and found him sitting cross-legged on the floor, naked, the barrel of the M-14 in his mouth, and a quivering finger on the trigger. She screamed, begging and pleading for him to put the gun down.

His eyes were at half mast, blank and as deep and empty as a Cu Chi well in April. He had left his body long ago. He was traveling far and light, soaring above Nguyen Hue Street, swooping down among the memories of a happier, auspicious time. A time filled with promise and grand expectations. Lilting piano music, deep conversation, laughter, meaning. And now he wallowed in the stench of his failures and broken promises. No matter how inspired they may have been or how well-intentioned, they had ended as tragically as the war itself. He had turned his back and walked away, leaving them to fend for themselves, wondering what the fuck had gone wrong, but still without answers.

What hurt Nick the most was the realization that he had become the very thing that he had tried to rescue the Amerasians from. He was not the answer. He was the problem. Charlie had been right all along. He was just like him. Maybe there is something to this PTSD, he thought. Maybe we both have it.

Eventually, like all the times before, Nick came back to the now and put the gun away. But it would only be a matter of time before something else would set off a sense of futility, hopelessness, and failure, and his finger would be on the trigger again.

He sought solace in drugs. It became all too apparent that the fix was not only temporary, but made the extreme mood swings even worse. Over the next year their life became a living hell. Nick emptied their bank account to fuel his self-medication. The only recompense was the wild, uninhibited sex that the cocaine afforded him with Malia. But she grew quickly tired of it because she was able to see the irreversible damage it caused. Nick was too far gone. He was a hopeless addict.

In the end, Malia packed up her and Keoki's belongings and moved back to her mother's in Lahaina. She demanded a divorce but would do nothing to facilitate it. Then one chilly February morning in 1991, Nick awoke to the roaring silence in his house. The recently completed cottage stood empty as well. He threw some icy water in his face and walked out onto his deck. The north wind cut cold into him as he surveyed the disheveled carnation farm around him. The only sound was the whining of Zeke, the huge German shepherd tethered nearby. It came painfully onto him then that the dog would have left him too, if not for the chain.

Nick sought help, finally, at the newly opened Vet Center that he and the other Vietnam Veterans of Maui had founded in Wailuku. A counselor named Bob Morton helped Nick file a claim for PTSD. The tests that Nick had been given indicated overwhelmingly that he did indeed suffer from the condition.

CHAPTER 33
Maui
April 1991

Nick received another letter from Fredy Champagne. Fredy and a new team of vets had built a small clinic in DaNang. They also had planted Peace Poles all over Vietnam, including one at the elementary school in the village of Lai Khe where he and Nick had served with the First Infantry Division. It was not far from Ma and Phuong and Hai's house, where they had given him his farewell dinner in 1966. Would Nick be interested in helping fund-raise for the nearby orphanage? Or even going back to Vietnam to assist with a growing list of humanitarian projects?

Nick's hand began trembling as he read the letter. Fredy really knows how to get to me, he thought to himself. A sudden epiphany rose like the sun. There was nothing and no one standing in his way now. Except, he still had two farms to work and no one to help him. Doing it all alone seemed impossible. But he would try, even while his destiny beckoned.

One July morning, he sat atop his big Ford tractor plowing his fields in preparation for a new planting when he felt the powerful machine lurch to a grinding halt, straining against an unseen obstacle. He looked back over his shoulder and watched one of the plowshares break off at the soil line where it had caught on a bedrock slab. Something inside his head went numb.

He was quite calm and unexcited. He simply stood up and climbed down from the struggling, still-in-gear tractor and plow, pulling against the ledge. He walked slowly to his truck and drove home, leaving the tractor running in the field.

He packed his suitcase after calling his good friend Mark. "I got a huge favor to ask, brother. "

The Texas drawl returned, "Just name it, brah."

"Can you take care of Zeke for a month or so?"

"A month or so?" The surprise was obvious in Mark's voice.

"Yeah." Nick paused, questioning his own sanity. "I'm going back."

"Oh my God! Are you serious? What about the farms, what about…?"

"Fuck it! Don't mean nothin', brah! You can sell whatever flowers and vegetables you can find. It's all yours."

"It's as good as done but listen, me and Tim Campbell are headin' down to Ray's lounge for a quick one. Why don't you join us?"

"I'll see you in thirty. And, Mark. Thanks, my brother."

Ray's was a local tavern that had replaced Michelle's as their favorite hang out. Most of the vets still had a lingering fear or resentment about the Vietnamese, even while being envious and in awe of Nick for his fearless forays back to the land of the dragon. Nick spotted them both in the corner booth that the vets had commandeered as their own. No one ever objected. They had been joined by a third vet, none other than Zach Christopher, who glanced over as Nick approached their booth. "Hey Nick!" he called out, "What the fuck, over?" They had been hunched over in a conspiratorial conversation, but stood to hug Nick as he arrived.

During the Tet Offensive in January 1968, Tim had been shot in the head. When he regained consciousness, he was in a hospital in Japan. He was given one of the largest metal plates available in the back of his skull. His entire left side was paralyzed, and he had a pronounced slur. Despite his disabilities he was loved and respected as everyone's hero. He smiled crookedly at Nick then in his New England accent asked, "Damn, Nick! Did I hear Mark right?" Nick nodded, grinning bashfully.

"When are you leaving?" asked Zach.

"A soon as I can get a flight."

"Where are you going exactly?" Zach persisted.

Nick smiled at the pretty Korean waitress as she put down his beer. "First Thailand, then over to Nam."

"Why can't you go straight to the Nam?" asked Mark.

"Because of the trade embargo. No one is supposed to do any business with Vietnam. So you have to go through a third country."

He watched Tim, who was suddenly into the thousand-yard stare, yet with a strange dreamy smile on his face. "Tim. You OK?" Tim nodded slowly, but his eyes were focused elsewhere.

Zach looked around to insure their privacy then lowered his voice. "Listen, Nick, you already know about the MIA group that I'm affiliated with, right?" They all leaned in on cue. Nick nodded. "Lately we've been getting reports of actual live sightings in Vietnam." There was an audible sigh around the booth as this news sunk in. "If I can get you the coordinates and locations, would you be willing to investigate for us?"

Nick stared Zach in the eye unflinchingly. "Hell yes! But you need to move fast."

Zach nodded. "You know, there are over two thousand MIAs over there. And we know some are POW's who never came home with the rest of them in 1973."

Mark squirmed excitedly. "How come?"

"Because Kissinger promised the Vietnamese nearly $4 billion in war reparations if they gave us back our boys. But the Vietnamese only gave back some of them, and Kissinger reneged on the deal. So they're still holding 'em until we pay up."

Nick stared steadily at Zach. "So how do I proceed? Where do I look? Will I have contacts over there?"

Zach shook his head. "You'll be on your own. But you know your way around. You speak the language, and I know you're 100 percent trustworthy."

Nick was embarrassed. "Thanks, brah."

"You should look in hospitals and clinics. There are rumors that many are sick and being treated, but their cover will be that they're Russians or other Soviet bloc citizens. If you can get in and search the medical facilities there's a good chance you could walk right up to them. But be damn careful. We don't want the gooks grabbing you too."

Nick could feel the butterflies in the pit of his stomach. He trembled with excitement as the adrenaline surged. "Zach. You get me the locations, and I'll give it my best shot. Goddamn! Wouldn't it be great if we could get some of our guys out?"

The others grinned from ear to ear, sharing the exhilaration of this exciting yet dangerous mission.

Tim came back from his mental journey and stared Nick straight in the eye. "Nick." A long pause.

"Yeah. What?"

"You want some company?" Tim smiled.

Nick studied his face. "You serious?"

"As an ambush."

"But Tim, you realize if we get caught, we won't be coming back."

Tim snorted his disgust. "Hey, Nick. Look at me. What have I got to lose?"

Nick envisioned the future. A tall, half-paralyzed ex-marine who spoke no Vietnamese and would be totally dependent on Nick for virtually all of his needs, as well as wants. It would not be easy. He would definitely slow Nick down. Especially in light of this new development. But he thought of the old war slogan, "We don't leave anyone behind." Tim had made a major sacrifice for his country. If Tim wanted to go, by God, he was going to take him! He reached out and shook Tim's hand. "I'd be proud to take you, brother!"

It took three weeks for Nick to arrange their trip. His Vietnamese travel agent in Honolulu had to send the passports to the Vietnamese embassy in Mexico for entry visas, since there was still no diplomatic recognition with the U.S.

CHAPTER 34
Philippine Airlines Flight
August 1991

Finally, he and Tim began a journey that included a one-week stay in Bangkok, then an Air Vietnam flight to Ho Chi Minh City for a one-month stay. Coming home they planned a week in Bangkok, another week in Hong Kong, and returning to Maui in mid-September.

They strapped themselves into their seats and grinned excitedly to each other as the Boeing 737 sped down the runway toward the ocean at Sprecklesville and on to Honolulu. Peering out the window, Nick watched Mount Haleakala rush past and out of sight. He felt the wheels lift off the *aina,* and a peaceful calm came over him.

It was now out of his hands. He simply gave it up. His destiny was no longer under his control. He surrendered his life to fate or luck or God. The moth was headed into the flame, one more time.

After a short layover in Honolulu, they boarded their Philippine Airlines flight to Manila. Nick was jubilant as the stewardess poured his first beer with the deep blue Pacific spread out below them. He and Tim clinked glasses.

"Well, Timmy. Here we go, brother!"

Tim chuckled, with foam on his upper lip. "Nick, I really want to thank you for taking me along. I hope I won't be too much trouble."

"Don't worry about it, brah. We'll be fine."

"So how many times have you gone back now, Nick?"

"This is the third."

"By the way. Is your divorce final yet?"

Nick gazed out the window at the fluffy cumulous clouds sliding away beneath the wing. "No. But I've filed all the papers. It's just a matter of waiting for the court to get off their ass."

Tim sipped his beer and glanced over at him. "I was wondering because I noticed you brought about a hundred condoms with you."

"Yeah, and that's just for the first week in Bangkok." Nick teased. "I wanna line up a bunch of beautiful chicks and take 'em on, three at a time!" He nudged Tim's elbow laughing. "Fuck 'em till they're dry!"

Tim laughed along. "I was able to talk with my old buddy Alan Roth. He'll meet us at the airport in Bangkok tomorrow, and he says he'll give us a sex tour down Patpong Road whenever we're ready."

Nick sighed, "Sounds good to me, brah. So what's he doing over there anyway?"

"He's still a lawyer. He's part of a Thai firm that does international stuff."

Nick nodded, impressed. He recalled meeting Alan one afternoon at Michelle's just after Nick had returned from his first trip back to Nam in '87. Alan was on his way to Southeast Asia and had heard about the crazy grunt who had tossed the dice again and lived to tell about it. Nick had watched the fire behind Alan's eyes when he talked about how Vietnam looked now and how well he had been received by the people. Alan ended up going to Vietnam as well as Thailand. As soon as he returned to Boston, he closed up his law practice, sold his house, and moved to Bangkok.

Nick liked Alan immediately. He was very short but thick and stocky and tougher than a nickel steak. He had also been a grunt with the Twenty-Fifth Infantry Division at Tay Ninh, which had been in Nick's area of operation. Back in 1988 he had helped Alan hit the ground running. Now maybe Alan could return the favor. It would be a huge help to have a friend in Bangkok if he got into trouble in Vietnam. Especially a lawyer who was into international law. He turned to Tim.

"So, how did you meet Alan?"

"It was back in Massachusetts, Nick. Him and me and a guy named Steve Foster, nicknamed Dixie, belonged to a club of Vietnam combat veterans. Then we all came to Maui together. After Dixie checked out, Alan went back to Massachusetts because of his business."

"What happened to Dixie?

"One night he had a party down in Kihei, so me and Alan and a bunch of people were there. Everybody getting high, you know. Some jerk started mouthing off to Dixie about Vietnam vets being pussies. Dixie goes and gets his shotgun. He sits down on the floor in the middle of everybody and says, "So, you think you're bad, eh, motherfucker? I'll show you bad!" He put the gun in his mouth and blew his fucking head off right there. Blood and brains splattered all over everybody, including his wife and daughter." Tim paused and swallowed hard. "So the party broke up kinda early."

Tim's grunt humor touched off intensely bitter laughter. Nick's chicken skin faded as he watched the clouds again.

"You know, I wish I had a dollar for every time I thought about checkin' out." Nick sipped his beer. "Back in '74, I moved up to Volcano, on the Big Island, with my first ex-wife and our five-year-old son. We lived in this cottage out in the boonies. It was winter and freezing cold. It rained for weeks on end. We never saw the sun. The only income we had was my unemployment, and after six months it was about to expire. We had no phone. No TV. Our radio only got one Oahu station and real scratchy. Once a week we would splurge and buy a six-pack. We had electricity, but we had to catch our water from the sky. That was the only easy thing about living there."

"It sounds pretty depressing, Nick," Tim observed.

"It was. Dark, hopeless. I kept thinking about how I lost my job. I can get pretty gnarly, ya know? Being a point man taught me to follow my instincts, and I never took orders very well. I'd go off on people I worked with because they were so fucking stupid. No common sense, ya know? I got fired and felt like a total fuck up. I started sticking the gun to my head.

"Luckily a previous employer gave me the chance to move back to Maui and start a landscape company. So I put the gun away. But you know what? Another Vietnam vet that I knew moved into that house in Volcano after we left. Six months later he blew his head off too."

They looked up into each other's eyes with an empty, deadpan stare for a moment, then turned away to reflect in the darkness of their mutual torment.

"There's a lot of us like that, Nick. A lot. Me too, ya know? How do you think it feels to lose half of your body? I mean, it's there, but I can't feel it or use it. I'm half a man. Chicks don't want half a man. I get really lonely. I need love and understanding too, but American women are too into themselves. A lot of them say that I deserve it because I went to Vietnam. Do you believe that?"

Nick was furious. "Fuck them bitches, man! Fuck 'em all! How dare they say something like that?"

Tim shrugged. "I don't know, but maybe I can find a poor Asian girl who would trade a new life in the U.S. for a little TLC." They chuckled together.

Nick gazed out the window again. "Not me. I just got rid of one. The last thing I want is another wife. Endless pussy is what I'm after. When I think of all the times I had a chance to... but didn't, I like to stick that gun in my mouth again." He laughed with his friend, flying into a golden sunset, 40,000 feet above the sea.

CHAPTER 35
Bangkok
August 1991

In Manila the next morning they had a two-hour layover and changed planes for Bangkok. When they finally disembarked at Don Muang Airport, memories swept over Nick. They stepped out onto the sidewalk outside the terminal and instantly spotted Alan's stout figure, dressed in slacks, white shirt, and tie and carrying the first cellular phone that they had ever seen. He was all smiles and laughed robustly as he waded through the throngs of passengers and greeted them with hugs.

"Well, you two are a sight for sore eyes. How was the trip?"

"It's all good, Alan!" said Tim. "Thanks for meeting us."

Nick grinned slyly. "Tim kept talking about some sex tour that you had planned. I couldn't sleep the whole time."

Alan beckoned a white taxi and Nick could not help thinking of Lek. When they squeezed inside Nick looked anxiously at the driver.

"Do you know Khun Lek? He drives cab # 579."

The man glanced sadly over at Nick. "How you know Lek?"

"He's my friend. Two years ago he helped me very much."

The driver turned back to his job. "He die two months ago. Accident. Very bad."

Stunned, Nick silently wondered who would take care of his two wives and families.

Alan screwed up his mouth in an Edward G. Robinson impersonation. "Yeah, things are tough, OK? But in Thailand we have a saying. *May pen ray.*"

Tim was lost. "What's that mean?"

Nick turned to him. "Same like we always said in the war. It don't mean nothin'."

Alan was impressed. "That's right. But tonight I'll show you what DOES mean something. More beautiful, sexy, available chicks than you can imagine."

Nick forced a weak smile. He took a deep breath, unnoticed by the others. Yeah. *May pen ray*, he thought.

Alan tried to get Nick away from it. "I made reservations for you guys at the PO Court hotel. It's close to my condo and was used by the Special Forces during the war. It's owned by the crown prince of Thailand. He's a good friend of mine," he beamed proudly. Nick and Tim looked at each other with raised eyebrows.

"What's his name?" Nick asked.

Alan grinned. "It's about fifty letters long, so we just call him Moonrock. Don't ask me why. He's kinda nuts. Let me rephrase that. He's REALLY fucking nuts. But he loves Vietnam vets and is a serious wannabe. I'll introduce you sometime. He has a penthouse at the hotel, complete with cooks, maids, servants, concubines, and body guards. You'll be frisked down when we go in. But keep your hands where they can be seen cause he has guns under every pillow in the house."

"Sounds kinda paranoid, Alan," Tim offered.

"You would be too if you were the prince. Lots of people would love to kidnap him. So wherever he goes he has heavily armed guards and decoy vehicles. When we go out to party together, it's like being in a James Bond movie."

"Does he have any extra concubines?" Nick winked.

Alan laughed, "Don't worry, man. You can find all the pussy you can handle. Here's the hotel. You guys go check in and clean up. I'll round up some beers and be up shortly."

The PO Court was a sprawling, two-story, U-shaped complex surrounding a large pool area with flowering trees and a small snack shop. In the courtyard area was a gilded Buddha shrine surrounded by flowers and a miniature waterfall. It was old and quaint, yet comfortable. They were given rooms on the second floor where they could collect whatever breeze flowed through the louvered windows. There was a small black-and-white TV with rabbit ears, hot water, and a functioning refrigerator. The double bed allowed only enough room for a threesome, Nick observed. But hey, *may pen ray*.

As the broiling sun finally began its descent behind the nearby high-rises, the three comrades hailed a taxi out front. They went down Inthramara Road to Paholyothin Road then turned south and proceeded past the Victory Monument roundabout into the embassy district. Soon, Alan ordered the driver to let them out at the edge of a huge open market. He paid the cabbie and wheeled around at a brisk pace through the blaring music, sizzling food booths, and racks of everything imaginable. "Welcome to Patpong!" he announced. "Follow me!"

Nick tried in vain to keep up with the stubby-legged Alan, while also ushering along the badly limping Tim. The sensory bombardment was dizzying, and more than once he lost their point man in the crowd. Tim's face registered fear and excitement at the same time, but the ex-marine would not abort this mission. They were closing on their destination.

Then, there was Alan, waiting impatiently by the front door of a gaudily decorated entrance to their first girlie bar. The multi-colored lights flashed in rhythm to the fiercely-pounding disco music, which was short on melody but long on bass and drums. Nick figured the decibel level to be well over 100, and he could feel the vibrations pummeling his entire body. The three men formed up at the door, handed over 100 *baht* each to the Thai bouncer and entered the den of sin with lecherous smiles from ear to ear.

The lascivious scene was thrust into their eager faces as they peered anxiously through blue cigarette smoke at dozens of bikini-clad beauties up on the elevated U-shaped bar. The girls were all grinding and gyrating around their chrome poles and fondling each other to shouts and cheers from the wildly intoxicated mob of men. They were all packed in like sardines, and the heat that radiated off the steamy bodies drew copious rivers of sweat from the newcomers. Tim yelled something to Alan, but the sound was totally overwhelmed by the deafening bedlam. Then he tapped on Alan's shoulder and leaned down close.

"How come the chicks all have numbered tags on their panties?" he all but screamed.

Alan laughed, "So you can tell the mamasan which ones you want!" This brought on a fit of laughter from all three men.

Nick counted at least thirty of the most beautiful, sexy women he had ever seen. He howled, "I'll take numbers one through twenty-seven! You guys can have the rest!"

They made their way slowly to the bar, where the Thai bartender looked up and shouted, "*Khun* Alan! Do you want your bottle?" Tim and Nick exchanged surprised looks.

"Hell yes! But give my two friends here *Sing Haa* beer!"

The bartender produced a bottle of Chivas, and handed it to Alan, who inspected the label carefully.

"What are you doing, Alan?" asked Tim.

"Checking the level in the bottle with my signature from the last time I was here. They hold it for me until I come in again. The locals make a cheap imitation and bootleg it under the same name, but it can eat a hole through a marble floor. I have a bottle of the good stuff at every bar in Patpong."

Nick laughed, chugged down some beer and surveyed the meat market at his fingertips. He became hypnotized by the bevy of beauties who eyed him coyly and seduced him with their sultry gyrations. Next to him he watched Tim standing with his mouth open in absolute shock. Then above the din he heard Alan telling him something.

"What's that?" he yelled.

"See anything you like?" Alan asked.

"Yeah! All of em!"

"Well, be careful. Two of them aren't women!"

Nick was shocked. "Are you serious?"

Alan nodded knowingly. "I've fucked every chick up there, including the two girlie boys!"

Nick was disgusted and let it show.

"Hey!" retorted Alan. "They got tits and a pussy just like the girls. What's the difference?"

Nick shook his head and gulped more beer. Alan was perturbed. He watched Tim for a second, then turned to Nick. "Watch this! Hey, Tim! You like that one don't you?" Tim grinned like a bashful school boy. Alan whistled loudly and beckoned the girl to come down with them. She was tall and stunningly beautiful. Nick saw that her tits were real.

Alan introduced Tim. "Tim, this is Amanda." He winked at Nick. "Buy her a drink." Tim did, and stood gawking foolishly as the girl toasted him as well as Nick and Alan, who both laughed conspiratorially. Nick pointed to the lovely creature behind her back with a questioning look, and Alan nodded emphatically.

Nick was embarrassed, because even he could not tell if Alan was just having fun with the two FNGs. Alan abruptly signed his bottle and led them outside the steamy den. Tim's "girl" returned to the stage, pouting professionally.

The short man sprinted away to the next bar, and on and on. When Nick finally lost track, they had visited over twenty bars and seen hundreds of gorgeous whores. With jet lag kicking in, he and Tim began dragging behind the energetic Alan.

At a place called the Pink Pussycat, Nick called down the two most beautiful, sexy chicks he had ever seen. Drunkenly, he sat one on each of his knees and could barely feel their weight. They were delightfully slinky and petite with small tight breasts, asses like cantaloupes, and long black silky hair. He looked deeply into their dark, exotic eyes and was mesmerized. They were slippery with oily sweat from dancing, so Nick ordered them drinks and paid the ten dollars gladly.

"What are your names?" he asked. The one in the tiger-striped bikini on his left knee said, "Mimi." The other was Kiki. "I'm Nick. And I think you are the most gorgeous girls I have ever met." They both smiled and toasted him with their watered down whiskey. "You look very young. How old are you?"

In unison they replied, "Eighteen."

"How old do you think I am?" he asked wincing.

Mi Mi examined his angular face and large, balding head. She screwed up her mouth slightly. "Forty," She said and looked away, embarrassed.

Nick took a deep breath. I don't want to marry 'em, just fuck their brains out, he said to himself. "Do you know *Khun* Alan?" he asked. They nodded. "We are all going to an island called Coh Samui in a day or two. Would you like to go with me?" They looked at each other, smiling, then nodded eagerly.

"You mean, we be your girlfriends?" Kiki asked. Nick nodded. "You pay our way and our bar fines while we go?"

"Of course. What is it, fourteen dollars a day per girl?" They nodded. "OK, no problem I'll come back for you in two days, alright?" They nodded again, smiling. "OK, how about one more drink to seal the deal?"

Later as the three men stumbled out the door, Alan questioned

Nick about the girls. "Did you make a date with those two?"

Nick grinned broadly. "Yeah. I'm bringing them to *Coh Samui* with us."

Alan shook his head in a solemn warning. "Did you know that two-thirds of these Thai chicks have AIDS?"

Nick stopped dead. "What? Now you tell us! Tim, did you know?" Tim shook his head in shock. Turning to Alan, Nick said, "I don't know much about AIDS except it'll kill you, and there's no cure."

Alan shrugged. "Just letting you know. Don't ever fuck 'em without a condom. Anyway, I've heard one of those chicks is infected."

Nick was in shock. "What happens if my condom breaks?"

Alan laughed. "Then you're toast, buddy!"

Fear swept over Nick like a cold shower. On the way back to the PO Court, Nick tossed it over in his mind. He felt his bubble being broken. Was it worth the risk? Maybe that's why God invented drugs and pornography, he mused. He took that dilemma to his lonely bed. In the morning, he popped some Alka-Seltzer into a glass of mineral water and decided to take his chances back in Vietnam instead. There were no reports of AIDS in the closed communist society yet.

He began thinking of Thanh. She was no turn-on, but there was something solid and appealing about her and their relationship. For a while, the thought of sex left his mind entirely. For a while.

Over the next several days, they would rest up during the day and party late into the morning. More than once they would stumble into the PO Court while the sun rose over the Bangkok smog. They postponed the trip to Coh Samui until their return next month.

One afternoon, they were all lounging by the pool, drinking beer and munching on some spicy Thai spring rolls and deep-fried shrimp. Nick nudged Alan. "Hey, brah. You haven't told us about your trip to Vietnam in '88."

"Oh yeah! In fact, I'm glad you reminded me. You know, I went back to my old base camp at Dau Tieng, just north of Nui Ba Den. The whole region is under water. It's a gigantic lake now. I guess they dammed up the river and use it as a reservoir. Anyway, I met this Vietnamese guy who is a really powerful man in the Communist Party for that district. He spoke good English and actually fought on the other side during the war. We went to lunch and talked all day about getting the embargo lifted and normalizing relations. He said that us vets are the key to that whole problem. I also told him about you. How you went to college and studied the language and tropical agriculture. He said he would really like to meet you the next time you go back. His name is Le Hoang Nghia, and I'll give you a snapshot that we took together, along with his address. Maybe you guys could work together on some agricultural development."

Nick could barely contain his excitement at this prospect of finally living his dream. But there was the other matter that Nick wanted to discuss. "That sounds great, but I need to ask you something point blank."

Alan drank from his beer. "Go for it."

"What are your feelings about the POW/MIA issue? Do you think there are still some there?"

"When I was in Ho Chi Minh City, I ran across a guy on a motorbike with a Vietnamese chick on the back. He was Caucasian. When he saw the look of shock on my face he started to get all nervous. I went up to him and tried to speak English with him. He got really scared and put up his hands to wave me away, then he took off fast. I'm damn sure he was one of us. But it looked like he had become one of them."

Nick decided to take a chance. "Look brah, if we get into trouble over there, for whatever reason, could I count on you to help us?"

Alan looked over at Tim, then eyed Nick carefully. "You're looking for POWs aren't you?"

Nick nodded sheepishly. Alan turned to Tim. "Are you in on this too?"

"Hell yes! What do I look like, Nick's baggage boy?" They all laughed.

Alan stared out over the pool and watched the plumeria petals floating on the surface. "Tonight I'll take you up to Moonrock's pad. He's the guy to talk to." They all agreed to get cleaned up and meet back at the pool at six.

꿈 ꞏ

As Alan had said, they were greeted at the heavy teakwood-and-iron-framed door by two burly and mean-looking Thai men in slacks and white silk shirts stretched over bulging muscles. Each wore an automatic pistol in a hip holster. They grunted a greeting to Alan, then frisked Tim and Nick, including a groin search that was not gentle. After they removed their shoes on the doorstep, they were ushered inside the prince's penthouse apartment.

The place reminded Nick of a movie set. There were red and blue tapestries and curtains embroidered with twenty-four-carat gold. Golden statues of Buddha, large ornate vases with cut lotus flowers and bird of paradise with ferns adorned the small but elegant living room. There was a wall of sophisticated electronic equipment, a large-screen TV, hand-carved mahogany cabinets and a fully stocked bar. Languid streams of smoke rose up from smoldering incense sticks. Long, plush sofas surrounded a large glass coffee table.

One of the guards motioned for them to sit. The other bowed politely with his hands brought together in front of him as if praying. "*Khun* Alan, can we offer you and your friends some refreshments?"

Alan smiled so politely that Nick thought he was someone else. "Yes. Thank you so much." He returned the bow. "Nick, Tim, what would you like?"

"Beer would be fine, thank you," answered Nick. Tim nodded in agreement.

The drinks were served individually on a silver tray holding the bottle, a cut crystal glass and a small silver bucket of ice with tongs. Nick bowed Thai-style to the man. "*Khop khun maak kap!*"

The man broke a smile and replied, "*May pen ray, kap.* I will announce you to the prince," and retreated up a flight of stairs. His partner stood guard at the foot of the stairs. Tim gawked at their surroundings. Nick felt he had stepped into a childhood dream. Roger's chest puffed up, watching his friends admiring the rich appointments.

They heard a soft and warm voice calling from the stairs. "*Khun* Alan, my friend! How nice of you to come for a visit! Please introduce me to your friends!"

"Moonrock!" Alan, stood abruptly and bowed to the man dressed in a long-sleeved, white silk, embroidered shirt and dark slacks. Like everyone else, he was barefoot. Medium height and build with manicured black hair above a handsome face. Looked about thirty, but was probably ten years older than that. Close to my age. Nick thought. Asians rarely showed their real age, especially a well-groomed prince. Moonrock hugged Alan warmly.

Alan gestured, "This is my old friend, Tim Campbell. We know each other from Massachusetts."

Moonrock reached out and grasped Tim's hand with both of his. "I am honored, Tim!"

"Please, no," said Tim. "I am honored. You have no idea!" Moonrock laughed humbly.

"And this is our good friend, Nick Dwyer, from Maui." Nick again bowed, but this time, very low.

"*Sawat dii kap.*"

"Oh! *Sawat dii. Khun phut phasaa Thai may?*"

Nick grinned shyly. "*Nitnoy tawnan.*"

Smiling his appreciation, Moonrock motioned toward the sofas. "Please, call me Moonrock. And please sit down before your beers get warm." He laughed, snapped his fingers, and pointed at the beer. His guard-servant quickly brought Moonrock the same tray, poured the beer into the glass and served it with two hands.

The prince lifted his glass to his guests. "Welcome to my humble palace! Alan has told me so many good things about you both that I feel I know you already."

Moonrock drained the glass and absently reached back behind himself with one hand. Nick watched it linger under a small pillow. The prince nodded ever so slightly to himself. Hidden handgun, Nick guessed. It was all Nick could do to keep from checking his pillow, but Alan's warning stuck in his head.

Moonrock naturally led the conversation with inquiries about Tim and Nick. He seemed very impressed and appreciated that they had, like Alan, been grunts in the war. He eyed them keenly. "I could use men like you on my yacht. Do you all have experience with machine guns?" The three surprised men looked at each other and nodded in unison. "How about quad-fifties?"

Alan shook his head. "Only single barrel. How about you, Nick?"

"The same. When I went back stateside after the war, they made me track commander and I fired the fifty. Why do you ask, Moonrock?"

"As Alan can tell you, we have a growing and quite serious problem with pirates in the waters off southern Thailand. I am in the process of updating my defensive capabilities, like installing three quad-fifties along with mortars and rocket launchers on my boat. It is a constant battle to outgun the enemy."

He was interrupted by the sound of a gong. The two bodyguards leaped into action and manned the entrance at the ready. One peered through a spy slot in the thick door and looked back at Moonrock. "*Khun* Warwick, your highness."

The prince laughed and clapped his hands in delight. "Just in time! Alan, it is our mercenary friend, Warwick. I invited him when you told me you would visit tonight."

Tim and Nick looked at each other in excitement, beaming electric smiles. This just kept getting better and better. The guards ushered in a tall, lean white man with very short-cropped blond hair. He was dressed in a faded blue T-shirt and khaki bush shorts with button-down pockets.

He was trailed by a very attractive Asian girl. She wore tight jeans and a beige blouse that showed her small breasts above a tiny waist. They were all smiles as they greeted Moonrock and Alan with hugs.

Moonrock introduced them to Nick and Tim. "Gentlemen, may I introduce you to my dear friends, Warwick Dunn and his beautiful fiance, Olivia." They sat on the long couch next to Nick and were served the now customary beer.

Warwick turned to Nick. "Are you the Vietnam veteran who keeps going back all the time?" He had a heavy British accent.

"Well, this is only my third time." Nick said.

"I am very curious about Vietnam. Maybe later you could fill me in on some things."

"Sure, if I can."

"You see, being an English subject, I never served in that war, but I did fight in Angola and Uganda."

"I didn't know England was directly involved in those countries."

Warwick smiled slyly. "Well, I don't fight for politics, just money." He laughed. "Eh, Alan?"

Alan chuckled with him, amused at the confused expressions on Nick and Tim's faces. "I guess you guys didn't know about me and those damn Egyptians, eh?"

Tim's jaw dropped. "Egyptians, Alan? What the hell are you talking about?"

"Yeah, after the Nam, I read about a mercenary job in *Soldier of Fortune* magazine. I went over there and went right back at it with them." His fiery blue eyes lit up as he laughed. "I'll tell you about it sometime, but right now we have another problem." His face hardened, and he took a deep breath before he looked up at Moonrock. "Nick and Tim are going back into Vietnam tomorrow." He paused for effect and scanned everyone's faces. "What I'm going to tell you must stay right here, OK?" They all nodded solemnly. "But they're not just tourists. They'll be looking for American POWs."

All eyes were suddenly on Nick. "Yeah, that's right. It's nothing official though. We're just doing it because we were grunts and we care. Back in the U.S., nobody else gives a shit. Our concern is that if we get into trouble, there's nobody to turn to for help. No embassy, nobody. We'll be on our own. But I was wondering if there is anything that any of you could do if we get caught."

Moonrock leaned so far forward in his seat that he almost fell on the floor. His eyes were bulging with excitement as the wheels turned. He looked intently at Alan and Warwick, then back at Nick.

"I can tell you right now, Nick. If you can contact Alan and let us know where you are and what you need, then you can count on me to pull all the strings I can to get you out." In a lighter tone. "Maybe Warwick here would volunteer to go in on a secret mission to break you out of jail." He laughed.

Warwick smiled weakly, but shook his head sadly. "When the Angolan rebels captured me the second time, they tied me to a tree and drove bamboo spikes up under my fingernails. They left them in for three weeks, then they pulled them out. The fibres had begun to grow under my skin." He winced at the memory. "The pain was so excruciating that there are no words to describe it. After thirteen surgeries, there is still no cure. I take morphine every day. " He shook his head apologetically. "I'm sorry, Nick. I won't be any help."

With visible compassion Nick grasped Warwick by the shoulder. "Don't give it another thought." He turned back to Moonrock. "I don't know what to say about your generous offer. I mean, you just met us. Why would you want to help?"

Moonrock lifted his glass in a salute. "During the war, I would listen to the Green Berets' stories when they came here for R&R. I always wanted to be part of it, but I was too young." He looked Nick in the eye. "But now is a different story. To your success!"

The next morning Alan arrived with a cab and a packet of photos, phone numbers, and other information that he deemed helpful to the fledgling commandos. He also gave them some locally produced medications that would be more effective than the stateside types that they had brought.

Once they had loaded the taxi with their luggage, Alan shook their hands. "OK, you guys, I'll leave you now. I've got a meeting this morning with one of the top Thai Army generals. He needs our help with some problem. You take care of each other. Call me if you need help."

Nick and Tim waved goodbye as the little white taxi sped them off through the noisy streets under a smog-filled sky.

CHAPTER 36
Ho Chi Minh City
August 1991

That afternoon, after a three-hour flight, Nick gazed out the plane's window and down through the scattered clouds at the now familiar Saigon River as it wound through the lush green rice paddies. When they hit the runway and could feel Vietnam beneath their rumbling wheels, Nick sensed once again that he was home.

He grabbed a luggage cart and loaded it with their bags, and guided the ecstatic Tim through Customs and Immigration. Tim reminded Nick of a school boy on his first trip away from home. He was constantly asking questions and making irritating observations, while Nick had to deal with all the formalities. Outwardly, Nick was patient and understanding and focused on the task at hand.

Soon they were in a private car headed toward the Bong Sen Hotel in the center of town. Nick had negotiated the price with the driver who had approached them as soon as they stepped out of the terminal.

"Nick, look at all the bicycles and motorbikes! I've only seen two other cars. They all drive like they're crazy. It's total chaos out there! My God! I can't believe there are no accidents!"

"Don't worry. There are. But nobody can go fast enough to get really hurt."

"God, Nick! The girls are so beautiful in those long flowing dresses, slit up the side. What do you call them again?"

"*Ao dai's*. It's the traditional dress. OK, Timmy, here we are. This is Dong Khoi street and this is our hotel. Let's go check in and then, after we get settled in our rooms, I'll come find you." Nick paid the driver while the bellmen grabbed their bags.

"Actually, I'm kinda tired," Tim said. "Can I take a nap first and meet you later for dinner?"

"Sure, that's cool. I'll go over to Vietnam Tourism. I want to visit an old friend there and talk about travel arrangements and permits. I'll meet you in your room at six, OK? Remember. Don't drink the water or you'll be sick for the duration. Only beer or soda." They laughed.

Nick went up to room 208, brushed his teeth and splashed on some cologne. He unpacked a box of Maui-grown macadamia nuts and walked down the street at a brisk pace that even Alan would have been hard pressed to match.

There had been some changes in the office. The desks were still arranged in the same order, but the repainted beige walls were paneled in dark wood halfway up. Ho Chi Minh still looked down from the same portrait. Brilliant white teeth were smiling at Nick as if it had been only two days, not two years, since the last time.

"So you're back again, eh?" she called out as he approached her desk. He wanted to go around behind it and grab her in the warm and tender embrace that he had dreamed of. Maybe even kiss her. But she calmly shook his hand gently and briefly.

Nick's smile faded at the cool reception. He handed her the box of nuts and quickly snapped a photo of her before she could protest. She gestured with her hand at the wooden chair. He slowly sat. Nick noticed that she avoided direct eye contact.

"Well, how are you, Thanh? I've been waiting a long time to see you again. You look as lovely as ever."

"Thank you. Yes, I'm fine... and you?"

"I'm so happy to be back here again, just like you said in your letters. I feel like I belong here."

"And how long will you be in Vietnam this time?"

"About a month. Listen, we can talk about that later. Actually, I just came half-way around the world to take you out to dinner. Shall we go to the Palace tonight? I want to ask our friend at the piano to play our old favorites. How about it?"

Pham Thai Than placed the box of nuts on her desk and slid her hands toward Nick. He noticed the small gold ring. "I have something to tell you." She paused, gathering her courage and stared directly into his troubled eyes. "About three weeks ago, I... I got married."

Sitting in stunned silence, with his mouth slightly open, Nick stared straight at her and felt his world begin to crumble. He knew he had no right to her. He never even knew how he truly felt about her. He had come with no real expectations. There had been no promises, either way. Yet the pain was very real and quite confusing. He took her hand.

"I guess congratulations are in order. What's the lucky man's name?"

"His name is Loc. I think you met him once briefly on your last trip when we ran into you at the souvenir shop on Nguyen Hue Street. Do you remember?"

Nick nodded vacantly, and spoke in a monotone. "Yes, of course. Well. I'll be going then. Could I see you tomorrow? I need help with travel arrangements. I'd like to go north to Hanoi, if that's possible."

She pulled her hand away. "Yes, of course. I'll be here all day."

"Goodbye, Thanh. It's good to see you." Nick ambled toward the front door.

"Oh, Nick!" He spun around hopefully. "Thank you for the nuts."

He nodded absently and walked out the door. As he crossed Nguyen Hue St. the bicycles and motorbikes swirled around him—a current in a strong river. He was oblivious to it. He stared straight ahead. What did I expect? he asked himself. Was everything supposed to stay on hold for me until I made up my mind to return? Remember, I told her I wasn't coming back. Besides, I was married then. I guess this is where I should be grateful that I read *A Course in Miracles*. The key to happiness is acceptance, forgiveness and unconditional love. But goddamn, it isn't easy! Trying to focus on that thought process, he began to shed his cloak of self pity. He heard the familiar voice calling his name.

"Ly! Ly!" Running jubilantly towards him, was the short, round figure with the beaming face.

"Mot! *Troi dat oi!*" They embraced each other tightly and laughed happily.

"*Troi oi*, Ly! Why you no write and tell me you are coming back?" He feigned a scolding look, then laughed again. His white shirt was threadbare and there was some grease on his dark slacks. Nick could feel the callouses on his hands.

"I'm sorry, Mot. Things happened kind of fast. I didn't know I was coming until I left."

"Why you come back again?"

Nick looked far away. "I don't really know. But here I am."

"You need me to drive you, like before?" he asked hopefully.

"Yes. Actually there is a place I need to go." He fumbled in his jeans pocket and pulled out the wrinkled paper. "51 Binh Thoi Street. Do you know it?"

"Yes! Maybe six kilometers. I take you now?"

Nick smiled. "OK." They straddled the same old black Honda 50cc motorbike and sputtered out into the flow, leaving a trail of blue exhaust smoke and all Nick's cares behind them. He felt the wind in his face and smelled the garlic, mint, and wood fires as they weaved through the memories of Ho Chi Minh City. When they pulled up in front of the slightly leaning hardwood-slat house, Nick could smell the open sewer that ran through the front yard. Chickens foraged in the hard-packed red dirt.

"I wait here for you, Ly." Mot pushed the bike into the shadows of the building.

Before Nick reached the doorway, a very tall, wispy man with wire-rimmed glasses came out and bowed his head slightly. With a look of serious concern, he spoke in a surprisingly deep voice. Nick sensed the tone was one of a man who was accustomed to being in command. "Good afternoon. Are you lost?"

Nick grinned. "I'm looking for Mr. Dinh Cong Vy."

The man returned the smile, revealing many missing teeth. "Yes?"

"Is that you?"

"Yes. And who are you?"

"Nick Dwyer. But you can call me Ly. I am a good friend of Fredy Champagne. He asked me to come talk to you."

The deep booming laugh was genuine and disarming. "Where is Fredy?"

"Still in California."

They shook hands firmly. The man turned and welcomed Nick into the house. "Please sit down. *Em oi!*" He called to a tall, big-boned woman with short curly hair. She had a very warm and friendly smile that somehow looked familiar to Nick. "This is *Anh* Ly. A friend of Fredy's." He turned to Nick. "My wife, Vui."

Nick smiled. "Vui means happy, doesn't it? I think it's a good name for you."

"You speak Vietnamese?"

"Just a little."

"How you learn?"

"I started during the war, from my girlfriend and a Vietnamese interpreter that I worked with at Lai Khe."

Vui looked straight at Nick. She lost her sweet smile momentarily. Then it reappeared. "I will make some tea." She retreated to a cast-iron, wood-burning stove and placed a pot of water on it to boil.

"So, how do you know Fredy?" Vy asked.

"We were in the same unit."

"That means you were in Alpha company, Second Battalion, Second Infantry Regiment. Right?"

"I'm impressed! How did you know?"

From the stove, Vui watched Nick as her husband answered. "I was a major in the ARVN. Vui and I are from the village of Lai Khe where your base camp was."

Now it all made sense. Nick nodded appreciatively. "Fredy said the elementary school and orphanage in Lai Khe need assistance. I would like very much to go up there and see what needs to be done. Could you take me?"

Vy smiled. "Of course. When do you want to go?"

Nick thought for a moment. He needed some time for himself first. He had a date with his endless pussy fantasy. "We just arrived today. How about in two days?"

"Thursday. Where are you staying?"

"The Bong Sen."

Vy nodded. "I will come pick you up on my motorcycle. About 0700?"

Nick chuckled. Old habits are hard to break, he thought to himself. Vui brought the tea, and seeing *Anh* Mot outside, beckoned him in to join them. After twenty minutes of sipping tea and smoking the obligatory cigarettes, Mot drove Nick back to his hotel. Nick paid him, then ran upstairs to meet Tim for dinner.

They walked to Brodard's on the corner and ordered cream of chicken soup, steak, fries, and salad, with French bread and butter. They toasted with their Heinekens.

"Thanks for this trip, brother," Tim said. "I can't believe I'm back again. It's like a dream. I don't ever want to wake up, you know?"

Nick laughed. "Well, don't thank me yet. Wait 'til you try to eat your water buffalo steak. It's usually like trying to chew on a rubber slipper." And it was. Tim couldn't slice it because of his weak left hand. Nick pulled his plate over, and did it for him then buttered his bread.

"I'm sorry, Nick. I don't want to be a burden for you."

"Hey, fuck you! I knew what I was getting into. But I hope you won't need any help putting Joe Cocker into all your beautiful girlfriends."

"I think I can handle that all right, Nick."

After they finished eating, Nick led Tim toward the Palace Hotel where there was a discotheque on the second floor. As they slowly made their way over the disintegrating sidewalks, rats scurried alongside their feet. Next to a tree trunk, they nearly stumbled over an emaciated Vietnamese man, dressed in rags, squatting low on the ground. Nick saw that he had a broken chopstick in his bony hand and was digging carefully through a pile of human feces. When his stick pulled out an undigested kernel of corn the man began breathing heavily. The panting turned into a low moan as he lifted it toward his mouth. Nick read the man's tortured face. He was asking himself if he was really that hungry. Overwhelmed with compassion, Nick gently pushed the withered hand away and placed a handful of money in it. They could hear the man's wailing cry of gratitude as they walked away in the evening still.

From the lobby they could hear the band playing. They followed some chic young girls into the club. The girls turned around and smiled demurely at the two men.

Nick beamed his best smile. "*Xin Loi, cac co biet noi tieng Anh khong?*"

Their faces lit up, shocked. Giggling excitedly, they shook their heads. One girl looked to be in her twenties. She was slim and very attractive. She wore her long hair up in a French roll and sported a grey two-piece suit with a ruffled pink blouse and high heels. The other girl's dress was long and blue. It was slit up the thigh on one side. She had shoulder-length hair and was beautiful. Nick guessed her to be still in her late teens.

"What do you think of these two, Tim?"

Tim nodded emphatically, panting like a puppy.

"They don't speak English, though."

"That's OK, Nick. I don't plan on doing much talking."

They learned that the first girl's name was Nga. She had an obvious interest in Nick. The other was Thuy, and Tim latched on to her. Nick invited them for drinks and dancing and slid in close to Nga on the plush seat of the booth.

Tim was like a teenager on his first date. He was visibly nervous but enjoying himself immensely. "Already, this is better than Bangkok." he told Nick. "At least here I feel like I'm on a real date." However, Thuy was very conscious of Tim's physical disability and let it show in her expression.

Hearing Nick speak in their language made him the focus of their attention but it was also a burden. As the evening turned to night, they danced several times and kept plying the girls with liquor. Even Tim attempted to dance but tried to remain inconspicuous along the wall, while Thuy moved freely in perfect rhythm to the music.

Back in their booth, Nick asked them if they would accompany them back to the Bong Sen. The girls looked at their watches and shook their heads sadly.

"Vietnam still has curfew," said Nga." We must be home in half an hour. There is not enough time." She smiled coyly. "But we will come back early tomorrow night and meet you here if you like. Then…" She eyed Nick flirtatiously.

"That's a date!" he crowed. He and Tim ordered another beer as they watched the two gorgeous girls swaying out the front door. Suddenly, Pham Thai Thanh seemed like a total stranger.

The next morning was chilled with rain. After a buffet breakfast in the hotel restaurant, Nick led Tim across Nguyen Hue Street to Vietnam Tourism. They sloshed through the door and stood dripping in front of Thanh's desk, staring at her empty chair. There was no one else in the office.

"Have a seat, Tim. I'll go find her." Nick said as he went through a wooden door behind her desk and down a dimly lit hallway until he reached another door. He stepped out into a parking garage built under the tall office building. But what he saw froze him in his tracks. There were several white Harley-Davidson motorcycles with blue lights parked along one wall. They obviously belonged to the police. Right next to them were rack after rack of AK-47 assault rifles. Nick estimated them to number in the hundreds. He stared open-mouthed, wondering what Thanh's job really was, when he was startled by the sharp male voice behind him.

"What are you doing?" The voice demanded. Nick spun around, quickly on the defensive. There was a slim Vietnamese man in his thirties. He wore a light-blue short-sleeve shirt and dark blue slacks with slippers. His face was angry. He came up to Nick, grabbed his arm and guided him roughly back inside the door. Nick fought to quell his surprise and anger at being manhandled. The war beast roared and shook the bars of its cage. But he knew it would be futile to resist. He grasped control of himself and smiled respectfully at the man.

"I'm sorry. I am looking for my friend, Pham Thai Thanh. She is supposed to help me make travel arrangements today. Do you know where she is?"

The man relented and tried to cover a deep breath. "OK. Excuse me." He forced a fake smile. "Please wait at her desk. I will find her." He climbed the stairs just off the hallway.

Nick went back in to sit with Tim and gave him a look that said, "Wait 'til I tell you what I saw!"

Thanh burst through the door. There was no pearly white smile, only an intense scrutiny.

"Yes, Nick. What do you want?"

Nick paused, wondering where everything had gone wrong, but feeling quite certain now that Thanh was not who she pretended to be. That's OK, he thought. Two can play that game. He smiled disarmingly. "I came to persuade you to be our personal tour guide as we travel throughout Vietnam. Oh, I'm sorry. This is my good friend Tim, from Maui. He is also a veteran and wants to go back where he served in the war."

The famous smile returned. "How do you do, Tim? I am quite pleased to meet you. But do you know that you are in dangerous company?"

Tim smiled nervously and glanced over at Nick. "Well, I guess that makes two of us," he teased, right on cue. Nick struggled to stifle his laughter.

Thanh smiled as if trying to decide if she had been the butt of a joke. "So, where would you like to go in Vietnam?"

"First, I want to go up in the mountains to Dalat," said Nick.

"Then, up Highway One, along the coast to Nha Trang, DaNang, Hue, Quang Tri, and Hanoi. Is that possible?"

"Yes. With the exception of Dalat. No foreigners are allowed to go there. I will need your passports, visas, and plane tickets, along with your registration papers. Then I can apply for your travel permits and plan your itinerary. But I will not be your guide. I can provide you with a government car and driver. You won't need an interpreter since you can speak fluent Vietnamese. Tim, do you speak our language?"

Tim shook his head apologetically and asked, "Why do we need travel permits? Can't we just go?"

"No, absolutely not. Unless you want to spend your vacation in one of our jails," Thanh warned.

Nick broke in. "Why can't we go to Dalat? I went there before, in 1987, on a government tour. Why not now?"

Her face turned solemn. She stared coolly at Nick. "There have been problems lately with some Americans who went there offering large rewards for information about POWs." She watched Nick closely.

Nick nodded and stole a quick glance at Tom. "That's too bad. It's such a beautiful area."

"And why do you want to visit Hanoi?"

"Do you remember my friend, Fredy Champagne? He's the one who built the clinic in Vung Tau in 1989."

"Oh yes, of course."

"He is in Hanoi right now organizing what he calls a Peace Walk. He wants us to join him with other Americans and some of our former enemy soldiers to walk from Hanoi to Ho Chi Minh City, to garner support for lifting the trade embargo and normalization of relations with Vietnam."

This sobering revelation brought a look of surprise and respect to Thanh's face. She nodded thoughtfully.

Nick smiled. "We'll go get our papers together, and I will bring them to you this afternoon."

Thanh nodded as they stood and exited out into large drops of rain loudly smacking the pavement. They were oblivious to the small, dark, sinister figure that leaned against the wall near the door watching them. They made their way across the street as quickly as Tim's hobbled gait allowed. When they finally reached the Bong Sen, they were drenched and cold.

"How about a cup of hot coffee? I got some interesting news, brah." Nick said.

"Sounds good to me." Tim replied through chattering teeth. They found a table as far away as possible from the air conditioner and sat waiting for the brew to drip down through the demitasse.

Nick lowered his voice. "Man, I went out the back door, looking for Thanh, and I stumbled on a whole shit load of weapons. AKs, RPGs, the works."

"I thought you said it was a tourism office."

"Yeah, but that's just a front. I think they're all part of the secret police. That's how they keep track of foreign tourists. I thought Thanh was a good friend but..." Nick paused. "Well, she is a good friend. All I'm saying is, we gotta be careful. Don't trust anybody." Tim was suddenly deep in thought and far away.

As they sat shivering, a short, thin man abruptly appeared and sat uninvited in the chair next to Nick. He looked around the room furtively and whispered. "You American?"

Nick looked up skeptically at Tim, then gave the intruder the once over. "Yeah. Why?"

"You look for powmias?"

Nick frowned. "What?"

"Powmias. Missing Americans." He gave the words a melodramatic flair.

Nick and Tim burst out laughing. Tim corrected him. "You mean P-O-Ws or M-I-As."

He looked down, embarrassed. "Yes, yes," he conceded.

Nick examined the rodent face. He was perhaps forty-five with long hair and acne scars. He wore wire-rimmed glasses and a dilapidated baseball cap. His natural expression was one of somebody who had just bitten into a lemon. Nick disliked him immediately, but the temptation was irresistible. "What's your name?" Nick played along.

"Mr. Song," He replied.

"Well, I'm Mr. Dwyer and this is my colleague, Mr. Campbell." They all shook hands.

Mr. Song, glanced around the room again, and whispered. "Can I trust you?"

Nick called on his best thespian talents, and replied in his own whisper. "Yes, of course." He winked at Tim. "What do you have for us?"

Mr. Song reached into his shirt pocket and produced a slip of folded paper. On it were the shaded impressions of several dog tags. Nick studied them carefully. He read the names, serial numbers, blood type and religion of each tag. "OK, so who are these guys?" he asked.

Mr. Song raised his eyebrows. "Missing American soldiers," he whispered. "Are they worth money to you?"

"Hey, man." Tim said. "You give us a few days to check these out. If they're for real we'll talk money. OK?"

"OK, you buy me soda?" Nick nodded. After the waiter had come and gone, Mr. Song began his monologue. "You know? After the war, the dirty communists took everything I had. My house, my money, my car. Everything. They put me in a re-education camp for five long years. While I was there, I heard about these American prisoners. Now I want to help them escape. But I need money. Can you help me a little bit?"

Nick played along. "OK. I've heard that there is a big reward for information about POWs. But we have nothing to do with that. We are here on vacation. That's all. But if this is real, we can put you in touch with other people who are involved with this. OK?"

Mr. Song looked disappointed. "OK, but we must be very careful. The communists will make big trouble for us if they find out. Please do not discuss our meeting with anyone. I will contact you here in three days. What is your room number?"

Nick paused, then answered, "208."

Mr. Song drained his Coke, shook their hands, and made a stealthy exit. Nick and Tim tried to stifle their laughter at his cloak-and-dagger routine but when the door closed behind him they let out a howl. But no sooner had they stopped laughing than they eyed each other seriously.

"I don't know, Nick. Do you think there could be anything to this?" Tim asked, still smiling.

Nick nodded. "He acts about as phony as a three-dollar bill. But what if there's a chance? We'd hate ourselves forever if we passed it up."

"How about we give Alan a call? He can check out this info for us." Tim said.

They went up to Nick's room. He threw Tim a towel and sat down by the phone. "Front desk? I would like to place a call to Bangkok please. No, I will pay for the call. Thank you."

"I am sorry, Mr. Nick," said the female voice. "But it will take a while to connect to Bangkok. I will call you when I have made the connection. OK?"

Nick took a deep breath, "OK. How long?"

"I do not know sir. Perhaps thirty minutes. Maybe more. We must go through many operators to call overseas. I am sorry, but the embargo makes everything difficult."

An hour later, Alan picked up his cell phone. "Goddamn, Nick! Are you in trouble already? You've only been gone two days."

"Hey, I work fast. Listen. We've already been approached by someone with some dog tags. Can you check them out for us?"

"Sure. But I need some time. How soon do you want it?"

"Three days, max. There are four of them. Here's the names and serial numbers." He read everything slowly to Alan who repeated it back for verification. "Thanks, brah. Call me."

"Wait a minute. Have you used up all your condoms yet?"

"I'm working on it." He hung up and turned to Tim. "You better get up to your room and have a hot shower. Get your papers together. I'll come up for them in an hour and take them to Thanh."

CHAPTER 37
Ho Chi Minh City
August 1991

That evening, Nick entered the restaurant through the French doors on the twelfth floor of the Palace Hotel. The look of shock on *Anh* Chau's face made Nick feel totally at home once again. They shook hands warmly.

"*Anh* Ly! You come back again, huh?" He began falling all over himself trying to find an appropriate way to welcome his old friend. "You like eat dinner or…" He smiled slyly, "maybe a beer first?" They both laughed heartily.

"Sounds like a great idea!"

"Where you like sit? Same like before?" He gestured to the corner table where a wall met the windows at a perpendicular angle. Nick liked it because he had his back covered and a view of whoever entered the restaurant before they saw him. He nodded.

When Chau brought the Heineken with a glass of ice, Nick also ordered a plate of *cha gio*, the deep-fried summer rolls, for pupus.

The restaurant was basically empty except for a couple of waiters who sat polishing the silverware. It was just six-thirty, still early by Vietnamese standards. Most patrons would arrive well after seven for dinner. Nick sat alone reflecting on a myriad of memories that stretched back decades. Tim would surely be late. SOP for him. Being severely handicapped slowed him down considerably, but Nick had decided to exercise tough love and let Tim fend for himself as much as possible.

Chau brought the platter of rolls and a fresh beer. "*Anh* Ly. How long has it been?"

"Over two years."

"You see things different?"

Nick nodded. "Yes. There are some new buildings going up. The streets are cleaner, but you still look the same. Very young."

Chau smiled appreciatively of the flattery. *"Cam on, anh, nhieu lam!"* He left to attend to a Caucasian family of four who sat down several tables away along the windows. Nick sipped his beer and watched the bats swarming in the evening dusk, like so many times before.

In the distance he heard a man's voice say, in English, " I heard him speaking Vietnamese with the waiter." Nick recognized the American accent immediately but paid it no mind. He was anxious to return to the discotheque downstairs on the second floor and meet up with Nga and Thuy. Maybe he could get away without having to wear a condom.

Anh Chau appeared at his shoulder. "Excuse me, *Anh* Ly. That family wants to invite you to dinner. Would you like to join them?"

Nick peered up over the rim of his glass at the family. They were younger, perhaps in their 30s. The wife was pudgy with curled blond hair and blue eyes that bugged out of her face. The man was dark and slim but had the appearance of a Tuesday-night bowling league member. The boy and girl were probably about ten and were so fat and white that they were almost blue. Everything that turned him off about his race and his country. They were loud and arrogant, and berated Chau when he was out of earshot.

Nick glanced up at his friend with an obvious frown. "No, thank you. I'd rather be alone."

Chau looked at him curiously, then bowed and went back to the other table. After a minute Nick heard the boy ask his mother something quietly. Then the woman, obviously feeling offended, said loudly, "Don't worry, honey! That's HIS problem!"

Nick took another drink. I didn't come ten thousand miles to hang out with a bunch of ugly Americans. He thought. Then it hit him. He actually felt much more comfortable with the Vietnamese than his own people. There was something very repulsive about them, and he wanted to distance himself from them, though the reasons why were still obscure.

Nick suddenly realized there was another man sitting alone, farther down the room, also along the windows. He sat facing Nick, and there was something quite familiar about him. He was, like Nick, in his 40s, balding, with a dark moustache below a large broken nose.

He had a muscular build and a weathered face that showed not only character but an underlying fierceness. And yet Nick felt somehow drawn to him, although he was one of those distasteful Caucasians too.

After studying the man for a while, Nick decided that he was quite possibly a veteran. There was something in the dark eyes, like he was looking in a mirror. Before he knew it, he was walking past the family approaching the lone stranger. The man looked up at Nick when he stopped at his table. He had a surly smirk on his face, and he nodded at Nick with his eyebrows raised, as if asking silently, " What the fuck do you want?"

Nick nodded. "Speak English?"

"A little," he answered sarcastically.

"You a vet too?"

The man sized up Nick. "Have a seat."

Nick slid into a chair across the table. He saw the man's 33 beer was nearly empty. "*Anh* Chau *oi!*" He called. "Two more beers, please. I buy." He extended his hand. "Nick." The man took it, and looked Nick in the eye, scrutinizing him carefully.

"Stu," he replied. The beers arrived. "So, what unit were you with?" Stu asked.

"First, I was an advisor with MACV. Then I went to the Big Red One. You?"

Stu's mouth broke into an appreciative grin. "Yeah. I was a grunt too. Up around the Iron Triangle. You know it?"

"Oh, yeah. That was my AO too."

An awkward silence followed. Neither man wanted to be the first to open up old wounds, especially with a total stranger. Finally Nick blurted out. "Fuck it, brother! Don't mean nothin'! What are you doin' here anyway?"

Stu pulled out a pack of Winstons and offered it to Nick, who took one and nodded thanks. Each man clanked open his Zippo, lit up behind cupped hands, then lowered them under the table out of sight, except for the rising smoke. Nick smiled at the old combat reflex.

"Trying to find myself, I guess." Stu finally answered the question.

"Any luck?"

Stu smiled off into space, then back at Nick. "Maybe. What about you?"

"This is my third time back. I guess I was like you before. Now, I just wanna get laid." They chuckled together. Nick knew he had to take the point. "When I came back here in '87 and again in '89, I felt like I really belonged here. Like it's my destiny or something, you know?"

Stu nodded in agreement, then looked past Nick to the family's table behind him. "They friends of yours?" He pointed with his chin.

They could hear the boy whining, "I wanna go to McDonald's, Mom! This food is yukky!"

"I'm sorry, honey, but they don't have McDonald's here. You just eat your rice now, OK?"

The girl chimed in, "Mom, I wanna go watch TV in our room. This is boring!"

The father got in the act. "Listen, Veronica, they don't have TV either, OK? Now just be quiet, and I'll order some fruit for dessert." He glared at his wife. "What a messed up country. I don't know why we fought a war over this place. The commies can have it, if you ask me. It's filthy, poor, backwards, and disgusting."

Without turning, Nick said with a sneer, "Fuck them. I don't know why, but I want nothing to do with 'em. What are they doin' here anyway? They'll probably go home and tell everybody how brave they were because they went to Vietnam. They'll be instant experts and go on the lecture circuit to tell the masses what the Nam is REALLY like. This is OUR Vietnam, brother. Fuck them!"

Stu leaned back against his chair and blew smoke out in a long stream. "So why does this feel like home? Because you can speak the language? Because you can eat the food? Because you love the women?"

"There's more to it than that. I feel accepted here. For what I am. In SPITE of what I am."

"You might FEEL like that. But to the Vietnamese you see on the street, it don't matter how good you speak the lingo or how well you can handle chopsticks. When they see you and me coming, brother, we're just two guilt-ridden white guys with a lot of money, that they'll try to separate us from. I wish it wasn't like that, but it is."

"Bullshit! They love us, man! They appreciate everything we're trying to do for them. I know 'cause I've been involved in some humanitarian aid projects here."

Stu looked Nick directly in the eyes. Gently. "And why did you? What was in it for you?"

Nick squirmed. "I don't know. Maybe it was like paying off some of that guilt you were talking about, or getting the parade that they never gave us when we came back from the war. At least these people know how to say thank you. Has anybody back in the States ever told you thanks for what you did?"

Stu looked down at the table and shook his head.

"There you go! Fuck them! Fuck America and everybody in it! I don't care if I ever go back." Feeling deflated by their argument, Nick tried to change the subject. "Look, my friend Tim will be here soon. We're going downstairs to the disco to meet some chicks. Wanna come along?" Stu suddenly glanced up. Nick could feel someone behind him. He turned quickly.

"Still talking to yourself, I see." No mistaking the British accent. Thanh smiled broadly to the embarrassed Nick. He returned her smile and laughed briefly while standing to greet her.

"No. I'd like you to meet my new friend, Stu…" He turned back to the empty table and his jaw dropped. He quickly searched around the room. "He was just here."

Pham Thai Thanh smiled warmly but blushed in sympathetic embarrassment for Nick. She patted his shoulder. "You know, I think you need to do something about this drinking problem." She tittered behind her hand. Nick looked around, sputtering helplessly. Stu had disappeared into thin air.

Thanh turned serious. "So, are you having dinner here?"

"Yeah, I think so," he answered distantly. "I'm waiting for Tim. Then we're going dancing downstairs. Would you join us?" he asked hopefully.

"No. I'm meeting my husband here with some of our friends."

"Oh, yeah. I forgot."

She reached into her purse and pulled out a bundle wrapped in a rubber band. She placed it on the table.

"Here are your passports and travel permits, along with your other papers and an itinerary. Please come by the office to pay us as soon as you can. If you want any changes you can tell me then."

"How did you know I would be here tonight?"

"Where else would you go?"

He stared at her silently for a minute. "Do I need a travel permit if I just go on a short day-trip?"

"No. Not as long as you return to Ho Chi Minh City before dark. But behave yourself." She waggled her finger at him. Then Thanh walked away, saying, "Have fun."

Nick checked his watch. Tim was very late. He sensed something was wrong. He paid Chau and hustled back to their hotel. He boarded the elevator alone and punched number seven. Suddenly he felt the pain of abdominal gas bloating his stomach. What the hell, he thought. I'm alone. So he farted, which helped somewhat but filled the elevator with the putrid stench. On the third floor, the doors opened and three Japanese businessmen in suits and carrying briefcases entered. As the doors closed, Nick saw them wrinkle their noses and one of them mumbled something in a deep guttural voice while motioning with his head at Nick. Nick knew it was something insulting like, "This white man must have just shit in his pants." The others laughed derisively while sneering at Nick. The continuing pain told Nick there was a lot more gas where that came from. When he reached the seventh floor, he paused just long enough for the doors to begin closing behind him before he cut loose a thunderous fart and escaped down the hall. He howled with laughter as the Japanese men yelled out what was surely insults and threats, while pounding wildly on the locked doors as the elevator took them up and away.

He knocked on Tim's door. No response. "Tim!" he yelled. "Are you OK, brah? Tim!"

A weak voice called out from behind the door. "Nick! Wait, I'm coming. Oh, my God!"

When the door opened, Nick was slapped with the stench of vomit and feces. Tim's face was chalky, eyes bloodshot, drool on his stubbled chin. He could barely stand. Nick was scared. He was responsible for Tim, and he had gone off and left him alone. "Here brother, let me help you. Sit down on the bed. What happened?"

"I've been shitting and puking for hours, Nick. I think that French onion soup that I had for lunch was bad. Do you have any meds?"

"Yeah. Alan gave me some Servipam that he says will cure anything. I'll go get it and be back in a flash."

Nick sprinted down to his room and then back. He helped Tim

to the bathroom and gently set him down in the shower. "I've learned from experience that it's best to just stay in here, let it fly from both ends, and drink lots of water. I'll open a few bottles and put them here by the door."

Soon Tim was over the worst and his body had stopped leaking. "Thanks Nick, I'm better now but I'll have to pass on the dance club tonight. You go on ahead and fuck 'em both. Tell me tomorrow which one was better, OK?"

Nick laughed and reluctantly left his friend with the pills and some Imodium in case he suffered another attack. He promised to return and check in on him in a few hours.

CHAPTER 38
Ho Chi Minh City
August 1991

Back at the Palace Hotel, Nick sat in the lobby while he waited for the disco to open. He picked up a Vietnamese language newspaper from the coffee table and sat back in his chair. He focused so intently on improving his reading skills that he failed to notice when she sat down and watched. His lips moved silently while he read. He was startled by a sweet little-girl voice.

"So, you speak Vietnamese?" she asked in English. Nick's head jerked up. He stared straight through her glasses into her beautiful, smiling, Vietnamese eyes. Her dark-brown hair was cut short, similar to Thanh's, but her body was very petite, almost fragile. She wore a blue flowered-print blouse with a very short and revealing black skirt and matching high-heeled shoes. The glasses were somewhat distracting but her round face and high cheekbones fit them well. Nick found her very attractive, but he had always fantasized about a girl with the traditional long black hair. Both Nga and Thuy had such hair. But there was something uniquely appealing about this girl. He could not describe it, but he certainly felt it. They locked eyes, and he returned her smile.

"*Mot chut thoi*," he admitted.

"And you can also read Vietnamese?" she pointed with her chin at the paper.

Nick couldn't help swelling with pride. "Yes, a little."

"And even upside down!" she kidded.

Flustered, Nick checked the folded-up paper and glanced quickly around him to see if anyone had been listening. Her bubbling laughter was genuine. Nick was forced to relent and join her amusement.

As they sat chatting, more patrons arrived. Soon it was standing room only. Dozens of young women and several male tourists waited anxiously by the elevator until the upstairs lounge opened its doors. Nick heard a girl's voice calling his name. He looked up to see Thuy.

"*Anh* Ly, where is my Tim?"

"Oh. I'm sorry, Thuy. He is very sick. He stayed back in his room. Where is Miss Nga?"

"She no come too. She stay home with husband tonight."

Nick raised his eyebrows. "Husband?"

"Yes. But no worry. Many girls here married, but need money. No problem."

Nick turned back to his new acquaintance with a smile. "Are you married?" he asked.

The girl frowned and glanced at him sideways. "Why do you ask such a personal question?"

Perplexed, Nick thought for a minute. "I don't know really. I guess I want to know if I'm wasting my time. It has happened before."

She nodded quickly at Thuy as if dismissing her. Thuy moved away. Turning back to Nick, she asked, "What is your name?"

"Nick. But in Vietnam I go by Ly."

"Why?"

"It all started in the war."

"So you were American soldier?" Nick nodded, scrutinizing her carefully. She stared curiously into his eyes. "I will call you Nick," she announced. "You can call me Hang. Are YOU married?"

Nick grinned. "Why do you ask ME such a personal question?" They laughed. The crowd started moving toward the elevators. Nick stood up and extended his hand. "Would you like to join me for dancing and drinks?"

The return smile shone in her mischievous eyes. She stood and placed her tiny hand in his, and they followed everyone up to the second floor. Once seated in the large ballroom, at a table against the wall, Nick ordered a Heineken and a Coke. Side by side, they faced the dance floor and the bandstand. The orchestra was tuning up. When the drinks arrived she turned to him and they toasted. She watched him carefully as he drank his beer.

He smiled. "Why are you looking at me like that?"

"You are the first American I have ever met. There are many French, Germans, and Australians, but no Americans. *Pourquoi? La guerre est finie, n' est-ce pas?"*

"*Oui, la guerre est finie. Mais beaucoup Americains sont...*" His voice trailed off as he searched in vain for the words. He laughed, embarrassed, and switched to English. "They are still very bitter, angry, and even afraid."

Hang looked puzzled. "*Pourquoi, peur?* Of what?"

"You speak excellent French." Nick took another drink. "Of the truth, I suppose. Some say we should never have come to Vietnam. Others say we could have won the war if our politicians had only let us. The truth is, they are both right." He waved away the subject like swatting at a fly. "I want to know about you. How old are you? Oh! I'm sorry. In America it is rude to ask a woman's age."

She lifted her chin slightly. "It is OK. This is Vietnam. Age is very important. It tells us how to greet people. For example, if I am older than you then you will call me...?"

"*Chi.*"

"Right! But if I'm younger?"

"*Co.*"

"Yes. Or, *em*, if we are very close."

"So how old are you then, *em?*"

Hang giggled. "*Trente-huit.*" She watched his eyes for a reaction but got none. "*Et toi?*"

"*Je suis quarante quatre,*" he replied haltingly. "So how did you learn to speak French so well?"

"I went to Saint Paul for many years. It is a French Catholic girls school. Do you know it?"

"Yes. It is very close to here, right?"

She nodded. "And how is it that you speak such fluent Vietnamese?"

He told her the whole story. While he spoke, Nick noticed her eyes often searching his face. Her interest was obvious as she read him. "...and then I just left the tractor running in the field and got on the next flight back here." He studied her as he gently held her hand. "So what do you see?"

"What?"

"In me. It has been a long time since a woman has looked at me like that."

She smiled shyly. "You are easy to understand. I guess because you are so expressive when you talk. I like it."

Nick could feel that strange warmth in his heart once again. For reasons he did not yet understand, he caressed her cheek ever so gently, and said. "I like you too. Very much. Like I have known you forever, somehow. Does that sound crazy?"

Her soft warm eyes drifted over his face, then stared deeply into his. "Yes, but it is interesting to be crazy."

The band broke into with a rousing rendition of "Black Magic Woman." She stood and pulled lightly on his hand. "Come, this is my song."

Nick tried to keep up with her movements but she was well practiced. He felt like the country bumpkin that he was and laughed, embarrassed. She joined his laughter but kept on, in time with the music, until the last note. Then, before they could move, the band segued into, "How Deep Is Your Love?" Nick pulled her close to him and she placed both her hands on his broad shoulders behind his neck. He felt the surge in his heart and the insistent stirring in his groin.

"Do you like the BGs?" she asked.

"I do now," he replied.

"They are my favorite group."

"I think you have many favorite groups."

She looked up at him with a dreamy expression in her eyes. "I think now, WE are my favorite group."

The song ended, Nick sat them back down. He glanced quickly at his watch. He tried to talk again before the next song drowned him out. "Listen, Hang. I enjoy dancing with you but I have a sick friend back at our hotel. I promised to check on him. Would you mind going with me? Besides, I really want to spend more time talking with you."

"Oh, yes. Tim, right?" He nodded. "OK, but I want you to agree that nothing is going to happen."

"That is up to you."

As they stepped out of the elevator at the Bong Sen, Nick was thankful they had not run into any Japanese businessmen. He led her to his room and unlocked the door. "Please make yourself comfortable. There is beer and soda and water in the *tu lanh*. I'll check on Tim and return in a few minutes. OK?" When he left, she was standing over his desk looking curiously at his blue copy of *A Course in Miracles*.

He banged on Tim's door. From inside came a stronger voice. "Just a minute! Who is it?"

"It's me, Timmy."

The door opened. He was still pale and smelled of vomit but appeared somewhat better. "Come on in, Nick. Thanks for coming back. I'm doing OK. That medicine from Alan really works. Did you see the girls?"

"Just Thuy. Mine stayed home with her husband."

Tim tried to laugh but coughed instead.

"But I met a different one. God, Tim, she's so nice! I can't believe it!"

Tim smiled appreciatively. "Good for you, Nick. I'm glad. So what the hell are you doing here? Go get her, brah!"

Nick gave Tim a high five and waved from the hallway. "I'll get you for breakfast, OK?"

"I should be hungry by then. Have fun!"

Nick found her sitting at the desk, reading intently.

She glanced up. "What is this book? Is it like a Beeble?" she asked.

He laughed. "What? What is a Beeble?"

"You know, the story of Jesus."

Now he laughed even harder. "You mean, Bible."

She pouted and squirmed in her chair. "In French we say Beeble. You are so cruel to tease me."

"Oh, yes," he agreed. "I am famous for being cruel to beautiful young maidens that I have just met." They giggled together. He grew serious. "Yes. It is like the Bible, but it has much more to it. It teaches about acceptance, forgiveness, and unconditional love. It says those are the keys to happiness."

Nick sat on the bed and pulled out his cigarettes. He offered her one and she took it. He lit hers, then his.

"Are you Catholic or Buddhist? " he asked, blowing out a stream of smoke.

"Of course I am Catholic. And you?"

"I guess I am more Buddhist than Christian. This book teaches lessons from both religions and incorporates psychology as well."

"Incorporates? What means?"

"I'm sorry. It means includes, or *bao gom*."

"Are you a priest?" she asked.

"Not hardly." He laughed. "I'm just trying to find myself, I guess. I've been lost for the last couple of years."

"Why?"

"It seemed like no matter where I was, I felt I should be someplace else. Have you ever felt like that?"

"No."

He took a deep breath. "I always felt like I belonged here, but I felt guilty about not being with my family. And when I was with them, I felt that they were keeping me away from here. In the end, I lost everything. My wife, my kids, my farm, my sanity.

"I had an uncle who owned a farm up in Wisconsin. I would go there to work when I was a kid. He and my aunt were like my second parents. Earlier this year he wrote me a long letter about this thing called *A Course in Miracles* and how it really helped him. A month later, he died. Then in April I went to California to visit an old girlfriend. One Sunday she took me to her Unity Church, where they teach this course. When I returned to Maui, I went to the Vet Center for counseling and discovered that the psychologist there also taught the course at the Unity Church on Maui. It seemed like I had been flying around in space for so long and then, here were the runway lights showing me where to land. Am I making any sense to you?"

She smiled and shook her head slightly. "I don't understand all you say, but I think I understand what you feel. I think you are a good man."

"Thank you."

"So, you not married?"

He shook his head. "We're getting divorced."

"And you love Vietnam?"

"Very much. Do you ever think about going to France or the U.S.?"

"No. I have been offered to go, by my parents in the U.S., and by many French men. But I love it here too."

Nick studied her curiously. Many Asian women tried to snag American husbands so they could immigrate to the U.S. But this one was different. He could feel it. There was no doubt. They sat on the bed and smoked and drank and talked in three languages for hours.

At one point he leaned close to her and asked, "Could I please kiss you?"

She looked at him with her now bloodshot eyes, and smiled. "Later."

And so it went.

Later, when he guessed it to be near dawn, and during a silent moment, he slowly reached over and pulled her face to his and kissed her full lips ever so gently. He felt her put her arms around him and they lay back on the bed. He slid his tongue into her mouth and she responded with hers. Slowly, deliberately, he caressed her calves, then her thighs. When he felt her open her legs and sigh he slid his hand up along her panties, where he felt her wetness. She had been ready for a long time. He was throbbing and hard. They finished undressing each other, and he opened her again and eased himself slowly into her as she moaned loudly.

Their mutual passion surged and flowed together as they writhed screaming on the bed. They came perfectly and forcefully at the same instant. The rapture that flowed through his body was like electricity. It felt like his very first time. Finally they lay panting and sweating on the love-soaked sheets. Nick knew beyond all doubt that during that magical evening he had just met the love of his life, his soul mate for all eternity. And he would never have need of a condom again.

Thoroughly exhausted they fell fast asleep in each other's arms until the room grew light. When he awoke, he heard her in the bathroom brushing her teeth. She came out and gestured apologetically for him to use it if he needed. When he went in to throw cold water in his face, he saw his toothpaste, toothbrush and a cap full of Listerine all laid out in a row for him. In all his life, no one had ever done that. It was a simple thing but with profound implications. When he finished he came out and held her in his arms and kissed her a long while. He was startled by the phone ringing on his desk. "Hello, Tim?" he asked.

A deep booming voice responded. "No. I am Vy. I am down in the lobby. Are you ready to go to Lai Khe?"

"Oh, my God! I'm sorry, Vy! Something has happened. My friend got very sick and I met this wonderful girl and… I completely forgot about our plan. I'm sorry." His head was swimming with emotion. "I will be down in a few minutes."

Holding his throbbing head in his hands he sat on the bed. He could not cancel this chance. He placed one hand on her tiny shoulder. "Here is my key. You can stay here until I get back if you like. If not, you can leave it with the front desk. But I must see you again… I cannot believe what I am feeling. It wasn't supposed to be this way. I never meant to fall in love…" He kissed her passionately.

"My darling." She held his jaw in her delicate hands. "I also fell in love with you. I will go home for a while. Then I will come back here and wait for you."

He quickly called Tim and explained. No problem. Tim would eat breakfast in the hotel restaurant and see Nick whenever he returned. Nick could hear rain splashing outside his window. He pulled on his blue jeans and a Levi jacket with dark sneakers and his Vietnam Veterans of Maui T-shirt and hat. He stuck a fresh pack of Marlboros in his pocket with his Zippo, kissed her, and was gone.

CHAPTER 39
Thunder Road
August 1991

Vy led him out the front door into the pounding rain. He wore only a light jacket, slacks and a baseball cap as well. He kick-started his Yamaha 250cc scooter. Nick swung his leg over the rear and found the foot pegs. He lightly held onto the waist of the thin man as they sloshed away into the morning rain. This would be a day that he would never forget.

With a biting wind and rain stinging their faces, there was little conversation. They wound through the morning smells and city traffic for nearly an hour before crossing the mud-brown river and entering the relatively quiet countryside.

Vy pulled over at a roadside soup stand in a thatched roof shack. The sign out front said *pho bo*, which Nick knew was a deliciously spicy beef noodle soup. He patted Vy's narrow shoulder. "Good idea! This will be my treat!"

Vy nodded. "Yes, it will."

Nick ordered in Vietnamese, which caught the attention of the dozen other patrons. Then he asked Vy. "This road looks very familiar. Is it Highway 13?"

"Yes. But as you remember, we called it Thunder Road, right?"

"Yeah. Because of all the mines, ambushes, and firefights that we had on it." Nick stared deeply into the past. The tape began to play.

Vy watched his eyes carefully. "So, you do that too."

Nick returned to the now, but his eyes brimmed beneath the rain drops on his face. He looked down at the red mud beneath the table, then up into Vy's eyes. "And you?"

Vy nodded. "Warriors are all brothers. No matter which war, or which side. I think you will find this truth after you stay here awhile."

Nick grinned. "Already."

The *pho bo* was hot and energizing. Nick paid the equivalent of fifty cents for the two large bowls. They slid out onto muddy Thunder Road, headed north. They passed a string of water buffalos being led by a small, barefoot boy in shorts, checkered shirt, and droopy baseball cap. The flooded rice paddies spread away from the road on both sides, stretching out through gray skies to the distant jungle, just as Nick remembered it from the war.

At one point, he asked Vy to slow down as a patch of jungle crept up alongside them on the west. His grip unconsciously tightened on Vy's waist. Sergeant McClintock lay in the dust with his leg hanging by a tendon. Travis' eyes rolled back in his pure white face as he died from the shock of losing his manhood. The screams of the others muffled by the pounding roar of the Huey dustoff. The silence was deafening once it had taken all the wounded away into the azure sky.

Vy turned his head to look questioningly at Nick, who patted his shoulder once again. "It's OK, Vy. Keep going." But Nick was trembling as he pressed his head up against Vy's back.

Soon, they passed an ancient cemetery on the east side of the road on a small wooded rise above the surrounding paddies. Nick remembered it was close to the town of Ben Cat, where there had been an ARVN fortress. Vy drove them past the old site and down a hill, then abruptly turned into a walled compound with a large French colonial building on the high ground. "Why are we stopping here, Vy?"

"We must check in with the police before we can go on to Lai Khe."

"What does that mean? Check in?" Nick asked.

"Show them your passport and travel permit."

Nick was shocked back into the present. "You never told me I needed to bring those things. I left them at my hotel."

Vy swiveled back, giving Nick a reprimanding scowl. He heaved a deep sigh as the rain dripped off his cap. "We must go back."

"But why?" Nick all but yelled. "Lai Khe is only a couple of clicks away. We've come almost fifty miles in the rain. Can't we just go for a little while, then head back?"

Vy gave him a stern, "No," and turned his scooter south, back toward Ho Chi Minh City.

When they finally arrived at the Bong Sen, Nick dismounted and stuck out his hand. "I'm really sorry, Vy. Here is some money for gas and your time." He handed over some wet bills.

The deep baritone voice replied, "Go get your papers. I will wait here."

Nick's jaw hung open. "Really?"

Vy snorted. "We are wet already."

Nick ran inside, but stopped at the front desk. "Is my key here?" he inquired. The girl behind the desk reached back and pulled it out of his pigeonhole. Nick nodded sadly and went up to get his papers.

Hang was gone.

An hour and a half later they approached the police station again. But this time Nick took charge. "Listen, Vy. We have the papers but not much time. Let's just go, and if we get stopped we will show them. OK?" Vy relented and soon they were passing the old check point on the left. Nothing remained but the stand of an old water tower. He thought of Ma, Phuong, and Hai.

Soon they arrived at the wall of rubber trees that marked the perimeter of his old base camp. On the right were the remnants of the PSP airstrip. It was covered by scrub brush and foraging cattle. When they finally turned left, down a red dirt road, Nick began feeling warm memories. There, up ahead, was the big tree, still standing after decades of war and reconciliation. It seemed stronger than ever. As they passed, Nick looked to the right for signs of the thatched roof over Ma's shack. Only bare dirt and weeds. How many more heartbreaks can I take? he asked himself.

They pulled up in front of the school. The rains had subsided, but the sky remained dark and threatening. Vy led Nick through a central courtyard that was surrounded by three classrooms. At the edge, under the overhang of the corrugated roof, Vy pointed at the white 4x4 Peace Pole. On two sides it said "PEACE" and on the other two, "HOA BINH."

"Fredy and I planted that pole a few months ago," Vy said as they made their way toward one of the classrooms. Exuberant children began cheering and calling out to them. They all smiled and laughed with delight when they recognized that Nick was a foreigner. Their faces beamed with anticipation, much as the Amerasian orphans had done a year and a half ago.

Nick sensed they saw him as some kind of rich and powerful savior, come to rescue them from their plight. He could not help but think of Charlie Brown, which tempered his emotions and kept him rooted to reality. He would not make that mistake again.

They entered the front doorway, which was simply an opening in the wall. The windows were open slatted louvers that had rotted and broken away long ago. The floor was concrete with standing pools of water from the many holes in the rusty tin roof. A middle-aged woman in a white blouse and light blue slacks and rubber slippers approached, smiling. Vy introduced her.

"*Anh* Nick, this is my sister-in-law, Yen. She is teacher here." Then he said to her, "*Day la ban cua Anh Fredy. Ong moun giup do tieu hoc nay.*"

Nick shook her hand, and spoke in her language. "That's right. But for now, I just want to see what is needed here. I cannot promise anything except that I will try to help you as much as I can."

Yen nodded smiling. "You speak Vietnamese very well. Where did you learn?"

"Right here in this village, about twenty five years ago."

"Would you like to speak to the children? I think they would love it."

Embarrassed at being put on the spot, Nick just said, "Hello, children. I am an American veteran who has come back to Vietnam to make peace. I hope we can all be friends." He was met with more cheering and applause.

Ms. Yen gave the class an assignment and escorted the two men out into the yard. She told Nick about the meager budget. The communists were very good at waging war, she said, but not so good at waging peace. The school needed generators and electric fans, a water-treatment plant, cooking facilities, new toilets, a new roof, and of course, basic school supplies. She hoped that he and Fredy could find a way to help the children of the village that their base camp had been built around, so many years ago.

Nick scribbled down everything in a small notebook. He glanced at his watch.

"Excuse me, Ms. Yen. Do you remember a family of orphans that lived two houses away from the big tree? The girl was named Phuong and the boy was Hai. I knew them in 1966."

Yen's smile spread across her face. "Yes. Phuong got married after the war and moved away. Hai was adopted by a family from Canada. He went there to start a new life." Then her smile vanished, and she looked away towards the black clouds coming in from Cambodia. Nick read her like a book.

"And what about their... well, I called her Ma?"

"She was killed in Ben Cat."

"But how, when, by who?"

Vy's deep voice cut Nick off. "It is getting late. We go now." He put his arm around Nick's shoulders as Yen turned away and walked with them toward their motor scooter.

They shook hands and bowed to each other. Vy drove them out the dirt path to the small road that led past the big tree. Nick stared over at the spot.

He could see them all sitting at the rickety table, feasting on their little roast chicken as his war came to an end. A tremendous wave of nostalgia rolled over him. He had meant to also visit a nearby orphanage, but time was short. There was one more thing he needed to do. "Vy. When we reach Thunder Road please turn left and head north."

"Ho Chi Minh City is south. We should go back soon." When they reached the intersection, Nick felt Vy turning right but with his superior weight advantage he leaned hard and forced Vy to turn left. Vy shook his head but resigned himself to his fate. This American was going to have his way, no matter what.

Gazing down the long green rows of rubber trees made a river of memories begin to flow.

CHAPTER 40
Lai Khe Base Camp
March 1966

I slung my rifle and strapped on my mess kit as I walked away from my bunker on the east perimeter, facing the jungle. I strode down the dirt road beneath the rubber's protective canopy of limbs and leaves. In the distance I saw an olive-green jeep approaching.

It was at least 500 meters away when I saw the unmistakable turquoise dress flapping in the breeze. Above it was bright red hair. That was a white woman! But how could that be? We were just a hundred meters off the line! They got closer and closer. My jaw dropped wide open as the jeep sped by me, so close I could have easily reached out and touched the beautiful, sexy, and smiling Ann Margaret.

When I reached the CP tent I couldn't wait to tell the others what I had just seen. But all eyes were fixed on Captain Bradley, who stood in front of his personal tent and opened a plastic bag. He pulled out a brand new red-and-blue flag with a gold star in the middle. It was a VC flag. Bradley ripped it, stomped it into the dirt, even cut himself with his bayonet and smeared his blood on it. We all stood around watching the spectacle while eating our powdered eggs with canned white bread, washing it down with Tang.

Within minutes the same jeep pulled up into the CP area, and the Old Man scurried over to take Ann Margaret's hand as she disembarked the dirty jeep. I was too far away to hear their conversation at first but soon they headed in closer to our group of grunts as we finished off our breakfast.

"Men! We are indeed honored today to have this famous movie star grace us with a visit to our humble abode." There was hearty applause, cheers, and wolf whistles. "Now I would like to present Miss Margaret with this Viet Cong flag that we captured on a recent operation." He handed her the flag as she wept and trembled. She was truly overwhelmed.

A grunt standing next to me leaned over and whispered, "I hope the Old Man remembered to remove the price tag."

CHAPTER 41
Thunder Road
August 1991

They drove on through the cold rain for half an hour before they reached the spot. There, on the right side of the road was the large white concrete wall beneath a vaulted pedestal supporting larger-than-life statues of a Viet Cong guerilla aiming an RPG and a woman guerilla carrying ammo and a pack. The words *"Bia Chien Thang Bau Bang"* were written in red letters on the face of the wall. It meant "Victory Monument to the battle of Bau Bang." Vy stopped, dismounted and looked hard at Nick.

"How did you know this was here?" he asked. "Even Fredy did not come here."

Nick shook his head. "I didn't."

"Do you remember this battle?"

"It was our battalion. The Second of the Second. The *dinky dau* battalion. They got ambushed right here and lost about a hundred and eighty men. But we killed nearly seven hundred of them. I guess that means that we won."

Vy pointed at the red inscription. "That's not what it says here."

Nick's face grew dark and solemn. "Yeah. That's why they call it, his-story. In the end, the victors get to write it." Nick went in front of the monument, squatted down like a Vietnamese. He placed his folded hands in front of him and whispered, "Acceptance… forgiveness… unconditional love. To all the brothers. On both sides. There were no winners here. We all lost."

He stood, came to attention, and snapped an Honor Guard salute to all of them. He walked stiffly over to Vy and climbed back on the bike. He patted Vy's frail shoulder. "I'm sorry, my friend. But there is just one more place I need to go. Turn north again."

The narrow strip of asphalt was threatened on both sides by encroaching vegetation. There were no other vehicles now. They sped along for a ways then Vy called back over his shoulder. "Where are we going?"

Nick peered through the slicing rain. "I'll know when I see it. It's on the far side of a bridge over a small river."

Vy nodded. "Cau Tham Rot."

"I don't know the name."

"I do." He twisted the throttle.

The rows of rubber trees seemed endless. Nick had spent the second half of his tour in and around them. He could not help but remember.

CHAPTER 42
War Zone C
March 1966

It was called Operation Mastiff. The entire third brigade swept around the southern border of the huge Michelin plantation, searching for the infamous 272nd VC Regiment. We set up a base camp in a wide-open expanse of paddies.

Spec 4 Rivera and I squatted bare chested in our two-man foxhole along the western perimeter. Sergeant Davis made his rounds along the line, passing down the word that every man was to clean his weapon for a field inspection. We looked skeptically at each other. "What you talkin' bout, Sarge?" queried Rivera. "Inspection for who?"

Davis grinned and shook his head. "Now goddamn it, boy, you know better than to ask me that shit! Just follow orders like everybody else, and make damn sure you do a good job. The Old Man will be checkin'."

We shrugged and broke down our M-16s, laying out the pieces on our fatigue jackets in the hot sun. We were so engrossed we hardly noticed when Staff Sergeant Murphy appeared on the brim of the hole with two strangers.

"Nick, Rivera. This here FNG is Private Williams. He's assigned to your squad, so you teach him everything he needs to know."

He was a husky young black man whose shiny jungle fatigues still smelled new. His boots were actually polished black, and his eyes bugged out white with fear. Standing next to Williams was a middle-aged white man with longish, curly, gray hair. He also wore jungle fatigues, but his were well worn. He was bare-headed and carried a camera and a thick notebook. His expression was calm and confident. He was a civilian but had been around for awhile.

Sergeant Murphy turned to the civilian. "This is Williams' shadow,

Mr. John Sack of *Esquire* magazine. He's doing a story about Williams and will be going every place that Williams goes. You treat him like everyone else and answer any questions he has. Mr. Sack, you can tag along all you want to, but you follow orders like the rest of us."

Nick scrutinized the newcomers. "Have a seat. You make a fine target standing up there." Williams dropped obediently to the ground but Sergeant Murphy lit a cigarette and remained perched over the hole.

John Sack sat on the red dirt and scanned the line of foxholes. "Sergeant Murphy. Do you think it's a good idea to have every one of your men clean their rifles at the same time? What if Charlie decides to attack right now?"

The old sergeant's face burned red with humiliation. "Men! One man in each hole, put your weapons back together! Who's the dumb ass that ordered you all to clean 'em at the same time?"

Someone yelled out, "Davis said it was you, Sarge!"

"Hey! Fuck you, Standridge! Nobody likes a smart ass!" The chuckling echoed down the line as Murphy stalked away. "Carry on, goddamn it!"

Nick shook hands with the two men. "That was good thinking, Mr. Sack. Where did you learn that?"

"I was in the Korean War," he replied, and pulled out his pen and notebook.

"What was that like?" asked Rivera.

Sack peered wistfully out at the horizon. "Actually, I've tried to forget about it. Everyone else has."

Rivera and I exchanged looks. I slapped Williams on the arm, which made the FNG jump. He was plenty scared already. "Williams. Come on over here and dig a two-man hole."

"Who's it fo'?"

"You and me. So make it big. I don't wanna get too cozy on our first date."

Williams low-crawled a few meters away and unstrapped his entrenching tool. I raised a questioning eyebrow at Sack, who silently held out his hand and let it shake from side to side.

"So, Nick. Tell me about yourself. What's your full name, where are you from, all that bullshit."

I told my story.

Rivera scanned the perimeter. "Holy shit, you guys! Look at this!" Several holes down the line, troops were scurrying around. We were shocked. A four-man group approached. It was led by Captain Bradley who darted back and forth in front of a taller second man like a dog waiting for his owner to throw him a stick.

Our jaws dropped. We were looking up at the monolithic silhouette of four-star General William Westmoreland. Standing over us, it seemed his head touched the sky.

Captain Bradley spoke first. "Don't salute, men! We're following bush rules, right, sir?"

"That's right." The fatherly face smiled. "Mr. Sack, are you men settled yet?"

"Yes, General. Williams there is digging in."

Westmoreland reached down and shook hands with both us sunburned grunts.

I said, "Good afternoon, sir. It's great to see you again!"

"We've met before?" the general asked.

"Yes, sir. In June last year when I got off the plane in Saigon. You shook my hand and told me to become Vietnamese, win their hearts and minds, all that bullshit." Too late, I realized what I had just said.

The general burst out laughing. "So, tell me. How's that all going?"

I froze momentarily, debating prudence versus honesty. I looked down sheepishly then up into the inquisitive dark eyes. I opened my mouth to speak several times but nothing came with it. My eyes searched the red dirt and rice straw around my hole for the answer. It left me empty. I finally came up with: "Well sir, I did learn to speak Vietnamese, but... well, things have changed a lot in the last year. Out here, things are different."

Westmoreland gazed out across the paddies toward the Black Virgin Mountain as the sun set fire to the sky. He nodded calmly. "That's OK, son. You just go home in one piece." He moved off down the line.

John Sack, Rivera, and I spent the rest of the evening basking in the fading sun, smoking and talking, while Williams grunted and sweated on his hole. When the interview was over, Sack wandered back to the CP, where he was the captain's guest. When I finally approved of the hole, I transferred my pack and rifle over to join Williams.

"Listen up, Williams. I'm gonna tell you everything I can think of to keep you alive. We've taken lots of casualties lately, and we don't want any more." Williams nodded, eagerly waiting for any information he could get. The man was clearly frightened. "When the sun goes down, we're gonna stop talking and start watching, listening, and smelling. Charlie might try to probe the perimeter.

"Here's the detonator for the Claymore. It's right out there in front along with our trip flares. These stakes in the ground define our sector of responsibility. We alternate guard shifts. Two hours at a shot until dawn. Then we both stay awake 'til it gets light and we move out. Got it?"

Williams nodded, fidgeting with his rifle sling. "I ain't never killed anything before in my life. Have you? I mean, what does it feel like? Were you scared? I mean, what if I freeze up?"

No one had ever asked me that before. Not even myself. "Where did you take AIT?"

"Fort Dix."

"Yeah? Me too. If they trained you the same way they trained me, then you won't have any trouble. It kinda just takes care of itself. Don't mean nothin'."

We settled down in the hole and I lit the last cigarette of the night. Sunrise and the next smoke was a long way off. We shot the shit in the impending dusk. Typical foxhole talk. But Williams' fear was becoming contagious. For some unknown reason, I started telling the FNG about some of my buddies who had gotten killed and what to avoid to stay alive.

Williams persisted, "Don't you ever get real scared? Cause man, I'm really scared!"

"Yeah, I get scared. Hell. I'm scared right now. Sometimes I get bad feelings, you know? Like I can tell when something bad is gonna happen."

"You gettin' bad feelin's now?"

I crushed out my cigarette in the dirt. "Yeah, I am. But don't worry about it. You're an FNG and got plenty to learn. The only way to learn is to go out and do it."

But he kept it up. Until now, nobody had dared discuss fear. It was taboo. It was unmanly. It was dangerous. Once a man gave in to his inner fear he would be worthless and unreliable. Williams and I were about to discover firsthand the consequences of such folly.

At 2200 we started our guard rotation. A can of demons had been opened and a premonition loomed large. I saw my own death. It would happen tomorrow when I took the point. I couldn't see past the fire and smoke, but death was waiting for me on the other side.

For the first time in my tour I surrendered to the fear. I was trembling badly as I placed the flash suppressor of my M-16 against my left boot. I planned to claim that a sniper got me when I stood up to take a leak. The loss of a few toes beat the hell out of getting killed. Before I pulled the trigger, I felt Williams shaking me. It was 0400.

"Listen, Williams. I ain't goin' out today."

"What? Oh man! What you mean you ain't goin' out? Can we do that?"

"I'm doin' it."

Williams sat watching me, an old-timer, as the first light crept into the last day of my life. Sergeant Davis appeared.

"I ain't goin' out today, Sarge." My voice was shaking.

"The hell you ain't! You saddle up, soldier! I don't wanna hear another word."

"I don't care what you do to me, Sarge. I ain't goin' and that's that."

Williams chimed in, "Sarge, I ain't goin' either!"

Davis stormed off. Minutes later he brought in the platoon sergeant, platoon leader and finally Captain Bradley. I refused all of their direct orders. They looked helplessly at each other. Lieutenant Arthur calmly asked, "What about tomorrow, Nick? Are you saying you won't go out ever again or what?"

The feeling of dread seemed to apply only to that one day. "No. I'll go out tomorrow and the day after that, you know. But not today."

"And what about you Private Williams?"

"I'll do whatever Nick does, sir. "

The officers all looked at each other again. Captain Bradley nodded. "All right, you two stay here on perimeter guard today. But tomorrow you go out and kick ass! Carry on!"

When the platoon returned that evening, they all filed past our position. Each and every man stared at us with blatant loathing and yet with a certain awe. The man who took my place on point was missing. He had hit a mine.

CHAPTER 43
Thunder Road
August 1991

When Vy began slowing down, Nick looked past him and saw the white concrete bridge. To the left was a broad flat plain with scattered eucalyptus trees.

Nick pointed to it. "There used to be an ARVN fort over there." Vy crossed the bridge and stopped when Nick tapped his shoulder.

"Yes, I know. I was the commander at that fort."

"You? Were you here in 1966?"

"Of course."

Nick looked at Vy carefully, then got off and walked slowly away. He went onto the shoulder and searched the surrounding terrain for familiar features. It did not take long.

From the scooter, Vy watched as Nick fell to the ground on his knees and began sobbing. He dug both his calloused hands into the earth and pulled up a clump of sticky clay. He held it to his chest momentarily, then lifted it to his mouth and began to eat it.

Vy respectfully kept his distance while the crazy American talked with his ghosts. Then Nick stood up, facing off to the west side of the road and saluted into the sky with a muddy hand. He came back to the bike, wiped his chin on his jacket sleeve, and offered Vy a cigarette. They both squatted in the mud and smoked. Vy waited. Nick lay his finger on the side of his nose and blew out thick snot.

"It was March 1966. We had a brand new squad leader named Sergeant Hickman. Then one day, my platoon sergeant came through asking if anybody was from California, because a congressman from there was visiting the company to find out how the war was going. Nobody spoke up, so I said I had been there enough to bullshit the politician if I needed to. So I got the job, even though I'm from Illinois.

But they wanted a sergeant, and I was only a PFC, so I traded shirts with Sergeant Hickman, and I played out my role.

"The next day, we were up here on Thunder Road. I was on point. I had a Vietnamese sergeant, named Son, with me because we were both interpreters. After we crossed the bridge, my position was on the road. Hickman was supposed to be down in that rice paddy with the rest of our squad, but he was really exhausted. He asked me to trade places, so I went down there with the others. Son was supposed to stay with me but he was tired too. He stayed with Hickman on the road.

"When we began moving forward, on line, there was a huge explosion on the road. The concussion knocked me down. I looked up and saw a leg fly through the smoke and land in the paddy. I went running up this slope to the crater of the big mine. They were both in it. Hickman had no arms or legs. His face was all burned black but he was still alive. He saw me and reached up a stump of his arm then collapsed dead, back down in the hole on top of Son. Son's head was gone." Nick pulled deep on his cigarette and exhaled slowly. "It took our whole squad nearly an hour to find it."

Vy watched in awe as Nick knocked the glowing head off of his cigarette and began chewing the butt, just as he had that day. Nick was off into the thousand-yard stare.

"That was the first time that I finally said, fuck it. I didn't care any more if I lived or died. I was so tired of being afraid. Trying to survive was futile. I just gave it up. I knew beyond all doubt that I was going to die, and I accepted it. You know something, Vy? That's a good place to go, if you have to."

Vy stared out across the paddy and stubbed out his cigarette in the mud. "I remember that day. Your battalion came through here on a road sweep and you stopped at our fort over there. After you all crossed the river there was a big explosion on the road. Yes, I remember. You said, March 1966, *phai khong*?"

Nick nodded numbly. The surprise of this revelation did not sink in at first. He thought back. Vy was correct. They had stopped and eaten some C rations with the ARVN soldiers at the fort. He and Son had accompanied the LT to talk with some Vietnamese officers. One of them had been a tall, thin, major with a deep voice. After they talked and ate together, they all smoked, and nearby they heard some grunt begin playing an old folk song on his harmonica. The Americans were all surprised to hear the major break out singing the song in English.

Nick turned and began to sing in a quavering voice while watching Vy's face. "Oh my darlin', oh my darlin', oh my darlin' Clementine…"

In a booming baritone, Vy chimed in, "You are lost and gone forever, oh my darlin' Clementine."

Twenty-five long years disappeared in a flash. Reunited, they squatted in the mud on the side of Thunder Road, singing together in the rain.

Heading south now, with yesterday behind them but still fresh in their minds, Nick recalled how, many years later, the author John Sack, had written a book called *M* which was about his old buddy Williams and his entire unit during 1966. The incident with the California Congressman was mentioned, but Sack had given him someone else's name. Nick's photo appeared on the back cover but was also given another's name. Once again, Nick had been sentenced to anonymity.

Now he was drenched. His clothes were plastered to his skin, but soon they would be back in Ho Chi Minh City. He could not wait to see Hang and hold her and make passionate love to her again. He would have a very hot shower and take her to dinner and introduce her to Tim.

Neat rows of rubber trees, perfectly spaced, lay out before them in a checkerboard pattern as they approached Lai Khe. The plantation seemed to go on forever. Then he remembered the Michelin…

CHAPTER 44
Thunder Road
1966

After we had policed up Son and Hickman's body parts from the paddy, we were loaded into deuce-and-a-halfs and sent roaring up Thunder Road towards Loc Ninh. Hatred and rage seethed inside of my being. "KILL VC! GET SOME!" My only thoughts were of revenge. Nothing else existed. I could taste the blood-lust in my mouth. I loved it, craved it, needed it. As we rumbled down the potholed road the wind rushed into my helmet, obliterating all other sound except for the growling engines.

Suddenly I heard the unmistakable crack of bullets whistling past my head. "Sniper! Ambush!" came the cries of the others in the squad. In less than a heartbeat I was on my feet trying to stand and fire from the lurching floor of the truck. Without thinking, I aimed across the other side of the truck and fired on full automatic into the woodline along the roadside. The other men also stood to shoot, and their helmets came up into my line of fire. My rifle muzzle was violently shoved up into the sky by the enraged Sergeant Lopez of second squad, whose men I had nearly decapitated with my reckless reaction.

"What the fuck are you doin', dumb ass?" he screamed. "You turn around and cover your own sector!"

I went into the sergeant's face and yelled back, "I saw muzzle flashes, goddamn it! I gotta get some, Sarge! I gotta kill 'em all!"

Lopez jammed his finger into my chest and pressed his face up against mine. "You listen to me, you son of a bitch! If you ever see the enemy, you hold your weapon up over your shoulder and point it towards where they are! We don't need some trigger-happy bastard killing our own men! Do you understand me, soldier?"

I was huffing deeply through gritted teeth, but it finally sank in.

I had really fucked up. I could have... Suddenly I was perfectly calm. "I'm sorry, Sarge."

We rolled on for another 10 kilometers without incident. The convoy turned west onto a red-dirt road that led through the outskirts of the Michelin plantation. Then the trucks stopped in huge clouds of choking dust, and the troops immediately leaped down and ran out to establish a defensive perimeter.

Lieutenant Arthur strode up behind our platoon. "All right, men! Form up in a single file. Right here! Third squad take the point!"

Sergeant Davis stepped up and beckoned his squad. "OK ! Saddle up! Nick..."

"Yeah, yeah. I know. Take the fucking point. But you know what, Sarge? I want it! I want it bad!" I was deadly serious and was glaring hard at Davis when I noticed an FNG in relatively new fatigues walk up. He was tall, handsome, and somehow familiar. He wore a bush hat, and a pistol on his belt but carried a huge camera, two canteens, and a pack on his back. He looked around and nodded at the men.

Davis said. "Men, this here is Sean Flynn. He's a photographer for some French magazine called *Match*. He's doing a story about the war and has been assigned to us, so take care of him. Is there anything you want to say, Mr. Flynn?"

The FNG searched the men's faces again, confidently but with a certain humility. His eyes were not afraid. "I'm really proud to be here with you guys. I've heard this is a good outfit." There was sarcastic snickering. He grinned broadly. "I like to be where the action is so, Sergeant Davis if it's OK with you, I'd like to be up front with your point man."

Davis nodded. "Nick?"

I stared straight into the man's eyes and smirked. "I like to work alone, and if you go with me, you'll be on your own too. I won't babysit you."

Sean Flynn reached out his hand. Slowly I took it and was surprised at the callouses. Sean grasped me tightly. "Don't even try to babysit me! I've been over here a while, and I can take care of myself."

I returned the grin and nodded my approval. "We'll see. Which way, Sarge?"

By early afternoon I had led the platoon on a western path. Then Lieutenant Arthur relayed the company commander's orders and had me turn south, then back east again. The plan was to zigzag through the rubber until we made contact with a large force of VC that had set up a base camp in the plantation.

Another FNG, PFC Jerry Blanton, was close behind me and Sean. He carried the M-79 thump gun. He and I had hit it off after he was assigned to me for orientation. Since I had more time in-country than anyone else in the division, I was always given the job of teaching the FNGs about the bush. I was uncomfortable with this role, as I preferred being a loner, but did what I could.

I walked close to the tree trunks for cover as we began up a small rise. When I reached the top and searched down the row as far as I could see, I saw something strange. The sun was to my right, but about 200 meters down, the shadows of the trees were also on the right. I froze instantly. There was not a breath of wind but the black shadows moved! Remembering my earlier mistake, I dropped to one knee and held my rifle over my shoulder at the target. The shadows grew straw hats and carried rifles and were sprinting hard to the right.

Cursing myself for being overly cautious, I brought my M-16 up and aimed at the place where I had a 45-degree opening in the tree trunks. I opened up on full automatic but the two VC never showed up. They had gone only a few rows over, then turned away, using the trunks for cover. Sean was snapping shots with his camera, and Derby ran up on line with us and began firing.

Blanton was in a panic. The FNG ran up, and forgetting about the tight cover of the rubber tree canopy, popped a high explosive round toward the enemy before I could stop him. The 40mm round hit a large branch just overhead and exploded in a fiery ball. I reached over and grabbed Sean by the arm and dragged him down to the ground. I felt the shrapnel skidding off of my helmet and heard Sean yelling in pain. When the smoke cleared, Sean was writhing on the ground clutching his knee. Blood was flowing down and quickly filling his combat boot. I pulled the man's hands away to see a huge gash in his knee cap. I yelled out, "Medic! Medic! We got a man hit up here!" Doc arrived and placed a small tourniquet around Sean's thigh and shot him up with some morphine.

Lieutenant Arthur stood over him watching. "How bad is it, Doc?"

"We need a dustoff sir. He could lose the leg if we don't."

The LT scanned the rubber trees stretching for an eternity. He radioed Captain Bradley who decided to have us carry Flynn about one kilometer to a stand of young trees. When we arrived, the LT surveyed the area and called me over. "Nick. Break out your machete and cut down a one-hundred-foot wide swath of trees so we can get a chopper in here."

I stared down at the tree trunks that were four to five inches in diameter, shook my head, took a deep breath and started swinging my big knife at a steep angle into the trees. Sean lay on the ground and watched me struggle. When I finally surrendered the machete to Blanton, who begged to help, I sat down with Sean and shared a smoke. Sean gazed at me with droopy eyes as the morphine worked its magic. "Goddamn it, Nick! I told you not to babysit me!" We both choked out a laugh.

I pulled long on the Pall Mall. "Why do you seem so familiar?" I asked and passed it over to Sean.

"Ever hear of Errol Flynn, the actor?"

I nodded. "Of course. Oh shit!"

Sean nodded dreamily. "He's my father."

I sat up to face him directly. "So what the hell is a guy like you doin' out here? You could be in Hollywood with all those good looking babes livin' the good life."

"What comes to mind when you think of Errol Flynn?" Sean retorted.

"I guess, a dashing buccaneer, a hard-living hero who always wins the fight and the girl. You know, Captain Blood."

"Exactly. It isn't easy being Errol Flynn's son. Lots of preconceptions to live up to, you know?"

The slapping, pounding rotor blades were just barely audible in the distance. We stared at each other. Blanton sat down quietly and all but wrung his hands. "I'm sorry, Sean. I lost my head. I hope you'll be OK."

"At least now I've got something my dad doesn't have. A battle scar. Tonight I'll have a cold beer for you guys."

Someone popped an orange smoke grenade. Blanton and I lifted Sean up by the arms and draped them over our shoulders. We stumbled over through the red back wash. We lay Sean down on the throbbing floor of the Huey and stepped back.

Sean yelled out, "Thanks, you guys! *Au revoir!*"

"How about in Hollywood next time?" I yelled.

Sean gave me a grin and a thumbs up. Blanton and I stood waving in the storm of red dust as the chopper lifted up and took Flynn away into the fiery sunset. We would never meet again.

CHAPTER 45
Ho Chi Minh City
September 1987

Twenty one years later, I met a *Los Angeles Times* correspondent named Jack Halsey in the bar atop the Rex Hotel in Ho Chi Minh City. He told me Sean Flynn had been wounded several more times as a war correspondent in the Vietnam War, but had been killed by the Khmer Rouge in Cambodia in 1979.

When I heard, it seemed a high price to pay for trying to live up to your father's legacy. I remembered my own father's derisive smirk that morning in June, 1961 when I shouldered my pack and pulled on my cowboy hat and boots.

"So, Nickie, where do think you're going? Camping out in the woods again?" he asked as he straightened his red-and-white polka-dot tie and slid on his suit jacket.

I took a deep breath. "California."

Donald Dwyer stopped dead in his tracks and turned back to face me, only fourteen, but tall and burly. His mouth grimaced and started laughing. "You idiot! That's over two thousand miles from here! How're you going to get there? Walk?"

I nodded proudly. "Yep."

I could still hear the sardonic laughter while my father walked out the back door. "Well, we'll see you back here by tomorrow night!"

I remember hissing under my breath, "The hell you will, you chicken-shit, draft dodger!"

Dear old Dad was declared 4-F and escaped the draft during World War II. Instead, he had worked for International Harvester building torpedos. I always suspected my rich grandparents had bribed somebody.

It's funny. I had failed freshman English while writing feverishly all winter long on a movie script that I hoped to sell in Hollywood.

In order to finance the long journey, I sold Star, my Holstein cow, and her calf to a tall, fat man named Dieter. Then I killed, plucked, and cleaned my thirty chickens and sold them. I had a total of $160 in my pocket as the screen door banged behind me. I headed west down a dusty road... I wouldn't be back for more than two months.

Hollywood may have chewed me up and spit me out, but Dad would never laugh at me again. And neither would the cocky little prick with the pompadour hairdo and a tuxedo that I encountered one sweltering afternoon at the gates of Paramount Studios. With my dust-covered and trail-worn cowboy outfit and sporting a six-week beard, I passed the guard shack and was nearly on the way to selling my script to become a famous movie writer when the uniformed guard and the Liberace look-alike called me over.

"You got a pass, boy?" asked the guard, while they looked me up and down.

I shook my head. "I just wanna sell my script and collect my money. Then I'll be on my way."

The guard and the pompous little asshole looked at each other and sputtered disdainfully.

"You got an agent, boy?" asked the guard.

"What's an agent?" I asked.

The haughty duo could not contain themselves and howled straight into my face. The short man's white ruffled shirt, gold chains, and glittering diamonds slapped me right in my pride and self-respect.

"You gotta have an agent, you moron!" he sneered.

I edged closer and felt my face flushing scarlet in the hot sun. "So where do I find an agent, asshole?"

"Hey! Do you know who I am?" He puffed up only briefly before a lightning quick, overhand right found its mark on the left side of his make-up covered jaw. The startled man reeled backwards and the guard reached over to shove me away.

"Now, see here, you! You get outta here right now, or I'll call the police!"

I gave them both the finger and retreated out onto the sleazy back alleys of Hollywood.

Later, that fall, our family gathered around the TV one night to watch the new western series called *Bonanza*. As a steel guitar played the intro, four cowboys rode up to be introduced, one by one, to the American public. And there, astride his pony, sat the same pompous little asshole, with long, curly hair and dimpled cheeks smiling impudently. The new cowboy hero, Michael Landon.

CHAPTER 46
Thunder Road
August 1991

The wind blasted heavily across the front of the Yamaha which yawed to the right. Vy fought it back on course. Nick could feel the thin man shivering in his rain-soaked jacket as row after row of rubber trees fell away in the grayness. Is that what it's all about? he wondered. Competing with our fathers? Trying to prove ourselves worthy? How many wars have been caused by such frivolity? How many warriors have been maimed or killed in the search of redemption? How many innocents? Are we all innocent? Are any of us?

Shivering in the wind rush, Nick's fantasies were suddenly shattered as they approached the north entrance into Lai Khe. Three motorcycles roared up next to them. The uniformed police in their gray shirts with olive-drab pants, brandishing 9mm pistols, surrounded them and roughly ordered Vy to pull over. Their facial expressions told Nick that this was serious trouble, more than a routine traffic stop. The commanding officer, who appeared to be a captain, walked briskly up to Vy while sneering dramatically at Nick. He was very short but robust and strong. "Where are you going?" he demanded.

"Back to the city," Vy replied calmly.

"What are you doing in Song Be province?"

"My friend asked me to bring him here."

"What is his nationality?"

Vy's voice dropped slightly. "American."

The captain stepped up close to Nick and glared into Nick's dripping face. Having just faced the dragon of his past gave Nick a huge psychological advantage. Nothing or nobody was going to intimidate him at this point. He looked straight back into the captain's eyes unflinchingly, but with a calm, confident smile as well. He knew macho bravado was out of the question. But so was subservience. I will be myself and I will be honest, Nick thought to himself. I am here on an honorable mission; to help the local people. Surely they will appreciate that.

"What does he want here?" the captain continued.

"To help the school and orphanage in Lai Khe," Vy answered.

The captain surveyed them both suspiciously. "You come with us into Lai Khe!" he ordered. The police motorcycles hung close and guided them down Thunder Road until they reached the same red-dirt road that led to the school. Nick was surprised when they all came to a halt beneath the big tree. They were ushered inside a small shack by the four policemen. Small stools around a low table. They were ordered to sit. Nick and three of the policemen sat on one side while Vy sat next to the captain across from them. The captain unslung his leather pouch and placed it on the table. He scrutinized Nick cautiously. "*Anh biet noi tieng Viet khong?*" he asked.

Nick nodded. "*Da co,*" he answered respectfully. "Do you speak English?" The captain shook his head. The situation was delicate. It was one thing to order food in a restaurant, but now his life was on the line. Vy would have to interpret if needed.

Nick decided to take the initiative. "Excuse me, sir. What is your name?"

"Captain Dung. Do you have your passport, visa and travel permit?" His tone mellowed somewhat when he heard Nick speak his language.

Nick pulled the plastic bag from his jacket, removed the papers, and lay them on the table with two hands. The other three police looked at Nick with so much disdain it was almost comical. Nick remained calm.

Captain Dung glared when he saw the American passport. "American devil!" he yelled. "Did you fight here in the war?"

Nick looked him in the eye and nodded. "Did you?"

Dung waved his arm around the room. "We all are veterans." Nick checked out the others. The hatred in their eyes was unmistakable. Nick missed their preoccupation with his VVM hat which displayed the flag of the Republic of South Vietnam.

"Why did you come to Lai Khe?"

"To offer help to the school and orphanage. I was stationed here.

I would like to give something back to the village, because they were once my friends."

Vy spoke quietly to Nick in English. "Do you have more cigarettes?" He motioned with his eyes around the table. Nick pulled out his pack and offered them to Dung and the others. After Dung accepted, the others followed. Dung exhaled slowly, watching Nick's eyes.

"If you came to help Lai Khe, then why did you go north?"

Vy answered for Nick. "He wanted to visit some battlefield sites from the war. We stopped at Bau Bang, then we went to Cau Tham Rot. He paid his respects and saluted all the fallen soldiers, on both sides."

Dung read Nick's travel permit. "Ah ha!" he exclaimed. "Your permit says, Vung Tau, Nha Trang, Da Nang, Hue, and Hanoi. But it does not say Song Be province. You are here illegally. Now you will have to be punished." Nick and Vy exchanged worried looks. "You must sign a confession of your crimes! Then we will put you before a people's tribunal to determine your fate."

He motioned to the man next to Nick, who began writing something in Vietnamese in a notebook. When he finished he showed it to Dung for approval. Dung handed it to Nick with a pen and a menacing scowl. "You sign this now!" he ordered.

Nick tried to read it but could not decipher more than 10 percent of it. He shrugged and handed it back. "I cannot understand this."

"You sign!" he screamed in Nick's face.

But Nick calmly shook his head. "I'm sorry, but I cannot sign what I don't understand."

"But you speak Vietnamese!" cried Captain Dung.

"Yes, but reading it is still difficult. Besides, his handwriting is terrible. It looks like Chinese."

This insult infuriated the author, who was medium height, lean, and sinewy with sunken cheeks and old acne scars. He came off of his stool and stood over Nick with his right hand on the grip of his pistol.

"You sign now!" the policeman ordered.

Nick looked up and shook his head slowly. "I'm sorry, but I cannot."

Captain Dung looked around the room at each of his men. He turned and said something to Vy that Nick did not understand, but he saw the fear in Vy's eyes. "*Anh* Nick. The captain says that we are under arrest and must go to the jail in Ben Cat." Nick felt the adrenaline surging in his body. He knew that once they had him behind bars, they could keep him forever, just like the POWs. He immediately focused on his only three options. He could go along peacefully and trust fate or God to get him out. Or, he could run… Or, he could fight.

At once he discarded the first two options. He had never been big on trust because it had to be earned, not given. The war had taught him that the only one he could really trust was himself. So many of his friends had believed in God but ended up in body bags anyway. Secondly, being the only white man between Lai Khe and Ho Chi Minh City, made running a suicidal choice. And they already had his passport. He quickly surveyed everyone's position in the room. He knew that officers usually carried a snub nosed .38 in their pouches. Pretending to stretch, he leaned forward ever so slightly and glanced into Dung's open pouch on the table. He could see no gun. Perhaps Dung wasn't carrying one. All the better. The mean one, on his left, wore a holstered 9mm right next to Nick's left hand. Just before leaving Maui, Mark had showed him one just like it. Nick tried desperately to recall where the safety was located in case it was on.

Jab left elbow into his ribs. Backfist punch to the head. Use right hand to pull out the gun. Chamber a round. Kill him first, then the other two on his right. The unarmed captain last. I think I'm fast enough to kill them all, he thought, but what if I'm not? His breath became quick and shallow as he prepared himself to die.

Nick saw Dung watching him intently, with a sly, knowing smile on his face. Nick decided to confirm the situation with Vy before he made his move. "Vy. Did you say they are going to put us in jail?"

Vy shook his head. "Not in jail. We are only under arrest. They want us to go to the police station in Ben Cat."

Nick came back from the dark and evil place. He nodded and looked back at Dung. "OK. We go."

Captain Dung kept smiling. He looked into Nick's eyes and brought up his hands and a .38 snubnose from beneath the table. He eased down the hammer, and slid it slowly into his pouch. It had been pointing directly at Nick's balls. Nick returned his own sly smile, but tinged with respect.

As they all climbed onto their motorcycles, Nick thought of the irony of surviving the war only to be killed beneath the big tree, twenty-five years after his tour of duty had ended.

When they arrived at the large colonial building in Ben Cat they dismounted and were led to an old mildew-streaked concrete bunker. It had a big, heavy, and well-rusted iron door with bars in the window. Nick peered in and saw the dirt floor and walls scribbled with Vietnamese graffiti. The mean cop gestured for Nick and Vy to go in. Nick was outraged. "Goddamn it, Vy! What's this bullshit? You said no jail!"

Vy talked briefly with the cop. "He says it is only temporary. Do not worry."

Nick suddenly grew calm. It was OK now. It all came back to him. Fuck it! Don't mean nothin'! All of it, every bit of it. Life. Death. Meaningless. It's inevitable. If there IS any meaning, then it is not when you die, but how you die that matters. I will die now, and I will die free. Outside those walls, not behind them. I will embrace my death and rejoice in it. He turned and put his face up against that of the mean one, with dead-pan eyes full of acceptance. He would call his bluff the only way he knew how. "If you want me in there, you must kill me here first."

Nick watched the eyes of the mean one fill with fear and confusion. He was not prepared for this. It had not been in his policeman's training manual about how to deal with stubborn American war veterans who came back to Vietnam and refused to follow the rules. The satisfaction of this small victory warmed Nick's insides.

After watching the man squirm for a moment, Nick decided to give him an out. He patted the mean one's wet shoulder. "It is OK. We will accompany you to your office and remain there as long as it takes to solve this problem. *Duoc khong*?" The mean one sighed with relief and led the way.

When they all trudged in out of the rain and sat at a long wooden table on the tiled floor, Captain Dung appeared and began yelling. "Why didn't you lock them up?" he cried.

"He said I would have to kill him," came the embarrassed reply. Dung sat down next to Vy, across the table from Nick and the three others, much the same as before.

Seeing Dung glaring at Nick's hat, Vy leaned over and grabbed the hat off of Nick's head and slapped it down on the table. Seeing that reminder of their sworn enemy had only infuriated the police further. Nick was not going to let it go.

He stood and pulled off his rain-soaked jacket and lay it next to his hat, exposing the same flag on his VVM shirt, right over his heart. He smiled innocently at Dung, who now returned the smile, but honed with the threat of vengeance. "Are you hot?" Dung asked sarcastically.

Nick saw Vy shaking his head in disgust. He wondered which side Vy would take if it came down to it. Vy lives here. He cannot afford to make trouble with the authorities. He has a wife and family. What do I have to lose? My life maybe, but not my pride. Then again, I came here to make peace, not trouble. And besides, they have all the guns. He passed out more cigarettes and said, "Captain, if I may, I would like to show you something." Dung nodded. Nick pulled out his plastic bag again and produced the damp photograph of Alan Roth and his former VC friend. "This man is named Le Hoang Nghia. He invited me to come to Song Be to discuss agricultural development for the province. That is my specialty."

Dung took the picture and his eyes immediately bulged. "*Troi dat oi! Ong Nghia day!*" he exclaimed, and passed it around to his men. Nick could feel the tension drain out of the room. They even giggled with relief. Being the only white farmer in the Japanese-run cooperative back on Maui had taught Nick that the worst thing you could do to an Asian man was to make him lose face. The police had overcommitted themselves and were too embarrassed to back down. This was their way out. A tray with tiny cups and hot tea appeared. Everyone was all smiles. Dung toasted his new-found guests. "Why didn't you say so before?" he said with a reprimanding smile. They all laughed self-consciously.

Nick saw an opening. "You know, Captain. In America, when we are arrested, we are allowed one phone call to ask a friend or a lawyer to help us. Would you please demonstrate to us that Vietnam has the same compassion for its prisoners and allow me to make a call?"

Dung thought for a moment. "Who do you wish to call?"

"The person at Vietnam Tourism who told me that I could visit Song Be province as long as I returned to the city before dark. Her name is Pham Thai Thanh. This is her number."

Dung went to his desk in the corner and picked up the antique dial phone. After a ten-minute wait for the various connections to go through, Dung finally yelled into the receiver. "Hello! Pham Thai Thanh? This is Captain Dung of the Song Be police! Do you know an American named Nick Dwyer? Yes, we have arrested him and his friend! He says you gave him permission to come here!" There was a long silence as Dung listened to Thanh for what seemed like about five minutes. Nick watched his face intently. Dung began replying with, *"Roi! Roi!"* Nick knew this was equivalent to a soldier saying, "Yes, sir!" to a superior. Then Dung hung up and made another call. When he returned to the table he ordered more tea. "Please make yourselves comfortable. We must wait for someone. He will decide what to do next."

After more smoking, tea drinking, and even cordial conversation, Nick heard a booming male voice from behind, in perfect English. "Good afternoon, gentlemen! Sir, are they treating you well?" And in walked an elderly, but brawny, Vietnamese man in a blue rain jacket and slacks that matched his gray hair. He extended his hand and shook Nick's warmly. "I am Colonel Nguyen Dang Linh, of the People's Army."

Nick introduced himself and Vy. "I'm sorry sir, but you speak English with no accent. Where did you learn?"

Colonel Linh laughed heartily. "I received my master's degree in engineering from Denver University in 1970. Now, tell me why you are here. I understand you know Mr. Nghia."

"Actually, I was invited here through a mutual friend to help this province with agricultural development. I also came to help the Lai Khe school and orphanage. Later we plan to participate in the Hanoi-to-Ho Chi Minh City Peace Walk that another Lai Khe veteran is organizing. We want to initiate the reconciliation process between our two countries."

Linh beamed a genuinely appreciative smile. "That is wonderful, and I wish you great success, but there is this matter of today that we must rectify. We need you to sign a confession of your breaking our laws before we can release you."

The weight returned to Nick's mind. "I already explained to them that Vietnam Tourism gave me permission to come here. What is the problem?"

"If you won't confess your crime, then we must hold you. But don't worry, not in jail, there is a small hotel here. You will stay there under guard until we can consult with Mr. Nghia."

Nick thought carefully. "Can I write an explanation in English?"

"Why, yes! Yes, of course! That would be wonderful! Please!" He motioned for pen and paper. Nick grinned over at Vy and began writing.

"To the people of Song Be province: I am an American veteran who has returned to Vietnam to make peace. I did not intend to break any laws or to make trouble. I only wanted to help the people here and to close the gap between our countries. I apologize for any misunderstanding." Nick signed his name.

"Excellent! Excellent!" cheered Colonel Linh triumphantly. He handed the paper back to Captain Dung. "Now, you may go back to Ho Chi Minh City as soon as you wish. But there is one personal favor I would like to ask of you."

Nick raised one eyebrow suspiciously.

Linh's voice dropped to barely a whisper. "Do you know anyone in ODP?"

"Yes, actually I do," Nick replied.

Linh could not contain himself. "This is my IV number. Can you please investigate what is the status of my immigration request? I and my family have been trying to go to the U.S. for three years already."

Nick tried hard not to show his shock, as well as amusement, at the idea of a communist officer trying to emigrate to the land of his enemy. He stood and shook hands. "I will do what I can," he assured the colonel.

As he and Vy bid farewell to the policemen, Nick realized he had no more cigarettes. Captain Dung sprang back to his desk and handed Nick four of his own *Jet*-brand smokes for their return trip. He smiled at Nick while obviously searching for a word in his mind. "A souvenir!" he offered, laughing.

Nick shook his hand. "Don't worry, Captain. Today I have MANY souvenirs."

Two hours later they pulled up, wet and shivering, in front of the Bong Sen. Nick reached into his wallet and gave Vy a long hug.

"Here is something to help with the gas and... all the trouble. Thank you, Vy."

Vy stared down at the soggy one-hundred-dollar bill in his hand. "It wasn't that much trouble."

Nick grinned and called back over his shoulder, "It could have been."

Nick sprinted into the lobby, but the man at the desk pointed upstairs. Nick grinned broadly and flew into the elevator. He pounded on his door and heard movement inside as the chain was released. Hang opened the door and leaped into his arms. "Oh, my God! You are so wet and cold! Come take off those clothes, and we will have a hot shower!"

Nick kissed her passionately before putting her down. "Yes we will!" he agreed. He eagerly began stripping off his rain-soaked shirt and fought with his belt. He was startled by the phone ringing loudly on his desk. He kissed Hang quickly again and picked up the receiver.

Alan's voice seemed very far away. "Where the hell have you been? I've been calling all day."

"In jail."

"What? Are you OK?"

"Yeah. Thanks in part to that photo of you and Mr. Nghia. It's a long story."

Alan laughed, "All your stories are long. Listen, I checked out those dog tags. They're all bogus. Sorry."

Nick sighed. "I figured they would be, but I had to try."

"Yeah, I know. Well, stay in touch and out of jail, you bastard."

"Thanks, Alan." He turned back to Hang, who stood naked in the bathroom doorway. "Now, where were we?"

The next morning came washed in sunshine. Old women swept the sidewalks with their short leaf brooms. Beggars clung like leeches to Nick and Tim. Exasperated, Nick shook them off and pointed at Tim limping along behind. "He's got all the money!" he said smirking.

"Oh, thanks a lot, Nick!" Tim called sarcastically with the poor wretches clutching his paralyzed arm and chanting their begging songs.

They walked with Hang to the Palace Hotel for breakfast and met Mot on the way. They invited him to join them. Over eggs and coffee they all decided to visit Vung Tau for a few days, and Mot readily volunteered to have Lai drive them down in his old Peugeot.

CHAPTER 47
Vung Tau
August 1991

The following morning they all met on the curb by the Bong Sen. Thuy apparently had decided that Tim might just be her ticket to the U.S. after all. She was all fake smiles and ass wiggling, but Nick had to admit she was entertaining. The unlikely group crammed into Lai's old car and one just like it driven by his friend for a three day in-country R&R.

Suddenly Nick saw Mr. Song's face peering at him through the window. He let Song see his disgust as he rolled down the window. "What the hell do you want?" Nick demanded.

Song registered shock at Nick's direct insult then humbly asked, "Did you check out the information I gave you?"

"Yeah, I checked it out, and they are all phony names! You wasted my time! Now get away from me, or I'll kick your scrawny little ass!" He yelled. Tim glowered out of the other car at Song in support of Nick.

But Song protested. "No! No! Mr. Dwyer. My information is correct. Please!"

"Forget it!" Nick retorted. "I'm not interested in dog tags. But there is a two-million-dollar reward for live POWs. If you get information on that, then you contact me."

Song's eyes popped open in shock. He was momentarily stunned. "Why, yes, yes!" he stammered. "I will look into it immediately. I will…" His voice trailed off as Lai pulled away from the curb, and Nick waved him off. It was time for fun, and Nick felt light and carefree as the cool breeze swept in through the open window. He sucked in the street smells and revelled in their foreignness. He was free and alive and in love. He felt that he was beginning the best part of his whole life.

Nick was amazed at how well Hang fit in with the others—like a life-long friend. She and Mot kept everyone laughing with their antics and jokes. It was the happiest time that Nick had ever had in Vietnam.

They arrived on Le Loi Street before he knew it. They checked into the Hoa Binh Hotel, where he had stayed in 1989, and went up to their rooms. Nick and Hang were given a large three-room suite, while Tim and Thuy had the usual studio.

Tim came banging on their door. "Nick, can you talk to Thuy? She's all pissed off because our room is so small." Nick and Hang went across the hall and had a look.

Hang held his hand and spoke quietly. "Honey *oi*. Let's trade rooms with them. We have real love. They don't. OK?"

Tim patted Nick on the shoulder, while Thuy broke out in a real smile. "Thanks Hang, for saving the day."

After Tim and Thuy left, Nick took out his tape cassette that he had brought from Maui. On it were many songs that somehow reminded him of Vietnam during the war. Not the words, really. But the melodies. That mellow Motown sound. He inserted it into the tape player that came with every hotel room in those days. He sat with Hang on the balcony and listened to "Are You Ready?" and "For the Rest of Our Lives, Love Always." They began singing together as Nick held her close and they gazed out over the bay.

"I love this song," she said as she lay her head on his shoulder. "I think from now on, it will be our song. Is that OK?"

"It is more than OK. Yes, it will be our song, for the rest of our lives…"

That evening's plan was to meet down on the terrace for dinner. The girls were slow to get themselves together, so Tim and Nick went down first for a quick beer while they waited. As Nick ordered he noticed that Tim seemed reticent. "What's up, brah? You look distracted."

Tim looked over shyly and said. "Thuy just came out and asked me point blank if I would marry her and take her to the U.S. She said her family would pay me. Then, once she got there, we would divorce. I don't know, Nick. What the fuck, over?"

"Are you serious, man?" Nick was angry but not surprised.

"Yeah, that's what she said. What should I do?"

"Fuck that bitch! That's what!"

Tim laughed. "Well, yeah, I've been trying! But she won't go for it!"

"Listen. When we get back to the city, dump her. You don't need that shit. We'll find you a better one. OK?"

"OK. Thanks, man. So tell me about your adventure the other day. What happened, anyway?"

Nick gave him the short version. Then, "You know, Tim, two years ago I sat right over there at that table with a bunch of Aussie vets and two VC colonels. We ate and drank together and talked from our hearts about the war. By the end of the night we were like brothers. But the other day, up in Lai Khe... those bastards! There was absolutely no forgiveness or acceptance."

Tim smiled faintly, "I don't think the police are in the forgiveness business. They probably just figured you were a CIA spy or something. They did their job, that's all." He gulped some beer. "I think it's like that Tai Chi symbol. There's a little bad in the best of us and a little good in the worst of us, but nobody is pure one or the other."

Nick lit a cigarette. "Yeah? Well, since when did you get so goddamn understanding?"

Tim shrugged, "I don't know. Maybe lying naked on the floor of the shower, puking and squirting shit all over the walls, helped me to see the world in a new light." They clunked cans and growled with laughter.Tim frowned. "You should quit those damn things, man. They're gonna kill you."

Nick shook his head and exhaled. "You know, those years that they say smoking and drinking take off of your life? They don't come off the beginning or the middle. They come off the END! They can have those fucking years in a wheelchair!" Tim roared with laughter. Then Nick took a pull on his 333 beer. "Anyway, like I was saying. There was no forgiveness or acceptance."

Tim got a far-away look in his eyes. "I remember once, in the war. We were up by the DMZ. It was just before Tet 1968. We got pinned down in this rice paddy, and it was pounding rain for days. The sky was so low that choppers couldn't even get in. We had no food, or clean water, and we were running out of ammo. We hid behind the flooding paddy dikes, and every time we raised up to take a breath we got shot at. It was like, drown or get shot. We lay submerged in water for three days. When we had piss or take a shit, we just did it in our pants. I guess that gave me a new perspective on things too."

Nick was confused. "So, what's all that got to do with forgiveness?"

"Nothing," replied Tim. "But it sure taught me a lot about acceptance." Nick nodded and stared out at the sunlight sparkling on the sea.

After the girls arrived, they enjoyed a steak dinner with fries, salad, and bread. The contrast between the two couples was increasingly obvious. Thuy kept her distance from Tim, although she pretended to care for him by cutting up his steak into small pieces and even feeding him occasionally. Hang and Nick stared dreamily into each others eyes and were so enamored that Tim and Thuy felt awkward. They called it a night and retired early.

In the morning, Mot and Lai picked them up and drove them along Front Beach beneath the ironwood trees. Nick directed them to turn north along VC Hill, until he recognized the small tree-lined lane. They turned in and parked in front of the sign that read "Friendship Clinic—Built by American veterans in 1989." Nick posed proudly next to it as Hang took his picture. Behind him stood the completed building that he had helped to build a year and a half before.

A young Vietnamese woman in a nurse-uniform came out of the front door and graciously invited them into the waiting room. When Nick explained who he was, she giggled excitedly and scurried away to an adjoining office. She returned with a small elderly man with glasses and a huge smile. "My name is Doctor Lam, and I am so glad to meet you!" he exclaimed while shaking hands. "Please sit down and share a cup of tea with us!" He seemed quite honored to be receiving a visit from this delegation and wanted to adhere to the universal protocol, which always began with the tea ceremony. As the nurse poured the golden liquid, Doctor Lam eyed the pack of Marlboros in Nick's pocket. Nick sighed quietly and offered him one. They both smoked while the others sipped from the tiny cups. "Have you come to bring us medical supplies?" The doctor finally asked. "Mr. Fredy promised us that he would send us supplies periodically."

"No, I'm sorry we didn't." Nick replied. "I just wanted to show my friends the clinic."

"Yes, yes. We are so grateful to all of you veterans who built it for us. Did you know that soon after the grand opening ceremony, the local people's committee came here to remove the sign out front. They did not want the people to know that the clinic was built by Americans. Especially veterans of the war. But I protested, along with some others, and persuaded them to change their minds."

Nick's eyes narrowed. He could feel the heat surging in his chest. He glanced over at Tim whose face also registered the outrage that Nick could feel erupting inside of him. He felt obliged to be the group's spokesman. "But we did all the fund-raising, paid our way here, bought all the materials, and built it ourselves. We only wanted to help open the door between our two countries so we can all make peace."

"Yes, of course. We all know that too. That is what I told the committee. They would look bad if they tried to take credit for all your sacrifices. But they are politicians, yes? They only think of themselves. Is it the same in America?"

Nick took a deep breath. "Yeah. I guess it is," he admitted. "But thank you for supporting us. I will tell Fredy about it."

After tea, Dr. Lam gave them a brief tour of the clinic and they were gratified to see several patients being attended to. Nick and Tim both kept a lookout for Caucasian patients but saw none.

After bidding the staff farewell they drove out to Back Beach for a seafood lunch in one of the open-air restaurants with sand drifts on the tile floors. The brown waves broke long on the dirty beach. The powerful stench of rotting fish could not be dispelled by the tepid breeze coming in off the sea. During a lull in the conversation Nick could still see Lieu running gaily through the surf, dark-skinned breasts bouncing in her bikini. Then the vision faded, and he could see only Hang's beautiful face smiling at him quizzically, as if she knew.

He returned to the now, smiled back, and grasped her tiny hand. How ironic is the course of fate, he thought. These last few days especially. The here-and-now in direct contrast with the there-and-then. How could I have ever guessed, twenty-five years ago, that I would someday be arrested inside Lai Khe, and to be sitting here on Back Beach where I met her, but now with another woman. I'm getting a second chance. But this time I will do it right.

It did not take the beggars long. They seemed to always sense when rich foreigners were nearby. First, there was the young woman, with a dirt-streaked face, tattered clothes, and a desperate look in her eyes. She held a baby boy in her skinny arms. The baby's head was thrown back, with milky-white eyes rolling uncontrollably in his head. "You! You!" she pleaded with an outstretched grimy hand. She pointed at the baby again. "You! You!" Mot and Lai tried to gently shoo her away and said something in Vietnamese, but she would not budge. Tim looked over at Nick for a clue. Nick shrugged and exhaled loudly.

Tim seemed exasperated. He was not yet accustomed to the constant harassment wherever they went. He reached into his shirt pocket with his good hand and pulled out some small bills that he kept there for this very purpose. "Here! Use birth control next time, goddamn it!" he yelled. The woman bowed and slunk away out towards the beach where some vendors were cooking food on their portable charcoal fires.

Hang smiled at Tim and patted his paralyzed arm. "Thank you, Tim, for helping my people. We are very poor."

Tim grinned begrudgingly and took a swig of beer. No sooner had he set down the bottle than a middle-aged man in army fatigues and missing a leg hobbled in the doorway from the road and leaned on their table. "You! You!" he begged. Again with his hand out and a pouting face. Now it was Nick's turn.

"Here!" he said in English. "Talk to your local VA, like we do! You won the war, after all!" The man smiled meekly, but took Nick's money and limped triumphantly out the door. Nick called after him, "You people need to study more English so you can beg properly, by God!" He watched the old veteran dragging through the sand. "Shit, Tim! Maybe you could go around here begging for money. You're more fucked up than a lot of them are!" He and Tim laughed and toasted each other. Hang shook her head at their demented humor and studied the men curiously as if wondering what she had gotten herself into, but still with love in her eyes.

Two days later they returned to Ho Chi Minh City and checked back in at the Bong Sen. They prepared to say goodbye to Thuy, Mot, and Lai in the lobby.

"*Anh* Ly. When will you go north?" asked Mot.

"Tomorrow morning, my friend."

"When you come back?"

Nick looked at Hang's worried face. He stroked her cheek. "I don't know Mot, but I will come back. Tim and I will leave from Hanoi and fly back to Bangkok. After that…"

Hang put her small arms around his waist and buried her face in his chest. He glanced over at Tim, whose eyes brimmed with compassion as he watched Hang begin to cry. Nick lifted her chin to face him. "Would you like to go with us?"

She smiled through her tears and grabbed him tightly, nodding happily. "Yes, but I cannot go to Bangkok. I must return here after Hanoi, if you can help me. I have no money."

Nick laughed. "Of course!" And they all cheered. Nick patted her on the butt. "You go home and pack. Mot, can you and *Anh* Lai please take her, then bring her back when she's ready?"

"*Duoc cho!*" laughed Mot. "But Ly. Do you promise to come back someday soon? I think now you have a good reason."

Nick nodded emphatically. "I promise! But you know me, Mot. I always come back."

Tim yawned and stretched as best he could with one arm. "OK. I'm going up for a nap, then I'll pack."

Nick patted his shoulder. "I'll be over at Thanh's office to finalize everything. This will be a great trip, brother!"

Minutes later he strolled in the door and saw Thanh at her desk. She was talking quietly with a long, lanky Vietnamese man dressed in grey slacks and a white silk short-sleeved shirt. He had a rice-bowl haircut and sunken cheeks. To Nick, he had NVA written all over him. He stood and extended his hand while towering over Nick. He was at least six foot two.

Thanh smiled, "Nick, this is *Anh* Cuong. He will be your driver on your trip to Hanoi."

"*Chau anh.*" Nick greeted him with a firm grip. It was returned with a calloused hand. This man is tough, thought Nick.

Cuong's smile seemed real, and there was a gentleness in his eyes. "*Za. Chau ang. Ang biet noi tieng Viet khong?*" came the strong northern accent.

Nick nodded and smiled at Thanh. "*Anh ay la nguoi bac phai khong?*"

"Yes, he is also from Hanoi. We have been friends for a long time. He does not speak any English, but you speak our language well enough. And Cuong is a really good guy. You should have a good time. And where is Mr. Tim?"

"He's packing. Here is the money to cover the trip. Could I please have a receipt?"

"Yes, of course." She bent over a receipt book of ultra-thin paper and carbons.

"By the way. I will be bringing a girl with me. I hope that won't be a problem."

"What? What girl?" Nick sensed anger, perhaps even a hint of jealousy.

"Her name is Hang. I'm afraid we have fallen in love."

Thanh took a breath to calm herself. Then she chastised him "You Americans fall in love too easily."

Nick laughed under his breath. "Yeah, but maybe it's better than never falling in love at all."

Thanh shook her head and said something with a sneer to Cuong. "It is against regulations for Vietnamese nationals to ride in government vehicles, Nick. But knowing you as I do... You're going to do it your way, no matter what. Right?"

Nick grinned victoriously. "It's the only way to live. What time tomorrow?" he looked at Cuong who looked to Thanh.

"Eight o'clock. In front of your hotel. And have your girlfriend bring her papers to show *Anh* Cuong," She handed Nick his receipt. Their fingers touched briefly and she pulled away. "Will we ever see you again?"

"Oh yeah. In English we say, I'll keep coming back like a bad check."

Thanh looked puzzled. "I don't understand that. Is it like a recurring nightmare?"

Nick grinned and winked at her as he turned away. "Close enough." He walked out the door into the afternoon heat. Yeah, this place is full of recurring nightmares, he thought.

CHAPTER 48
Highway One
August 1991

The next morning was cloudy and cool. They loaded their bags into the trunk of Cuong's Ford sedan while Nick made introductions and Hang showed Cuong her ID. Nick looked around when he heard Mot calling his name. Mot unstrapped a small package on his little black Honda. He bowed to Hang and Tim while beaming his perpetual smile. Mot handed it to Nick with both hands. "*Anh* Ly, I have a little souvenir so you won't forget me."

Nick stared at it appreciatively then gently placed it on the rear seat. "*Cam on, Anh Mot*. But you know I will never forget you!" He glanced over at Mot's decrepit motorbike, reached into his jeans pocket and pulled out a hundred-dollar bill. "Here is a little something to help repair your Honda. It has traveled many kilometers and given us some happy memories, yes?"

Mot grinned. "Yes. Many good souvenirs. Thank you, Ly! And remember your promise! OK?"

"OK." Nick hugged the short man tightly, then let him go and turned quickly to join Hang in the back of the car. Cuong started the motor. Nick unwrapped the package and saw another black lacquerware ashtray. This one was shaped like a globe on a stand and tilted on its axis. The gold engraved letters read, "*Anh* Ly and *Chi* Hang. Love each other, OK! Your friend Mot. Aug. 21, 1991."

Hang pulled his face down and began to kiss away the tears. "Don't worry, my darling. You will see him again. Right?"

Nick smiled and whispered. "I'll see you both again." Then he caught a glimpse of Cuong's curious eyes in the mirror looking quickly away. Tim climbed into the shotgun seat. "You know, Tim? This is one of the toughest places on Earth to say goodbye."

"How come?"

"I guess everything is more intense here. The tastes, smells, memories. The best and the worst of everything. I'm more alive here, you know?"

Tim turned back to the front and gazed out the windshield at the passing sights of Ho Chi Minh City. "Yeah, Nick. I DO know. When you risk your whole life for a place and its people, you become a part of it like nowhere else. And it becomes a part of you, whether you like it or not."

Nick nodded and squeezed Hang's hand. "Welcome home, brother."

Tim turned back slightly. "Welcome home, Nick."

They spent the overcast morning fighting their way through the relentless horn-blowing, swerving, dodging, speeding, and braking insanity of everyday Vietnamese traffic. By noon they finally eased out into the rubber plantations of Xuan Loc. Hang rested her head on Nick's lap and slept peacefully while Tim and Nick chatted sporadically. Cuong concentrated on driving. Then Nick spotted the sign that said Gia Ray 12 km. He automatically thought of Big John again, and for some reason told Tim the story of the 1965 ambush. The pain of the memories was muted by the newfound love in his heart and the growing peace in his mind.

On the coast, they stopped at a seaside restaurant in Phan Thiet and enjoyed an aromatic seafood lunch. When the food arrived, Hang grabbed her chopsticks and placed generous portions on everyone else's plate before taking any for herself. Tim and Nick washed it down with beer. Hang and Cuong had Coca-Cola.

Back out on Highway One, Cuong gassed the old Ford and sped them on to Nha Trang, bouncing and careening around huge potholes. The shoulder of the road was pitted by many ancient bomb craters, now filled with rainwater. They passed ox carts, motorbikes, large trucks and buses. On the right side of the car they stared out at the shimmering blue South China Sea. Before sunset they pulled into the fresh and breezy town of Nha Trang with long, wide, white-sand beaches and checked into the Vien Dong Hotel.

The next morning rose quietly with soft sunlight streaming in through an open window. A salty breeze stirred the lacy curtains. They lay naked on top of the sheets with Hang's head lying on Nick's arm.

"Do you know this song?" she asked, and began to sing. " Dre-e-e-e-eam, dream dream dre-eam. Dre-e-e-e-eam, dream dream dre-eam. When I want you, in my arms, when I want you, and all your charms, whenever I want you, all I have to do is dre-e-e-e-eam."

Nick joined in, "I can make you mine, taste your lips of wine, anytime, night or day, only trouble is, gee whiz, I'm dreamin' my life away."

She kissed him sensually and stroked the morning stubble on his chin. "Yes, but I think right now the dream is coming true." She sat up in bed. "Where will we go on this trip?"

"Tomorrow we will go to DaNang, then up over Hai Van pass to Hue. After that we'll go to Dong Ha, and I will take Tom back to the place along the Cua Viet river where he got shot during Tet 1968. We also can visit Khe Sanh and go over to the Ho Chi Minh trail on the Laotian border. Then we return to DaNang and fly up to Hanoi. Cuong will meet us there with the car."

"Why don't we drive up with him?" she asked.

"He says the road is very rough. They have been unable to repair it after all the American bombings destroyed it in the war."

"OK. What we do in Hanoi?"

"Do you remember me telling you about my friend from the war, Fredy Champagne?"

Hang nodded, "Of course. You helped him and the other veterans build the clinic in Vung Tau."

"Right. He is organizing a peace walk to persuade the U.S. to lift the trade embargo against Vietnam and to normalize relations. He asked me to join them."

Hang nodded thoughtfully. "I think this Fredy is a very good man." She kissed him again. "I think you are a very good man too."

"Don't be so sure. There are many people who would argue with you about that."

"I don't care. As long as you are faithful to me. But if you are ever unfaithful, I will kill you, or maybe I will cry." She smiled.

He laughed. "I think better if you cry. Now, get dressed. We are going to visit my mother today."

"What? Where is your mother?"

"Her name is Kauthara. She is in the Tap Ponaga on a hill next to the river."

"I don't understand. You mean the Cham pagoda?"

"Yes. When I visited there in 1987 I went inside and bowed down to her statue and asked her to help me find Lieu. I told you the story, remember?"

"Yes."

"Now I must go and thank her. It is the right thing to do."

They climbed the ancient stone steps past dozens of chanting beggars and others suffering from all types of afflictions. Tim limped and struggled awkwardly behind them but grinned happily through the pain, refusing a helping hand from Cuong. Nick kept looking back to watch his progress. "You OK, Tim?"

"No worries." Tim laughed. "I'm looking for a spot to set up my own begging station."

Nick handed out random offerings of small change to the beggars. At the top, Nick led them to the crumbling ruins of the eight-hundred-year-old red brick pagoda. They marveled at its unique design, basically a square shape, perched upon a brick foundation, with external arched doorways on all sides. The walls rose straight up 20 feet to the first of five tiers with successively decreasing dimensions and ornate carved stone corner pieces. The front door, led into a pitch-black chamber. At the entrance sat an old man in a brown shirt and slacks. He wore wire rimmed glasses and a perpetual, gentle smile. Nick returned the smile and reached out both his hands. The old man took them in his and studied Nick curiously. When Nick's smile broadened the old man laughed and wagged a finger at him.

"I remember you!" he said in Vietnamese. "You come here long ago and worship Kauthara, right?"

"Yes. In 1987. You remember, eh?"

"Of course. I have never seen a white man bow down to Kauthara and cry from his heart, until you came that day. You asked her for help, in Vietnamese. You were sincere. I have never seen such a thing."

"And I had never done such a thing, until that day. But after I left, she did help me. I came to give her an offering of gratitude. Is that OK?"

The old man patted Nick's shoulder, and stretched out his hand to the darkened step. Nick kicked off his tennis shoes and turned to the others. "There is something I have to do alone first, then you can all come in if you want. OK?"

They nodded silently. Nick bowed to the doorway and stepped over the primeval stone threshold that had been worn halfway through by centuries of bare feet.

The overpowering aroma of incense and sweat and ripened fruit poured over him as he slowly dropped to his knees on the grass mats. It took his eyes a moment to adjust to the steamy darkness. Smoke rose in thin streams from joss sticks in an urn of sand. He took three sticks and lit them with his Zippo. Holding them with both hands above his head, he bowed to the benevolent statue, who was adorned with flowing garments and a shroud. Strands of beads were draped around her neck, and when Nick looked up at her eyes, it seemed like she was watching him.

He felt the syrupy air stir slightly as the old man slipped past him and took up his position by the gong. Nick bowed three times. The old man struck the gong three times. Nick placed the incense in the urn and spoke in Vietnamese as best he could. "Thank you, mother, for helping me when I came to you four years ago. It was the beginning of my long journey to find peace. I am still on it. But now I have another request. Will you please help me to find the three things that I need in my life?"

Kauthara waited patiently.

"Acceptance, forgiveness, and unconditional love."

Kauthara's face beamed in the blackness. Nick felt her presence enfolding him. A calm came over him as streams of sweat trickled down his face. Nick placed the bills in the offering tray and bowed for the last time. "*Da. Cam on, Me.*"

He stood and bowed to the old monk and stepped back out into the light of day. Hang's loving arms reached out to hold him. He noticed the two tall men watching them with astonished expressions. Tim's face reflected envy. Cuong was awed.

Nick waited while the three of them went in to pay their respects. The old monk came out with them. His hands were full of exotic fruit from the altar. He handed them to Nick. "Your heart may have pain. But it is a good heart. I hope to meet you again."

Nick grinned. "I promise. We will meet again." Then he turned to the others. "How about a beer?"

They returned to the Vien Dong for an afternoon at the beach where they indulged in fresh crab, fruit, sandwiches and, of course, cold beer. Heineken was only fifty cents a can. After drinking several, Tom and Nick vowed to come back and live forever on this beautiful, clean beach.

"This is probably the only place in the world where I can afford to live on my VA disability." Tim said.

Nick nodded. "You know Tim, that's not a bad idea."

Hang dipped a piece of fresh crab into a paste of lemon juice, salt, and pepper, then put it in Nick's mouth.

"I think that is a VERY good idea," she said.

The next morning, Cuong maneuvered the big Ford out onto Highway One and headed north. They crossed the bridge that spanned the river next to the Tap Ponaga. Nick noticed the old guard bunkers at each end of the bridge. They were among the many remnants of the war strewn across the countryside. There were blown-up and abandoned trucks, jeeps, and tanks. Derelict buildings of the former government still stood with bullet-scarred and partially destroyed walls.

They passed a familiar-shaped monument on a knoll. The large sign outside said, "Cemetery for the heroes of the liberation." They had seen them all over Vietnam.

Tim looked back over his shoulder at Nick and sneered, "Yeah! Get some!"

Nick chuckled. "Yeah. If you just go around and count the graves then you would think we won the war."

Tim looked puzzled. "I don't remember seeing any cemeteries for the ARVN, just the VC. How come?"

"You know how it is, Timmy. The victors always get to write the history, even if it's bullshit. The guys who were on our side were just plowed under like the straw from the last rice crop. Like they don't mean nothin'."

Tim shook his head and turned back to the front. His voice was loaded with bitter resignation. "Yeah. It don't mean nothin'. Don't mean a fuckin' thing."

Nick craned his neck to see out the windows. He had never been past this point before, and was curious as to what lay ahead. "I wish I had my map," he said to Tim in English. Then he was shocked when Cuong immediately reached into the console compartment, pulled out his map, and handed it back to Nick.

"Tim. Did you see that?"

"See what, Nick?"

"This dude speaks our lingo, brah. He's been playin' possum."

In the rear-view mirror, Cuong's eyes registered fear. He tried desperately to cover his mistake but only dug himself a deeper hole by saying quickly in Vietnamese, "No! You asked for the map in Vietnamese! I don't speak English!"

"Then how do you know what I just told Tim? You liar! You probably speak English better than we do, by God!" At this, Cuong could only laugh, red faced, as his cover was blown.

Hang seemed puzzled. "Honey *oi*. So what, if he speaks English?"

"Thanh told me he doesn't. So he sits here listening to everything we say and can report it back." Nick had to laugh at Cuong's amateur mistake and also to keep it light to draw Cuong's suspicions away from their real intentions. "Cuong. Admit it. You speak English, right?" The whole car erupted in laughter as Cuong again denied it, in Vietnamese. For the next two days, Tim and Nick spoke in Hawaiian pidgin, or contemporary American slang when in Cuong's company.

After they arrived in DaNang, Nick decided to try an investigation of a local clinic, but needed a cover of his own. "Hey, Cuong. We would like to visit a medical clinic here that treats western patients. Can you help us?" he asked in Vietnamese so as not to rub Cuong's nose in his failed deception.

"Why do you want to do that?" Cuong asked suspiciously.

"We brought some new medications with us, and we want to donate them. Also, we would like to show people back in the U.S. that Vietnam is treating westerners with the same care as their own patients."

"Very good idea," Cuong agreed. "I will ask around and take you this afternoon."

True to his word, Cuong drove them through the outskirts of the city and arrived at a small clinic on a side street. When they got out of the car a young doctor in a white coat appeared and shook hands all around.

"Hello! I am Doctor Bao. What can I do for you?" he greeted them in English.

Nick smiled innocently. "We are American war veterans who have come back to help Vietnam in any way we can. We have brought some new American antibiotics to give you."

"Oh! Yes! Yes! We are very grateful! As you can see, we are very poor." Dr. Bao almost literally wrung his hands.

"We understand that you treat western patients here as well as Vietnamese. Is that true?"

Dr. Thanh nodded tentatively. "Yes, why?"

"We want to show that the Vietnamese have no animosity towards those of us who were involved in the war. May we visit with some of those patients now?"

The good doctor looked uncomfortably at Cuong, then back to the two Americans. "Well, I'm sorry but we don't have any westerners here right now. But if we should ever receive them then you are most welcome to come back."

Disappointed, Nick shook his head. "I'm sorry, but we are leaving tomorrow."

The doctor ushered them all toward the reception room, where an attractive nurse poured the traditional tea.

"Please sit down and enjoy some tea and cigarettes. Then we will be happy to receive the medicine you mentioned."

"Hey Tim, does this movie look familiar?"

"Yeah. Same movie, different theatre."

Nick turned to the doctor. "I'm sorry, doc. No patients, no medicine. Thanks for your time." They walked back to the car while the poor doctor blubbered along behind.

Hang lightly held onto Nick's arm and whispered, "Honey *oi*, why don't you give him the medicine?"

Nick looked down at her beautiful pleading eyes. "Because..." He trailed off. He glanced over at Tim and shrugged. "Cuong *oi*. Can you please open the trunk? "He dug into his pack and pulled out some packs of samples that his doctor friend on Maui had donated. But he saved some for the next clinic. Everyone was all smiles as they waved and drove off in the sunset.

The next morning, Nick helped Cuong load their luggage while Tim got situated in the front passenger seat. A hotel official came out to speak with Cuong and presented a bill of some kind. Cuong looked in at Tim apprehensively then reached in past him and unlocked the glove box. Tim's eyes got huge and he immediately turned back to

Nick and Hang but had to wait until Cuong exited with a handful of money to pay the man. Then he whispered his secret to Nick.

"Nick! He has a gigantic wad of money in there, and a .38 revolver! Who is this guy?"

Nick grinned knowingly. "Only the police are allowed to have guns, brother. Shhh!"

Cuong got in and pulled back out on Highway One. They headed north toward the ancient imperial city of Hue. They soon began a steep ascent over the tall mountains on the coast known as Hai Van Pass. Along the way, Hang asked Nick for some money and had Cuong stop to purchase fresh snacks. One was a wrinkled little fruit called *trai coc*. They dipped it into a mixture of salt and chilli-pepper juice and crunched the fiery concoction while sucking wind noisily through their clenched teeth to alleviate their burning mouths. She also taught Nick and Tim to eat the seeds of the lotus flower and a soft flexible pancake type of sweet bread called *banh phong sua*.

The two American guinea pigs sampled the local fare, chuckled self-consciously, and rolled their eyes at each other. The two Vietnamese smacked their lips and ate ravenously while proclaiming all the health benefits offered by each food.

Tim scoffed under his breath, "I don't know about you, Nick, but I sure wish we could find a McDonald's," he laughed.

Nick agreed, "I heard that. I guess this is like Vietnamese survival training. It always amazes me how these people can find something to eat just about anywhere. If it were up to us, we'd starve to death in no time."

At the top of the pass they were rewarded with a sweeping view, both north and south, as the emerald sea and white-sand beaches stretched away into infinity. Down the other side, the switchback road was quickly covered by dark clouds unleashing a huge downpour. The road was awash with gushing streams across their path. By the time they reached the coast on the north side of the pass, the entire basin was flooding.

Cuong slowed and hunched over the wheel as they plowed through the surging, knee-deep, muddy water. Wind whipped through the dancing ironwoods and wreaked havoc with the many pedestrians forced to wade through the flood pushing bicycles or leading livestock to higher ground. Others sat in doorways smoking or drinking hot tea while laughing helplessly at their plight.

Nick shook his head in admiration. "You know, honey *oi*," he said as he squeezed Hang's tiny hand, "I just don't understand how your people can always smile and laugh no matter what tragedy occurs."

She smiled gently and looked up at him. "What would you have us do? Cry? What good does that do? It is our fate, our destiny, either good luck or bad. We have no control over it. We have no choice but to accept it."

Nick stared deep into her beautiful almond eyes. He smiled, thinking. Well, I did ask Kauthara to teach me acceptance. Perhaps this is lesson number one. He kissed Hang softly and resumed watching the passers-by coping with their world.

When they reached the old Huong Giang Hotel, on the southern bank of the Perfume River, the rain subsided. Nick and Hang checked in and were assigned a room next to Tim's on the third floor. The rooms had balconies overlooking the swollen, muddy green river. Nick immediately noticed the absence of any odor resembling perfume, but found it incredibly romantic none-the-less.

Anh Cuong would again stay in the drivers' rooms and eat separately unless otherwise directed from his passengers. After a lovely dinner at the rooftop restaurant, Tim, Nick, and Hang retired to their rooms and agreed to meet for breakfast the next morning before heading out for a tour of the Minh Mang Tomb and the famous Thien Mu Pagoda.

The morning sun brightened their drive to Vietnam Tourism's office, where a local guide would take over for the tour. She was a very attractive girl, named Mai, in a straw *non la* hat, and a purple *ao dai* dress which certainly caught Tim's eye, and she spoke good English. Before returning for lunch at the hotel, they walked around the ancient temples, gardens, and lagoons where Emporer Thu Duc kept his one hundred concubines. Hang periodically asked Nick for change to buy sodas or trinkets, but he noticed that she never kept a penny for herself.

After lunch, they all walked down to the boat launch on the river. Nick dropped back with Hang and gave her $50 in Dong. "This is for you to spend on whatever you want for yourself. Of course, I will buy everything else as we go along. OK? And please let me know when you need more." The smile she gave to him looked as if he had just handed her a fortune.

She hugged him tightly. "Oh! Thank you very much, honey *oi*! You always take such good care of me!" She literally pranced down the path to the long cabin cruiser that awaited them at the dock. Her dance evoked hearty laughter from Nick, Tim, and Mai.

The green-and-white boat idled out into the river. The captain turned the bow west, into the afternoon sun. The boat was in a state of serious disrepair, peeling paint, standing water on the floor of the main cabin, and black smoke coughing from the aft manifolds. Nick and Tim shared some of their Heinekens with the captain, much to Mai's dismay. She and Hang sipped their iced tea. The three-mile trip ended all too soon. The slightly inebriated skipper rammed the boat into the dock and stumbled forward to secure his craft before the current dragged her off.

Mai walked slowly beside them up the gravel path to the tall, seven-tiered temple. "Welcome to the fabled Thien Mu Pagoda." She said, smiling. Out of nowhere, an old crippled man dressed in rags appeared, with a grimy outstretched hand begging for money. Nick shook his head and turned away. Tim did the same. The old man looked around helplessly then stumbled away.

"It is a very romantic spot, don't you think?" Mai continued. "It is also a very historic place. Like many Buddhist shrines in Vietnam, this represents a symbol of resistance to the American puppet regime of Ngo Dinh Diem in the early 1960s. In here you can see the actual car that drove the venerable Thich Quang Duc to Saigon in 1963, where he committed suicide by self immolation to protest the discrimination of the Diem Regime against Buddhists."

Tim gave Nick a scornful look. "Puppet regime, Nick? Where does this chick get her info?"

Nick shrugged. "Well, actually it was, brah."

Mai continued. "And did you know that during the victorious Tet Offensive in 1968, the head Buddhist monk of Thien Mu was named Thich Don Hau. He was responsible for organizing and directing the communist forces that overran and occupied the Citadel just down river in Hue City." At this, Tim began growling under his breath as he limped off angrily to be alone. "Mr. Nick. What is wrong with your friend?" she asked, genuinely concerned.

Nick let go of Hang's hand and faced her sternly. "Listen, Mai. I know you have a job to do, but do you see how difficult it is for Tim to walk?"

"Yes, of course," she said. "Am I walking too fast for him?"

Nick snorted sarcastically. "He walks that way because, during your 'victorious Tet Offensive,' which, in reality, destroyed the vast majority of the Viet Cong forces, Tim was a U.S. Marine who got shot in the head not far from here on the Cua Viet River. He has been half paralyzed ever since."

"Oh, Mr. Nick, Miss Hang, I am so sorry! I didn't mean..."

"Just show us the sights, but forget about the propaganda from now on, OK?" Nick's face grew red. His breathing was labored. "In fact, why don't you just leave us alone and meet us down at the boat in a little while."

Embarrassed, Mai put her head down and obediently scurried away. Nick left Hang and caught up with his friend. Tim sat on the stone steps of the pagoda, staring down over the slow-rolling Perfume River.

"Hey, I'm sorry Tim. I just gave her shit and told her to fuck off. I hope you're not pissed off at me for my remarks."

"No. Jesus Christ! You're fine. I guess there's still a lot of pain inside me. I didn't really know it 'til now. But I still feel guilty, you know?"

"Guilty? For what?" Nick asked.

"You know, getting shot and never finishing my tour."

"Are you fucking nuts? You feel guilty for getting shot?"

Tim nodded sheepishly. "Hey! I'm a Marine! We always..."

"Shit man!" Nick cut him off. "I feel guilty for NOT getting shot! Do you know how many guys took my place on point and got wasted? Why them, and not me? Over and over again! And I come out with hardly a scratch! Fuck it, brah! Fuck it!"

Tim nodded slowly. "Yeah, but I really don't understand that either, Nick."

Nick took a deep breath. "Yeah, well I bet there's a lot more guys who feel like I do. For example, you remember Kenny Chapman, the chopper pilot that flew for the First Cav? He was in our group at the vet center for a while." He lit a cigarette behind cupped hands and exhaled. "He flew a lot of dustoffs, going into pitched battles to pick up the dead and wounded when nobody else would go. He told me about this one time when he came into a really hot LZ. They were taking heavy machine gun fire from two directions as the grunts loaded the body bags and a few critically wounded into his Huey.

"He said they were taking so many hits that it sounded like a bunch of guys with baseball bats were outside beating on the chopper. As he took off and tried to clear the jungle, his copilot took a round in the head and died immediately. The wounded grunts were lying in the back moaning and screaming with blood running all over the floor.

"The chopper was hit in the hydraulic lines and he was fighting for control as they swerved and dived with smoke pouring out the back. Then he feels this grunt crawling up over the controls and into his lap. He could feel the hot blood pouring down between his legs onto his seat, and the guy was looking him in the face, clutching his arms around Ken's neck. Ken yelled to him, 'Hey! Let go! I'm kinda busy here!'

"The grunt just put his head on Ken's shoulder and says, 'I love you, Mom!' and died right there in his arms… When Kenny finally crash-lands the chopper back in An Khe, they had to pry the dude's arms off of him. Kenny was the only survivor… It haunts him to this day. Fucking guilt!"

The two friends sat in the hot, dripping stillness. The only sound was the buzzing of thousands of unseen insects. Finally, Nick gently crushed out his butt and put it in his shirt pocket so that later he could still smell it and would remember to throw it away.

Tim returned to the present. "Hey! Where's Hang anyway?"

Nick looked around and then spotted her a hundred yards away, quietly and unobtrusively handing the old beggar some folded-up money. Not blatantly or obviously or with some fake gesture of generosity aimed at making herself look good. She gave away what Nick had given her for herself. And right there, Nick knew without question that Le Thi Ngoc Hang was the one.

That evening, Nick and Hang sipped some excellent Bulgarian wine while overlooking the river. They decided that tomorrow would be Tim's day. In the morning, they arranged with Cuong to drive them all up to Dong Ha, where they checked into the dilapidated Hotel Truong Son.

The building was quite old, with streaky green paint, broken louvered windows, and sinks without drain pipes so that everything poured out onto the warped wood-and-tile floor. The cabinets were leaning, with broken doors, and the floors strewn with dirt and miscellaneous rubbish. The AC didn't work. Only cold water trickled from the shower head and disappeared through a hole in the floor which also served as the toilet. Cuong listened patiently to their complaints but insisted that this was Dong Ha's best hotel.

Later, they drove to pick up a local guide who would show them around what used to be called I Corps. On the way, they passed a dusty roundabout built around an abandoned tower bunker from the war. At the base of the tower was the remains of a destroyed American tank. Flying proudly from a pole on top was a red flag with gold star. Passers-by gave them hostile looks.

"It seems the farther north we go, the more unfriendly the people are." Tim said.

Nick nodded, "I see the same thing, brother. And we still have to make Hanoi." They both laughed nervously.

The guide was a Hmong who stood four-foot-seven at the most. The Hmong hill people had been fiercely loyal allies of the U.S. Special Forces during the war. Mr. Duy was employed by the communist government because he spoke excellent English and would be their token representative minority person to show that there was no prejudice in the current government. He seemed very friendly, had a good sense of humor, and kept praising Nick on his fluency in Vietnamese. He began by asking where they wanted to go.

Nick turned to Tim. "Well, brother, this was your AO. Where to?"

Tim was caught off guard and smiled self-consciously. "Really, Nick? Wow! OK. I guess I'd like to visit my old base camp at Camp Carrol, maybe the Rock Pile and Khe Sanh if it's not too far. But most of all I'd really like to go up to the Cua Viet River." His smile faded, replaced by the look. "That's where I got hit." Tim was suddenly lost in the past. He stared beyond the rice paddies along Highway 9-A. Toward the coast where the Cua Viet would feed its load of brown silt into the patiently waiting South China Sea. His jaw slackened and then a deep sigh. He refocused on Nick and Hang. The smile returned. "Is that OK?"

Nick turned to Duy. "Mr. Duy, can we take Tim to the place that changed his life?"

"Yes, of course! But first we head west towards Laos and the Ho Chi Minh Trail." He grinned excitedly and his enthusiasm was immediately contagious.

Tim sat up front with Cuong so he could have a better view. The tiny, balding tour guide kept pointing out sites of interest and beamed proudly as he gestured down into a wooded valley where there lay a small hamlet. "That is my village. We were proud supporters of the victorious communist troops that controlled this area for most of the war."

Nick and Tim exchanged angry looks then sneered openly at Duy who immediately realized his mistake, and changed the subject. "Is anyone hungry? We can stop for lunch any time you like."

They remained silent and cast glares of contempt. Duy was quiet for awhile until Tim chirped up. "Hey, you guys! This is old Camp Carrol!" he announced gleefully.

"Yes, that's right. And how did you know that, Mr. Tim?" Duy inquired.

"I was stationed here in '67 and '68. The camp stretched from here over toward those hills and across this valley. Not the best place for a camp but the Marines got their own way of doin' stuff." Nick watched Tim closely as they got out to stretch their legs and saw Tim's expression change from happy go lucky to the brink of tears.

"Tim, you wanna talk about it, brother?"

The ex-Marine shook his head as he scanned the old perimeter. "It's personal, Nick."

"OK, brah." Nick herded the others away and let Tim have time with his own past. When Tim got back into the car he stared silently ahead until they approached Khe Sanh, where the U.S. Marine base once stood.

Duy deferred to Tim by asking, "Mr. Tim, if you like, you can take over as tour guide here also."

"I was only here once. Just before the siege began. Then we shipped out to the Cua Viet." Tim said.

The group hiked around the grassy plains covered with sparse clumps of shrubs and bushes. Here and there were clusters of Vietnamese people with bicycles, rakes, and shovels. They slowly dug through the laterite clay, unearthing left-over ordinance from the huge battle in 1968 for the last bastion of American power in the area, a barrier intended to halt invading forces from North Vietnam.

The visitors watched skittishly as a middle-aged woman prodded cautiously around an old 105mm Howitzer round, then carefully rolled it into a sling and draped it over her handlebars for a trip to the local pawn shop.

Tim grinned. "Hell of a way to make a living, eh Nick?"

Hang grabbed Nick's arm and pulled him back towards the car. "Honey *oi*! Let's go. I think it is very dangerous here."

Nick bent over and pried a handful of 5.56mm from the mud. Tim found some 7.62mm, and both men stuffed their pockets with the souvenirs.

Duy glanced nervously over at Cuong. He spoke obligingly as the tall man stared at him through the intimidating government-issue sunglasses. "Yes, this was the site of the biggest battle in the Vietnam War." He turned to the Americans and emphasized, "According to communist newspaper, the People's Army inflicted heavy casualties on the Americans here. They killed over twenty-five-thousand of them in a few days."

Nick and Tim howled with laughter at this ridiculous claim. Their expressions held such disdain, Duy squirmed with embarrassment. He repeated with a raised index finger, "I SAY, ACCORDING TO COMMUNIST NEWSPAPER!" Which made the American vets laugh even louder as they high-fived their small victory. Behind his dark glasses, even Cuong seemed humbled and hung his head as they made their way back to the car.

Within an hour, Cuong maneuvered the dust covered sedan across the Da Krong iron bridge that spanned a small river as it wound through the jungle-covered mountains. Duy sat forward in the rear seat. "We are now leaving Vietnam and entering Laos. This road is part of what was once called the Ho Chi Minh Trail. It is a series of winding, interconnected trails, roads, and highways that enabled the North Vietnamese Army to send troops and supplies all the way to Saigon."

Nick and Tim took several deep breaths to settle their nerves. They were seeing first-hand an infamous, feared, and reviled remnant of the war that had cost so many lives, and America its pride, not to mention the veterans their sanity. Nick's skin prickled with electricity. He scanned the sides of the trail furtively and unconsciously felt around his body for a nonexistent weapon.

They drove slowly on. Roadside weeds turned to towering elephant grass whose sharp edges sliced and scratched at the fenders and rooftop. Nothing could have prepared them for the terrifying culmination of their collective fears as they came around a bend. Stretched out as far as they could see was a company-sized group of Vietnamese soldiers in camouflaged fatigues, AK-47's, and pith helmets, all bivouacked along the fringe of the trail.

Even Cuong was shocked and quickly braked next to the first of the soldiers. "*Za. Chao ang. Cho phep di nua khong?*" he asked, smiling meekly.

The rugged face peered into the car at the passengers. He also smiled politely. "What nationality are they?" he asked.

Cuong hesitated briefly. "American. They are both veterans."

At this, Nick and Hang looked into each other's worried eyes. Was this how it would end? Nick wondered. Tim's expression asked the same question. What's to keep them from wasting our asses right here, right now? How easy! They have all the guns.

The NVA stared directly at Nick, who now knew exactly what he had to do. The soldier became Captain Dung, back in Lai Khe.

Nick looked him square in the eye and smiled genuinely but confidently. "*Da. Cho anh,*" he greeted him. With two hands he offered the man his pack of cigarettes. Smiles blossomed all around as the soldier took them and gestured toward his comrades with a questioning look. "Yes, of course!" Nick laughed. He saw Cuong's eyes watching him in the mirror now. Without his dark glasses, the relief was obvious. Nick winked at him. "No sweat, GI!" Within a few minutes they were on their way, and they never looked back.

Hours later they made their way back into Dong Ha. Nick poked Duy's ribs to awaken him. "Hey, Duy. Now it's time to take Tim up to the Cua Viet."

Duy squinted around at the long shadows and the setting sun. "It is too late now. Next time I will take him there," came his rude reply, and he closed his eyes again.

Nick was furious. "Hey! You little sawed-off piece of shit! You promised to take him today! And now we're going, so show Cuong the way!" he commanded.

Of course now he had overcommitted, and Duy had him over a

barrel. "I'm sorry Mr. Nick, but I cannot take him now. You come again sometime, and I will take him. I'm tired now. I go back to sleep."

"It's OK, Nick," said Tim over his shoulder. "It might be a lot to handle after all we've been through today."

"No! Fuck you, Tim! He promised, by God!"

Hang began stroking Nick's neck. "Honey *oi*. Please forget about it and let it go, OK?"

But Nick was into it now. There was no going back. "Cuong! Pull over, right here!"

Cuong obeyed, but with a questioning look on his face. The car came to a halt, Nick reached over the shocked Mr. Duy and opened the door. Nick twisted, shoved, and kicked the little man out onto the shoulder of Highway 9A, slammed and locked the door and ordered Cuong back to the hotel. Duy was left standing in a cloud of red dust, sputtering helplessly in the sunset. They pulled back out into traffic with Nick trying to remember how to breathe again. All eyes were on Nick as Hang playfully slapped his arm.

"You! Beaucoup dinky dau!" She laughed. "Why you do that to him? Now he must walk a long way to get home."

"Fuck him! That's what he gets for lying! "Nick fumed.

The others looked at each other as if making mental notes never lie to Nick.

CHAPTER 49
Hanoi
August 1991

The aging Tupulev 134, with bald tires and pieces of fuselage flapping in the wind, made a hard landing on the bumpy runway of Noi Bai Airport in Hanoi. Nick, Hang, and Tim disembarked down the ladder onto the tarmac and into the single-story terminal. They found *Anh* Cuong waiting jubilantly at the baggage claim. He had driven the car up over the still bombed-out Highway One and had arrived in time to deliver them to the old classic Thang Loi (victory) Hotel. It stood perched on the shore of West Lake on the west side of the city, just over a narrow spit of land from the famed Red River. They checked in to adjacent rooms and planned to meet for dinner in the hotel dining room at seven.

Hang opened the glass doors that led out onto a porch which stood just above the water line. Gentle waves lapped against the concrete pilings below. Nick came up behind her and put his arms around her thin waist. She leaned back into him and he could feel himself hardening against her. She turned suddenly and drew his mouth down. They kissed passionately.

They soon found themselves naked on one of the twin beds, in front of the open doors. They screamed, moaned, and panted as he filled her. They soon climaxed as one. An eternity later, they awoke in the light of the setting sun.

They were immediately stunned to see a long, multidecked boat just yards off their porch. It was headed north. Hard rock music blared from tinny speakers. A huge banner was draped from stem to stern with the words "USA & VIETNAM PEACE WALK—AUGUST 1991" emblazoned in red, white, and blue across it. Dozens of people were drinking, dancing, laughing lewdly, and pointing at the naked couple.

They scrambled to cover themselves, but laughed self-consciously. Nick recognized one of the passengers. It was an old friend. He quickly slid on his shorts. "Fredy! Fredy Champagne!"

The round, brown, bearded face peered intently over at him, then hooted, "Nick, you bastard! Welcome home! We're staying at the Hoa Binh Hotel just up the road! Come up tonight!"

"You got it, brother! We'll be there about nine!"

"OK, but wear some clothes, goddamn it!" he pointed at Hang who had pulled a sheet over herself. "Of course, she don't have to!"

Nick grinned and shot him the finger.

That evening, Hang dressed in the same outfit that she had worn the night they met. Nick dressed in olive colored slacks with a white, short-sleeved shirt and loafers. They stopped and knocked at Tim's door.

"Come on in, you guys. I'm sorry, I fell asleep. I'm not quite ready for dinner." Tim greeted them groggily, wearing only swim trunks and a tattered T-shirt. His room was a shambles. Nick realized once again how difficult it must be for Tim to live with his disability.

"Hey Tim, do you need help getting things organized?"

Tim chuckled. "No thanks. This is how I live. I'm used to it. Sorry if you're not."

"We have a date with Fredy Champagne tonight at his hotel. We'll have to go down and eat and be on our way."

"That's OK, Nick. I'm still fighting the runs from breakfast. I just can't get used to the food here. You go on ahead, maybe I'll catch you tomorrow."

Hang hugged Tim warmly. "Will you be OK, Tim? I think you need to eat something to stay strong. There are many beautiful girls in Hanoi," she teased.

Tim tried to smile but his face quickly twisted into a painful grimace as he hurried to the bathroom. "I'll see you tomorrow!"

In the dining room, Hang marvelled at the lovely view out the open windows to the lake. "*Troi oi*, honey *oi!* This is so beautiful! How can I ever thank you for bringing me here? Do you know how few people from the south get a chance to see Hanoi? You have shown me my country in a way that I never could have seen, if I never met you."

He grasped her hands and gently massaged her small but strong fingers. "Yeah, this is a dream come true. I can never tell you in words how much this means to me and how much I love you."

As they gazed dreamily into each other's eyes, the young attractive waitress in a long maroon *ao dai* looked on. "*Troi oi*, sister. You are very lucky to be so in love. What nationality is he? French? Russian?"

"American," Hang said proudly.

"My God! American? But he speaks our language! I have never seen an American before…" Her expression went from envy through shock and awe to fear.

Nick read her like a book. He smiled at her warmly. "Please don't be afraid. Yes, I was here in the war. But I and some others have come back to make peace. Did you lose someone?" He reached out and gently held her hands. He saw her eyes glaze over.

She pulled away and forced a smile. "It is over now. Thank you. Would you like a drink before dinner?" They ordered iced coffee for Hang, Heineken for Nick, spring rolls, pig's ear and lotus salad, bread and butter, and grilled meat on a stick with a bowl of white rice.

They sipped their drinks, and enjoyed listening to the traditional music show being performed at the head of the restaurant. The musicians wore mandarin-style outfits with silk sashes around their waists. Nick was enthralled by the instruments, most of which were made from bamboo. Some had but one string and could make the haunting whining melody typical of the Far East. There was a drum, and a set of bamboo tubes, sawed off at different lengths and stacked in a triangle. A lithe young man stood in front and clapped his hands in front of them, and each produced a different note. Then another man stepped forward with a wooden flute and amazed the audience with his incredible talents. When they finally concluded their performance, only Nick and Hang applauded them, much to their surprise. The rest of the audience, obviously Asian, simply returned quietly to their meals.

Nick and Hang's enthusiastic appreciation was not lost on the flutist, who made his way to their table. Nick stood, shook the musician's hand firmly and invited him to sit.

"*Za. Cam on zat nhieu*," he said, "I'm sorry, I only speak Vietnamese. My name is Le Pho. And yours?"

Hang bowed, "I am Le Thi Ngoc Hang and this is Nick Dwyer. Don't worry, Mr. Nick speaks our language. He very much liked your performance, as did I. Thank you so much."

Nick offered him a drink.

"A beer would be fine, thank you."

When it arrived they all toasted each other. "To *hoa binh*," said Nick. Le Pho grinned appreciatively and touched glasses. "How long did it take you to learn the flute so perfectly?" asked Nick.

"Since I was a little boy on my family farm. Do you play any instrument?"

Nick shook his head shyly. "Not really, but I think I would like to learn the flute. Is it difficult?"

Le Pho instantly pulled his bamboo flute from his waistband. "Here, please try. You must hold it like this. Then you place your fingers like so and blow down through this hole."

Nick followed his directions and tried, but only a squeaky high-pitched shriek escaped from the tube. They all shared in the embarrassed laughter. "It takes much practice," Le Pho said. "What country do you come from?"

"I'm American." And he braced himself for a response. "I fought here in the war."

Le Pho's smile vanished, then returned slowly. "Why do you come to Hanoi?"

"To learn more about the Vietnamese people that I fought against and to help make peace between us. There is a group of us veterans in Hanoi now who will make a Peace Walk in a few days. We hope it will bring attention to this issue."

Le Pho's eyes filled with admiration. He reached out and shook Nick's hand warmly. "Please wait here." He walked away into the lobby. He returned in a few minutes with a tape cassette.

"This is a collection of our music. I hope you will take it with you along with my flute as a souvenir of peace from your former enemy. I wish you great success. Now I must return for the rest of our show." Nick and Hang stood, shook hands, and bowed deeply. Le Pho returned the bow and said, "The next time we meet, perhaps we can play a duet together. We will sing a song of peace."

After dinner they stood and bowed to the musicians and went to the lobby. Nick asked the girl at the reception desk to call *Anh* Cuong.

"Oh, I'm sorry, sir, but he has gone to be with his family this evening. He said you had given him the night off," she explained.

"Now how do we get to the Hoa Binh Hotel?"

"There are cyclos outside the hotel, if you like, sir. The Hoa Binh is not far."

Nick and Hang found a driver waiting just outside the front door. Soon they were making their way along the narrow strip of land on Yen Phu Street. They enjoyed the romantic view of the mist rising off the lake and the sounds of the jungle that soon crept up on both sides of the dark little road. To Nick, it seemed more like a trail. He held Hang close on the small seat and felt the chill of chicken skin on his arms.

Within a half-hour they arrived at the new five-story building, perched on the edge of the water. The landscaping was not yet established, and the smell of fresh paint greeted them in the lobby. The desk clerk directed them to the fifth floor, where the peace delegation was quartered. When they disembarked the jerky elevator they were met by hoots and hollering from each open door down the hallway. Nick stuck his head in one room. "Hey guys! We're looking for Fredy."

A fat, bare-bellied Asian man wearing an NVA helmet and shorts waved at them as he took a hit from his pipe and tried to hold in the marijuana smoke and still choke out, "Two doors down." His bearded companion smiled languorously.

Hang was worried. Nick just chuckled. "Don't worry honey *oi*. These guys always smoke that stuff."

"Do you ever smoke drugs?"

"Sometimes. But since I met you, it's the furthest thing from my mind." He reassured her with a smile and a kiss. Nick walked into the open door and immediately smelled the beer. "Well, goddamn it! Did you guys come to make peace, or to get high?" he yelled.

The long-haired, bearded man in a sweaty tank top threw back his head and roared. "Nick! You son of a bitch! You finally made it! We've been waiting on ya!"

A short, middle-aged woman with long dark hair flowing out from under a black scarf jumped up. Smiling through clenched teeth and with glassy blue eyes she threw her arms around Nick. "Welcome, my brother! Long time no see! And who is this lovely creature?"

Laughing, Nick pulled Hang closer to him. "This is the love of my life, Hang. Honey *oi*, these are my friends Fredy and Sherry

Champagne." Hang was suddenly smothered by Sherry's bear hug. It was followed by Fredy stumbling over to follow suit. Hang retreated to Nick's side where she held onto him tightly. She had come unprepared for this boisterous band of misfits, but smiled timidly and tried to fit in.

Fredy gestured at two other men. "Nick, Hang. These are our comrades, Steve Stratford and Louie Block. They are both vets who are part of our Peace Walk."

Steve was tall and bearded with curly brown hair. He wore a tank top with a peace sign on the front. Bare chested Louie's white, pasty skin hung over his belt and jeans. His long dark hair and beard were stringy. He was missing his front teeth and looked like a vampire. Nick shook their hands with the three-part grip that was in vogue among vets. Hang hid behind Nick and smiled self-consciously.

Fredy pulled a Vietnamese man off of his bed and thrust him out in front of the others. "And this is Pham Van Kiet, our Vietnamese government representative."

Nick and Hang both bowed and greeted him in Vietnamese. He seemed impressed and relieved that not all of these Americans were barbaric party animals. He instantly stood next to the newcomers and tried to shuttle them off to the side, but Fredy had other ideas. "Nick, have a beer! How about you, Hang?" Hang shook her head hesitantly and looked up at Nick.

"You got any soda? Hang doesn't drink." Nick said as he accepted his 333 can.

Sherry offered Hang a bottle of locally made orange juice. "Here, honey. We can share this. I don't drink either. But I sure do smoke!" she cheered, and snatched a joint out of Louie's hand.

Nick turned back to Fredy. "Brother, tell me about your peace walk plans. What can we do to help?"

Fredy stepped over to a large box and pulled out a T-shirt with both a Vietnamese and American flag printed on the front, along with the words PEACE—HOA BINH—WALK VIETNAM AUGUST 1991. "Here. You can start by wearing this wherever you go. Next, tell everybody you meet. Third, you can stick around 'til next week and join us walking through Hanoi. Lastly, but most importantly, we could sure use some financial help."

Nick nodded enthusiastically. "We're set to leave day after

tomorrow and fly out to Bangkok for the first leg of our return trip back to Maui. So we won't be able to walk with you, but all the other things are no problem. Hang and I can tell the Vietnamese people about it. In fact we already have. We've been spreading the word from Ho Chi Minh City to here." He reached under his shirt and unzipped the money belt around his waist. " I've got to make this money last a couple more weeks, but here's a few hundred. I hope it will help you out."

Fredy took the cash and waved it as his friends. "I told you we could count on Nick. Here, I'll try to find something to write out a receipt."

"No need, Fredy. I wouldn't give it to you if I didn't trust you. Besides, I don't think the IRS will be letting me deduct this from my taxes." Nick's laughter was infectious. "So tell me the plan."

"We're gonna start by marching through the streets of Hanoi and go past the Ho Chi Minh Mausoleum. The Vietnam News Agency is giving us coverage and will broadcast it all over the world. The general theme is to start the reconciliation process by lifting the trade embargo that the U.S. put in place against Vietnam immediately after the fall of Saigon on April 30, 1975. That will mean that guys like us won't have to sneak in here through third countries like we've been doing. Then we can open up communications and telephone links so people can talk directly instead of writing letters, which can take months. The next step will be American investment in Vietnam and opening businesses here, that will help the local economy and also be profitable for U.S. companies. The biggest goal, though, is to finally normalize relations between us so we can open embassies in both countries." He paused to chug down half of a beer. "After we leave Hanoi, we're heading south to Hue and continue the march there and then finally on to Ho Chi Minh City, where we'll end the march."

"So why do you think there has been so much resistance to these things back in the U.S.?" Nick asked.

Fredy looked frustrated. "Because of the POW/ MIA issue. A lot of our veteran groups and the League of Families have been pressuring our government not to ease up on Vietnam until they have accounted for all of the 2,238 missing American soldiers from the war."

Nick could feel a chill sweep over his arms again. "What do you think about that?"

"There ARE no POWs Nick!" he shouted. "That's just a crock of shit being fed to the media by people who don't know how to forgive and move on! The Vietnamese gave back all the POWs in 1973!"

Nick squirmed slightly. "I don't know, Fredy. What about Bobby Garwood? He turned up here in 1979. He had been a POW for over a decade. There could be others."

"Bullshit!" Fredy roared. He seemed possessed by some inner demon. Nick and Tim had planned to conduct another POW search at the International Hospital in Hanoi tomorrow morning, and Nick had thought of asking for Fredy's support. Now he bit his tongue.

"What do you mean, bullshit? How do you account for Garwood?" Nick asked calmly.

"He was a goddamn deserter! A traitor! Who gives a fuck about him?"

Nick couldn't let it go. "Well, there are people back in the world right now that think the same thing about you."

"Yeah? Well, fuck them and fuck you too, Nick! Do you want your goddamn money back?"

"No, I don't want my goddamn money back! I want you to shut up and drink your beer and mellow out, motherfucker! I don't want you having a heart attack before this thing even gets started! Wait until afterward, then we can all piss on your grave, you bastard!" Nick grinned and growled with laughter as the two old friends grabbed each other in a spirited hug. There was an audible sigh of relief from the others in the room.

Steve Stratford looked around at the others. "Well, this is sure a hell of a way to make peace!" He said laughing.

The old and new friends stayed up drinking, smoking, and planning for several more hours until finally Hang tugged on Nick's arm. "Honey *oi*. I think it is very late. We should go and let them go to sleep, OK?"

They all said their goodbyes and Fredy walked out with them to the shiny new elevator. "You know Nick, every time we've hooked up it's been in Vietnam. Maybe next time we should do it back home, I mean the U.S."

Nick grinned as he stepped into the elevator. "I'd rather do it at home too. I mean, HERE."

The cyclo driver lay draped over the ragged seat of his vehicle.

Startled by their approach, the driver jumped out from under a holey, green poncho. Nick told him, "OK, *anh oi. Xin ve khach san di.*" He and Hang squeezed into the seat between the bicycle tires. Hang snuggled under his arm. The night was cool, and pitch black. No moon and few stars. The driver pedaled slowly back toward the Thang Loi. Crickets and frogs sang in the swampy jungle on both sides of the road. Nick felt a chill again. There was something foreboding in the night air. Hang shivered, and Nick rubbed her arm and back to warm her.

"Thank you, Minh," she said. "But I will be warm as long as you just hold me."

"What did you call me?"

"Minh. It means, stronger than honey or darling. It is like me calling the other person myself, or you think of the other person as yourself. Usually, only people who have been in love for a very long time call each other that. But I think we are special and it is how I truly feel. Do you understand?"

"Yes, Minh. I understand."

At this, she purred and snuggled closer to him. "Are all Americans like your friends that I met tonight?"

"No. They are very different. Why do you ask?"

She paused, searching for words that were not hurtful. "I don't know. I'm sorry but, they are so hairy and dirty and wild looking. They scare me."

Nick laughed, "They are Vietnam vets, like me and Tim. We carry a lot of pain. Yeah, I agree. To look at them you would never suspect that beneath their rough exterior they have hearts of gold. Sometimes I think that we've been put down for so long, we have actually started to believe we deserved it. Now we're all looking for something good in our lives. Something that we can point to and say, 'See, we're not baby killers or cowards or demons. We only want to do what is right, so people will love and accept us.' Staring intently ahead, he added quietly, "Even if those people don't come from our own country. We are just trying very hard to prove ourselves."

"Well, I think what you are all doing is wonderful, I hope…"

"SHHHH!" he hissed.

"What is it, Minh?" she asked.

"The crickets and frogs have stopped!" he whispered.

He braced rigidly against the seat, as his senses flared in the darkness. But too late. The flashlights appeared immediately from both sides of the jungle. They were surrounded before they could blink. The raspy, guttural voice called out in Vietnamese. "Halt, or we will kill you!"

The driver immediately slid his slippered feet off the pedals to brake against the muddy road. Nick prepared himself to fight but could see the distinctive silhouettes of a half dozen AK-47s in the beam of the lights.

"*Minh oi*! Do not speak Vietnamese!" she whispered.

They won't take us alive! He vowed under his breath. Fuck it! I'm getting tired of this bullshit! Give it up Nick! Don't mean nothin'!

But much to Nick's chagrin, the ambushers were not interested in him or in Hang. He could see that they were all dressed in Army uniforms. He knew they could kill them all at their whim.

They grabbed the cyclo driver by the shirt and demanded his money. The poor wretch complied immediately but the leader slapped him hard across the face. "Give me the rest!" he ordered. "You have a rich foreigner here! I know he paid you more than this!" The driver hung his head and went to the cyclo and reached under the seat and pulled out the bundle that he had hidden there. The soldier slapped him again for lying but grunted in satisfaction.

Nick held his breath as the man came over and thrust his light squarely in Nick's face. Nick glared menacingly back into the light, waiting for the blow that would surely come.

Another of the group spoke to the leader. "He probably has a lot of money, boss." Nick cocked his fists.

The leader shook his head. "We don't want trouble with foreigners," and signaled for the others to withdraw. They faded back into the bushes as quickly as they had come. The driver was breathing hard as he stood on the pedals to gain speed, away toward the lights of the city. When they arrived at the lobby of the hotel Nick handed him twice the agreed-upon price, and patted his shoulder in sympathy. The humiliated man bowed low and thanked him profusely.

On the way back to their room they came upon Tim, limping down the corridor, returning from his late-night dinner. Nick related the story of their new adventure and Tim shook his head in frustration.

"Goddamn it, Nick! I always miss out on the fun! From now on I'm sticking with you guys whether you like it or not." He laughed.

They bid Tim goodnight at his door and then went on to their room. Once inside, Nick stripped and sat on the bed in his shorts. He opened a beer and lit a cigarette as he watched Hang undress.

"We were very lucky tonight," he said.

She came over to him in her slip and kissed him. She took his cigarette and sat down by the ashtray.

"Minh. We need to talk. What happens after tomorrow? You and Tim are going to Bangkok, yes?"

"Yes."

"And what about me?"

"You're on your own," he teased, laughing.

"Hey! I *cat cai dau* you!"

Then it came on him suddenly, without warning. He was sitting across the table from Lieu. Their last night in Saigon, 1966. Then there was Pham Thai Thanh at the Palace Hotel, 1989. And now... the end was coming... again. His tour would be over tomorrow, but hers would never end. Would he come back? How long would it take this time? Would he be too late... again?

"How much money do you need to live each month, back in Ho Chi Minh City?"

She thought carefully and crushed out the butt. "Maybe thirty dollars. Why?" She studied him while he sipped his beer.

He went to his wallet and pulled out two hundred. "Here. I should be back in two months, but... just in case."

She put her arms around his neck and squeezed him hard. She pulled back slightly and he saw the tears of gratitude flow down her cheeks. "In two months?" She squealed with joy as he nodded. "Thank you so much, Minh! I love how you always take care of me."

He kissed her tenderly. "I will always take care of you... I promise."

They each lay down on their separate twin beds and Nick turned off the lamp. Will you really, Nick? he asked himself silently. Will you keep this promise? And what about all the other promises?

In her small voice she called over, "*Chuc minh ngu ngon.*"

"*Cam on, Minh.* You sleep well too."

The rhythmic waves caressed them to sleep, and it was not long before Nick began the dream.

He's on a passenger train going through familiar mountains in

Idaho or Montana. He feels at home. The train slows as it enters a small town. Just before coming to a stop in front of the log-cabin station, it cruises past some school bleachers. Fans watch a football game. On the top row of seats there's a middle-aged couple in cowboy attire. They turn to look inside the passenger car where Nick is sitting. He starts to stand and collect his belongings. He's getting off the train. The couple frowns discouragingly, and wave their fingers at him and shake their heads. The woman points down the tracks in the direction the train was moving. She's a white, American woman but she suddenly yells out in Vietnamese… "*Day noi*!" Nick is shocked and puzzled. He shrugs at her and she yells again, "*Day noi*!"

Nick awoke trembling. "Minh! Minh *oi*!" he pleaded and turned on the lamp.

"What is it, Minh?" she replied groggily.

Still half asleep, he tried to focus. "What does it mean? *Day noi*. What does it mean?"

Hang rubbed her eyes, "*Day noi? Day noi* means, teach to speak. Why, Minh? I'm trying to sleep. We study Vietnamese tomorrow, OK?"

"Teach to speak? " he repeated, dumbfounded.

"Yes. Goodnight, Minh."

Nick lay back down in the darkness. He smelled the Vietnamese night and listened to the rhythmic sounds of her breathing. He felt something profound had just happened; even prophetic. He tried to calm his mind and go back to sleep, but he quickly found himself in the rubber trees on the red-dirt road.

Once again, out of the mist, marched the ghost platoon. They hobbled along. The maimed and the dead. They were led by the same beefy point man. All their eyes were on Nick. It was just like all the other times. Nick stood and watched them approach and prepared to join them as soon as he was beckoned. As the troops got closer they were smiling at him. Not like before. He saw love and respect in their eyes. Confused and baffled, he stepped forward to join the procession as usual. The point man gave him a stern look of rebuke. Nick froze, alone, on the side of the dusty road and watched the smile return to the point man's bloody face. He nodded at Nick and turned off the road to cross the clearing and plunge into the jungle. Finally, the last man paused briefly, and turned to wave at Nick before disappearing into the mist. And they were gone.

When the sky lightened enough to see, Nick stepped into the dawn. Hang still slept. Bewilderment had kept him awake the entire night, but it was going to be a day, whether he was ready or not.

— —

They met Tim and Cuong in the hotel restaurant for breakfast. Nick ordered massive amounts of thick black coffee and his hands were soon twitching violently as the strong caffeine worked its magic.

Tim stared into Nick's face. "Damn, Nick! Your eyes look like two piss holes in a snowdrift!" He laughed.

"Yeah, well at least they look how they feel, goddamn it," Nick mumbled, downing another hit of coffee. "Rough night. By the way, Tim. After we finish our business at the hospital today, I'd like to have a beer with you. Just us. OK?"

Hang was concerned. "Minh *oi*. You go with Tim today? But this is our last day together."

Nick massaged her neck reassuringly. "It's OK, Minh. Just for a little while. We have been ignoring Tim for most of the trip. I need his help with a few things. *Duoc khong?*"

"OK, Minh." She relented with an understanding smile.

Nick turned to Cuong. "*Anh* Cuong *oi*. Can you please drive us to the International Hospital this morning? I have some more medicine that I want to give them." He winked at Tim.

Cuong straightened stiffly in his chair and grinned. "Of course, *Anh* Nick. Will you need me this afternoon?"

"No. I think we will stay here and pack. What time will you take us to Noi Bai Airport tomorrow?"

Cuong thought for a minute. "Sister Hang's flight is at 10:00. You and brother Tim will depart for Thailand at 12:30. We should leave here by 7:30. OK?"

Nick nodded and translated for Tim. After breakfast they returned to their rooms briefly. When Nick came out of the toilet he found his dental kit again laid out in a neat row on the wooden counter next to the metal basin. The ritual had been repeated each morning and night for the whole trip. It hit him hard. Hang's loving gesture would soon be over. He peered around the corner and watched her putting on her makeup. He saw her eyes smile when she spotted him in the mirror. They gazed at each other with so much emotion that he thought sure his heart would break.

Cuong drove them southeast toward the city center, then turned right, and soon they came out on Hung Vuong boulevard with its broad parade grounds and flower-lined walkways. Cuong slowed and pointed at the huge stone monument rising up on the right side of the car. His voice began to break, "This is the final resting place for Uncle Ho." Nick saw him swallow hard as they passed by two armed sentries dressed in white uniforms with blue trim. They stood firmly at attention.

Nick motioned Cuong to pull over. In his white polo shirt and khaki shorts Nick faced the tomb of the legendary leader. In his best honor-guard tribute, he drew himself up into attention, and snapped a quivering salute to his once-sworn enemy. Hang shot a photo with his camera. He bowed and returned to the car. Tim looked back at him with open contempt.

"What's the matter, brother?" Nick asked.

"You salute that fucking commie, Nick?"

Nick shook his head as Cuong continued down Le Duan Avenue. "Tim, did you know, 'that fucking commie,' actually worshipped George Washington and was once our ally, along with a guy named Vo Nguyen Giap, against the Japanese in World War II?" Tim's mouth dropped open.

Nick continued, "Did you know that the fucking French, who were in control of their Indochinese colonies, were actually puppets of the Japanese and collaborated with them in ruling Vietnam while Ho Chi Minh and Vo Nguyen Giap worked with us behind enemy lines?" Tim shook his head in shock.

Nick was on a roll. "Did you know that just before we finally won the war, President Roosevelt promised Ho Chi Minh that Vietnam would be independent and never go back to the traitorous French? But shortly after that, Roosevelt died and Truman took over. De Gaulle convinced him to give Vietnam back to France. Ho Chi Minh justifiably felt betrayed and started his war against the French by declaring independence here on Sept. 2, 1945. He stood right here in Hanoi at Ba Dinh Square and read the declaration which started out, 'We hold the truth that all men are created equal, that they are endowed by their creator with certain unalienable rights, among them are life, liberty, and the pursuit of happiness.' Do those words sound familiar, Tim?"

"Yeah, they do," Tim said, still in shock. "Aren't they from OUR Declaration of Independence?"

"You got it, brother. And while we turned our back on him and started to help the frogs reassert their domination over Vietnam again, he had no choice but to fight. And once he and General Giap defeated the French in 1954, he thought that Vietnam would finally be free and united. But the international community separated Vietnam at the 17th parallel. The deal was for everybody who supported Ho Chi Minh to go north and those who supported Ngo Dinh Diem to go south. There were supposed to be free elections in 1956 so that the Vietnamese could determine their leader. But the U.S. and our puppet, Ngo Dinh Diem, refused to honor the elections because we knew Ho Chi Minh would win. That's when Uncle Ho started his attacks on the south. And the rest we know already. Right?"

Tim was incredulous. "Are you sure, Nick?"

"One hundred percent! And it blows my mind how so many hard-headed people just won't accept the truth! Even now! And I can tell you one more thing, Tim. Until we can face the truth and accept our mistakes, we ain't never gonna heal, brother! Never!"

Cuong's eyes were watching Nick with obvious admiration in the rear view mirror as he pulled into the shaded parking lot of the five-story brick hospital.

Nick took several deep breaths. "I'm sorry Tim. I got a little carried away."

Tim chuckled. "A little, Nick?"

"OK, look bruddah." Nick said to Tim in island code. "We goin use da same MO like befo. Get em to give us da tour and look for haoles or popolos. And if dey get some, we no say nutting. Bumbye we talk. OK?"

Nick noticed that Cuong's eyes went from admiration to consternation. But he stayed with the car as the others walked up the steps. Once inside, a gentle, well-spoken doctor and a middle-aged nurse went through the customary tea ceremony. Then Nick asked if there were any foreign patients currently at the hospital. He was shocked when the doctor nodded. "Yes, we have two."

Nick could barely contain his excitement. He and Tim exchanged high-five looks. Hang watched them both with more than mild curiosity as the doctor led them up the stairs to the third floor.

As they turned through the doorway of the first room, Nick actually held his breath. He followed the doctor up to the bed and watched him pull back the mosquito net. A young man turned over to face his visitors. Nick exhaled and looked at the doctor. "Excuse me, doctor. I thought you said you had foreign patients. Who is this?"

The doctor smiled calmly. "Oh yes, he is a foreigner. He is Cambodian." The trio looked at each other, perplexed.

Nick again found his voice. "No doctor, I mean do you have any foreigners from the West, like Europe or Canada, for example?"

The doctor shook his head emphatically. "No, I'm sorry. Not at the moment. But we do treat them occasionally."

"Then who is the other patient you mentioned?"

"Oh, she is the wife of a Thai diplomat. She is pregnant. Would you like to meet her?"

"No. That won't be necessary. Can we go back downstairs? I have some medical samples to give you."

After shaking hands all around and agreeing to keep in touch in the future, the disappointed would-be heroes went back to the car and returned in silence to the Thang Loi Hotel. Hang took their room key and left to go pack.

Nick and Tim took a table by a window overlooking the lake, which shimmered happily in the midday sun. When the waiter brought their beers they toasted, drank deeply, and sighed. A cool breeze stirred Tim's hair as he finally broke the silence. "At least we tried."

"Yeah, but I feel like I let everybody down. Maybe I could have done more if I hadn't lost my focus."

"I don't get it."

"I had no business falling in love. That was the last thing on my mind."

"Hey, Nick. No more guilt, OK? You're goddamn lucky, brah. I wish I could find someone like Hang."

"I know that. And yet… What about that 'endless pussy' fantasy, goddamn it?"

Tim roared with laughter and the sound of it brought Nick back to his own belly laugh. But it was short lived. "You asking me?" Tim said. "A guy with half a brain?"

"You make more sense than a lot of people, Timmy. Besides, you know my situation back there as well as here."

Tim thought for a minute. "It seems to me you already had a shot at endless pussy in Bangkok. Fear of AIDS changed all that. You ended up here. There are risks with everything, Nick. Either you risk your life for your ego, or you risk your heart for love. Pick one, drive on, and don't look back."

Nick hung his head and nodded. "Yeah, but technically I'm still married to Malia until the divorce papers go through. And here I am promising Hang that I'll be back here in two months. Part of me wants to live out my dream of staying in Vietnam and working to help the country, but what will I do here? There are no American companies, no jobs. There are no Americans, period. The only money I have will come from the VA, and what about my mortgage? Is it worth risking everything I've worked for, over the last twenty years?"

Tim pulled on his beer and watched his friend intently.

Nick continued. "Sometimes, I even think about trying to work it out with Malia. You know, bring the kids back and work the farm again. They deserve better than what they got now."

"OK, but what about your PTSD? Can you control it back there? Aren't you afraid of it coming out and ruining everything again?"

"Hell yeah! But I'm also afraid of it following me over here and ruining this too."

"Hey, Nick. I got news for you. It don't follow you, brother. It's inside you all the time. I don't care how far you run."

Nick emptied his beer and motioned the waiter for two more. He scanned the horizon, smelled the air, and for the first time that day, listened to the Vietnamese music coming from a nearby stereo. The wailing female voice hit poignant notes and struck hidden yet familiar chords, deep within his heart. They came from another time, perhaps another life, but not from another place. Vietnam was a part of him, now and forever. Maybe it always had been. And now, just like so many other times... "Tim. Do you feel at home here?"

Tim snorted out a brief laugh. "No." He took a swallow and followed Nick's gaze across West Lake, in the city of Hanoi, in the country of Vietnam, and his eyes brimmed. His mouth began to move several times but nothing came. He shrugged. "Home, Nick? Where the hell is home?"

"That's right, Tim. Where the hell is home? Is it back in the U.S. where they spit on us? Is it in Hawaii, the land of aloha? Or, is it here where they truly understand war and what it costs? I don't think anyone knows the price of war better than the Vietnamese." Then Nick stared hard at his friend. "I'm really scared about tomorrow, Timmy."

"Tomorrow? There is no tomorrow. You know that. We only get today, Nick. That's all we ever get."

As the tropical sun began its descent into Ho Tay, the two grunts made their way along the raised walkway back to their rooms. At Tim's door they stopped and faced each other.

"Thanks for listening, brother."

"Forget it. Thanks for bringing me. This will stay with me the rest of my life."

The old friends hugged tightly. Nick stepped back and walked away. When he closed his door behind him Hang jumped up from her bed and ran to his arms. They kissed deeply.

"Oh, Minh *oi*! I will miss you so much!" she whispered as she clung to him tightly.

He stroked her hair and felt her small body and memorized each curve for all time. Then he held her chin lightly and kissed her lips. He avoided her eyes. "Please sit down, Minh. We have to talk."

They sat, holding hands, on the couch facing out to the lake. Her eyes searched his. "What is it, Minh?"

"I hate goodbyes. Especially this one. When I came on this trip I had different plans. Meeting my soul mate and falling hopelessly in love wasn't part of it. But it happened. Now, I'm confused."

Hang smiled sweetly, stood and went to the tape cassette. "For the rest of our lives, love always," filled the room with the powerful melody and emotions.

The shadows grew long as they clutched each other desperately and made love for the last time. Nick knew now what he had to do.

CHAPTER 50
Bangkok
September 1991

Alan, Tim, and Nick sat together under an umbrella at the poolside bar of PO Court. Nick heard the other two laughing in the distance. He still saw Hang's tear-stained face at Noi Bai airport. He still felt the choking in his throat. He could feel his body boarding the plane, but his heart was not with him. He wondered if the soldiers who lost their limbs in the war felt the same when they got on the freedom bird.

He tuned into Alan's voice as he crowed triumphantly about his latest sexual conquest.

"You should have been here, Tim! I had three chicks at the same time! While I was fucking one, the other two were getting it on with each other. I could've used some help. Man, they wore me out!"

Tim giggled. "How many times did you change condoms?"

"I lost track! But that reminds me. I've got to get resupplied. Tonight's another night. I just love these LBFMs!"

"What's that?" Tim asked.

"Little brown fucking machines!" he laughed. "I'm telling you. This is the life!"

Tim glanced over at Nick. "Come on, man. Snap out of it! We're going out to party! I got a feeling we're gonna get lucky tonight!"

Alan joined in with Tim's laughter. "Damn, Nick! Looking at your forlorn face is making me lose my hard-on! Forget about that chick. She's in Vietnam. You're here. Case closed."

Nick stood and drained his beer. "You guys go on ahead and fuck a couple of 'em for me. I'll see you tomorrow. But don't forget, Tim. We need to be at the airport by 1:00 to check in for the flight to Coh Samui."

Alan looked puzzled. "You want me to bring back those two little hotties that you invited last month?"

Nick hated himself and yet was proud at the same time. He shuddered, "No thanks, brother. I've got new promises to keep."

Alan and Tim looked at each other with disgust. Alan smirked. "Who invited him along anyway?"

Nick gave them a *shaka* and returned to his room.

Nick and Tim spent the next few days stretched out on the beach at Coh Samui, riding motorcycles, and enjoying the local cuisine. The tiny island was a welcome respite from Bangkok and reminded them of Hawaii. The adventure was not over, but Nick felt a longing for Maui. He would have much to do when he got back. His ailing father crossed his mind.

Donald Dwyer was an invalid in a Florida nursing home. He suffered from advanced Parkinson's disease. Nick and his kid brother Dan had visited their father in April and found that he could no longer take care of his finances. Since Dan had taken care of their mother's affairs before her death, it fell to Nick to take on this responsibility. Nick now worried that this long journey might make some bills come past due.

When they returned to Bangkok, Alan greeted them excitedly at the PO Court. "Hey, Nick! Guess what! I just met an old friend of yours. Do you remember a Tom O'Rourke? He went to the University of Hawaii."

Nick smiled. "Yeah! He was a roommate of two other friends, Frank Hollister and Shayne Fair. He was in pre-med."

"Exactly what he told me!" Alan shouted. "He's a doctor now, serving with the International Organization for Migration. Part of the United Nations. He's going to Hong Kong to meet up with that other guy, Shayne Fair. Here. He gave me that guy's number. If you want to call them you can use the phone at my condo. It's cheaper than the hotel phone."

Later, they sat on Alan's eighth-floor balcony overlooking the smoggy skyline in the afternoon sun. Nick dialed the overseas operator. The connection took less than a minute. The high cost kept the call short. After the excitement of the surprise wore off, Nick learned that O'Rourke had been called up to the Burmese border and was not going to Hong Kong after all. But Shayne invited Nick and Tim to come stay at his house on Lamma Island. Tim immediately agreed, and by nightfall they had their tickets to Hong Kong in hand for the next day's departure.

That night, Alan decided to have Pizza Hut deliver to the condo instead of going out. Nick was shocked. Vietnam was just two hours away but still remained in some ancient time zone. Hang's face came to him again for the millionth time. The aching in his chest persisted. "Hey, Alan. Can I make another overseas call?"

Alan grinned. "Come on, Tim. Let's eat ours in the living room."

Twenty minutes later Dr. Hung, Hang's next door neighbor, answered. Nick apologized for the intrusion but asked if the doctor could send his maid to fetch Hang to the phone. Hearing Nick's Vietnamese tinged with lovesickness warmed the doctor's heart. After three long minutes Nick heard her small and humble voice, breathless on the other end.

"Minh *oi!* Oh, honey *oi!* Tell me you miss me! Tell me you love me, honey!" Her voice seemed to come from another time, another planet, another life.

"You know I miss you. You know I love you. I just wanted to make sure you got home OK. This will be the last time I can talk to you. As soon as I get back to Maui I will write and tell you when I'll return to Vietnam. Until then, just remember… For the rest of our lives…"

"Love always. And we will. I know it, Minh."

CHAPTER 51
Hong Kong
September 1991

"Excuse me! Can you tell me which boat belongs to Mr. Chen?" Nick asked.

The short, dark-skinned Chinese sailor peered up from beneath his straw hat at Tim and Nick. The two tall white men stood out in contrast to the throngs of boat people who milled around the docks of Aberdeen Harbor. Hundreds of Chinese junks and sampans bobbed in the brown, trash-filled water that reeked of salt and rotten fish. "You go that way." He pointed. "Look for blue boat." He returned to coiling his rope on the weathered wooden deck.

Tim looked down the line of boats which stretched for a quarter mile. He laughed. "I can see at least a dozen blue boats from here, Nick."

Nick shrugged and led the way. At the second blue boat, a smiling Mr. Chen welcomed them, bowing and shaking their hands repeatedly. "Yes, yes. Miss Suzanne say you come. Now, we wait for her. She come soon." He continued smiling and gestured for them to sit along the gunwales.

They ducked under a canvas roof stretched over curved metal hoops. It covered about half of the 30-foot boat. Nick stowed their travel-worn suitcases on wooden slats above filthy ankle-deep water that sloshed in the bottom of the boat. They looked at each other with grins of apprehension.

"You like beer? One dollah." Mr. Chen smiled.

"Sounds good to me, Nick. Whadiya say?" said Tim.

"Hey, you can't drink the water!"

They toasted each other and gazed across the hazy, three-mile channel that lay between them and Lamma Island. It was a major shipping lane and was filled with ocean-going freighters, sampans, junks, trawlers, and barges of every description.

Soon they heard a shrill female voice calling from the gangplank. A tall, blonde, woman dressed in a long blue frock led a small, chubby, blond-haired boy by the hand. "Nick? Tim? I'm Suzanne, Shayne's wife. This is our son, Jesse." They shook hands all around and got settled on the wooden seats. Mr. Chen fired up the diesel engine while a young woman in baggy silk clothes cast off.

They chugged out around a small island and swung into the current of the sea lane. Mr. Chen expertly dodged the huge ships that blasted their horns in warning.

"So, what brought you folks to Hong Kong?" Nick asked. "The last time I saw Shayne he was a wild party animal at the University of Hawaii. Obviously things have changed."

Suzanne laughed. "Yeah, we've been married for four years. Shayne is a song writer, but I'm involved in the silk trade. I wholesale to markets in the U.S. Shayne stays in his studio in our house and composes. He's really eager to show you his set-up and find out about all your Vietnam experiences. He'll meet us at the dock at Picnic Bay. Our house is a short hike up Caroline Hill."

A half-hour later they spotted the lanky, long-haired figure pacing on the dock. He was silhouetted against a low-lying hill covered with scrub brush and light jungle. Three large dogs sat nearby. He caught the mooring rope from Mr. Chen's mate and tied it off. Laughing and shouting the old friends hugged. "Goddamn it, Shayne! Why don't you live a little closer to home? Tim and I had to travel half way around the world to see you!" Nick teased.

Shayne grinned from under a wide-brimmed jungle hat. "This IS home. We've been here a couple of years and loving every minute." He tousled little Jesse's hair, then stuck out his hand. "Hi Tim, nice to meet you. But I should warn you. You're in dangerous company."

"So I've been told. Suzanne says you're a song writer. Wouldn't it be easier back in the States or over in Hong Kong? This place looks kinda wild and isolated."

"It is. That's why I like it. No distractions. Here, follow the dogs. They know the trail and will kill any snakes along the way. This island is crawling with cobras, so always watch your step."

This solemn warning immediately focused the two grunts on the trail. Tim limped along behind dragging his suitcase through the mud. Seeing Tim's difficulty Shayne tried to take it from him but the ex-marine shook his head. "No thanks, brother. I can handle."

"Why do you walk like that?" asked Jesse.

"Shhh! Don't ask such personal questions." Suzanne scolded.

"I got shot in the war, Jesse."

"What does war mean?"

"I hope you never find out."

Jesse looked puzzled but took hold of Tim's paralyzed hand and guided him up the path.

That evening, Suzanne barbequed some local steaks out on the lawn. A low rock wall ran the perimeter of the property. It separated the yard from the jungle that crept up the side of Caroline Hill. The dogs patrolled constantly, which put their minds at ease. The men enjoyed a view of the channel below and Hong Kong in the distance.

"What's the story on Tom O'Rourke?" Nick asked. "Do you guys stay in touch pretty regularly?"

"Oh yeah," Shayne said. "He'll be sorry he missed you. But if you're ever in Vietnam again you'll be able to find him in Ho Chi Minh City. He's being transferred there to help with the processing of refugees out of the country."

Nick nearly jumped out of his wicker chair. "Jesus Christ! I'll be back there as soon as I take care of old business on Maui." Hang's beautiful smile flashed in his mind's eye. "How can I get in touch with him?"

"You can't. He's up in the golden triangle. There's some trouble brewing between the drug-dealing warlords and the Thai Army. Lots of refugees, but no phones. Sorry."

Tim leaned forward. "What a small world, Nick. Remember? That's how Alan met O'Rourke. Alan was representing one of the Thai generals in some corruption case involving the drug cartels up there."

Nick's insides fluttered excitedly. What a blessing to have an old friend in Hong Kong as well as Thailand, and now in Vietnam. A new adventure loomed on the horizon. He felt an intense exhilaration blossoming inside. He could feel a new life unfolding, and he wasn't going to miss this for anything.

For the next two days Tim and Nick enjoyed Shayne and

Suzanne's boundless hospitality. Young Jesse became Tim's shadow in a protective kind of way. His innate empathy and compassion touched Tim deeply. Nick was astonished that a four-year-old could exhibit these traits so naturally. It seemed to Nick that back in the States, boys his age would be playing aggressively with toy guns. Whatever Shayne and Suzanne had taught him was commendable.

When their last day on the island arrived, the three men sat out on the veranda in the cool evening air. They watched the ship traffic in the channel as the lights of Aberdeen and Stanley twinkled in the distance. Shayne was obviously struggling with a way to broach a sensitive subject. He shrugged, started to speak, then stopped, twice.

Nick broke the silence. "Spit it out, brother."

Shayne looked almost apologetic. "I'm Canadian, not American, so I didn't go to Vietnam. I never even went to the military. I don't know what war is like any more than Jesse does. My grandfather fought in World War I. He was in France at a place called the Somme. When I was a kid, I asked him about it. His hands would start to tremble and his lips would move, but nothing came out. He would always go away somewhere to be alone, but I could hear him crying.

"I'm sorry, I hope I'm not out of line. I just want to know what the war did to you. What was it like going back? How did it feel to give back to your enemies by building clinics and schools or whatever? Tim, you paid a terrible price. Can you forgive them? Did they forgive you?"

Tim and Nick stared at each other. Nick spoke first. "During the war I gave it everything I had. Every day was a living hell. The killing, the terror, the hatred, and the rage. I just wanted to survive until my one-year tour was over. Every day we moved through the jungle. Every night we dug holes in the ground. We lived like animals. We drank dirty rice-paddy water and ate twenty-year-old C-rations that tasted like dog food. We fought for our lives and for our brothers in the squad.

"When I came home I expected a warm welcome, pats on the back, gratitude. What I got was spit, rotten vegetables, curses, and insults. I started hating my own country. I certainly didn't call it home anymore. But then I went back to Vietnam in 1987. I felt more at home there than I ever did in the U.S. After my second trip back in '89 those feelings intensified. Now, I've decided to move there and live forever. Is that weird, or what? I don't understand it, but it feels right. I carry a heavy pack around with me all the time. It's full of guilt. But every time I help a Vietnamese it seems to get lighter." Nick snorted out a sarcastic laugh. "Sorry you asked?"

Shayne shook his head. "That's beautiful, man. Thank you. Tim?"

Tim squirmed uncomfortably in the wicker chair. His reluctance to talk was obvious. He grinned bashfully at Nick. "Feels like we're in a therapy group back at the Vet Center, eh Nick? I don't know, Shayne. I guess I ditto everything Nick said about the war itself. I was a gung ho marine, you know? Then I got hit just three months into my tour. This was my first time back. I don't know about forgiveness, either way. But I sure don't hate them. Sorry. I'm still processing all the feelings. Call me in a year or two."

Shayne was far away. "Don't be surprised if someday I write a song about it."

"Shayne!" Suzanne called out as she ran out of the house. "There's a typhoon coming! I just heard it on TV. It's a category 3!"

Tim looked worried. "What the hell does that mean?" he asked.

"A hurricane," replied Suzanne. "They are rated from 1 to 5 depending on their intensity. Category 3 is really bad. Do you guys want to ride it out here with us or over on Hong Kong island?"

Nick looked at Tim. "I think we should get to the airport ASAP. What time does Mr. Chen sail in the morning?"

"Whenever you can get down to the dock." Shayne answered. "I'll call him right now. What time shall I tell him?"

"Dawn," said Nick. "But what about you guys? Will you be OK?"

Shayne grinned. "The house is strong. We've been through a bunch of these things. Have a good trip!"

CHAPTER 52
Kula, Maui
September 12, 1991

Nick hadn't slept in over two days. Their hurried escape from Hong Kong took them to Korea, Japan, and Honolulu. Then they caught an Aloha Airlines flight back to Maui.

He unlocked the front door of his house in the midday sun, but the chilly mountain air that rushed out to greet him reminded him of the loneliness he had left behind six weeks before. He tossed the box of mail onto his desk, showered, and collapsed on the sofa in the living room. He was asleep before his head hit the armrest.

The ringing phone woke him. It took him several minutes to remember where he was. It looked like it was morning. "Hello. Yeah, I'm Nicholas Dwyer, I think. That's right. He's my father."

"Mr. Dwyer, this is Larry Buchold calling from the Palm Gardens Nursing Home in Sarasota. I'm very sorry to inform you that your father passed away just ten minutes ago…"

Nick's first thought was, I guess there's no rush paying those bills now. A surge of adrenaline swept through his chest. "I'll be there as soon as I can get a flight."

He hung up and stared quietly at his unopened suitcase. Yeah. Welcome home, Nick. One more time.

Coffee mug in hand, he stepped out onto the deck and smelled the clean, crisp air. The deep blue Pacific stretched out below him as far as he could see. James Taylor's voice called out from the stereo…

"Father, let us build a boat and sail away. There's nothing for you here. And brother, let us throw our lot on the open sea. It's been done before. I'm talking about a broken heart. I been talking about the break of dawn. You love me while I'm here. Now you can miss me when I'm gone.

Sweet misunderstanding. Won't you leave a poor boy alone.
I'm the one-eyed seed of a tumbleweed in the belly of a rolling stone.
Back on the highway, yeah, yeah, yeah, back on the road again."

After making all the flight reservations, he wrote to Hang and placed the letter in his mailbox with the flag up. He hoped it would get there before he did.

Brother Dan and his girlfriend Susan flew down to meet Nick in Florida. They made arrangements for the memorial service and shipping the body to Chicago for burial next to Nick's little sister, Kathy. That painful time came back to haunt Nick again as he stood before the small gathering of his father's friends.

After Kathy's death, in 1951, Donald Dwyer had rarely been home and when he was, he would not talk. They all became strangers residing under the same roof. Their only interaction came through conflict. When the Parkinson's finally took control of his father's body, communication ceased altogether. But at least then there was a good excuse.

All his life, Nick thought their estrangement was because he had left the gate open and Kathy had followed him out onto the road where she was killed. Nick felt that his father never forgave him, until thirty years later, at his mother's funeral. Standing over her grave, Nick had tried to apologize for his terrible mistake. "Dad... Dad I'm so sorry for leaving the gate open." But Donald Dwyer did not even blink. "Dad. Did you hear me?"

His father swallowed hard. "What?"

"I'm sorry about the gate."

"The gate?" Then his father turned to face him. "What are you talking about? You mean, you thought you... all these years? Oh my God!" And with a look of incredulous horror Donald Dwyer shook his head. "Nick, you didn't leave the gate open... I did!"

Now, Nick took a deep breath and faced the small congregation. "Thank you all for making time to say farewell to my father. I wish I could tell you all about him and the wonderful things that he did. I wish I could tell you about his lofty achievements and awards for his contributions to humanity. But I can't. I can only tell you what I know. That he was honest, hard-working and frugal. He would use the same paper napkin for a week. He always said, "Don't spend a quarter if you only have a dime." He never lied… never. He never cheated. He was too gentle to kill a fly. He was a deeply religious man. In my whole life I only heard him say 'damn' one time. When I was a teenager, we used to fight a lot. I wish I could take back some of the things I said and did. He worked double shifts and weekends to provide what he could for us. He gave us all he had. In the end, his reward was being divorced by my mother so she could run off and marry her college sweetheart. Then he left Illinois and moved here, looking for a new home. I hope he found it."

Without warning, a place called Thunder Road flashed in Nick's eyes. Painful memories cut into him like the stinging rain on the back of Vy's motorbike. He saw Sean Flynn's face as they laid him on the floor of the chopper. Suddenly he realized there are many roads to manhood. Not all of them lead to war, or two thousand miles across the country to Hollywood. Sometimes they lead only a few miles to a dead-end job where you grind out a meager living everyday, with no gratitude or recognition. But you do it for those you love, even if they don't love you back…

He felt chicken skin as the memories of his homecoming from the war at Travis Air Force base appeared from the mist. He suddenly realized that he and his father had more in common than he thought.

Donald Dwyer's journey was over. It had led him to a place of peace, love, and acceptance. He was finally home. Nick could only hope that someday he would be too.

CHAPTER 53
Ouray, Colorado
September 21, 1991

She pulled the long, strawberry blonde hair away from her face. Her wide-set blue English eyes studied him. "So, what exactly are you doing here? I mean, we've been divorced for fourteen years," she said and sipped her Coors. Her voice was gentle, caring, and he thought, maybe even hopeful. Maybe not.

Nick stared into his own beer as he swirled it in his glass. He had to be honest, above all else. A John Denver song played in the background. He liked the melody.

"Janet. We had our differences. But aside from everything else, we have always been good friends. I hope we still are."

She reached over the checkered tablecloth and grasped his hand. "Always. What's up? Do you want some Kleenex?"

"No, I don't want some Kleenex!" He pawed at his eyes and looked at her bashfully. "I just buried Dad a few days ago."

"Oh, Nick! I'm so sorry!"

"Don't mean nothin'. I didn't come looking for sympathy."

"What then?"

He lit a cigarette behind cupped hands. "Where did we go wrong? I mean, was it me? Was it you?"

She stared out the window of McHale's Bar & Grill at the lightly dusted peaks across the valley. "We were the most beautiful couple in the world. We had the most beautiful son. Remember how people would always come up to us and rave about him? From Colorado Springs to Illinois to Honolulu."

"Where is he now?"

"Phoenix. How long has it been since you've talked?"

"Too long. Does he still hate me?"

"He just wants to understand you."

"Hell, I don't understand me. How can he?"

"Well, he told me what happened with Charlie Brown last Thanksgiving." She paused and lit her own cigarette. "You asked where we went wrong. I don't know. I think I was always competing with Vietnam for your love. For your soul. I just wanted to be as important to you as IT was. I could share you with other women, but not with Vietnam."

"Why?"

"Because I knew the other women were only one-night stands. Vietnam was like your second wife. Are you in love with someone?"

"Yeah." He sipped his beer and followed her gaze out at the mountains. The song filled the ensuing silence…

"I didn't think it could happen again. I'm too old and set in my ways.
I was convinced I would always be lonely, all the rest of my days.
Maybe I gave up on romance in my longing to give up the pain.
I never thought I would ever love again…"

She turned back to him. "Are you talking about Malia, the Filipina you married after we split up?"

He shook his head. "We're getting divorced too."

"Oh shit! I'm sorry, Nick. Why do I keep saying that?"

Nick shrugged. "I'm sorry too. I keep hurting people. Especially the ones I love, and I don't know why. I have to stop but I don't know how. I've been going to the Vet Center. They say I have PTSD. I've been studying the *Course in Miracles* too. It helps a lot, but there's so much more.

"Anyway, her name is Hang. I just met her in Vietnam, and she's wonderful. You'd love her. Everybody does. She's the one, Janet. She really is the one. But I'm scared." He took a puff. "Would you help me?"

She laughed. "If anyone else heard this conversation they would think we're nuts. But if they knew how many times we watched each other make love with someone else maybe they'd understand. Remember that foursome we did with Jim and Alice in Honolulu?"

"Forget about it."

"Have you?"

338   STUART NICHOLLS

"No. But there's no payoff in it. Jim's dead, she got off easy, and we're here. At least for now." He took a long puff. "Tell me about your boyfriend."

She came back to the now. "His name is Peter. I think you'll like him. He's a Vietnam vet too. He's into hunting and survival living and making jewelry."

Nick laughed. "Interesting combo. Does he know I'm here?"

"Yes. But he's afraid that you came here to take me away with you. Did you?"

"No. Are you sorry?"

"I'm glad you're happy with, what's her name?"

"Hang."

"Yeah. Hang... Peter should be here any minute. Then we can load up your bags and head out to our cabin. You're welcome to stay in our bunkhouse. It's small, but it has a couple of cots and a heater."

"I don't want to upset Peter."

"Don't worry. Well, speak of the devil!"

A tall, forty-something man with long, wavy brown hair came up to their table. He kissed Janet as if marking his territory, then coldly sized up Nick when he stood to shake hands. Nick gave him a warm smile and a firm grip. "Welcome home, brother." This brought a surprised smile to Peter's face. "That's right. Janet said you were there too. When?"

"Sixty-five to sixty-six. Then again in '87, '89, and last month."

"Last month? Holy shit! What's it like? How'd they treat you? Where did you go?"

"If you'll let me buy you a beer, I'll tell you all about it."

"Well gee, OK."

For the next hour the two vets became so engrossed in their conversation that they never noticed Janet get up and visit some friends at a distant table.

"Did you ever get up to Hue?" Peter asked.

"Yeah. Just a couple of weeks ago. We went down the Perfume River and stopped at a beautiful pagoda."

Peter came unglued. "Thien Mu pagoda!" he shouted. Other patrons turned and eyed them curiously, then resumed their conversations.

Janet came back and giggled as she sat down. "What are you yelling about?"

Peter ignored her. His eyes were glassy and far away. "I was in the Navy. I ran a Swift boat on that river in '69 and '70. We'd stop in there all the time to visit the old monk who ran the place. I helped support his orphanage. We became good friends. Did you happen to meet him?"

A sly smile crept across Nick's face. "Was his name Thich Don Hau?"

"Yeah, I think it was! So you DID meet him!"

"No. We tried but he was very sick. You said you were friends?"

"Good friends!" Peter was beaming.

"I've got some bad news for you, brother. He was a Viet Cong commander who engineered the 1968 Tet Offensive in Hue."

Peter was shocked into silence. When the stare came into his eyes Nick patted his shoulder. "Don't mean nothin', brah. That was the nature of the beast. It's all good now."

Peter stared at Nick. "You said 'we' went there. Who else went?"

"Another vet friend and a Vietnamese lady who has become the love of my life. No offense, Janet." Janet smiled and looked down at her clasped hands on the table. "Like I said. I'm happy for you."

Peter could not conceal his relief. "So you're not here trying to hook up again?"

Nick laughed and shook his head. "Janet and I made a lot of mistakes. I don't want to make them again with Hang. I just need her help. Is that OK with you?"

"You're welcome at our place any time. Should we go?"

As Nick paid the tab Janet said, "Nick, you can ride with me and we'll meet Peter at the house."

"If it's all the same to you, I'll ride with Peter. Is that cool?"

Peter grasped Nick's hand. "Welcome home."

The old Ford pickup weaved along the two-lane highway. The aspens were beginning to turn gold against the dark-green spruce on the steep slopes of the valley.

"How did you and Janet meet anyway?" Peter asked.

"I had just gotten back from Nam in '66 and was stationed at Fort Carson. One night I was in this cowboy bar with a dance floor and a good band. After our first dance we sat down and got into a ferocious argument about the Nam. She was anti-war and anti-veteran like everybody else. But she was beautiful. I couldn't make up my mind which I wanted more. To fuck her or kill her. I remember her asking me, 'What do you want, a medal?' I told her, 'Already got some. I want respect. I want acceptance. I want you and everybody like you to get off our backs and put the blame where it belongs. On the government. Nobody hates war more than those who have to fight it. So shut up and give me your phone number!'

"Nine months later she was pregnant and we got married."

Peter had to laugh. "If it's any consolation, she and I started pretty much the same way."

"Well, I hope it doesn't end the same way. You seem like a pretty decent dude to me."

After a dinner of bear and venison chili, Janet went to do dishes. Peter handed Nick another beer. "Come in here, man. I got something I need to show you." In a small cluttered den Peter moved some dusty cardboard boxes off an old olive-green footlocker. He pulled it away from the wall. Nick noticed a well-rusted padlock in the hasp. Peter sat and sighed deeply. He stared hard at Nick. "I brought this back from Nam in '70. In over twenty years, it has never been opened." From a nearby shelf he produced a hammer and chisel. It took four good raps to break loose the lock.

Nick held up his hands. "Hey, brother. You don't need to do this now. This doesn't involve me."

"Bullshit! I'm honored to show you this. There'll never be a better time than now."

Nick stood and they hugged hard just as Janet came around the corner. "Well, I see you two are getting along all right."

Peter chuckled and wiped his eyes. "If it's OK, Nick and I are gonna be up for a while. You can go to bed."

She stared at them a moment, studying their faces, then nodded. "Goodnight, guys. Oh! And welcome home!"

One by one, Peter removed hundreds of photographs wrapped in brown paper bags and rubber bands. There were also stained silk clothes, lacquerware paintings and some jungle fatigues. With each photo he would give Nick its history and meaning. Then he pulled one out and smiled triumphantly. "Ah ha! Here it is! Check this out, man! This is me and the old monk at Thien Mu pagoda standing in front of a huge tree that has been there forever. Do you remember seeing it?"

"It's still there, brah."

Peter stared at it so long that Nick thought he had fallen asleep. His watch read 0348. Then Peter handed Nick the photograph. "I want you to have this."

"What? Are you fucking nuts? You keep that, man!"

"Do you think you'll ever go back there again?"

"I'll be back in a couple of weeks. Why?"

"Would you take this to the pagoda and give it to the old monk? Tell him I will always remember him and our friendship. No matter which side he was on."

Before the sun rose over the jagged peaks, Nick had made another promise.

Janet's rosy red cheeks were wet with tears as they hugged for the last time at the Montrose airport.

"Nick, I'm really worried about Peter. I've never seen him like this. He's just sitting there on the floor going through his box. You've only been here one day. How did you get him to open it?"

He wiped her face with his fingers. "I didn't. But I believe that all vets have a Pandora's box somewhere. Sooner or later we have to open them and let the demons out. It's just Peter's time, that's all. He's a good man, Janet. Try to be there for him."

"What are you going to do over there, anyway?"

"Live out the dream I guess. Remember when I studied at University of Hawaii?"

"Yes. Then the war ended, and we couldn't go. I would have, you know. If we had won."

He nodded. "But you still would've had to share me with Vietnam. Funny how things work out."

Her eyes brimmed again. "Will we ever see you again?"

"If the fates allow."

"What should I tell Eric?"

He looked far away and long ago. "That it was me who left the gate open."

"What?"

He shook himself back to the now. "It was all my fault, not his. I'm sorry." He burned her eyes into his memory, then turned away. "Have a good life."

CHAPTER 54
Maui
September 28,1991

When Nick picked up his mail at the post office, he found the final divorce papers had been signed and recorded. Two days later, a squad of his veteran friends came up to his house and helped him move all his furniture down to his shed. They had a GI party and cleaned the entire house. It was now ready for tenants. Nick hired a property manager who would rent out both his houses and deposit the money in his account. But there was no way to transfer the money to Vietnam because of the embargo. Nick would have to return every so often to fill his money belt with cash and go back.

The late morning sun played hide and seek with puffy clouds that drifted lazily on the trade wind.

He stood on his deck for the last time. His suitcase and two large crates waited patiently. Custer's small portable radio played a Michael McDonald song...

"Now here I stand. I wonder why, I'm on my own. Why did it end this way? On my own...

This isn't how it was supposed to be... I wish that we could do it all again.

So many times, I could have told you, losing you, it cut like a knife. You walked out and there went my life...

I've got to learn where I belong again, I've got to learn to be strong again... On my own."

Mark, Custer, and the Grizz began loading Tim's car as Nick surveyed the world he was leaving behind. He felt his death was imminent, but he didn't care. He would give it up and take what comes. His first life had begun at birth and ended the first time he set foot in Vietnam. His second life began then and there. Now the twenty-five years of waiting was over. The third lifetime was about to begin.

His small going away party got underway at Saigon Café in Wailuku at three. His flight was at nine. The waiter, *Anh* Nguyen, paused at the edge of their table. He picked up the empty bottles and asked, "*Mot chai nua khong, Anh Ly?*"

Nick nodded. It was only his third one, and the day was still young. Sitting next to him was Mark, the stocky, sandy-haired Texan. His drawl somehow escaped between clenched teeth and tight lips. It had always fascinated Nick.

"Mark, I gotta ask you, man. How come everybody from Texas talks through their teeth?"

Mark took a long pull on his beer. "Nick, you ain't never been to Texas, have ya?" Nick shook his head. "Well, ah'll tell you what. See, down 'ere we got plenty cows and horses and lots of them big ol' black flahs flahin around. Man, if you don't talk through your teeth, why they'll flah down in 'ere and fill you raht up! You won't have to ba lunch for a week, and I ain't bullshittin', motherfucker!"

Sharing the laughter was Custer who, like Nick, came from a small town in Illinois. He had served with the First Cavalry Division in the same unit as Jack Smith. His dark-gray hair was curly above sunburned cheeks. He had a slight paunch hanging over his belt. He had been Nick's best friend for over thirty years and they had much in common. They had worked, traveled, fought, hunted, fished, farmed, and played music together. They had even shared a girlfriend once.

Outside, the afternoon trade wind rustled the bamboo in a concrete planter box by the restaurant's front door. Saigon Café was nestled in the older, poorer part of Wailuku. It was surrounded by plantation style wooden houses and two-story apartments with an abundance of coconut and bauhinia trees. Inside, the pungent aroma of fried onions and garlic danced hand in hand with basil and fresh snapper.

After *Anh* Nguyen returned with fresh beers, the Grizz raised his glass to his friends. "*Bon voyage*, Nick! You crazy son of a bitch!" They all drained their brew and grinned sloppily at each other like a band of pirates.

Nick turned to the beer-bellied Grizz, whose long red hair fell over thick shoulders to present the classic picture of his Viking ancestry. "Hey, Grizz. Ain't it your turn to buy a round?"

The Grizz shook his head. "I'd love to Nick, but I'm so broke I can't even pay attention!" Dissatisfied with the response of mild chuckling, he added, "Why, I'm so broke I had to jack off the dog to feed the cat!" The table roared with knee-slapping appreciation as the Grizz leaned forward at them with wild eyes and open mouth, forcing them to share his ribald laughter. An older tourist couple, sitting at the next table, was obviously repulsed by their rowdy behavior and glared over at the men.

The Grizz didn't miss a beat. "I'm sorry, folks. I know that sounds kinda rude, vulgar and disgusting." He pulled himself up and pretended to straighten an imaginary tie. "But hey! That's JUST the kinda guy I am!" Again the table erupted in unrepentant glee, leaving the neighboring couple shaking their heads and looking for the exit.

Just then, Custer returned from the men's room in time to appreciate the exchange between the tables. He stood over the Grizz, put his hands on the big man's shoulders and shook him playfully. "That's what we love about you, Grizz. Your self-deprecating humor."

Grizz emptied his glass, and with red eyes watering, he sputtered, "Yeah, that's my specialty, that self-defecating humor!" Then, lifting his bulbous ass off the bench seat he punctuated his *faux pas* with a thunderous fart for emphasis.

"Har! Har! Har!" growled the unruly crew. That was enough for the elderly couple, who stood up abruptly and made a hasty retreat out the front door, mumbling to each other in disgust.

The Grizz slapped Nick's arm. "Nick, I wanna thank you for gettin' me to go down to the Vet Center. I'm tellin' ya, since you been gone I made lots of progress, by God!"

Nick chuckled. "Yes, I can see that!"

The Grizz looked hurt and pretended to be on the brink of tears. "Come on now. I'm tryin' to be serious here."

Nick turned sincere. "I'm glad to hear that, brother. What did you learn about yourself?"

The Grizz winked around the table. "Well, just the other day the doc told me that I made a major breakthrough, and he was real proud of me."

"What was it?" Nick asked. "Did you acknowledge you have

problems with survivor guilt, or you figured out why you keep having the nightmares?"

The Grizz looked around the table again, "Hell no! I found out, I'm a LESBIAN!" he roared and put the bear hug on Nick and shook him while they all laughed uproariously.

The outburst died down to a chuckle again as the petite and beautiful owner, Jennifer Nguyen, arrived through the kitchen door carrying a paper bag and her purse.

"Hello, *Anh* Ly! Hi, guys!"

Nick nodded, "*Chao, em! Khoe khong?*"

"*Da, khoe.*" She smiled, shaking her head. "I can hear you guys way out in the parking lot. You know I want you to have your party for *Anh* Ly but please don't scare off my other customers, OK?"

"*Xin loi, em,*" said Nick.

She smiled at him and waved it away. Then she reached into her bag. "Ly *oi*, I brought you a present from home. This is the first fruit off my tree that I planted a few years ago. Do you know what it is?"

Everyone at the table was stunned by the immediate shock that swept over Nick's face as he took the gold colored fruit with a curved red appendage at the bottom. His mouth fell open and his eyes widened as he stared at it incredulously.

"What is it, Nick?" asked Tim. The others exchanged quizzical looks as Nick gazed through and past them to a private place far away. They knew the look. At one time or another they all had it. It was cold, empty, and hard. It could pierce concrete walls, cross vast oceans, or transcend time and space. It saw reality with frightening clarity and could bring there and then to here and now at hair-trigger speed.

Mark put his hand on Nick's shoulder. "Nick, you OK, brother?" There was a long silence. "Nick?"

Without blinking Nick said, "Did I ever tell you guys the story about Sergeant Xuong?" They all looked at each other and shook their heads. Nick emptied his beer, took a deep breath, and surveyed his friends.

The booth grew quiet as the men sipped their beer and listened. In a heavy voice, thick with emotion, he began, "We were in War Zone C. April '66. It was ungodly hot. We had been out in the bush for three weeks straight.

"What was left of Alpha company had not been resupplied for

days. None of us had any C-rations left and no water in our canteens. The dry season was upon us in full force. The tropical sun was relentless and laid everything dusty and brittle. The bamboo thickets that stood in the parched red clay would rattle whenever a timid breeze would dare to creep in off the Cambodian plains.

"I was on point, again. Panting and groaning, I swung my machete automatically, like a machine. I had to fight the natural urge to let my mind drift off to other places and happier times. My fatigues were crusted white with salt from my sweat that had stopped flowing hours before. I began playing games with my mind to keep focused on the present. I debated which was better, swinging my big knife in the dark, humid greeness of the jungle or trudging, arms free, across the wide open expanse of dry paddies. My chance to find out came as I spotted sky, behind some foliage to my front. I instinctively crouched down and clenched a fist over my head. The column behind me came to a welcome halt. I heard the rustling of bushes, then Sergeant Xuong's small hand grasped my shoulder.

"'*Anh Ly, khoe khong?*' " he asked.

"I turned grinning, '*Suc may ma khoe! Met lam!*' We giggled quietly at the edge of the tree line. Xuong could easily see the exhaustion on my face but in typical Vietnamese fashion felt he should keep it light and underplay the obvious difficulty.

"Sergeant Davis quietly made his way up to the point. 'What's the hold up, Nick?' he whispered.

" 'There's clear ground ahead, Sarge. How should we handle it?'

" 'Let's go look,' he said. So the three of us crawled forward cautiously to where the edge of the gently rolling jungle met the flat expanse of open plains. It was interspersed with small stands of arecas and fan palms. The vast stretch of yellow grass loomed forbiddingly. We could think of little else but water. Davis surveyed the horizon. 'Damn! There ain't much cover out there.'

"Sergeant Xuong turned to me, '*Anh co nuoc khong?*'

"I pulled a canteen out of its pouch, shook it, but heard nothing. 'No. How about you?'

"Xuong nodded and began to offer me and Davis a swig of filthy, black paddy water. But we rolled our eyes and I said, 'We're OK for now, thanks.' I turned back to the front, searching carefully for signs of danger.

"Xuong nudged me slightly. 'Ly, you see bamboo poles stick up like dis?' He held his hand and forearm at a 45-degree angle. I spotted a half dozen about thirty meters apart. I nodded. Xuong said. "Dat mean wews."

" 'Wews?' "I raised a questioning eyebrow. 'Oh. You mean wells. For water. *Cai gieng?*'

" 'Yes. Wews.'

"I smiled and wondered silently how many Vietnamese words I myself had butchered.

"Davis asked, 'If there's wells then there must be a village closeby, right?'

"Xuong nodded, *'Dung roi.'*

"I couldn't contain my excitement. 'And wells means water, right?'

" 'I don't know. Maybe. Maybe dry too. Very hot now.'

"I scanned the area but only spotted some pole frames that were charred and leaning. It looked like the ruins of an abandoned hamlet. The remains were shaded by several large trees. There was no movement except for the rippling heat mirage that rose up off the sun-baked paddies in the foreground. I tried to swallow but couldn't. I began reconsidering Xuong's offer of paddy water but decided against it. The chances of contracting dysentery or cholera were too high to risk it. At least for now.

"There came movement from the rear. The three of us turned as Lieutenant Arthur crawled up on us, followed by Spec 4 Simmons, his RTO. They were breathing heavily. We all had scarlet flushed faces, except for Sergeant Xuong who smiled quietly, seemingly immune from the onslaught of the deadly heat.

"Davis spoke in a hoarse whisper. 'Sir, there's open ground ahead and what looks like an abandoned ville about half a click away. Sergeant Xuong says there are some wells out there too. We really need some water, sir.'

"The LT nodded weakly. 'I know, but orders are that we proceed about ten more clicks to a rendezvous point with the rest of the company. We're supposed to maintain cover and concealment until then because a large force of hard-core VC has been sighted in the area. We're only an under-strength platoon, and I don't want to get caught out in the open.'

"A tense hush fell over our group. We eyed each other uncomfortably. Davis spoke up. 'LT, there ain't none of us got water, except Xuong, and I wouldn't even give Charlie that shit to drink.'

"Xuong's handsome face beamed with innate Vietnamese pride. Us Americans were all larger, stronger, richer, and better equipped than him, but he was lean and tough. He could take the heat and survive on paddy water without getting sick. No sweat, GI.

"The LT retorted, 'Orders are orders, Sergeant Davis, you know that.'

" 'Yes sir. But I've been here long enough to know that you can only go so far without water. I think you should reconsider, sir.'

"While they debated, I reconned out to the front. I focused on the patches of trees that randomly dotted the paddies. If the enemy was around, that's where he would be. Suddenly I detected slight movement in a bamboo thicket close to the ruins of the ville. 'Psst! LT! I got movement out there!'

"We fell silent and crouched low on the jungle floor. We spotted two black-clad figures emerging from the bamboo and trudging toward the wells. Each had a rifle slung on their shoulders. My eyes were wild with excitement. I turned quickly to the LT with questioning raised eyebrows. The LT thought aloud. 'There isn't enough cover to hide a sizeable force unless they're sequestered in the ville. We have the protection of the jungle. Fuck it! Take 'em, Nick!'

"I quickly brought up my M-16 to my shoulder, sighted in on the leader, and squeezed off a six round burst. But in my excitement I had forgotten to allow for the 500-meter distance, which was considerable for my weapon. An M-14, with its flat trajectory, would have had no problem at that range, but the shorter, lighter, and faster Armalite was designed for close quarters in the jungle. Red dirt flew up at the feet of the two VC, and they began sprinting for the wells. Making adjustments, I delivered a longer burst. This time, the second man fell forward onto his knees. The first one turned back, grabbed his comrade by the arm and dragged him stumbling to where a long pole signified a well. Suddenly the pole bent over and down and they both disappeared.

"The LT was on the horn immediately. 'Six, this is three six, over! Sir, we spotted two VC in an abandoned ville and fired on them! I think we got one! Request permission to pursue, sir!'

" 'What's your position, over?'

"Xuong nudged my arm and gave me a thumbs up. I shook my head, ashamed. I knew better than to let my emotions take over. I should have been able to kill them both, but I had fired too quickly. Still focused on the area around the wells, I searched desperately for more movement. The two men were probably sentries for a larger unit that could be hiding in the ruins and surrounding brush.

"Yes, sir. Three six out." The LT's voice was coarse and dry. "Sergeant Davis. Take your squad out to that well. Second squad will be on your left and first squad will be on their left. We'll leap frog. Questions?"

Shaking his head, Davis motioned us out into the direct heat of the sun, leaving the refuge of the jungle behind. I labored heavily while I ran with my pack banging and slapping my back and shoulders. I sprinted for a short paddy dike about a hundred meters to the front. Amazingly, we took no fire. When my squad hit the dirt we laid down cover fire for the other two squads while they moved up parallel to us. We rotated like that until we were at the well. We still took no return fire. With my rifle at the ready, I approached the long leaning pole with a stout woven rope descending from it down into the hole, which was one meter in diameter. Carefully, I peered over the edge, down into the abyss, searching first for the enemy and secondly for the reflection of water. I saw neither. But only a short way down was a small tunnel entrance burrowed into the wall. I beckoned the others.

"Xuong smiled and shook his head. 'VC go down rope then into tunnel.' He pointed to a spot on the rope that was red with fresh blood. 'Good shooting, Ly!' Still mad at myself, I shrugged it off.

"The LT swept his arm in an arc. 'Sergeant Davis, take your squad and set up a defensive perimeter out to the front, facing those ruins.' He then called in second squad under Sergeant Wheeler, a burly black man from Ohio whose most impressive feature was his strong, square jaw. 'Sergeant Wheeler, you and your men check out the other wells. Watch out for booby traps.'

"After several tense minutes the search ended in frustration. No VC, and no water. We all looked at each other despondently. Lieutenant Arthur sighed with downcast eyes. 'OK, men. We're going to move out and make for the rendezvous point. I don't like it, but we'll have to travel across these plains because going through the jungle will take too much time and energy. We need water! Saddle up! Nick, take the..."

"Yeah, I know, LT.'

"With our jungle fatigues crusted red and brown with white salt stripes, our ragged platoon spaced ourselves five meters apart and filed off toward the western horizon under the merciless Asian sun.

"Hours later, I was becoming delirious as I led the platoon across the red, sun-baked clay. I thought I saw a cluster of trees in front of me, or was it a mirage? I was stumbling more than walking now. I looked back over my burning shoulders at the others. They were all looking at the ground as they plodded on in my footsteps."

Nick took a another swallow of beer. "So we end up in this small grove of trees at the rendezvous point. By then, even Xuong's paddy water is long gone and we're about to die from thirst. I mean REALLY! Xuong comes up to me and says, with a sly smile, 'Ly, you thirsty?' Duh! So he reaches up into this tree and pulls out this yellow fruit with a red thing at the bottom and gives it to me. 'Eat this,' he says. So, I do. Suddenly my mouth turns into cotton and I start to gag. I swear, we'd been working together as interpreters for months already, and I thought I could trust him, but here he is trying to kill me! So I jump up and go for his throat when he says, 'No! No! Just wait!' And then my thirst totally disappears.

"Later on, the choppers came and took us back to our base camp, and we went our separate ways. I shipped out two months later and I never saw Sergeant Xuong again. As the years passed I would think of him often and wish I could thank him for saving me and my platoon that day. When I went back to Nam, a couple of years ago, I found out it was a cashew fruit that had saved us. And this, right here, is the first one I've ever seen outside of Vietnam."

The others in the booth sat looking at Nick with mouths agape. Mark spoke first. "Goddamn, Nick! That's a hell of a story, and I ain't bullshittin'. But man, you can turn a short story into a novel better than anybody I know." Their laughter made Nick blush.

Tim patted Nick's shoulder. "That's right! Nick always gets right to the point... no matter how long it takes!"

Nick chuckled. "I'm gonna miss you sorry bastards."

Custer suddenly shuddered and jumped like he was being shot with electricity. "What the hell you goin' back there for, anyway? You already been back three times! What the fuck, over?"

"*Anh* Ly." It was Jennifer. "Aren't you afraid? Us Vietnamese are. We don't dare go back. What if they put you in jail or kill you?"

"They already had their chance. Don't mean nothin'." Nick could feel their collective surge of angst. It caught him off guard. "Listen up. This started off being one thing, but now it's something else. I don't know where the trail will end, but I'm gonna cut it. What happens, happens."

Custer stood and drained his beer. "You're committin' suicide by default! That's what you're doin'. I want no part of it. Fuck you, Nick!" He threw down some money and stormed out the door.

Nick sat back in the booth. He watched out the window as his best friend moved through the shadows of the treeline by the street. "Anybody else got a problem with this? I mean, do I need to call a cab?"

Tim Campbell smiled. "My car's outside. If you don't mind riding with a half-paralyzed jarhead."

Nick stood up. "I gotta piss first."

Minutes later, Nick found Tim sitting alone. "Where'd everybody go?"

Tim shrugged, "I guess saying goodbye ain't easy. Especially when a brother is going back to Nam for good. Remember in the war when we DEROS'd back to the world? We were ecstatic to be going home but felt guilty as hell for leaving the others behind. I think this is a twisted version of that."

"Timmy, for a guy with half a brain you sure got a handle on things."

Both slightly drunk, they stumbled to Tim's sedan. Once inside, the finality of it all hit Nick full force. It left him feeling numb yet content. Once again, he gave it up. Tim pulled away from the curb. As they headed down Kaahumanu Avenue in the gathering darkness another car pulled along side and blew its horn. They recognized the driver as Mike Murphy, who was yelling farewell to Nick. And next to him, hanging his entire torso out the passenger side window was Babaloo. He saluted Nick, then reached for the sky with both arms open wide.

Nick would never forget the look on Babaloo's face as they sped past them in the night. He had that same look that they give you when they're hit really bad, and you lay them down in a pool of blood on the throbbing floor of the Huey, with the blades pounding and slapping over your head.

They look into your eyes, and you both know that you'll never see each other again. They look at you with a profound love for the living hell that you have endured together, with fear of the inevitable, and the desperate hope that it wasn't all for nothing.

Within fifteen minutes Tim pulled his car over to the curb in front of the departure gates. Nick called the porters to help with the luggage.

Tim reached out with his good arm and gave Nick a strong hug. "You know, I kinda wish I was going back with you."

"I kinda wish you were too. But this time is different. I ain't comin' back til my money runs out. Then I'll fill my pockets and go again."

"What about your mail? Who's gonna keep it for you, the post office?"

"No. Actually, I had it forwarded to Alan, in Bangkok. He'll get it to me or I'll go pick it up once in a while."

Tim nodded. "How are you gonna pull this off, Nick? I mean, if it's illegal to even BE in Vietnam, how can you stay forever?"

"Do you believe in destiny?"

"I live day to day."

Nick nodded. "I've been pointed toward this all my life." He drew his right hand into a salute. "Aloha, brah."

CHAPTER 55
Tan Son Nhat Airport, Vietnam
October 1991

Being the only westerner, Nick easily stood out as he pushed his luggage cart through the ill-tempered, sweating mob of Asian passengers to the Hai Quan inspection desk. Just beyond, he searched the sea of Vietnamese faces pressed up against the chain-link fence. Thousands of people anxiously awaited a glimpse of their loved ones coming through Customs. There was waving, shouting, and chaos. The air was thick with the stench of an open sewer, mildew, minty antiseptic, and the nauseating sweetness of decaying fruits.

Above the din he heard the shrill voice calling, "Minh *oi!* Minh *oi!*" Somehow he spotted her small figure amid the throng. She wore a white dress and a red ribbon in her hair. She carried a bouquet of roses. His heart leapt into his throat as he also began waving, shouting, and becoming part of the insanity.

Minutes later, he passed through the final gate and she was in his arms. They kissed long and passionately, in defiance of traditional Vietnamese morals. The crowd stared at them in shock but was not about to chastise the rugged, broad-shouldered foreigner. The couple's love was so obvious that it was hard not to accept. Finally she released her arms from around his neck and stared at him breathlessly. "Minh *oi*, welcome home!"

Once again, Nicholas Dwyer felt the emotional surge welling up inside his chest, filling his throat, and burning behind his eyes. Yes, he thought, this is it! I really am home!

The driver, named Chanh, took them down narrow, tree-lined Pasteur Street in the morning sun. The shadows were cool, and the scents of the curbside kitchens enticing. Young girls rode their bikes in flowing, white *ao dai* and *non la* straw hats. Occasionally a motorbike would putter by, leading a trail of blue smoke. They sat in the back holding hands and kissing.

Chanh could not help but watch them in his mirror. "*Xin loi, chi Hang.* What nationality is he?"

"American," she replied without looking at him.

His face registered surprise. "*Troi oi!* Was he a soldier in the war?"

"Yes. Why?"

Chanh sighed and stared out the windshield. His eyes grew sad. He looked back into the mirror. "My wife's whole family was killed by an American helicopter. She was badly wounded."

As Nick listened and translated in his mind, a wave of empathy washed over him. He let go of Hang's hand and reached up over the seat. He gently squeezed Chanh's shoulder. "Brother, I am very sorry for her loss."

Chanh was shocked. "My God, you speak Vietnamese!"

"Just a little. Does she still hate Americans?"

Chanh slowed down and turned left into a horseshoe-shaped driveway. It led up to a beautiful two-story French villa. He stopped under the marquee and shut off the engine. He turned to face Nick. "I don't know what she feels now. But she was very saddened at the time. We don't talk about it anymore. We must move on."

"That's easy for you to say. You won the war. For us it's different."

"I'm sorry, brother, but nobody won the war."

Nick nodded, remembering Thunder Road with Vy. "Would it be OK for us to meet your wife sometime? I think it might help us both to heal."

"I will ask her. Now, here you are. The Pasteur Institute guest house. I will help you carry the boxes upstairs."

Nick was amazed. The building was freshly painted beige with a terra-cotta-tiled roof and stood in a lovely park-like setting of a one-acre lawn. There were poinciana, tamarind, and African tulip trees, whose blooms softened the air with color. Other buildings were arranged in a rectangular pattern surrounding the lawn. Nick thought it too good to be true. "*Minh oi!* How did you find such a beautiful place for us?"

"I want you to be happy here. We have a room on the second floor. There is a breeze and a view. But it is expensive because you are

American. It is $500 per month. Is it OK?"

Nick nodded. "It's OK."

Across the street was the famous Pho Hoa Pasteur restaurant. They served the best *pho* in Ho Chi Minh City. The tree-lined street was magnificent and, combined with the French colonial architecture, Nick felt as if he had gone back in time for a second chance. Then he remembered that MACV Headquarters had been just up the street, where he had reunited with A.J., back in 1965.

After unloading Nick's luggage they went out to buy bottled water, beer, and soda. Hang picked up some litchee, mangosteen, grapefruit, and bananas. A local street vendor supplied fresh-baked French bread and *La Vache Qui Rit* cheese. The final touch was *nem*, a raw, pickled pork wrapped in banana leaf with a clove of garlic. Nick's reluctance to try it surrendered to Hang's reassurances that Vietnamese had eaten it for centuries with no major problems.

Their room had a high ceiling, tall French windows with lace curtains, and a rattling air conditioner that provided relatively cool air. By dark, they had all Nick's clothes hanging in the spacious closet next to Hang's wardrobe. The only drawback was the toilet, which had no seat, just the cold rim of the bowl to sit on. But better than a hole in the floor with two rocks.

The next morning, Hang went out to the street vendors and brought back two loaves of French bread filled with ground pork omelettes and garnished with green onions and hot chili peppers. The maid delivered some tiny cups of powerful and delicious Vietnamese coffee. After Nick drank two he felt like he was being electrocuted. They ate breakfast by the windows that opened onto a peaceful view of the gardens below. Hang delivered the *coup de grace* when she inserted the tape cassette that Nick had left with her six weeks prior. "For the rest of our lives, love always" pulled on their heartstrings in the morning stillness. Nick felt his dream was finally coming true.

The first order of business was for Nick to register with the police. The paranoid communist government required it of all foreigners. An hour later, they climbed out of the cyclo beneath the shaded entrance to Vietnam Tourism and walked up to the familiar desk of Pham Thai Thanh.

Thanh looked up in shock, then seeing Hang, broke into her famous pearly white smile.

"So, the bad check returns, eh?" she teased Nick. Then she turned to Hang. "*Chao, chi. Khoe khong?*"

Hang returned the smile. "*Da, khoe. Cam on, chi.* It's nice to finally meet you."

"Me too. But I must warn you, I think your boyfriend is a CIA spy," she laughed.

"Yes, and Thanh is KGB," Nick countered.

Thanh came around the desk and pulled up another chair. "Please sit down. So, how long will you be in Vietnam this time, Nick?"

"Forever."

She chuckled. "No, really."

"Really. Forever."

Thanh looked at Hang, who nodded in affirmation.

"But Nick, as you know, the maximum visa is for only one month. Then you must leave."

"And go where?"

"Home."

"I AM home."

"I don't think you understand. It is illegal for foreigners to stay longer than a month."

Nick leaned forward in his chair. "I don't think YOU understand. I have nothing to go back to. No job, no house, nothing. I'm living here."

"But you need to have a job here also, or do business of some kind. And it's impossible because of your country's embargo. I'm sorry, Nick. You will have to leave."

Nick let go of Hang's hand and reached over to grasp Thanh's. "You know, this is your own damn fault. If it wasn't for you, and everyone else, making me feel so welcome here, I never would have come back."

Thanh smiled at Hang. "I think it's obvious why you came back. But it wasn't because of me."

He and Hang looked at each other with love pouring from their eyes. "You're right. But you know my story, Thanh. I've waited twenty-five years for this. Now, I'm sorry, but I'm not going anywhere." He placed his papers on the desk. "We're staying at the Pasteur Institute guest house. I'll be waiting to hear from you."

Hang and Nick stood up, bowed, then smiled benignly and walked out the door holding hands. Thanh sat looking helplessly around the room.

Once outside, Hang laughed aloud. "You *dien cai dau*! You know that? She work for the government! How can you just tell her no like that?"

Nick grinned at her. "I never did take orders very well. Don't worry, she'll let me stay. This is meant to be."

As they crossed Nguyen Hue Street and approached the corner by the Palace Hotel, they heard the familiar voice shouting. "*Anh Ly! Chi Hang! Troi dat oi!*" *Anh* Mot came running up, laughing and hugged them both warmly. "You come back again! I know. You always keep your promise, right?"

Nick held his old friend with one arm and his new love with the other. Suddenly, Carmine Genovese's face flashed in his eyes. "Yes, Mot... I do now."

For the next few weeks, Mot and Hang drove Nick around the city and the surrounding countryside on their motorbikes, trying to reacclimate him while he looked for some kind of work. He started with the Department of Agriculture. Thanh made an appointment for him with the director, Mr. Nguyen Van Tim, and the external relations chief, Mr. Tran Ngoc Lang.

Nick was received warmly and within minutes of the initial tea ceremony they fell into the easy rapport known to all farmers. They discussed the weather, crop pests, marketing problems, and the trade embargo. They hoped that Nick could somehow have a positive influence with the American government to lift the embargo and open up world markets to Vietnamese products. Nick promised he would do all he could.

The next day, Nick brought them all his old college textbooks to use as reference material. He brought them volumes of technical data on a variety of crops and his own research records from working at Alexander & Baldwin's Maui papaya plantation. They were fascinated by his experience working with the so-called miracle rice, IR-8, at the University of Hawaii, as well as his knowledge about various vegetable crops, gained at his Kula Agricultural Park farm.

They invited Nick to visit their experimental farm in Hoc Mon, outside the city near Cu Chi. After studying their planting techniques and variety trials, Nick was able to offer some ideas to help with crop protection. He also promised to bring seed from new vegetable strains in the U.S. the next time he returned to Maui.

In response to the favorable reports that Thanh received from the Department of Agriculture, Nick was rewarded with a three-month visa. The only condition was that he not mention it to anyone, especially any other visiting Americans.

Each day, Nick met many Vietnamese officials and foreign businessmen. Most of the latter were from Asian countries such as Taiwan, Japan and Korea, Australia, Singapore, and the Philippines. As his contacts expanded, so did his influence and acceptance by the Vietnamese government. He was on a first-name basis with the directors of Vietnam Tourism and soon became a familiar figure in Thanh's office. He also enjoyed the celebrity status of being one of the very first American veterans to live in Vietnam after the war.

He made it a point to learn at least ten new Vietnamese words a day and soon became fluent enough to get much more than the "beer, bed, and a blowjob" that he had joked about two years before with the Aussie veterans.

Hang would often drive him out to the tunnels of Cu Chi, where he had fought during the war. He soon became very good friends with the soldiers who worked as tunnel guides to the increasing number of tourists. Their problem, however, was their lack of English-language training. This made it very difficult to answer questions, and they had to give their lectures in Vietnamese while someone else translated. Soon Nick was giving them basic English lessons three times a week.

One Sunday afternoon Nick and Hang were enjoying the rare and precious private time that Nick had taken for granted back on Maui. They lay in bed, naked, munching exotic snacks and talking intimately. They heard a knock on the door. Nick yelled out, "*Di di!* We don't want visitors today!"

The persistent knocking aroused his anger. He slipped on his shorts and flung open the door. Standing humbly with hands clasped in front of them was the driver Chanh and a stout woman with a strong jaw and short hair. They both bowed and smiled, very much embarrassed. "*Da, xin loi, Anh Ly.* I am sorry to bother you. I would like you to meet my wife, Hien. You remember the first day I meet you?"

Fully ashamed now at his rude behavior, Nick bowed low to them. He had to forgive their unannounced visit. Telephones were a luxury enjoyed by only a handful of people in those days. "Please forgive me. Minh *oi*! Get dressed. We have important guests."

Nick pulled on a T-shirt and ushered them in to sit on the couch. Hang brought them sodas from the fridge. The young couple kept smiling shyly and nodding politely while Hang made small talk. Nick made a conscious effort to be calm and friendly. He and Hien stole quick glances at each other while the others talked. During a lull they all turned to Nick. It was his cue.

"*Anh* Chanh and *Chi* Hien. I want to thank you very much for coming today. I know it must be very difficult to be with an American veteran who you fought against."

Hien looked at her husband and searched his eyes. He nodded. She turned back to Nick. "You are the first American I have ever met since the war. You are not what I expected."

"How is that?"

"You seem so nice. Not like the American devils that we hated for so long. I am sorry." She laughed uncomfortably. "Have you met other soldiers from the National Liberation Front?"

"Yes, many. I would like to tell you the same thing I told them. Our two governments might not be friends, but that doesn't mean that we cannot be. I am very sorry for what my country did here during the war and for some things that I did. I'm especially sorry to hear about the loss of your family."

"*Cam on, anh.*" Her eyes stopped smiling and went blank. She was gone. Nick knew that look all too well.

"Hien *oi*. Can I ask you how they died, or is it too painful?"

She kept looking far away, then spoke in a monotone. "We were crossing a small river by the Cambodian border. My mother, father, two older brothers, and me. I was only six. We were on our way to a camp of freedom fighters.

"An American gunship appeared suddenly and opened fire on us with machine guns and rockets. I felt the bullets hitting my legs. I fell in the muddy water. When I tried to stand up I saw the bodies of my family floating away. The worst part was not being able to catch them. I could hear crazy laughter coming from the helicopter, then they flew off. I crawled out of the river and waited for some of our other soldiers to come help me."

She was startled back into the present as she felt Nick's hands on her shoulders. He was oblivious to the presence of Hang and Chanh. At that moment, Nick was in the muddy river with her. He could smell the death, the aviation fuel, the cordite. He gently took her face in his hands and stroked her cheeks. She watched the tears streaming down from his eyes. The two former enemies stood and held each other in a tender embrace as their loved ones watched in silent awe. Nick was overwhelmed once again by decades of time, thousands of miles, two different races and different sexes, melting into one. He could feel rage and hatred being transformed into love and understanding. The power and intensity of his emotions were truly frightening. Nick and Hien felt the encircling arms of Hang and Chanh as they joined the embrace. It was one of the most magical moments of his life.

CHAPTER 56
Ho Chi Minh City
November 1991

As the weeks passed, Nick and Hang fell into a comfortable routine. It became impossible for him to walk the streets downtown and not be greeted by dozens of locals, from cyclo drivers and shop-keepers to police officers. Eventually, even the beggars started to ignore him. A sure sign of acceptance in the community. They found it more productive to play on the guilt of first-time tourists.

Toward the end of November, Hang drove them out to visit his old friends, Vy and Vui. Hang and Vui hit it off immediately and kept the men laughing with their jokes and good natured antics. Vy and Vui introduced their two young children, Truong and Mai, who begged Nick to teach them English. It seemed that wherever Nick went, this was a common request, and he complied as often as time and patience allowed.

Before they left, Hang invited them to Pasteur Guest House to celebrate Nick's forty-fifth birthday at the end of the month. They excitedly agreed.

The morning of the big day, Nick went to the closet but could not find his favorite dress shirt. He had a meeting with Mr. Tim at the Department of Agriculture. "Minh *oi*. Have you seen my green aloha shirt?"

"Maybe the maid has it in the laundry. Wear a different one," she said, hiding a smile.

That evening they heard knocking at the door. It was Vy, Vui, and the kids. They came in and made clucking sounds of envy as they took in the stylish apartment. Hang played hostess and seated the children at a table of fruit and pastries. She handed Vui a soda, but gave Vy and Nick cold cans of Heineken. As they took their seats, she passed around a bowl of roasted cashew nuts. Nick looked at them for a moment before slowly putting one in his mouth.

Vy spoke up in his booming baritone voice. "I propose a toast!" And he drank some beer. "I propose another toast. To Chi Hang!" And they all drank. "I propose another toast to *hoa binh* and *huu nigh*." They laughed and drank some more but tried to catch their breath. "Oh yes, and Happy Birthday, *Anh* Nick!"

There was another knock at the door. A young man came in carrying a large cardboard box. Hang placed it on the bigger table and opened it, exposing a huge cake. It read "Happy Birthday Minh! Love Always!"

After they sang to Nick and finished their cake, Nick and Vy had more beer. Hang handed Nick a soft package wrapped in brown paper. "For you, Minh. I hope you like them."

He tore open the paper and there was his green aloha shirt along with four other brand new shirts that had been tailored using his for the model. "I stole your shirt last week and took it to the tailor. Are you mad at me?" she asked innocently.

Feigning anger Nick scowled, "Yes, and I will punish you all night long after our guests leave."

When the lascivious laughter died down, Vui sat next to Nick and pulled out a photo album from a worn plastic bag. "*Anh* Nick, I think you will find something very interesting in here. Happy Birthday!"

Nick put down his beer and began thumbing through the pages. There were pictures of many Vietnamese people, young and old. Among them were Vy, Vui, and the kids. Some were taken in a rubber plantation.

He recognized the village of Lai Khe. Then he stopped and stared long at a photo of a handsome young soldier in sunglasses and an ARVN uniform. "You know, Vui. For some reason, I think I know this guy right here."

Vui smiled that sad Vietnamese smile and took his hand. "He was my brother-in-law. He was killed by the VC when they overran Ben Cat in 1974. Yes, Nick. You did know him. He served as interpreter for Alpha Company Second of the Second in the First Infantry Division. His name was Sergeant Xuong."

CHAPTER 57
Ho Chi Minh City
December 1991

"*Anh* Ly! *Anh* Ly! You have a telephone call downstairs in the office!" called out Tuyet, their maid. Nick quickly opened the door and followed her downstairs.

"Hello, Thanh! Yes, we are free this morning. Can you speak louder? The line is very scratchy. The Mondial Hotel? OK. On Dong Khoi Street? Didn't it used to be called Tu Do Street? In half an hour? You know I'm never late. What's the surprise? OK. See you there."

Hang swerved her Honda up onto the sidewalk and gave it to the attendant, who handed her a receipt. A short, thick bellman in a blue uniform opened the heavy, sliding glass doors and growled a greeting in the northern accent. The Mondial was a small boutique hotel in the French style. It was six stories tall, white, and shaded by huge, lacy mimosa trees. The lobby was tastefully decorated with large potted plants, mirrors, hand-carved trim and plush upholstery.

Thanh sat in a chair facing the door, holding a small briefcase. Seated next to her was a young man in a white shirt, tie, and dress slacks. He had longish hair and a pleasant face. They stood, smiling as Hang and Nick entered. Thanh and Hang hugged briefly. Nick reached out for his, but was met with a reprimanding frown. They all giggled. "Nick, Hang, I want you to meet my good friend, Nguyen Viet Trung. He is the manager of this hotel."

"*Da, Chao anh. Anh khoe khong?*" Nick greeted him.

Visibly impressed, Mr. Trung beamed while shaking Nick's hand and bowing to Hang. "Your Vietnamese accent is perfect!" he exclaimed in equally perfect English.

Now it was Nick's turn to be impressed. He grinned. "Thank you. But I think your English is better than my Vietnamese."

"I doubt that, but if you like, we can speak English. Please come into our Orchid Lounge for a glass of iced tea. It can be so refreshing when you come in out of the heat. Don't you agree?"

After they were all seated and a lovely young waitress had delivered their drinks, Mr. Trung sat forward and clasped his hands. "Thanh has told me all about you and that you have come back to Vietnam several times. She also says you are a war veteran."

Nick nodded. "Yes. And you?"

"No, no. I was too young. But I saw the war from my home, in Hanoi." He watched Nick's eyes.

Nick raised his glass. "To *hoa binh*!" They all toasted.

"Have you been to Hanoi?" Trung asked.

"Yes. Thanh arranged a trip there for us a couple of months ago. It's a beautiful city. So much history and culture." Suddenly, Nick had chicken skin.

"Where did you stay in Hanoi?"

"The Thang Loi Hotel on West Lake. Do you know it?" Something was coming. Nick could feel it.

"Yes, of course. It is one of Vietnam Tourism's many hotels."

"So you work for Vietnam Tourism as well?" he glanced at Thanh, who nodded along with Trung.

Thanh said, "We are both connected."

Nick's mind sparked for a split second as he recalled the racks of AK-47s. He smiled at Thanh. "So what is the big surprise you mentioned on the phone? We Americans are not known for our patience."

Thanh grinned at Trung conspiratorially. "Do you still want to stay in Vietnam, forever?"

Nick leaned forward. "Absolutely."

Thanh seemed to enjoy watching Nick squirm. "Well, maybe we have a job for you."

"What is it? I'll do anything! Just tell me! You don't even have to pay me!"

Mr. Trung laughed. "Listen, Nick. I have a problem." He gestured around the room with open arms. "I have this lovely hotel in the center of Ho Chi Minh City. A prime location for all the tourists who will come if we can only get the U.S. trade embargo lifted. But my staff cannot speak much English! How can we welcome visitors here if we can't communicate?"

Nick was becoming agitated. "Mr. Trung, please just tell me what you want."

Trung looked Nick in the eye. "Would you be interested in teaching my staff to speak English?"

KABOOM!

Nick and Hang turned to each other and shouted in unison, "*Day Noi!*" They began laughing hysterically as Thanh and Trung looked on in bewilderment. The dream in the middle of a Hanoi night "teach to speak" had just been proven prophetic. Nick's first thought was, maybe there's something to the *Course in Miracles* after all!

Mr. Trung waited for calm. "It will be better if we don't actually pay you. However, we are prepared to offer you free room, free meals in our restaurant, and free laundry and maid service. You can work six days a week with Sunday off. Of course we will give you a long-term visa. What do you think?"

Nick looked at Hang. "When can we move in?" he asked euphorically.

"What do you mean we?" Trung replied.

"Hang and I."

Trung shot a worried glance at Thanh. "I'm very sorry, Nick. No Vietnamese guests are allowed at our hotel."

"What?" Nick was aghast. "Why not?"

Trung was apologetic. "It is against regulations. Again, I'm sorry."

Hang tried to grab Nick's hand. "Minh *oi*, it's OK..."

Nick stood abruptly with fire in his eyes. "I'm sorry too, Mr. Trung. If Hang cannot stay here, then neither can I. Thank you anyway." He pulled Hang from her chair and nodded to them.

A silent, desperate look passed between Thanh and Trung. "OK. Wait, Nick. Please sit down." Trung took a deep breath. "If you feel that strongly about it, well, I guess we can make an exception. But please don't tell anyone. I could get in big trouble. Is it a deal?"

Nick smiled, relieved. "How can I ever thank the both of you?"

Thanh gave him a deadpan stare. "Don't forget. We wouldn't do this for anyone else. Do a good job for us and you will be rewarded. If you make trouble..." She tried to smile and raised her eyebrows in warning.

Nick smiled around the table. "When can we move in?"

Room 406 was plush. Wall-to-wall carpeting, remote-controlled AC, closed-circuit TV, twin beds, and a real bathtub. The rooftop restaurant had an enclosed dining room and outdoor tables on the patio with a view of the city down to the Saigon River and beyond. Nick and Hang felt like king and queen. Everything far exceeded what he had anticipated. Before leaving Maui, he had hoped for the best while expecting the worst, but things could not be better.

By the end of the week, Nick was teaching six classes a day. Reception, restaurant and bar, housekeeping, security, office, and maintenance. There was a total of seventy students. The language ability varied widely, and the classes were held in vacant rooms which changed daily according to availability. He used *American Streamline English* textbooks which had Vietnamese translations for each word and phrase.

He had learned from the "Course in Miracles" that it is impossible to give without receiving or to teach without learning. This was proven true on a daily basis. His Vietnamese language ability increased exponentially. He also found that teaching came naturally to him, as he had always been an animated storyteller, and his uninhibited sense of humor made him appear much less threatening than the mentally disturbed combat veteran that he really was. It also encouraged his students to risk making mistakes.

Soon, his reputation of being a talented teacher spread throughout the city, and he had more offers than he could accept. Two nights a week he taught at an architectural firm owned by another friend of Thanh's. He was paid the outrageously high rate of $13/ hour, which went a long way on the local economy, although he was always charged higher prices because he was American.

One night, he stopped at the lobby bar for a cold beer after class. As he sat talking to the bartender he overheard two white men speaking English at a nearby table. One was large, red faced, with soft gray eyes and brown hair in a duck's ass style from the fifties. He spoke in a southern accent, "You know, the other night I was down at the Apocalypse Now bar. I ran into this ol' boy named Tom O'Rourke. He's a doctor. Gonna work for IOM, he says. I reckon he's gonna give the physical exams to all our refugees before we ship 'em out to the states."

The other man was beefy, with a shaved head and a perpetual look of disgust on his fat face. Arrogance oozed from every pore. Nick recognized him immediately. He had seen him several times over the last few years in various airports throughout Southeast Asia. He had CIA written all over him and Nick disliked him at once. If there was ever an ugly American, he was it. He sneered, "Yeah, I met him. Skinny son of a bitch. Looks like he's ready to croak, his own self. I remember him going on *Sixty Minutes* a few years ago to expose the AIDS epidemic in Thailand. He's got guts though, I'll give him that."

"Sorry, guys. I couldn't help overhearing," Nick said. "Dr. Tom O'Rourke and I went to the University of Hawaii together. I heard he was in town. How can I get in touch with him?"

The ugly one snorted, "Who are you?"

Nick stared the man down before he replied. "Nick Dwyer. English teacher. And you?"

Baldy looked away and sipped his beer. His friend answered for him. "This is Bob Pritchard. Immigration and Naturalization Service. I'm Manley Daniel. Orderly Departure Program. Nice to meet you." He reached out his hand. Nick took it while smirking at Mr. INS. Walk softly, Nick, he told himself. This guy may be an asshole, but you might need him someday.

"So, you guys process all the people going to the U.S.?" Nick asked.

"What the hell you think?" sneered Mr. INS.

Seeing the hot flash of fury in Nick's eyes, Manley pulled out a chair and laughed. "Sorry, Nick. You'll have to excuse ol' Bob. He's havin' a bad-hair day. Here, sit down. Beer?"

"Sure."

"Did I hear you speakin' Vietnamese over there a while ago?" Manley asked.

Nick nodded. "How about you guys?"

Manley shook his head. "Bob does, a little. Where'd you learn?"

"Here. In the war. Are you vets?"

Bob finally spoke. "I am. Third Marine Regiment. Eye Corps. Manley was 4-F. His dick was too short."

Nick grinned at Manley and shook his head sympathetically. "I was with the Big Red One. Point man."

Bob looked at Nick for the first time and stuck out his stubby hand. "Welcome home."

Nick took it and squeezed hard. "Same to you, brother." Suddenly the air was cool at the table. Nick thought to himself about forgiveness. He's probably as fucked up as I am. We're all doing the best we can. He's a son of God, just like everybody else, even though he acts like a son of a bitch.

"You're not tryin' to get your girlfriend back to the states are ya?" Bob asked.

"How did you know I had a girlfriend?"

"Everybody got one."

"No. She doesn't want to go. Neither do I. We're home. Why?"

The skinhead stood up and pushed in his chair. "Lots of guys try to use us to get their whores out of here. See ya around."

Nick watched him go, then turned to Manley. "So, where can I find Tom O'Rourke?"

Manley dug in his wallet and pulled out a card. "Here. You can keep it. I got more. You live here at the hotel?"

Nick nodded.

"Us too. We come in every three weeks, then go back to the embassy in Bangkok."

Nick watched Bob get on the elevator. "We'll have to get together with Tom sometime. Maybe you can lose Bob somewhere."

"Bob's OK. But he's been out here too long, that's all. I've seen it before. It gets to you after a while. You'll see."

"No, I doubt that. I'm staying forever."

"Don't count on it. I've seen forever come and go a couple of times. You'll see."

Nick stood up. "Thanks for the beer. Next time, I'll buy." He walked away thinking, Manley doesn't understand how I feel about Vietnam. With me it's different. This is going to be the best time of my life. He'll see.

The next day, Nick broke for lunch and went up to their room. He dialed O'Rourke's number. There was a tinny ring tone in his ear, then a female voice said, "Alo. Who you call, please?"

Nick was confused. "Who is this?"

"Reception, sir."

"I want to call outside the hotel."

"Who you call, sir?"

"I already dialed the number. Why can't I just be connected?"

"I'm sorry, sir. I must know who you call. Then I connect you."

Nick felt the heat filling his head. "You mean I can't just call a number directly?"

"Yes, sir."

"Why? I never had this problem at any other hotel."

"This is the Mondial Hotel, sir."

Swearing under his breath he said tersely, "OK! I want to call Dr. Tom O'Rourke at the International Office of Migration! Is that OK with you, or do I need permission from higher authority?"

"Please wait, sir."

After a series of clicks and buzzs another female voice answered. "Hello. IOM, may I help you?"

"May I please speak to Dr. O'Rourke? My name is Nick Dwyer. I am an old friend of his."

"Please hold the line, sir." More clicking.

"Tom O'Rourke here. Is this the same Nick Dwyer that went to the University of Hawaii about a hundred light-years ago?"

"Damn right it is! How the hell are you, Tom?"

"I'm having more fun than a nymphomaniac in a dildo factory! I heard we missed each other a couple of months ago in Hong Kong. How's Shayne?"

"Still singing for his supper, but his wife brings in a steady paycheck. How about dinner? I want you to meet my girlfriend."

"You got it. I'll pick you up in my car. Where are you staying?"

"The Mondial on Dong Khoi. How about seven, tonight?"

"Can I bring my wife? Her name is Toy, and spare me the jokes, I've heard 'em all. She's Thai. You'll love her."

"It's a date, brother!"

Like all doctors, Tom was late. Hang and Nick waited out on the sidewalk in the evening heat. They had grown tired of the air-conditioned hotel environment. It cut them off from the reality of the world outside and began making their bodies dependent on the comfort indoors.

They watched in amusement as the beggars, most of them with phony afflictions, plied their trade with other foreigners. Then Nick noticed a wretched-looking man lying face down on a mechanic's dolly pulling himself along by using short wooden pegs in his crooked and bleeding hands. The man's face was severely disfigured with huge lumps and open sores. His heavy jacket was torn and encrusted with various types of dried and greasy fluids. His stubby legs stuck out below his tattered and filthy khaki shorts. There were longitudinal open wounds running from his knees down to his toeless feet. Blood and pus drained out of his blackened skin where the toes had once been. Bystanders backed away in horror, giving the pitiful leper a wide berth.

On his cart was a battered tin can with some small-denomination bills in it. He stopped at Hang's feet and mumbled something incoherently to her. Everyone else hissed and groaned at the sight of him and ordered him to go away. But Hang stood her ground and looked up pleadingly to Nick. "Honey *oi*. Can we please help him? He is for real. Not pretend like so many others."

Once again, Nick was reminded of her gentle heart. She showed her selflessness to him on many occasions and it seemed to him that her empathy and compassion were boundless. He smiled tenderly into her eyes and placed some money into the tin can. Hang nearly cried with gratitude.

They watched the poor man drag himself only a few meters before one of his blackened and oozing fingers came off and fell onto the pavement. The man was oblivious to his loss and kept struggling down the sidewalk into the encroaching darkness. A scroungy and mangy street dog immediately ran up and snatched the finger in its teeth, then ran off behind a tree trunk and devoured his prize. Nick squeezed Hang's trembling hand as she whimpered in dismay.

Minutes later, Tom's black United Nations staff car pulled up. The tall, thin figure emerged from the front passenger seat and grabbed Nick's hand and looked him up and down. "Damn, Nick! You look sharp in that fine silk shirt. Not like the old hippy days. I remember seeing scarecrows better dressed than you were!" he teased.

Nick laughed. "Tom, this is the love of my life, Hang."

Tom shook her tiny hand. "Yeah, I think she's a keeper, Nick. Way too beautiful for you. And speaking of beautiful." He opened the rear door. "This is Toy."

A small, dark-skinned woman with flashy Thai eyes beamed pleasantly from the back seat. "Hello, Nick. Hello, Hang. So nice to meet you both. Please get in."

Tom ushered them into the rear seat. He got back in the front. "So, where are we going for dinner?"

Nick saw the nausea in Hang's eyes. She sat silently, still in shock. He said, "I think, someplace with a good bar."

CHAPTER 58
Ho Chi Minh City
December 1991

By now, Nick sensed that he was becoming something of a celebrity. Strangers bought him drinks. Others left him notes at the front desk, requests for help with emigration papers or marriage proposals from women he had never met. Sometimes veterans needed counseling to deal with the trauma of returning to the land of the dragon. He often felt like he was running the Ho Chi Minh City Vet Center. He would help exchange currency, file registration papers, interpret, recommend hotels or restaurants, or lend a sympathetic ear to the lost souls seeking redemption.

All the while, he would socialize with Manley and other U.S. embassy personnel from Bangkok, as well as Tom O'Rourke. Through it all, Hang stood at his side to help with anything that arose. Except the marriage proposals.

One night, when he returned from teaching his night class, Miss Le at the front desk handed him a note. It read, 'Please call Dan Cutlip at the Riverside Hotel if you would be interested in guiding American veterans back to their old battlefields.' An attached business card read Travel Advantage, with a Hermosa Beach, California, address.

Up in their room, he asked Hang, "What do you think about this?"

She read it and came around behind him to massage his shoulders while he sat on the floor. "Aren't you busy enough already? I never see you as it is."

"But I know my way around pretty well. There will be a lot of vets coming back soon. They need to heal. I think it would be good for them to make peace with Vietnam. It might help to open up talks between our countries and lead to normalization. Maybe we could work with Vietnam Tourism to develop a veteran tour program. It would help everybody. Plus, maybe I could make some money to help cover expenses."

She leaned down and hugged him tightly. "Whatever you want. I will help you, Minh. I hope you know that."

He kissed her. "You're the best. Thank you, Minh." He picked up the phone.

At 8:00 p.m. sharp, a pudgy, balding man in his late fifties arrived at the downstairs Orchid lounge leading a much younger Vietnamese woman. "Nick? Hi, I'm Dan. This is my wife Thuan."

"And this is my girlfriend, Hang," said Nick. "Nice to meet you both. Would you join us for a drink?"

Hang and Thuan immediately began jabbering happily while sipping their sodas. Dan and Nick toasted with their Foster's Ale. Nick scrutinized Dan carefully, then asked, "You know, it's not often I get job offers from total strangers. How did you hear about me?"

Dan offered Nick a cigarette. They lit up. Dan seemed to be a man who was used to being in control, and he wore his confidence comfortably. "You ever hear of a guy named Fredy Champagne?"

Nick laughed. "Sounds kinda familiar. How do you know him?"

"Well, let's just say we are both connected to Le Ly Hayslip."

Nick nodded. "I've heard of her. What's her story?"

Dan looked smug. "She's about to become very famous. She's writing her memoirs about the war. Oliver Stone is going to make a movie about it. She enlisted Fredy to build a clinic for her up in DaNang to help the people of her village. I've been talking to him about opening up a Vietnam tour program. Especially for returning vets like yourselves, but I need someone on the ground here. He said you were in the same unit in the war." He paused, waiting for confirmation.

"Yeah. So?"

"He said I could trust you."

"That's nice, but I'm a little confused. There seems to be a lot going on here. Books, movies, clinics, tour programs. The last time I talked with Fredy he said he was going to build another clinic at Xuan Loc, about a hundred klicks east of here. Fredy has a lot of energy, but it sounds like he'll be spread a little thin."

Dan crushed out his cigarette and lit another. "That's why I need you. I understand you live here and that you teach English here at the hotel. Right?"

"Who told you that?"

"It's common knowledge." He winked.

Nick thought he caught the first scents of an ambush but kept his point man paranoia on hold. Dan Cutlip was not familiar, but his attitude was. "I'm pretty busy myself, but what you're doing is very interesting. What about pay?"

Dan blew smoke toward the ceiling in a thin stream. "Well, we won't be able to pay anything to start with, but after things get going, who knows? I think we all have to risk a little bit. The better we do, the more we all make." Dan looked at his watch. "Listen, we're going down to Shake's Pub for a sandwich. It's kind of like my office and meeting center for a lot of businessmen. Would you two like to join us? My treat."

Nick asked Hang with his eyes. She smiled and shrugged. Nick said, "OK. Let's go. Where exactly is it?"

"Down by the river. Three blocks from here. Hey, if you're gonna be a tour guide you'll have to get out more often."

After climbing a narrow stairway with low overhangs they entered the bar area of Shake's Pub. It was busy with robust laughter and shouting from a happily intoxicated clientele. The air was thick with smoke and "down under" accents. Nick immediately felt comfortable amidst the rowdy but friendly men, as it was a welcome respite from his more staid Vietnamese friends. Hang held his hand timidly and stayed close by his side, smiling shyly. Dan led them to a table, in a more secluded dining area away from the dartboard. Nick was pleasantly surprised to find hamburgers on the menu. "Is this for real, or are the hamburgers chopped up buffalo meat?" he asked Dan.

"One hundred percent Australian beef, Nick. They're great! Try one."

Nick looked at Hang's worried face. "Would you like to try, Minh? It's what we eat in America."

She shook her head. "You go ahead, Minh. I don't know how to eat."

Nick teased her. "It's easy. You put it in your mouth and chew with your teeth, then you swallow it."

She giggled and slapped his arm. "I will just have a Coke, please."

Thuan tried to encourage her but Hang politely refused.

After ordering burgers and drinks, Dan looked around the bar and saw someone he knew. "John!" he called out. "Over here!" A large heavy-set man with thinning brown hair waved and led a beautiful Asian lady by the hand over to their table.

"Nick, Hang. I'd like you to meet my good friend John D'angelo and his lovely wife Ming."

Nick stood and shook hands. "Where are you from, John?"

"Originally, New Jersey. But now we live in Singapore. That's where Ming is from."

Impressed, Nick asked, "What do you do there?"

"I used to work for the State Department." He watched Nick carefully.

"You mean like at the embassy?"

"Sometimes. But now I do consulting work." He reached into his wallet but came up empty. "Sorry. I'm fresh out of business cards."

Dan elbowed John in the ribs conspiratorially. "You don't have cards for the same reason I don't have cards." He laughed.

"Why is that?" Nick asked.

Dan ignored him. "Nick is going to help us set up a tour program over here, John. He's a war veteran."

John smiled obligingly. "Well, the best of luck. Hope to see you around Nick, Hang. Sorry, we have to get back to our friends. Later, Dan. Bye, Thuan."

As the evening passed, Dan dominated the conversation with name dropping and grandiose expectations of being the first American tour company in Vietnam, after the embargo was lifted. Through it all, Nick kept fighting his suspicious instincts, but soon the excitement of being involved in a unique project like this was too much for him. By the time they parted company to walk back to the Mondial he had agreed to represent Travel Advantage in Vietnam. But he would have to print and pay for his own business cards.

Halfway home, they walked briskly through the dark shadows. Nick always felt like he was walking point. Especially at night. There were frequent reports of muggings and stabbings by desperate thugs. Even the brutal communist police had problems controlling the city, hence a six-hour curfew from ten to four.

From a secluded doorway in a long, low building, Nick spotted a dark figure jump out into their path. He tightened his grip on Hang's hand. "Minh *oi*! Get ready to run. If he attacks us, I'll fight him off while you escape."

Hang bent down and took off her high heel shoes. "Minh! Please be careful!"

Nick tried to detour around the lone figure but he hopped over in front of them. Then Nick sighed with relief when he recognized the man Tim Campbell had once labeled "quarter soldier."

"*Anh Quy, phai khong?*"

"*Da, phai. Chao, Anh Ly, Chi Hang.* Can you please help me a little bit? I have nothing to eat today."

In the dim streetlight was one of the familiar beggars that patrolled downtown. *Anh* Quy was a really sad case, and Nick always gave him change to help him get by. Quy had only one leg. The other had been blown off at the knee. Both his arms had been lost at the elbows. He had only one eye. He still wore his only pair of army fatigues and a green baseball cap. Nick stuck several thousand Dong into his shirt pocket which was enough to buy food for a day. He patted Quy's shoulder. "Doesn't the government have an agency to help wounded war veterans?"

"Yes, but they only give us the clothes on our back, a medal, and enough money for one month. Then we are on our own."

Nick shook his head sadly. "But why? You sacrificed so much for your country."

Quy shrugged and tried to smile with his crooked mouth. "But we won the war. It was our duty. Thank you, *Anh* Ly. Thank you, *Chi* Hang." The poor veteran turned and hopped away, back toward the lights by the river.

Nick mumbled under his breath. "Yeah. We all lost."

CHAPTER 59
Ho Chi Minh City
January 1992

With each passing day, Nick felt more and more accepted and involved in Vietnam's future. He and Hang spent Sundays traveling outside the city with the Bangkok embassy people, if they were around. They visited My Tho, Tay Ninh, Cu Chi, Vung Tau, Ben Cat, and Dalat. They were assigned a van and a husky driver from the Vietnam Office of Foreign Affairs, and a tall, muscular young man who accompanied them as "guide and interpreter."

Sometimes they visited with Hang's family in District Five, just off Tran Hung Dao Street. The only ones left in Vietnam were Hang's son Huy, and her sisters, Hien and Huong, along with their four young children. Hang's parents had emigrated to the U.S. in 1985 with their three youngest children. They had offered to sponsor Hang to go also, but she refused.

Their family home had been deteriorating ever since liberation, because under the communist system, the government owned all real estate. No maintenance had been done on the confiscated house and it was in danger of collapse. Nick offered to chip in, and help finance demolition and rebuilding a new home. In February they hired a contractor to begin work.

Nick learned to drive Hang's small Honda motorbike through the insanity of traffic gridlock during rush hour. It was harrowing. The streets teemed with motorbikes that even drove up onto the sidewalks and scraped along the walls of the buildings. When he went out into it, he had to think like a drop of water flowing in a huge slow moving river. When he came to a stop light, he didn't need to put his feet down to balance, he simply leaned on the bikes tight in next to him. He also learned quickly that you could still drive with a flat tire or no lights, but you weren't going anywhere without your horn. He figured out that the Vietnamese used them like bats use sonar. It was deafening.

He connected with a Vietnamese tour company run by former Viet Cong officers. It was called CCB Friendship Tour Company and the head man was Colonel Tran Minh Son. He had been a commander in the 272nd Viet Cong Regiment during the war. This unit had been the main adversary of all the American forces in the area, including Nick's, especially around Cu Chi, where the tunnels were located. Nick and Hang spent every spare moment in negotiations with CCB trying to establish a joint venture. What better way to heal the wounds of war than to meet and break bread with your former enemies? It had already worked with Nick, Fredy, and so many others. Why not open up the possibilities to everyone else?

Colonel Son had joined the Viet Minh Army in 1945. He had fought the Japanese, the French, the Americans, and most recently the Khmer Rouge and Chinese in Cambodia during the 1977-79 war, and had beaten them all.

Nick and Hang became good friends with the seemingly kind-hearted colonel, although he and Nick had fought directly against each other many times. Nick began thinking of him as a venerable uncle with his warm smile and soft features, but he never forgot the potential ferocity of such an experienced warrior.

In the coming months, Dan sent American veterans to Nick, who worked with CCB and Vietnam Tourism to provide the vets, on both sides, the opportunity to make peace and grow. The word spread, and soon Nick was representing tour companies from California to Thailand. The only problem was, Nick didn't make a dime. He became so wrapped up in the healing that he would often feel like he was running a refugee center instead of a tour agency. But the sense of fulfillment brightened each day with happiness.

With the lovely and gentle Hang at his side he truly felt that this was the best time of his life. He was living his dream. He was committed to something bigger than himself. It was so vital and important that the act of giving became its own reward. That warm and fuzzy feeling that he first felt back in 1987 became his constant companion.

One morning, Nick and Hang took their breakfast outside on the sixth-floor patio of the Skyview restaurant. The sun burned orange through the mist that lay over the paddies in the distance.

Nick swallowed some of his ground pork and green onion omelette. He washed it down with some of the world's finest coffee from the highlands around Dalat. There was a platter of exotic fruit and fresh-squeezed orange juice. Another plate held fresh French bread and rich butter. He was in heaven. He paused and admired Hang's beautiful countenance in the cool morning shadows. He stared deep into her heart, and he saw what he had always searched for. He wanted to see it every morning for the rest of his life. There was no denying it now. The quest was over. "Minh *oi*. Will you marry me?"

She stopped chewing and looked over at him in shock. Then a sweet smile crossed her lips, and her eyes came moist. She reached over and took his hand…

"Teacher! Excuse me!" It was Mr. Duc, one of the waiters. Nick had taken an immediate liking to him during their first English class. Nick had told him about the famous American movie star named John Wayne whose nickname was, "the Duke." Nick told him, "From now on your nickname is John Wayne." The name stuck, and the boy was so honored that he adopted Nick as his surrogate father.

"Yes, John Wayne. What's up?"

Duc grinned and blushed with pride. "Teacher, here is an important message that just arrived."

"Thank you. Could you please bring *Chi* Hang a little more coffee?"

"Right away."

Nick opened the folded paper. He read it aloud. "Nick, I need help. They won't let us out of the airport because we don't have a visa. Sherry and I are stuck at the immigration hotel at Tan Son Nhat. Call me. Fredy."

"What are you going to do?" Hang asked.

"Call Thanh. Please finish your breakfast, Minh. I'll see you later, OK?" He kissed her quickly and walked away.

"Minh *oi*!" she called after him. "The answer is, yes!"

Nick ran back and kissed her again, laughing happily. The waitresses, Ms. Oanh and Ms. Van, watched enviously. They approached the couple shyly. Oanh began cleaning up the dishes. "*Chi* Hang, you are so lucky to find a love like that. I wish I could find true love someday."

Van agreed. "You know, *Chi* Hang, everybody can see how much you and teacher love each other. It gives us all hope."

Hang grasped both girls' hands. "Thank you, but don't worry. You are both beautiful with good hearts. It will come."

Nick bent over and kissed Hang again. "Thank you so much, Minh! *Troi oi!* I have never been happier in my whole life! Tonight we will go out and celebrate, but right now I must go help Fredy." He nodded to the waitresses and sprinted to the elevator.

Pham Thai Thanh made some calls and got Fredy and Sherry a temporary visa, but it only allowed them to leave the airport during daylight hours. At night they had to return to their immigration hotel.

That afternoon, Fredy stormed into the Mondial with a red face and sweat pouring off his furrowed brow. Nick stood and greeted him in the Orchid Lounge. They hugged briefly. Nick called over Ms. Dung, "Dung *oi*, please bring my good friend a beer. I think he needs one badly."

"You're goddamn right I do!" Fredy shouted. "Who the hell do they think they're fuckin' with, Nick! I'm Fredy Champagne! I built clinics all over this country and did a peace walk and got them all kinds of free publicity! I've worked my ass off tryin' to get the fuckin' embargo lifted, and this is the thanks I get?"

"OK, brah. Calm down. We'll figure something out. But first I want to know what you're doing here."

"Didn't you get my letter?"

"No."

"I sent you a letter three weeks ago. This fucked-up country hasn't changed a bit! Nothing works! We're here to build that clinic out in Xuan Loc. The rest of the team will here in a few days. How can I help them if I'm stuck in immigration?"

"Why didn't you get a visa before you left the U.S. like we always do? You know the drill. Until normalization happens, we have to go through other countries' embassies."

Fredy sucked down his beer and banged it on the table for more. "Because that fucking Dan Cutlip said he could get me one when we arrived! What bullshit! Did you ever meet him?"

"Yeah. He comes and goes. What do you think of him?"

"Not much, at the moment. I smell something fishy about him. So I've decided that you can do the tour thing with him if you want to, but I'm out of it. I'm gonna concentrate on building clinics. Listen. Can you help me get my team settled when they come in? I can't rely on anyone else. I need you to be a liaison between Steve Stratford, you remember him, and the local People's Committee. Help them with logistics, interpreting, whatever. Can you do that?"

"I'll do all I can, but I'm spread pretty thin already. Tell them to contact me here. What about their visas?"

"They went through Mexico, like I should've done. Fuckin' politics! Here I am, giving Vietnam all I've got, and they're shittin' on me!"

"Yeah, sounds kinda familiar doesn't it?"

"Fuck it! Don't mean nothin', Nick!" He stood, emptied his beer and gave Nick another hug. "I gotta get back before dark. See you tomorrow."

By the end of the week, Fredy's visa problem was solved. The team of veterans arrived and Nick got them quarters at the Saigon Hotel, a grenade's throw from the Mondial's front door. A few days later they moved out to the Hoa Binh Hotel in Xuan Loc.

On his first Sunday off, Nick and Hang went out with their old friends Mot and Lai to visit the men. As they passed the sign that said Gia Ray, Nick again thought of Big John. He thought about how ironic and appropriate it was that they were returning to build a clinic just a few klicks from where Big John had been killed back in 1965.

The team worked near Xuan Loc during the week but came back into Ho Chi Minh City for weekends and sought out Nick for help with various problems. One afternoon, Nick got a message from a Daniel Robinson, who was the Southeast Asia correspondent for Voice of America. He was also staying at the Mondial and wanted to do an interview with Nick and any other team members that were interested. Only Bill Harris volunteered. His political views were the same as Nick's, and they both worried that VOA would never broadcast the interviews for fear of upsetting the U.S. government. But they both agreed laughingly that they had nothing to lose. What would the government do, send them to Vietnam?

One night, Robinson took them up to his room and conducted an hour-long recorded interview. Bill Harris told about the medical clinics that the veterans had been building all over Vietnam and how it had helped them to heal by giving back to the Vietnamese people. He chastised the U.S. for not doing more to help Vietnam. He said basically that the war was over and it was time to forgive, even if we can't forget.

Nick implored the U.S. to immediately lift the trade embargo and normalize relations so that many more people could heal. His new battle cry was, "We are the veterans who fought this war. If we can forgive the Vietnamese and they can forgive us, then what the hell is the government's problem?"

Robinson was very moved by their candor and conviction. He assured them that he was taking the recording back to his office in Bangkok where it would be broadcast all over the world.

Soon, Nick was contacted by another reporter, named Joe Studwell, who claimed to be doing a story for the *South China Morning Post* out of Hong Kong. Like Dan Cutlip, he had no business card. His companion was a photographer named Greg Girard, who did "freelance work." Studwell had a British accent, was tall and lean with dark, curly hair. Girard sounded American and was shorter, with closely cropped brown hair. Nick sensed that there was some animosity between the two. It sometimes seemed that Greg was skeptical of things Joe would say. His expression said, "Do you really expect this guy to believe that bullshit?" He looked disgusted, but in too deep to back out. Although Nick's natural mistrust and point man instincts were screaming at him, he played out his part honestly and sincerely.

Studwell wanted Nick to take them on a guided tour of the clinics in Xuan Loc and Vung Tau so that they could document the veterans' peacemaking efforts. Nick was only too happy to oblige. Besides, all his expenses would be paid. After getting permission from Mr. Trung at the Mondial, they left on a two-day trip.

Nick arranged to use Chanh as their driver. Chanh had proven an adept driver in city traffic but was surprisingly clueless out in the countryside, as he could not read a map. Nick became the guide and had them on course after visiting Xuan Loc, but then Chanh veered off the road on a whim, despite Nick's protests, and got them lost in short order. Nick knew exactly where they were, but the bewildered Chanh kept driving in circles around an abandoned rubber plantation. Nick became livid but was helpless, as Chanh was behind the wheel. He flashed back to '66 when he had to read maps for the cherry lieutenants.

Joe finally said, "I say, Nick, does this chap know where the hell he's going?"

Nick snapped. He felt an emotional aneurysm raging inside of him. In his mind's eye, he imagined reaching over and turning off the ignition. The old Datsun jerking to a stop. Chanh yelling at Nick who then grabs Chanh's collar and drags him over the gear shift, pulling him out the passenger side door and beating him mercilessly. "Goddamn you! I'm the boss here, not you! Now you sit here and shut up or I'll kill your fucking ass and leave you in the bushes!" He saw himself throwing the bloody-faced Chanh into the passenger seat, then going around to the driver's side and taking the wheel while Chanh curled up whimpering on the floor. Suddenly Nick flashed back to Charlie Brown, and as quickly as it came, the vision disappeared.

He looked at poor Chanh, who was about to cry from losing face in front of Nick's clients. Nick's anger melted with sympathy. Instead of the imaginary beating, he said, "Chanh *oi*. Please stop here. Let's get out and have a smoke." He winked reassuringly to Joe and Greg. When they were out of earshot, he said. "Listen, Chanh. Follow this dirt road straight back the way we came. Turn left at the small shed, and then we will meet highway 15. It will take us right to Vung Tau. Trust me, OK?"

Chanh tried to smile. "OK, Ly."

An hour later, they arrived at the hotel, no one was hurt, and they were still friends. Nick smiled in the warmth of the sunset. Just another day on Thunder Road, and a little closer to home.

The next day Nick took them to the Friendship Clinic and again met Dr. Lam. More tea and cigarettes. By nightfall they had returned to Ho Chi Minh City, where they said farewell. Joe promised to send Nick a copy of the story when it was finished and went off to bed. Nick never heard from him again. A month later, when he tried calling Joe's Hong Kong phone number, it was not in service.

In the middle of March, Nick had another visitor. One night about eleven his phone rang. "Goddamn it, Nick! Get down here and pick up your mail! I've been hauling it all over Asia!" Alan yelled into the lobby phone. "There's a hefty delivery fee, you know. You owe me a few beers."

Laughing, Nick jogged out of the elevator. "I hope you paid all the bills for me and just brought all the checks!" he growled. They hugged and pounded each other's backs. Nick steered Alan into the Orchid

Lounge, and the pretty Ms. Dung brought them beer. Thumbing through the stack of envelopes Nick said, "Seriously. Thanks, Alan. I knew I could count on you. It's really good to be able to trust someone, especially way over here."

"Forget about it! Us vets gotta stick together. Nobody else gonna take care of us, right?" After they toasted and chugged down their beer, Nick ordered two more. "So, where's this wonder woman that's changed your life?" Alan asked.

"Upstairs asleep, where I'm supposed to be. You can meet her tomorrow. Where are you staying?"

"Over at the Saigon Hotel. It's close, cheap, and kinda clean." He reconned around the room. "So how's the POW hunting?"

Nick made a face. "I've been kinda busy living my life. I have it good here. But yeah, I haven't forgotten."

"Well, thanks for the beer. Go on upstairs and get some. I'll see you tomorrow. You're buying me breakfast."

"No problem. How long you here for?"

"Three days. Then it's back to Manila. I met a real hottie over there. I might be falling in love myself."

"The end of the world is coming soon!" Nick laughed. "Good night, my brother."

Nick saw little of Alan because of his teaching schedule, but once Alan met Hang he immediately understood Nick's commitment to her. On the day of Alan's departure he said, "I think you found a diamond in the coal pile, Nick, you lucky bastard."

In the coming weeks, Nick informed all of his students about the veterans building a clinic in Xuan Loc. He wanted to spread the word about their efforts to bring Vietnam and the U.S. together. Soon he was approached by a reporter for *Tuoi Tre*, a local magazine. Mr. Huy Quang wanted to write a story on the project. Nick and Dave Gallup, another team member, were interviewed, and the article was published on April 26, 1992.

A few days later, Nick received a call from another reporter with the *South China Morning Post*. His name was Michael Kikirchjou. He met Nick after class one evening and spent several hours in the interview. When asked what he did in Vietnam, Nick told the truth, that among many other things, he taught English at the Mondial. But because it was illegal for Americans to live in Vietnam, he told

Kikirchjou not to include that part in the story. It fell on deaf ears, and when Nick picked up a copy of the paper, his blunder was there for all to see.

The next morning, Nick went out on the street to buy cigarettes. As soon as he stepped out of the door, he felt the presence of a mousy little man slide up very close to him and whisper, "Hello, Mr. Dwyer. Do you remember me?"

He spun around and confronted the despicable face of Mr. Song. "What do you want?" he asked curtly.

"Do you remember what we talked about, last year?"

"Yeah, the weather." Nick sneered.

Song smirked. "Please, teacher. Do not be so rude. We are on the same side. Right?"

Nick was uneasy. He had become so wrapped up in his new life that he had all but forgotten. Guilt crept slowly into his mind. "Are we?"

Song looked around melodramatically. "Yes. Please come over here. I have information. Are you interested?"

"About what?"

Song paused for effect. "Live American POWs."

Nick felt the flutter of excitement rush through him like a cold chill. His breathing became shallow. He had chicken skin. "Seriously?"

"Yes. Can we go somewhere?"

Nick thought quickly. "I have a class in ten minutes. Can you come back this afternoon, about two?"

"Yes. I will call you from the lobby. Room 406?"

"How did you know that?"

Song smiled crookedly. "I know."

Precisely at 2:00 Nick's phone rang. Mr. Song's voice whispered, "Teacher, can you come down to the lobby? I have something very important to show you. Please come alone."

Before leaving, Nick sat on the bed and took a deep breath. He had a silent conversation with himself. Do I dare believe this shit? Last year he tried to con me with phony dog tags. If he wants money up front, I'll know it's a scam. Or what if it's a setup? I could get in big trouble. Is it worth the risk? What if I was the POW? Wouldn't I want somebody to take the risk? Don't they deserve a chance? Hell yes! Goddamn it! Just when things were looking up! If I don't, it will haunt me the rest of my life. Fuck it, Nick! Don't mean nothin'!

Stepping out of the small glass elevator, Nick spotted Song sitting against the wall of the nearly empty lobby. He also noticed another man sitting close by, near one of the mirrored pillars. He was older and wore military-style bush clothes and carried a briefcase. He studiously ignored Nick as he sat down with Song.

In a low voice Song said, "Teacher, I must ask you. Is there still a two-million-dollar reward for live American POWs?"

"As far as I know. Listen, Song. This better be for real. If not, you're gonna be in big trouble, understand?"

Song nodded vigorously. "Yes! It is real! Here. Look at this. But be careful. Are there cameras in this room?"

"I don't think so." Song slipped Nick an envelope. He took it but decided to look nonchalant. If he was being watched he did not want to arouse suspicion by acting guilty. He opened it and pulled out a handwritten note in English and a color photograph. The photo showed a middle-aged man with black hair and tan skin dressed in khakis squatting in a field. It was a profile shot which hid his eyes. As Nick studied it, he noticed the man by the mirror glance over.

Song whispered, "Do you know that man?"

"No, do you?"

Song shook his head. "Your friend wrote you a note."

Nick opened it. "Please help me. I have been prisoner long time. I want go home to U.S. Mr. Song will bring you here. Please hurry." He studied the photo again. The man looked Asian or possibly Mexican. Nick smelled bullshit, especially because of the incorrect grammar. The picture also looked bogus. But deep inside, he wanted very much to believe it. What if?

"Who took this picture?" he asked.

"A friend," said Song.

"What's this man's name?"

"I'm sorry. I don't know."

Nick's eyes narrowed. "Where is he?"

"In the central highlands, near Pleiku. Do you know it?"

"Never been there. So what do you want?"

"I will make arrangements to go there by car. But I will need help. Can you do that?"

"Let me think. I'll call you. What's your number?"

"I don't have telephone. I will contact you. When I do, I will call the POWs your students, OK?

Nick nodded and stood up.

"Teacher, wait. When will I get the money?"

Nick smirked and went back to the elevator. He got off on the fourth floor and met Ms. Mang, their maid, in the hallway. "Good afternoon, Teacher."

"Good afternoon. Have you been studying your English lesson for tomorrow?"

"Oh yes. I will see you then. I just finished cleaning your room." She gestured invitingly to his door, then bowed and walked away smiling sweetly.

He locked the door behind him and went into the toilet. While urinating he looked down at the floor and noticed some small pieces of plaster or concrete next to the tub. He flushed and zipped up. Turning, he saw more under the sink. Puzzled, he went back out in the hall. "Miss Mang! Are you there?"

Her maid station was right around the corner by the elevator. From there she could monitor all comings and goings. "Yes, Teacher!" she came around the corner.

"You said you cleaned my room?"

"Yes, sir."

"When?"

"I just finished, sir."

He beckoned her into the bathroom. "Then what is this?"

Blushing, she bowed low. "I am sorry, sir. Maybe they do repair in your bathroom."

"But there is nothing broken."

She scurried away and returned with a broom, dust pan, and Mr. Danh, the head maintenance man.

"I am so sorry, Teacher." He said. "We are doing repairs to your bathroom. Tomorrow we will return to finish, OK?"

"But why? Nothing is broken."

"Do not worry. I will take care of everything. Good afternoon."

Closing the door, he went to his desk and slid the envelope under a large pile of papers. He lit a cigarette and opened a beer. His head was swimming. The phone rang. It was Thanh. "Hello Nick. How are you?"

"Fine," he said. "I haven't heard from you in a while."

"Yes, well we've been quite busy. Can you come down to our office? We have a surprise for you."

"Again?" He smiled. "I'll be right there."

Hearing her voice was reassuring somehow. They had been through so much together, and he felt their friendship had been tried, tested, and proven. When he arrived, she led him upstairs to the office of the director, Mr. Tinh. They were greeted by Miss Thuy, his secretary, who had them sit down for a spot of tea. When she left the room to get something, Thanh put down her cup. "Nick, did you know that there is an American delegation in town?"

"Yeah. I think one of them is Senator John Kerry, right?"

"Yes. Do you know why they are here?"

"No, not really," he lied.

"They are trying to help resolve the issue of the POWs so that we can begin normalization." She watched his eyes. "As you know, that is the major stumbling block. Anyway, he will be staying at the Rex Hotel. Room 216, I believe."

Before Nick could respond, Miss Thuy returned carrying some papers and sat down across from them. "Nick," she said. "We have been very impressed with your accomplishments in Vietnam. You have been so helpful to us that Mr. Tinh has asked me to congratulate you and to offer you a small token of our appreciation. As you know, we have repeatedly extended your three-month visa so that you may stay here. That in itself is virtually unprecedented. But now we have decided to issue you a six-month visa. This is the first time we have ever done that for an American." She beamed a huge smile and passed the orange-colored papers over the desk. Not only was it for six months, but he was allowed multiple entries.

Nick was speechless. He looked from Thuy to Thanh and back again, in total shock. "My God! I just want to thank both of you and Mr. Tinh! I can't believe it!" He laughed self-consciously. His voice sounded like a school boy. "I won't let you down."

Then he thought about the envelope. He almost wanted to tell them about it and how he had been approached by this con man, but he had stood up for Vietnam knowing full well that there were no POWs. Peace, love, and normalization, by God! He would never betray his devotion to Vietnam!

But, on the other hand, if there were POWs and they could be returned to the U.S. in exchange for the restitution that Henry Kissinger had promised, then normalization would happen automatically. When Nick left the office he walked a thin line between disaster and cloud nine. That line led him to the front desk of the Rex Hotel.

CHAPTER 60
Ho Chi Minh City
April 30, 1992

"I'm sorry, sir. Senator Kerry is not in at the moment. If you would like to leave a message, please write it down. We will give it to him when he returns."

Just my luck, Nick thought. If I seal it, they'll open it anyway. I'll just play it straight. Face up on the table. Take that, goddamn it!

He wrote…

Dear Senator Kerry:
I'm a Vietnam combat vet, living here in HCMC. Need to talk ASAP. I have live sighting reports. Please advise. Call me at the Mondial Hotel, room 406.
Thank you, Nick Dwyer

He waited by the phone that night and the next morning. Nothing. Then the knock at the door. It was the repairmen. Three men filed in with toolboxes and a cardboard carton. Nick wanted to stay and watch them but his first class was starting in a few minutes. Hang had gone home for the day. He reluctantly left them alone in his room. To protest would be to invite scrutiny.

Two hours later he hurried back to his room. They had gone. The room was spotless except for some smudges on the bathroom mirror. He went to the phone and called the Rex. "Hello. I need to speak with Senator Kerry, please."

"Just a moment, sir."

"Hello. Yes, this is Senator Kerry."

"Senator, this is Nick Dwyer. Did you get my message?"

"Yes. But I'm leaving this morning. I'm just stepping into the shower. Can I call you back in fifteen minutes?"

"Yes, sir. I'm at the Mondial Hotel. Room 406. Phone number is 96291. It's important."

Nick waited a half hour. Nothing. He called the Rex again.

"Yes, sir. This is Colonel John Vann. I'm sorry, you just missed the Senator. He's on his way to the airport. Can I help you?"

"Colonel, I'm a Vietnam vet, living here. I have live sighting reports. How should I proceed?"

"You take whatever information you have to the Ho Chi Minh City People's Committee, right next door. They'll help you."

Nick was momentarily shocked. *What the hell is he talking about? I can't go to them. It's ridiculous.* Then reality hit the farmer turned spy. *He can't talk on the phone. I shouldn't have either, but it's too late now. I'm already committed. Drive on.*

"Mr. Dwyer, whenever you get back stateside, give us a call."

"Right." He hung up. His next class wasn't for two hours. He decided to exercise. He stripped and changed into a pair of swim trunks in front of the mirror. He did knee bends, push ups, and lifted his heavy suitcase head high, watching his muscles flex in the glass. *Not bad for forty-five,* he thought. After a half-hour he went in to shower.

That evening, Hang returned, and they decided to have the restaurant deliver dinner to the room. After a bottle of good Bulgarian wine and a romantic meal, they made love on the bed voyeuristically in front of the mirror, then drifted off to sleep in each other's arms.

The next afternoon, he went up to the restaurant after lunch to teach their class. He was early. While waiting for everyone to arrive, Ms. Dung, the very attractive cocktail waitress from the lobby bar came and sat next to him. She looked at him with her head tilted slightly. She placed her hand on his forearm and gently stroked it. "Teacher," she said slowly, "I think Miss Hang is very lucky. I wish I could be her." There was no mistaking the lust in her eyes. Surprised, he stared at her and felt his face flushing. He smiled and took her hand away but she held onto him. Then two other students arrived and the flirting came to an end, but his curiosity lingered.

At three that afternoon he walked into room 312 for the security staff's class. There were only a half dozen students, as there were always two on duty at the front door, twenty-four hours a day.

As everyone got settled, Mr. Hop came up and greeted Nick with a bow and a smile. Hop was a veteran of the war against the Khmer Rouge, and he had proudly shown Nick his various bullet wounds. There was another veteran in the class named Mr. An. He had fought against the Americans as an artilleryman at the battle for Khe Sanh in 1968. His voice was deep and guttural, as if his vocal chords had been crimped shut. But these two were among Nick's favorite students, and there was mutual respect.

Hop reached out and squeezed Nick's bicep. He nodded and looked over at An. "I told you, An." He said and turned back to Nick. "Teacher, I think you are VERY strong!" and he did the Vietnamese clucking sound which showed awe or envy. Again, Nick was puzzled by this unusual attention but he was flattered nonetheless.

Over the next few days, he received regular calls from Mr. Song. One came as he was teaching the office class. He picked up the ringing phone on the nightstand of the classroom. "Mr. Dwyer. It is me. Can you talk?"

Nick surveyed the students who watched him closely. "No. Please call me later."

"OK, but I have information about your students. I will call you this afternoon."

"I won't be here. I must go to a wedding. Maybe tomorrow."

"As you wish. Goodbye, Teacher."

Nick resumed the class, excited yet annoyed, and scared at the same time.

At five, he and Hang attended the wedding of one of Nick's students at the Rex Hotel ballroom. Nearly everyone there worked at the Mondial. Soon, Nick and several of his students at their table were well lubricated with beer. After the ceremony, they decided to stumble back to the Mondial together and have some more at the Orchid Lounge.

Upon arriving, they all took a shortcut to the bar through a dark, narrow passageway that led to an open area behind the hotel. Nick had never seen it before. As they passed by a large metal door, it suddenly opened and out stepped Mr. Ha, one of Nick's troublesome students. Before Ha could slam the door shut, Nick looked into the room and was shocked to see several people from the hotel sitting in front of a huge bank of electronic equipment. There were TV monitors and audio recordings playing. There were gasps of surprise and fear from everyone there. Someone yelled. "Quick, close the door! Teacher is here!" He and Hang were quickly spirited away to the lobby, but Nick feigned drunken oblivion. Though they all had another drink together, the tension was palpable.

Later, up in their room, Nick lit a cigarette and went to his desk. He went in under the pile of papers to find the envelope. It wasn't there. After searching for several minutes, he found it near the top. He had looked at it just that morning. He always put it back in the same place. He took Hang in his arms and held her close. Suddenly afraid. He kissed her. Ambush coming. Now it all made sense. The workmen, the flattery, the set-up with John Kerry, Mr. Song.

Thanh's voice came back to him from the past. "There are no secrets in Vietnam, Nick."

He led Hang to a corner where the mirror camera could not see them. He played a cassette tape loudly. Holding a finger in front of his lips he whispered in her ear, "Minh, come sit down." He had to tell her. He handed her the envelope. "Have you ever seen this before?"

"No. What is it?"

"Did you move it this morning? It was under this bunch of papers. It's OK. But I must know."

"No, Minh. I promise. Why?"

He told her the whole story. She held his hands and stared into his eyes. "Why you never tell me about this?"

"I was afraid to involve you. I didn't know if it was for real or not. But if there's any chance that it was, then I had to go for it. Understand?"

"But you can get in big trouble. What about your life in Vietnam? What about us? Can you throw all that away?"

He saw the fear in her eyes. She could see the end of their world, even if he didn't. "If I was a POW, I'd sure want somebody to get me out. They're my brothers. If there's anything I've learned about vets, it's that nobody cares about us but us. The government doesn't care. The POWs are just bargaining chips. Vietnam wants money, the U.S. wants the boys back."

"Then why doesn't America pay Vietnam and Vietnam give them back?"

"It's very complicated. The bottom line is, I don't trust either side to solve this problem, because they both have too much to lose. The POWs are going to be written off just like the Amerasian orphans, unless we can find them and get them out. It's up to us, the veterans, to take care of it, because the governments damn sure won't."

Hang stared off into space. The war had come back to haunt them once again. The phone rang. Nick turned down the cassette and answered. "Yes, Miss Thuy, how are you? You're working late tonight."

Miss Thuy's normally friendly voice sounded stern. "Please come to Vietnam Tourism office tomorrow morning."

"I have classes scheduled all day. Could I come the next day?"

"Forget about your classes. Come at 10:00 a.m. Bring your passport and visa with you."

"OK." He hung up. It was coming fast. There wasn't much time. He took Hang in his arms. "We need to find Manley."

The three of them met at Brodards. "If you're in a hurry then the best way is to file a K-1 fiance petition," Manley said as he chewed on his water buffalo steak. "You don't have to get married until she gets into the U.S. If you get married here, then it actually takes longer. Don't ask me why."

Nick sipped his crab and asparagus soup. "How long do you think for the K-1?"

"Hell, I don't know. Maybe a year or two. Haven't done that many."

"A year or two?" Nick shouted. "We can't wait that long!"

"Hey, Nick. I'll try my best to speed it up if you really want me to. Maybe Tom O'Rourke can help." Manley gulped his beer. "See, I told you it would get to you after a while."

"It ain't my choice, brother. But I need all the help you can give me."

Manley reached over his hand. "Don't worry, but be patient."

Nick grasped it tightly. "I don't have time to be patient. I need to file the papers tonight."

Manley studied his face and looked at Hang's pleading eyes. "Come up to my room after dinner."

By 3:00 a.m. Nick had completed the forms. He lay in the darkness and listened to hear sleep breathing. He could feel it coming, like so many times before. And just as helpless to stop it.

CHAPTER 61
Ho Chi Minh City
May 2, 1992

The crowds of people celebrating Communist May Day had subsided, and normalcy was returning to the city. Nick marched, bleary eyed, across Nguyen Hue Street and into Vietnam Tourism. Thanh was not at her desk. He went upstairs. After a short wait, Miss Thuy appeared from a door behind her desk. She sat down.

"Good morning, Miss Thuy. *Co khoe khong?*" he greeted her cordially.

She looked down at the papers in his hands. "Did you bring your passport and new visa?"

"Yes." He handed them over.

She scanned over them, slid his passport back across the desk to him but held up his six-month visa in both hands in front of his face. Looking him straight in the eye, she tore it in half. "It is time for you to leave Vietnam."

Though he had seen the ambush coming, he was outraged none the less. The beast within him poised to leap across the desk and rip out her throat with his teeth and leave her severed head on the desk for all to see. But his lessons in spirituality had provided enough of a delay in reaction time for him to see everything differently. He sat staring at her, waiting for the rage to subside, trying to think, instead of feel. He took a deep breath. "But why?"

She remained calm, almost sympathetic. "I think you know." She stood up, dismissing him. "You have overstayed your visa now. You must leave within forty-eight hours. Goodbye, Nick."

"I want to see Mr. Tinh or Ms. Thanh."

"They are not available." She pointed to the door.

Hang jumped up from the bed when he returned. His expression said it all. She held him tightly. They kissed long. He said, "I have only forty-eight hours."

"But, when will I see you again? They won't let you come back! I cannot leave until the K-1 goes through! Oh, Minh! What are we going to do? I cannot live without you!"

"Nor I without you. I'll find a way. Don't worry. But you need money to live and rebuild the family house that we have already torn down. I only have a couple hundred dollars. How long will it take to finish building?"

"At least a couple months. Where will I stay with you gone?"

He handed her a hundred. "I'll send you money from Manila. It'll be risky, but we have no choice. Wait for a letter from me. It will have cash inside."

"Are you sure you can do that?"

"I give you my word. I'll contact you through Manley. I can call him at the embassy in Bangkok, and he can relay messages. You may hear from Tom O'Rourke and Alan Roth also. It's the only way, until I can get back. And I promise you Minh, I will be back."

Despite repeated calls to Thanh and Mr. Trung, he got no reply. It was obviously over. He was suddenly alone, homeless, thousands of miles from Maui, with no money and soon to be separated from his soul mate.

She cried in front of Tan Son Nhat Airport, and they held each other until the last possible moment. Her tear-stained face, full of love, pain and fear, was burned into his memory for all time. As he turned to enter the terminal, the past rose up to torture him yet once again… How many more times must I endure this same pain? When will it end? When will I find peace? When will I get home? Where the hell is home?

When Nick arrived at Immigration, he showed them his old visa. The uniformed policeman glowered at him. "This visa expired a week ago!" he yelled. Another man came over. They conferred. Nick heard one of them say, "Yeah, that's him."

The first cop got into Nick's face. "There is penalty for overstaying your visa! Open your suitcase and carry-on, NOW!"

Nick obliged and calmly placed them both on the metal table. They went quickly through the carry-on but paused when they found Nick's stack of letters and papers in his large case. "Ah-ha!" they cried, and confiscated the bundle. "You wait here!" said the second cop, and he disappeared into a room behind a barred door. Fear surged through Nick's body. They had the envelope in that bundle. If they looked, they would have to find it. Then it was really over. They could keep him forever. He would never see Hang again. He considered confessing. Too late. He thought of running. Where? Fight them! They have all the guns. Suddenly, the tunnels of Cu Chi appeared in his mind. 1966. 1987. The Ben Cat police station a year ago. Accept my own death. Again. When you truly accept your own death, he thought… what the hell can anyone do to you? That's how you win. That's where your freedom comes from. You show them your acceptance. Show them now. They might keep you, but they won't break you. NEVER!

He turned to the first cop who had stayed with him during the wait. Nick got in very close to him and pierced the man's eyes with the look. "Yes, I made a mistake and overstayed my visa. But today I am going home. No problem. Right?"

The cop froze, searching the crazy American's face. He saw it. It humbled him. He nodded, entranced. "I think it will be no problem."

Nick offered the cop a Marlboro and lit it. He patted his shoulder. "Good boy."

Twenty minutes later, the second cop came strutting back. He tossed the papers into Nick's suitcase. Nick showed him the look too. The second cop's smirk faded. He gestured to the Departure Area. "I think you should be careful who you talk to. Goodbye, Mr. Dwyer."

When Nick arrived in Manila he took a cab to Makati. He had the driver wait while he went into Citi Bank and took out a $2,000 cash advance on his credit card. Then he went to the Municipal Post Office downtown. Checking to be sure he wasn't followed, he slipped $1,000, wrapped in a letter, into an envelope addressed to Hang. He went to three separate windows before mailing it, to throw off any would-be thieves. Then he said a silent prayer to God or Buddha or whoever else might be listening. He had done all he could. The rest was up to fate.

CHAPTER 62
Hawaii
May 5, 1992

From the Honolulu Airport, Nick called Thomas Lai at Pacific Ocean Travel and booked a return flight to Vietnam in three weeks. They would have to wait for visa approval. If it came through the embassy in Mexico there might not be a problem.

Then he called Mark, on Maui. He asked to sleep on Mark's couch until he could get back to Vietnam. "Hell yeah, Nick! You're welcome here anytime, for as long as you like. And I ain't bullshittin', mother fucker!"

Waiting for the Aloha Airlines flight he leaned against the concrete railing along the outdoor walkway. He smelled the ginger, gardenia, and plumeria. The air was clean and fresh. He watched the local officials as they interacted with passengers. They were smiling and warm. It was not because they wanted something in return. There was genuine caring and concern. There was something that you could only find in Hawaii. It's called Aloha. As his good friend Willy Koja had once said, "If I do something for you 'cause I like something back... I wrong already! You just go do something for somebody else. That's how you pay it back. No worry. Bumbye come back to me."

On May 27 he got the tickets and a three-month visa in the mail at Mark's house. Once again, the moth shook the dust off of its wings and the tears out of its eyes. A distant fire was calling, and his destiny would not be denied.

STUART NICHOLLS

CHAPTER 63
Ho Chi Minh City
June 1, 1992

Nick stared out the plane's window, trying to see through the thick clouds of rain that rolled silver out of the dark, Vietnamese sky. He had done it. He was back. But this time, instead of feeling unbridled joy, he viewed it with some trepidation. There was no telling how he would be received. Now slightly older, but much wiser, Nick knew how to play the game. Don't trust anybody. Be like them. Tell them what they want to hear and go along with the program until you can get Hang out.

They created another spectacle when they spotted each other in the massive throng outside Customs.

She sobbed uncontrollably as they hugged and kissed in the rain outside the terminal. He had kept his word and beaten the odds. "Did you get the money from Manila?" he asked anxiously.

"Oh yes, Minh! Thank you so much! We are finishing work on my family's house. Just in time!" she looked up at the heavens. "The monsoon season has started." They laughed ecstatically.

"And obviously you got the message from Manley that I was coming in today."

"Yes. He called me at Dr. Hung's house. He said that now we can telephone to America. A company named AT&T has opened up a system between Vietnam and the U.S. Did you know that?"

"Yes. So the next time I go back I can call you directly. Where are we staying, Minh? Did you find us a hotel?"

"Yes. The Bong Sen."

He frowned. "I think it'll be too dangerous living next door to the Mondial. I don't want anyone taking away my visa again."

"Don't worry, Minh. I have some ideas." She quickly led him to a small Renault. Out jumped the laughing, round-faced *Anh* Mot, who threw his arms around Nick and jumped up and down. "*Anh* Ly! Look inside! You have an old friend here!" Nick bent over and peered inside to see the beaming face of *Anh* Lai.

"Welcome home again, *Anh* Ly!" he called. "Get your suitcase inside! Very wet!"

Laughing together, Nick and Mot tossed his bags into the small trunk. Suddenly, Nick no longer felt the chilly wind as it drove sheets of rain across the pavement. He was warm with love and friendship. He was home.

Their room was a box on the fifth floor in the center of the Bong Sen with no windows. It had a small bathroom, air conditioning and intermittent electricity, but no phone or TV. They lived there for the next three months. Nick resumed teaching at night for the architectural firm whose owner was close friends with Thanh. Three days a week they drove out to Cu Chi on Hang's Honda to teach the tunnel guides. Strangely, Nick received no harassment from the government about returning to live in Vietnam.

In July, Nick received a letter from Tim Campbell. He would arrive in late August and was bringing a Maui friend named Tom Domsitz, a long-time supporter of the Vietnam Veterans of Maui and a world-class body builder. Tim still wanted Nick to get permission to visit the spot where he had been wounded up north near Dong Ha.

Nick and Hang stayed in close contact with the ODP people and Manley Daniel became their close friend. They would often meet at the Cyclo Bar on Dong Du Street, across from the Saigon Hotel.

The owner was a young-looking man named Hoang Van Cuong. He had been a photographer for UPI during the war. He had missed an opportunity to leave on a Huey from the U.S. Embassy roof on April 30, 1975, so he had made his way through the terrorized chaos to Independence Palace. Under the pretense of being a Japanese reporter, he photographed the victorious North Vietnamese invaders as their tanks broke through the palace gate. His famous photographs of that historic day were hung on every wall of the two-story bar. Whenever Nick, Hang, and Manley went in for happy hour, Cuong would come and join them for drinks and reminiscing. He would always show them old invoices that he had submitted to UPI, but still without reimbursement. "*Anh* Ly, could you please help me get paid?"

he would ask.

One day, Cuong mentioned that he had been born in the ancient capital city of Hue. Nick asked if he was familiar with Thien Mu pagoda. "Of course!" he replied. "In fact, my grandfather is a famous monk who still lives there."

Nick felt the chicken skin again. "What is his name?" he asked.

"Thich Don Hau. Why, do you know him?"

Nick looked at Hang. They shook their heads, laughing. Nick told Cuong about Peter Goble and the old photograph. "I still have that photo of your grandfather and my friend Peter during the war. My promise to deliver it is long overdue." He held Hang's hand. "Minh oi, I think it's time to head north."

"How far north will you go?" Cuong asked.

"To the old DMZ, you know, the Ben Hai River."

"Will you go to Khe Sanh?"

"Not this time. Why?"

Cuong scanned some nearby patrons and lowered his voice. "*Anh Ly.* I know where there is a crashed American helicopter in the jungle. Is the information valuable to you?"

Nick felt his heart sink. Here we go again. "I'm sorry, Cuong. If you have information like that then please take it to the Ho Chi Minh City People's Committee. They will help you."

Cuong nodded, perhaps disappointed, perhaps relieved. But Nick wasn't walking down that trail again.

The journey began the following month. Besides delivering the photograph, the goal was to research destinations for returning veterans and to gain access to old battlefields as well as the usual tourist attractions. Nick was still determined to develop a veterans' tour program that would take any vet anywhere he wanted to go.

While on this trip, they also planned to visit the Peace Village, Mothers' Love Clinic, and the Ky La Clinic. They had all been built by Fredy Champagne and his veteran teams for the owner and founder, Le Ly Hayslip. Oliver Stone, the Vietnam vet turned movie producer, was also a supporter. Nick and Hang had been working closely with Le Ly for several months after bringing in a married couple, Michael and Monica Rhodes, to be the managers of the Mothers' Love Clinic. Nick had also assisted with logistics by receiving and transferring supplies, finances, and personnel from Ho Chi Minh City north to

Da Nang, where the projects were located.

Their driver was a young man named Tam whom Nick had met back in 1987 when Tam was still a cyclo driver. He now owned a car and was a driver and guide. He brought along his girlfriend, Huong, to keep him company during long nights on the road.

Along the way, they stopped in Nha Trang and again visited the Tap Ponaga where Nick would always go for spiritual rejuvenation. The old monk, Chu Muoi, greeted them warmly. They sat inside the ancient chamber that housed the statue of Kauthara, the bluish incense smoke curling up along the red-brick walls.

Chu Muoi held Nick's hands and stared kindly into his eyes. "I feel you are still traveling a long and painful road. Perhaps you have taken a wrong turn. But do not worry. Kauthara will shine a light for you to follow. It will lead you home." He stood and disappeared into the darkness. The gong from within sounded three times, then was still. That prophesy would haunt Nick all the way to Quang Ngai, where they stopped to visit the infamous village of My Lai.

Known to the Vietnamese as Son My, My Lai was the site of the 1968 massacre of hundreds of unarmed civilians by the Americal Division. Permission was required to visit the shrine, so Nick had to first be interviewed by the local People's Committee. His obvious empathy and compassion for the victims won him immediate access. A local guide took them several kilometers off the main road to the site. After touring the grounds and seeing hundreds of tombstones that marked the location of the fallen, Nick bowed and burned incense at the foot of a huge stone statue. Then all four of them were asked to go inside a building that housed a gut-wrenching exhibit of photographs of the actual massacre. They were asked to sit and talk with the caretaker of the shrine. He was a young man, thin, with threadbare clothes and eyes that mirrored the horror of what he had witnessed on that bloody day while he was still a small boy. He had watched in horror as his family and friends were beaten, tortured, and slaughtered like animals. It was clear to Nick that his PTSD was nothing compared to that of the pitiful man who sat across the rickety table.

The man scrutinized Nick for a full minute before asking, "Did you participate in this atrocity?"

"No. I was a soldier, but far away from here."

The man's eyes narrowed. He eyed Hang with disdain, as if

accusing her of sleeping with the enemy. "But, please tell me. How can you come into a poor village of innocent, unarmed farmers and kill women, children, and old people?" His voice began to break. "How can you do that? They threatened no one!"

Nick stared back at him, first with a look of sympathy and understanding. "Though I was not here, I am very sorry for what happened that day. I can understand your pain and the hatred you must feel. Can you see the sincerity in my eyes?"

The man slowly nodded.

Then Nick decided to take a big risk. He could easily pretend to grovel and beg forgiveness to placate the blatant demand for guilt and retribution. Or he could show him what nobody else could, or would.

He lifted a blank page from the book where visitors signed in. "This paper has two sides. On one side can be written the story that you have to tell. If people read only that story, they will side with you." He turned the page. "But on this side can be written a different story. Can you imagine being a soldier and walking down the trail that leads to this village, over and over, for weeks or months, even years? And each time, a mine or a booby trap explodes that kills or maims your friends. And those innocent, unarmed farmers that you mentioned are sitting by, watching it happen. Those women, children, and old people never come out to warn us or lead us away from danger, because they are the ones who set the traps. Because your people are poor, they are forced to fight war in this way instead of direct combat. But the result is that you cause this type of revenge. It is inevitable. What do you expect the soldiers to do? Should they simply allow you to keep killing them without a response? I'm not trying to justify what they did, just explain it. The stress of combat can make even the best of us do terrible things. The experience of war has no equal on this earth. It is rarely understood even by those who fight it, let alone by those who have not."

The dark slits in the man's weathered face stared at Nick silently and unflinchingly.

Hang's tortured face begged Nick to walk softly. He reached out and took the man's hand. "It was a terrible war. I don't think we will ever forget. But at the very least, we must try to forgive. If not, we'll fight the war forever. And none of us will find peace." Nick stood up, patted the frail shoulder, bowed and said, "Aloha, brah," before walking back to the car.

CHAPTER 64
DaNang
August 1992

That evening, they checked into the new Non Nuoc hotel on China Beach. It was very close to Marble Mountain and not far from Ky La, the village where Le Ly Hayslip had been born and raised.

The next day, they visited the Mother's Love Clinic. Mike and Monica gave them a tour of the complex that Fredy had built. Nick made a large cash donation to help them with expenses. He also asked Mike if he might be able to come and work at the clinic, in case the veterans tour program didn't work out. Mike suggested they all talk with Le Ly about it.

Nick and Hang called Le Ly and invited her, Mike and Monica to dinner that evening. They agreed to meet at the Bach Dang Hotel, where Le Ly was staying, and walk from there.

At six they waited in the lobby bar with Mike, and Monica. Nick was surprised to see Le Ly walk in accompanied by a young, attractive Vietnamese couple. He was slightly annoyed that she had not asked if she could bring additional guests, but Nick had learned through long experience that this was a common practice in Vietnam. Le Ly wore simple black *ao ba ba* or farmer pajamas. She had no jewelry or make up.

"*Anh* Nick! How nice to see you again!" She shook his hand warmly, then hugged Hang. "*Chao, chi! Manh gioi khong?*"

"*Da, manh gioi! Cam on!*"

Le Ly turned to her young friends. "I would like you to meet my son Jimmy and his lovely friend, Miss Hiep."

They all shook hands. Jimmy was tall and handsome. Miss Hiep was very petite and beautiful. They both seemed quiet and humble. Throughout the evening they said very little, but listened respectfully.

Le Ly led them about three blocks to a small outdoor restaurant named Ngoc Anh. They sat under the stars, and a cool breeze gently stirred the trees above them in the courtyard. Hang ordered a small feast of fresh seafood, soup, noodles, steak, rice, fruit, bread, and drinks.

The conversation revolved around the progress of Le Ly's movie *Heaven and Earth* which was the story of her life in Vietnam before, during, and after the war. According to her, it was being filmed both locally and in Thailand. Nick was surprised to hear that some ODP people were also being hired as extras.

Over the years, Nick had met many Vietnamese who suffered from pie-in-the-sky expectations. As he listened to Le Ly talk about her upcoming book and the movie that Oliver Stone was producing, he felt that was the case here. But the clinic was real. It was up and running, and Nick felt a certain pride at having been involved.

Hang reached over with her chopsticks and placed fried shrimp on everyone's plate, Nick sipped his beer. Le Ly was telling about her life in Ky La during the war.

"The hardest part was being pulled in two directions. In the daytime the ARVN and American soldiers would come. They would demand our loyalty, and offer us rewards for turning in any Viet Cong in the village. They would leave before dark. Then at night, the Viet Cong would come and recruit soldiers to join them. They would punish anyone who cooperated with the government or the GIs." She paused and stared off into the darkness. Nick watched her eyes closely. She had the look also.

"We were being torn apart with no one to help us. I was raped, beaten, and tortured. I had no idea which side to take. They were both wrong. I felt helpless to change it. Finally, I escaped to America. But I could not escape the war. It raged on within me for a long time."

Nick leaned forward and took her hand. She returned to the now and smiled. "I'm sorry. I am ruining everyone's dinner."

"No," Nick said. "This is important. There are many of us who felt that conflict. Unfortunately, many of us still do. Did you ever find peace?"

She smiled again and nodded.

"How?"

She closed her eyes. "Violence, guilt, revenge all revolve in a vicious cycle. Without intervention, it goes on forever. The pain returns to haunt us again and again. There is only one way to break the cycle and attain true peace. We must truly forgive. It is as simple as that, and yet it may be the most difficult thing we ever do in this life. Our forgiveness of our enemies and our forgiveness of ourselves are inseparable."

Nick nodded and looked around the table. He stopped when he got to Hang. "Minh *oi*. Does any of this sound familiar?" They both laughed and stared at each other through the eyes of love. Nick raised his glass. "To forgiveness! The key to happiness!"

Though Le Ly had no openings at the clinic for someone with Nick's qualifications, or lack thereof, she urged him to continue to support the Peace Village and Mother's Love Clinic. "Without the involvement of you veterans, these vitally important projects would never have happened," she said. "I really appreciate all that guys like you and Fredy and Oliver Stone have done to give back to Vietnam. Thank you so much."

Nick paid the waiter and said, "Well, Le Ly, my part in all of this is very small compared to theirs, but please don't hesitate to call on us for any help. Hang and I look forward to working with all of you folks as long as you need us."

Le Ly stood and bowed. "Thank you so much for the wonderful dinner. If I can do anything to help with your veteran tour program here, please just ask, OK?"

Years later, Nick and Hang finally saw Oliver Stone's movie, *Heaven and Earth*. They were shocked to learn that the lovely young star who played Le Ly in the movie was none other than Le Thi Hiep, Jimmy's "friend", who had been their dinner guest that evening.

The next morning, Tam drove them out of Da Nang and up over Hai Van Pass. By noon they arrived in Hue and checked into the Hue Hotel. It was brand new and much cheaper than the Huong Giang where they had stayed with Tim Campbell the year before. Nick unpacked Mike's old photograph of him and the monk and got back into the car for the short drive to Thien Mu Pagoda.

Standing before a huge wooden door to the ancient temple, they smelled incense. The serenity was palpable. Nick could feel the presence of primeval spirits in the air. A young monk in a brown robe appeared. He bowed to them, smiling sadly. "You have returned. I remember you both from a year ago. How can I help you?"

Nick and Hang returned the bow. Nick spoke in a reverent voice. "Yes. Last year we wanted to meet the old monk Thich Don Hau but you said he was too sick. We hope now he is better so that we might meet him. I bring greetings from two old friends."

The monk bowed again. "I am very sorry to tell you, he recently passed on from this earth to the next life. But please tell me about his friends."

Nick and Hang looked at each other with a calm resignation. "One is his grandson Hoang Van Cuong who is a friend of ours in Ho Chi Minh City. The other is this man." He handed over the photo. "His name is Peter Goble. During the war they became friends, and Peter made donations to the temple and helped with the orphanage here. He asked me to take a picture in front of this same tree with Thich Don Hau and send it back to him in America."

The young monk smiled compassionately as the reality of the situation sank in. "If you like, I would be happy to take a picture with you in front of that tree."

"Yes, thank you. You are very kind."

The monk led them along a dirt path to the tree, which grew in an orchard of bananas and cashew trees. It stood atop a hill overlooking the Perfume River. Several sampans were working their way upstream in the evening sun, toward the mist-covered mountains in the distance. Hang snapped the picture of Nick and the monk. They bowed to each other and Nick said, "Peter wanted me to say that he and the old monk would always be friends, even if our countries are not."

The monk bowed low again. "Yes. I am sure that Thich Don Hau would agree with that. Please go in peace. And give our best wishes to your friend Peter."

CHAPTER 65
Highway One
August 1992

Over the next week, they made their way north. First, they stopped in Dong Ha to visit Quang Tri Tourism to make arrangements for Tim Campbell to finally visit the place on the Cua Viet River where he had been wounded in 1968. When Nick walked into the office he literally bumped into his old adversary, Mr. Duy. Both were shocked to see each other again and neither knew how to react. Nick waited for Duy to make a move.

"So, what are you doing back here again?" Duy asked gruffly.

"Do you remember my friend, Tim?"

"Yes, why?"

"He will be coming here to visit in a couple of weeks. And by God, this time you better take him to the Cua Viet, or I'll come back up here and..." He felt Hang's hand on his arm.

"Minh, do you remember what Le Ly told us back in Da Nang?"

Nick could feel his face flushing hot and red. His breathing was fast and shallow. He took a deep breath, then another one. He walked to a window and looked out at the city that had been nearly destroyed in the war. Is this why I came back? he thought. To fight again? Another deep breath. Break the cycle, Nick. Do it now.

"*Anh* Duy. The last time I saw you, we both acted badly. For my part, I'm sorry. Let's not do it again." He reached out his hand.

Duy walked slowly over and took it. "OK. I'm sorry too. Don't worry. If Tim comes back again, I will take him there. I promise." He handed Nick his card. "Please tell him to contact me here. OK?"

"Thank you, Duy." He flashed a *shaka*. "Aloha, brah!" And Nick took another step down Thunder Road.

The journey north continued. They visited the old American base camp at Con Thien near where the Ben Hai River had formed the DMZ, between North and South Vietnam from 1954 until 1975. From there, Highway One turned into a one-lane, pothole-riddled washboard, flanked on both sides by thousands of water-filled bomb craters. The ride got so rough that Tam worried aloud that the old car might be shaken to pieces.

Just over the old border they turned east onto a red-dirt trail. When they reached the coast there was a village of very hostile-looking people and ex-soldiers who still wore their old uniforms. Their local guide told them this was the site of the huge Vinh Moc tunnel complex that was dug during the war to provide a bomb shelter for upwards of twenty-five thousand people. A tiny young man guided them through the maze of tunnels carved from solid rock and ended in the face of a cliff that overlooked the South China Sea. This incredible engineering feat left Nick and Hang marveling at the fortitude and discipline of the northern people.

When they returned to the car, they found it surrounded by a crowd of young men. They were not smiling. Nick immediately noticed how tall and muscular they were compared to their southern cousins. In all the years he had spent in-country, he had never felt so vulnerable as he did at that moment. Hang grabbed his hand and huddled close, obviously very afraid.

The sickening reality swept over him that there was no way to either intimidate or fight them. The only choice left was to accept what came. But before it got to that point, he would try some good old-fashioned aloha. Taking the initiative, he walked up to them smiling confidently and bowed slightly. Just enough to show respect but not fear. "*Xin chao, cac ban*. Did any of you work on building these amazing tunnels?" he asked as he handed out cigarettes.

A lean, shirtless man in front spoke out. "We were all soldiers fighting in the south. The tunnels were dug by the women and farmers who stayed behind. Where you come from? Where you learn Vietnamese?"

Nick lit his cigarette and looked directly into his eyes. "I'm American. I was also a soldier who fought in the south." He waited.

The man's eyes widened in shock as he turned to his friends. "*Troi oi! Nghe khong? Ong la nguoi My!*" Suddenly they surged closer and surrounded them. Nick cocked his fists and lowered his center of gravity. But the men were smiling. Someone said, "You American?" Another asked, "You take me America, OK?"

They started shaking his hand and patting his shoulders. Tam sighed with relief. "They want to know if you will bring more Americans back here. They want to meet rich Americans." He laughed.

Once again, through acceptance and forgiveness, peace had prevailed.

After two more days in northern Vietnam, they turned around for the long ride south to Ho Chi Minh City. Along the way, Nick had Tam drive them up into the A Shau Valley, near the Laotian border, to the notorious battlefield known as Hamburger Hill, where the 101st Airborne Division had fought a bloody battle in early 1969. The road was just being constructed through the jungle and consisted of sharp-edged shards of granite that threatened to make hamburger out of Tam's tires. They had to drive through several streams that flowed across the freshly graded track. Tam finally insisted on returning to civilization, unless they wanted to finish the trip on foot.

By the time they arrived back in Ho Chi Minh City, Nick had compiled enough information to begin his veteran tour program. As soon as he had the film developed, he mailed the new photo from Thien Mu Pagoda to Peter in Colorado.

CHAPTER 66
Ho Chi Minh City
1992

As the weeks turned into months, Nick and Hang continued on as tour guides and English teachers. Tim Campbell and Domsitz arrived, went north, and thankfully, Mr. Duy took them to the very spot where Tim had been wounded. Walking through that same rice paddy, where his life had changed forever, brought Tim the closure that he had desperately needed for so long.

Shortly after Tim's return, Hang introduced him to one of her girlfriends named Tien. Tom was immediately smitten, and it wasn't long before he had also filed a K-1 petition.

Nick returned to Maui every three months to renew his visa and sometimes to pick up a tour group in Los Angeles from Dan. On one such trip, he and Dan were making their way to lunch in Hermosa Beach. Dan pointed at a well-dressed, long-haired man in a wheel chair. "Would you like to meet Ron Covic?"

Nick's jaw dropped. "You mean the guy from *Born on the Fourth of July?*"

Dan smiled smugly. "Come on."

"Dan! How are you?" The man greeted him like an old friend.

"Ron, I want you to meet Nick Dwyer." Nick reached out to shake hands. "Nick is a combat veteran too. He works for us in Vietnam."

Ron's face shone with admiration and respect. "Do you really? Holy shit! I can't imagine that. But hey, welcome home."

"Welcome home, brother. Yeah, it's true. But I'm still waiting for my first paycheck." He glared at Dan.

Dan gave him a reprimanding frown. "Come on, let's not air our dirty laundry. Nick has also worked with Le Ly Hayslip."

Ron nodded, smiling. "How is Le Ly?"

"Fine. How do you know her?"

"I'm also a supporter of her clinic in Da Nang. It's how I give back."

"That's terrific. Have you been back yet?"

Ron paused, looked out at the waves on the beach, then beyond to the horizon. He smiled gently. "Not yet. What's it like now?"

Nick followed his gaze. He shrugged. "Sometimes it feels like home. Sometimes it doesn't. But it's always my school."

Ron nodded sympathetically. "Well, if I decided to go, would you take me with you?"

"In a heartbeat. Just tell Dan."

"Thanks, Nick. I'm really proud of you."

Nick blushed. "Hell, I'm proud of YOU! You've done a lot more than I have, or probably ever will. It was an honor!"

That evening, Nick met his group at the Los Angeles International Airport. They were about twenty Vietnamese who were returning home for the first time. They were scared, but after hearing Nick reassure them that it was safe, their anxiety turned to giddy excitement.

During the thirteen-hour layover in Seoul, Korea, Nick was approached by an elderly man with white hair and glasses. He had a dark complexion and looked very fit. "I say there. Where did you learn to speak Vietnamese like that?" he asked in a British accent.

"Lots of practice over the last twenty-seven years. Have you been there before?"

"Oh my, yes! I lived there for years during the war. I still visit frequently. I'm Jamshed Fazdhar."

"Nick Dwyer. What did you do there?"

"Telecommunications, actually. Met all the reporters and correspondents. Politicians too."

"Did you know guys like Sean Flynn, Jack Halsey, Neil Sheehan?"

"Every one of them. They would always try to get me to attend the five o'clock follies but I never did."

"Why not?"

"I don't drink. I am a Bahai minister. Are you familiar with my faith?"

"Yes. I almost joined once."

"Why didn't you?"

"I DO drink!" Nick laughed.

"Well, why don't we go sit in the transit lounge and chat about it. But we'll have to talk fast. We only have twelve-and-a-half hours left before our flight to Ho Chi Minh City."

By the time they boarded the flight, Nick and Jamshed had become good friends, although Nick found him to be quite pushy and self-righteous about his religion. But the man was a walking encyclopedia and could converse on any subject that arose with impressive accuracy and knowledge. He resided at a place called the Peace Mansion in Singapore and was a world-renowned leader in the Bahai faith. Nick asked him if he was familiar with the Course in Miracles.

"I don't place much value in any book of miracles. The Bahai faith provides the only credible solutions to the quest for inner peace." he said. "But please stay in touch with me. If you are ever in Singapore, I insist that you be my guest at the mansion. Best of luck to you on your journey. But I hope you won't waste your time searching in the wrong places." Though they never met again, Nick kept up a running correspondence with Fazdhar for decades to come.

As Hang's immigration papers ran the long gauntlet of government bureaucracy, Nick found himself simply treading water in Vietnam, waiting to get Hang out. He could not accept the fact that the governments of their two respective countries had the power to interfere with their living their life together. Vietnam could pull his visa whenever they wanted, and the U.S. could refuse to let Hang into the country on a whim.

The longer he stayed in Vietnam, the more cultural differences became a problem for him. He truly began to miss the system in the U.S. It was so much more efficient and reliable. Soon, little things became big things, and it was obvious he wouldn't last until Hang's petition was approved. Manley Daniel and Tom O'Rourke helped speed things up as best they could, but Nick was growing impatient.

Anh Chanh, the driver, had given Nick a handmade acoustic guitar to entertain himself in their austere hotel room. One day, as he reflected on the recent events and circumstances of their life, he wrote a song with a country/western melody titled "I'd Rather Be In Hell With You Than In Paradise Alone" that seemed to tell it all.

"I went back to Nam again in 1991,
I met you on that August night and then we had some fun,

We checked into an old hotel down in district five,
I thought that I'd seen bad before but God it was a dive!
The roof, it leaked and the water's weak and the beds were hard as stone,
But I'd rather be in hell with you than in paradise alone.
I tried to cook some dinner but I damn near fried my brains,
The rice cooker's not grounded and I was standin' in the rain,
The dog meat was delicious and the rat was OK too,
But that old boiled goat dick sure did make me blue.
The doors are broke, the fan's a joke, and the maid took all I own,
But I'd rather be in hell with you than in paradise alone.
The toilet and the shower are both the same big hole,
It seems my bathroom basin is someone's old rice bowl,
The neighbors are all nosey and they play their music loud,
Sometimes it seems as though my life is hung beneath a cloud.
And all that I can think about is catching a plane home,
But I'd rather be in hell with you than in paradise alone.
We tried to drive to Hanoi and visit Halong Bay,
But we had to bribe policemen all along the way,
The road, it was so bumpy, we all went through the roof,
And if you don't believe me, my bald head is the proof,
But then I saw your smiling face and felt your love so true,
That suddenly I found myself in paradise with you!"

The truth was, that in order for them to live back on Maui, he would have to start up his carnation farm again. This meant asking his tenants to vacate his small house, clearing land, ordering plants, and preparing to open for business again. He would have to go first and wait for Hang on Maui.

Early in 1993, Nick prepared to leave. The going-away parties that were thrown by their friends went on for weeks. Even the staff at the Mondial lavished him with gifts and souvenirs. Every morning in January began with Alka-Seltzer and black coffee. Each night ended with feasting and massive amounts of beer.

One night, his former students from the Mondial actually stood in line twelve deep, each holding a full beer. One by one they would step up to Nick and say, "Teacher! One hundred percent!" then Nick would have to drain his glass with each student.

Hang was very worried. She confronted John Wayne, who was the instigator. "What are you trying to do? Kill the teacher?"

"Yes! Kill the teacher! Kill the teacher!" he chanted, laughing drunkenly.

Nick shook his head good-naturedly. "We'll see who kills who, you goddamn Viet Cong!" he roared. "Come on! One hundred percent!"

After several rounds, the students began dropping like flies. One vomited all over a table, another passed out on his plate. But Nick was well practiced, and by the time he reached his second wind, he wavered alone against the wall. Leaning on his beloved Hang for support, he weaved out of the restaurant laughing derisively and stepping over all the young men sprawled unconscious on the floor. He grinned sloppily at Hang. "You see that? As in the immortal words of William Shakespeare, 'They knoweth not with whom they are fucking, by God!'"

The only ones that he never saw were Thanh and Trung, and that gnawed away at him until the very end. When finally the last day arrived, Hang, Mot, and Lai drove him to Tan Son Nhat. Hang placed her arms around his neck and gazed up at him in the cool morning sun. "Minh *oi*. I don't want you to worry about me, OK? I will be staying at home with Hien and our family. I will go to school everyday to study English and computers. I talked with Dr. Hung. He said you can call me on his phone anytime. I will be good. I will be faithful to you. Forever, Minh. Even if we are not married... For the rest of our lives..."

"Love always." He kissed her tenderly. "Here is some money to help you for the next six months. If it looks like you won't be able to leave by then, I will send more. Don't worry, Minh. I will take care of you for the rest of your life."

"*Anh* Ly. Wait. I have something for you," said Mot as he handed Nick a package wrapped in brown paper. Nick grinned knowingly and opened it to find another lacquerware box inlaid with mother-of-pearl. The gold lettered inscription read, "To *Anh* Ly—a souvenir of your *que huong* (homeland) from Mot & Lai, 1993."

Nick grabbed them both in a two-armed bear hug. He let go, kissed Hang again for the last time and walked away wiping his eyes.

CHAPTER 67
Wailuku, Maui
March 1993

Since Nick's return, Saigon Café had become the regular site of Happy Wednesdays for him and his veteran friends. On one such occasion, Tim Campbell limped in to join the group with a huge smile on his face. "Hey, Nick! Guess what! I'm going back to Nam next month!"

"What? For real?"

"Yeah. I'm gonna stay there until I can get Tien's K-1 petition approved!"

Mark looked confused. "Sorry, Tim, I haven't seen you in a while. What the hell you talkin' 'bout?"

"Nick and Hang introduced me to this girl over there. We decided to get married, so I filed the same papers that Nick did."

Nick was suddenly far away. He missed Hang terribly. The wheels began to turn. He stared back at Tim. "You know, Hang's birthday is next month. God, I'd love to ambush her!"

Tim laughed, "Then why don't you go with me? It'd be like old times. I'd love to see the look on her face if you just showed up by surprise."

Six beers and lovesickness drove Nick up to the bar where Jennifer was working the register. "*Em oi*, can I use your phone to call Honolulu?"

"Who you call, *Anh* Ly?"

"Pacific Ocean Travel."

Her lovely face broke into a surprised grin. "*Troi oi*! You going back again already? You must really be in love." She laughed. "OK, go ahead."

Within minutes he had a reservation on the same flight as Tim.

But he would have to wait again for visa approval from the embassy in Mexico. He left that night as giddy as a teenager and went home to prepare for the trip. As usual, Mark had agreed to take care of things while he was gone.

Three weeks later, Nick was getting antsy. His bags had been packed for days. He was caught up on the farm work, and the anticipation was driving him crazy. Then one day, just after breakfast, his phone rang. It was Thomas Lai. "Hello, Nick. I'm sorry, but I have bad news. Your visa application was denied."

Nick immediately felt the shock of the adrenaline surge through his body. Anger and fear were tightly intertwined. "What? There must be a mistake!"

"No. I checked and double checked. They said it was denied from Vietnam. Your name is on some new computer list. There's nothing they can do. I'm sorry, Nick."

"OK, Thomas. Don't cancel anything. I'm going to call Vietnam Tourism and fix this thing. I'll call you back later, OK?"

"Good luck!"

Because of the time difference Nick had to wait until late afternoon to make calls. When he finally got through, he was first put in contact with Ms. Thuy, the one who had torn up his six-month visa the year before. "Actually Nick, you have returned to Vietnam illegally several times since our problem last year. You were lucky. But now, your luck has run out. Goodbye."

Now he was infuriated but also desperate. There was only one other person who might help. He dialed the old familiar number.

"Oh! Hello, Nick! What a surprise! It's been a long time. Where are you?"

Strangely, Nick was suddenly conscious of the distance between them. There was an ocean of differences that just could not be crossed, no matter how hard he tried. His mind was a whirlpool of emotions. "Hello, Thanh. I'm on Maui." Inexplicably, his eyes welled up. Then he saw Hang's smiling face in his mind's eye. "I'm trying to get back to Vietnam, but my visa has been denied. Look Thanh, we have been friends for a long time. No matter what else has happened, I hope we always will be. Can you help?"

There was a long pause. He could hear her breathing. "Yes, Nick. We'll always be friends. But I cannot help you with your problem. I'm sorry. Really, I am."

He took a deep breath. He was calm. The acceptance settled over him. "Yeah, me too. Aloha."

After hanging up, he went outside on his porch and felt the warmth of the sun. He surveyed the beauty of his island. He had spent the last twenty-three years working the 'aina, and he had become a part of it. It had also become a part of him and yet, without Hang, he felt empty.

He thought of the contemporary Vietnamese group called Que Huong and their beautiful haunting music. He was visited by a line from one of their songs. "Que huong (homeland) is like a mother... every person has only one." Yeah. He thought to himself. Except for some Vietnamese expatriates, Amerasians, or certain disillusioned veterans who feel a life-long connection to the place that they gave so much to, or took so much from.

His heart was torn. But he had lived on Maui longer than anywhere else. Halfway between the U.S. mainland and Asia, it was the most isolated place on earth. Perfect.

CHAPTER 68
Kula, Maui
August 17, 1993

In the cool mountain air, Nick walked to his mail box and pulled out the single envelope. It was the monthly phone bill. He opened it apprehensively. "Seven hundred sixty-two dollars!" he exclaimed. "It would be cheaper to fly back to Nam!" Then he laughed. But at least I can call her, he thought. In the old days it took two months to get a reply from a letter.

He went back inside the cottage and looked longingly at the photo of her in a flower-print shirt and blue jeans standing next to a rice paddy. Nui Ba Den (The Black Virgin Mountain) rose up from the jungle in the background. A lilting Kenny G. instrumental played on his radio. In a flash, he was there, holding her small body in his arms, watching the towering cumulous clouds drifting in from the west.

The totality of his Vietnam experience surged over him. The horror of war. The serenity of peace. The blood-lust of killing. The gut-wrenching guilt. Love. Hate. The surrender to the powers of the universe. The acceptance of death. The ecstasy of life. Extremes, always. No gray.

And the wait would soon be over. He sat back down on the floor and resumed stringing the double red-and-white carnation leis. Tomorrow he would fly to Honolulu on the early-bird flight. Tom O'Rourke had told him their flight number. Hang and her twenty-year-old son, Huy, would arrive at 11:30a.m. from Bangkok.

At eleven he found the exit gate for the Immigration and Naturalization Service and sat in the shade of a plumeria tree with his leis draped over his arm. Dozens of other sponsors milled about the area, chatting and exchanging information. Soon, the first few immigrants began coming through the doors and jumping into the arms of their loved ones. Nick watched anxiously as the reunions continued. Each time the doors opened he would leap up, only to feel the disappointment when it wasn't them. After three hours the crowd had disappeared and he found himself alone on the sidewalk. Finally he saw a uniformed female officer come out the door. He ran up to her. "Excuse me. I'm waiting for my fiance, Le Thi Ngoc Hang and her son, Huynh Thanh Huy. Can I please go back and look for them?"

"No. I'm sorry. Access is restricted to authorized personnel. Do you know their IV numbers?"

"Yeah, right here." He handed her his papers.

"I'll be right back," she said and the doors closed behind her.

Nick began pacing wildly. The beast within him was shaking its cage. What had happened? Why did everyone else arrive, but not them? What if they were lost somewhere without money or papers and stranded in some foreign country? They were helpless! She needed him, and he couldn't reach her! He could hear her small voice calling to him for help, but it came from an abyss! He couldn't take any more! He charged the thick metal doors and laid his shoulders into them. They flew open with a loud crash. And there were two large Hawaiian armed guards. They grabbed him and held him tightly just as he spotted her and Huy walking toward him dragging their heavy suitcases. "Sir! What are you doing?" one guard yelled at him. "This is a restricted area!"

"Minh *oi*!" he yelled. "Minh!" Somehow he broke free and they were in each other's arms crying, laughing, and kissing. He almost forgot the leis. "Here, Minh. Aloha! Welcome to Hawaii, Huy!" He placed the leis around their necks.

The guards looked at each other and shrugged, smiling. Soon they were laughing. Nick turned to face them. "Hey, sorry eh, you guys. This is my fiancé and her son from Vietnam. I been waiting long time, eh."

The other guard stared hard at Nick, nodding. "Hey brah, you one vet?"

"Yeah. You?"

"No, brah. But, welcome home!"

Two hours later, Nick, Hang, and Huy arrived on Maui and were met by a boisterous crowd of Vietnam Veterans of Maui and their wives. They were welcomed with more hugs, kisses, and leis. They eventually made their way up the volcano to Nick's farm, and he proudly showed them the new addition that he and all the vets had built to make room for them in the small cottage. Nick had supplied the materials, but every man that worked on the construction did it for free.

Nick and Hang marveled that, nearly two years to the day after they had met, she was here. From that day forward, nothing or nobody could ever come between them again. Though Huy later moved to the excitement of Los Angeles, Nick and Hang were married on Veteran's Day 1993 and became inseparable. They were the envy of everyone they knew because of their fairy-tale kind of love.

Over the next twenty years, they returned to Vietnam often. In 1994 they took back two other vets, Mark, Andrew, and their old friend Tom Domsitz. They all checked in to the Bong Sen Hotel. One afternoon, Nick got on the elevator in the lobby. There was a plump, middle-aged white woman already aboard. She asked, "Where are you from?"

"Maui. And you?"

"Albany, New York. But now I work in Hanoi with the Amerasian refugee program." She extended her hand. "Rosemary."

Nick couldn't contain his laughter. "Rosemary Battisti, by any chance? I'm Nick Dwyer."

"Oh, my God! I think still have your letter on my desk! How is Charlie Brown?"

He told her the sad story. She nodded understandingly. "Isn't it a shame? So many of us have tried so hard, for so long, but we just can't seem to get it right."

"In Vietnam, that's the name of the game. *C'est la vie, n'est-ce pas?*"

She nodded sadly. "I'm leaving tonight for Hanoi. Will you be heading that way? I'd love to exchange notes sometime."

"Me too, but not this time."

The door opened. She shrugged. "This is my floor. I'm sorry." She reached out and hugged him.

He smiled. "Ships passing in the night, that sort of thing."

She laughed, "Yeah. We have to stop meeting like this! Good luck, Nick."

A few months later, in January of 1995, President Bill Clinton made history by lifting the trade embargo and normalizing relations with Vietnam. The boisterous street celebrations went on for weeks, but Nick and Hang were already farming intensively and unable to attend.

However, they went back again in 1997 to meet up with Fredy and Sherry Champagne in Lai Khe, where they donated thousands of dollars in cash and medical supplies to the local Red Cross and orphanage. Then they traveled north together and visited the brand new U.S. embassy in Hanoi. The former machine-gunner and point man from Alpha Company, Second Battalion of the Second Infantry Regiment, hugged each other on the front steps. Their eyes glistened as they saw that their common dream had finally come to fruition.

In 1998, they closed down the farm and moved to Vietnam for a year. Nick again taught English at night for a university in Ho Chi Minh City. His employer was a woman named Nguyen Thi Xuan Mai, introduced to him by his old friend, veteran and author, Peter Leonard.

Xuan Mai was a colonel in the Peoples' Army of Vietnam. During the war she had been a Viet Cong guerilla who had also lived in the village of Lai Khe, inside Nick's base camp. She had known Vy and Vui as well as Ma, Phuong, and Hai.

It was during the fall of 1998 that Nick and Hang decided to go on a dinner cruise, aboard the My Canh, on the Saigon River. Nick had always been leery of it because of the tragic bombing that he and A.J. had witnessed in 1965. But they had actually gone quite often over the years, and it was always enjoyable. The boat would sail up and down the rolling, muddy river in the sunset while the guests dined on such delicacies as pig-brain soup, fresh fish, snails, eel, and duck heads. This particular night, however, would end much differently.

When they docked, the patrons began leaving down the gangplank. Nick and Hang were among the first ones to disembark. They pushed through the throngs of beggars and vendors and crossed busy Ton Duc Thang Street. Just as they reached the far sidewalk they felt the roar of a huge explosion behind them. Agonized screams pierced the night air as debris rained down on them and a cloud of smoke swept through the trees. At first Nick thought he was having a flashback, but the reality was overwhelming. He grabbed Hang's hand and sprinted away, dragging her to the corner and then up a side street. They didn't stop running for two blocks, where they hailed a taxi and sped away to Hang's family home on Tran Binh Trong.

The news later reported that the bomb had been detonated by a counter-revolutionary group trying to wrest Vietnam from the communists. Several people were killed, and over a dozen wounded. When Nick read the report in the paper, he couldn't help but recall Le Ly's words of wisdom about the endless cycle of violence and revenge and how the only way to break the cycle is with true forgiveness. That night, as he lay in bed with Hang snuggled under his arm, he thought back over Vietnam's long and tragic history. They had been at war with someone for over a thousand years. It was going to take a whole lot of forgiveness to bring that to an end.

As the problems of the past faded into history, their friendship with Pham Thai Thanh resumed. She had retired from Vietnam Tourism and took a job with Air France. Her husband, Loc, rose through the ranks in the Office of Domestic Affairs, and his future brightened accordingly. The four of them would socialize frequently.

But as the days passed, Nick grew tired of loafing all day and teaching at night. The routine was in direct contrast to farm life back on Maui. He felt like a fish out of water. As this reality set in, his feelings of resentment and frustration began resurfacing after a few months, and they finally had to pack up and return home.

As soon as they reached Maui, the sense of relief and belonging was immediate and powerful. Their lives entered the time of long shadows with love and laughter.

One morning, shortly after they got back, they awoke in the comfort of their own bed, then walked outside with cups of coffee. They sat in lawn chairs under a cypress tree. Hang gazed out across the valley and giggled to herself.

"What?" he asked.

"I was just remembering. Why do you and your veteran friends insult each other all the time. You're all so rude!"

He sipped the rich Vietnamese coffee and grinned. "I guess we're trying to hide our true feelings. Men aren't supposed to feel things, you know. At least that's what we're taught from small-kid time."

"Who teaches you that?"

"Everybody. Especially our heroes. John Wayne, Robert Mitchum,

Errol Flynn… our fathers. We all want to be tough guys like them. No fear, no feeling, and especially no crying. That's how we prove ourselves as men. We go to war for the same reason. As if the act of killing, with no regrets, is our rite of passage into manhood."

"Do you still believe that?"

"It's a crock of shit. I hate to admit it, but maybe Charlie Brown was right. I was trying to hide who I really was. But I'm tired of hiding. I'm just gonna be me. Fuck them."

"And who are you really, Minh?"

He felt the heat surging through him, the pressure behind his eyes. "I'm… I'm not who they think I am. I'm not a baby killer. I'm not a coward… I'm…"

"Say it, honey *oi*! Say it! You know it's true." She squeezed his hand. He looked over at her, head bowed.

"Then I'LL say it. You are a good man. You and Fredy and all those other veterans who went back to my country. You went back to help make things right, to make peace, when nobody else would. I'm so proud and grateful to all of you." She watched him looking out at the horizon. "So what do you believe in, Minh?"

He grinned sheepishly. "Well, some people believe in Catholicism, or Judaism, or Buddhism. I believe in alcoholism!" he teased.

"No! Really!" she jabbed his ribs.

He chuckled. "I believe in the Golden Rule and Murphy's Law."

She laughed along with him then stroked his arm. "Is there anything else?"

He leaned over and kissed her sensuously. "I believe in you, and our love."

Her eyes shined back, then stared far away. "You know, Minh. Ever since we met, you have been looking for the place where you really belong. A place called "home," right?"

He nodded. "Yeah. It's crazy. It's like, when I'm here, I feel like I should be there. Whenever I'm there, I just wanna be here."

She grasped his hand. "And what about me? I left my family and my *que huong* to come here and start a new life with you. I came looking for home too. And I have found it." She surveyed the farm. "I don't know what more you want. Listen to the birds. Smell the scents of the flowers and the earth. It is quiet, peaceful. No traffic, no crowds, no beggars. The people here have love in their hearts. What you call aloha. They accept us for who we are, not for who we used to be. I think you have been searching for something that is right under your nose."

He nodded. "I know you're right, but I just don't feel I deserve it."

"Why? You still feel guilty?"

"Always. I know it's sick, but that's just how it is. Some things will never change." He sipped his coffee. "I've been reading the Teachings of Buddha lately."

"I know."

"There is something called The Truth of Suffering. Have you heard of it?"

"You know I'm Catholic."

"Well, it says that suffering is a natural part of life. Birth, sickness, old age, and death are all forms of suffering. No one is exempt. I've been thinking about my PTSD. It's suffering too. I don't believe there is a cure, but maybe this is the way to accept it and at least learn to live with it."

She smiled dreamily. "And home?"

He kissed her softly. "All those trips back and forth to Vietnam taught me something. Home is not in Vietnam, OR in the U.S.... but wherever YOU are... That's where HOME is."

CHAPTER 69
Home
Halloween 2009

Hang handed him the glass and stood beside him as the orange ball began its descent behind the West Maui Mountains. They embraced in the evening still and he whispered, *"Cam on, Minh."*

She lifted up her face and kissed him gently. "It's OK, Minh. Go do what you have to do. I'll make dinner."

The old man sipped his cabernet and stared out off his lanai at a cruise ship on the distant sea.

Nestled on the slope of Haleakala, their freshly painted cottage was planted in the middle of the carnation farm. It was surrounded by thousands of brilliant blossoms. The house commanded a panoramic view of the island, not unlike the bridge of the ship which sailed slowly through the Kealaikahiki Channel 4,000 feet below and more than fifty miles away.

It had been more than forty years now, and yet he still marveled at the pristine beauty of each sunset. Nowhere on Planet Earth could you find such diverse contrast of shape and color, clarity and depth as on this island of Maui. The natural beauty was so overwhelming that it made him want to weep with joy. A gentle trade wind ruffled the fronds of the tree ferns. Mynah birds sang a melody from the tops of the cypress trees bordering the road. The purple shadows lengthened beneath the gold and crimson sky. Far below on the floor of the central valley the streams and reservoirs shimmered silver and spread like jewels through the fields of sugar cane. Soft lavender jacaranda blooms fell silently onto the lawn and the delicate fragrance of pink roses wafted up from below the porch. Sipping the wine, he shook his head in disbelief.

"Heaven can't be any better than this," he said to himself. And then he felt the familiar aching in his heart and the lump forming in his throat. "I owe this moment to you, my brother. How can I ever repay such a precious gift?"

From deep within his soul the dark, lifeless eyes stared back at him. Blood streamed down from beneath the steel helmet and ran off the dead face onto Nick's arm as he cradled the body on the jungle floor. The small, round hole was hard to see at first. It was hidden by the tattered camouflage cloth cover that hung down over his forehead. Nick could not tell about the damage until he turned the man over and felt the hot, sticky slime saturating his jungle fatigue pants. The back of the man's skull was gone, and gray brain matter plopped out onto the red clay.

Eighteen-year-old Nick had been on point all day the day before. He had been on point all day the day before that, and the day before that.

Each day, at first light, third platoon tossed their empty C-ration cans into the two-man foxholes and filled them with dirt. Then they would smoke and await the dreaded words.

"Saddle up!" Invariably they were followed by, "Nick, take the point!"

"Fuck this shit, man!" came his reply. "Hey Sarge, how come I always got to take point?"

"Because you're good at it, Nick. And besides, you got those size-thirteen clown feet. If there's any mines out there, I know you'll find 'em. Now shut up and start swinging your big knife. We gotta make twenty klicks by noon."

"Man, you're fuckin' nuts! There ain't no way we gonna make that in this jungle. This is Cu Chi, Sarge. There's tunnels all over the place, man!"

"Sounds like a personal problem to me. I suggest you take it up with the chaplain."

"Sarge, you know how I operate. It's better to take your time and get there than to be in such a hurry that you don't. I got a bad feeling this morning."

Sergeant Murphy paused and stared into Nick's eyes. Then, "Time's a wastin'. Move out."

"OK, look, you can put me on point if you want to, but I'm gonna do it my way. If you got a problem with that, then get somebody else.

This'll be my fourth day in a row on point. We got three platoons out here, man. Why don't you stand up for us for once. Tell the old man it someone else's turn." A chorus of support arose from the rest of Nick's squad.

"Yeah, Sarge, Nick's right, man!" agreed Derby, a short, robust farm boy from South Dakota. He was normally the relief point man if Nick could not take any more. There was something in Nick's tone that spelled danger. Sensing it now, he pleaded Nick's case to lessen the likelihood of being sent in to replace him. Platoon Sergeant Murphy paused, then looked over to Oddo, the machine gunner, who was usually the most even-tempered member of the platoon. With a nod, he invited the big man's input.

"Nick needs a break, Sarge," came the quiet reply.

Sergeant Murphy pulled long on his Camel and scratched at his gray stubble. He knew the boy was right. Giving Nick a sidelong glance, he stepped over to his RTO.

"Hernandez, get six on the horn."

Squatting nearby, side by side, Chief and Cooper faced out to the jungle. They silently looked at each other with raised eyebrows. Cooper, being an FNG, had never witnessed this kind of insubordinate behavior. He whispered to Chief, "Is Nick nuts? He's only a PFC! How can he talk to the Sarge that way?"

Chief gave him a wry smile. "Nick's getting another bad feeling. That ain't good."

"Whatdya mean, a bad feeling?"

"Nick's been in-country longer than anybody, man. He's walked point so long that he can feel stuff the rest of us can't. I've seen it before. The first day he joined our unit we was doin' a road sweep, you know, checking for mines along Thunder Road. Sarge put him on point and there was two other FNG's right behind him. Well, Nick started walking down this trail running parallel with the road. He hadn't gone more than 20 meters when he just stopped in his tracks. Then after a minute he stepped off the trail and went into the jungle. One of the new guys was an E-5 and he asked Nick what he's doin'. Tells him to get back on the trail. Nick shakes his head and says, 'I got a bad feeling, Sarge. I think you guys should get off that trail too. That's a perfect place for a booby trap.' But the two new guys are lazy and decide to stay on the trail. They get about ten feet down it when a

Bouncing Betty goes off. That fuckin' mine blew the sergeant's leg off at the knee. The Spec 4 lost his cock and his balls and died right there from the shock. I got a big piece of shrapnel in my crotch. Standridge got a piece in his thigh. But Nick came out clean, man. When Nick gets a bad feeling, you better listen, cause he ain't never been wrong."

Sergeant Murphy held the handset to his ear with his grimy fingers. "Roger, six. Thank you, sir. This is three six Mike, out." He glanced back over his shoulder at Nick. "OK, hot-shot. You got your way. Happy now?"

"Thanks, Sarge. You're OK, man."

"Tell it to first platoon. You'd better hope they don't hit nothin', or you won't sleep good the rest of your life." Shaking his head Sergeant Murphy pulled on his pack. "Saddle up!"

Third platoon stood, grumbling and sweating, and pulled on their packs. Some lit cigarettes, others took a long swig from their canteens while they waited for first platoon to move into position in the rice paddy where they had spent the night. Nick took his place at the head of his platoon's column but fell in behind the sixteen men who made up what was left of first platoon.

Fredy Higdon, their short, thick machine gunner, waddled up past him with a head nod. "So what, Nick? Got a bad feeling again, uh?" He smirked as he gave Nick a sideways glance.

"Yeah, that's right. So?"

"Fucking pussy!"

"Hey, you try walkin' point everyday, man, and see how you like it. It's about time one of you fuckers earned your combat pay."

"Oh yeah? You try humpin' this 60 for a while and you'll beg to take point again."

Nick gave Higdon a shit-eating grin along with the finger. Higdon laughed and swung by him. He was followed by a tall and burly rifleman Nick had met only briefly one day back at the base-camp mess tent. He was a white, good-looking and cocky FNG who had fallen in with some of the black soldiers in first platoon. He loved to talk jive and sounded more black than the brothers at times. This was a constant source of amusement to the men, and he was well liked. As he strode past Nick he too nodded in a sarcastic way as if to chide him for having to take his place.

Nick's conscience began nagging him slightly, but since the normal policy was for the point to be rotated at least on a daily basis, he felt justified in demanding a break after three days in a row. Besides that, there was the ominous premonition that had come to him last night in his foxhole. He watched the rifleman take his place at the point, and first platoon's Sergeant Guerrero gave the order to move out.

The jive-talking point man unsheathed his machete and swung it in the air as if he was attacking an imaginary enemy. "OK, Charlie! Look out, motha fucka, here ah come, man! Ah'm goin' whoop you, boy! Ah'm goin' cut yo ass up and I ain't bullshittin', motha fucka!" Then he began strutting and prancing and bobbing his head like a young rooster, which brought howls of laughter from all along the single file behind him. Even Nick had to laugh. He had to admit that this FNG was cool. He made a mental note to buy the dude a beer when they got back to their base camp, whenever that would be.

First platoon, such as it was, led the company out of the paddy and into the triple-canopy jungle. Leaving the blistering tropical sun behind, they stepped into the darkness of the famed Ho Bo woods. It had become impossible to enter this brutal war zone without making enemy contact. Every American unit from the 173rd Airborne Brigade, to the First Infantry Division, which was Nick's unit, to the Twenty-Fifth Infantry Division had fought in this notorious place.

The men in Alpha company dreaded this most dangerous part of *Cu Chi* district for good reason. There were a myriad of tunnels dug beneath the jungle, which wound and interconnected for more than 200 kilometers. They were built in three levels, ranging in depth from 5 to 20 meters. Along the subterranean route there were air holes and fighting positions and spider holes, which were tiny openings in the jungle floor that could hide the small and perfectly camouflaged Viet Cong snipers. They could pop up beneath your feet, shoot you between the eyes and disappear before you knew what hit you.

As soon as they slipped into the forest all conversation and smoking and noise of any kind immediately ceased. All eyes suddenly focused with a frightening intensity at every leaf and tree and patch of red dirt. Nick could physically feel the fear taking over his body. Breathing was short and shallow. Every hair on his body bristled with electric energy like miniature antennas, straining to sense any hostile presence. His eyes widened and swept back and forth, then up and down, scanning like a radar screen. Unconciously, his nostrils flared and filtered the thick humid air, searching for anything out of place. He drew back his ears and opened them with a crackling sound inside his head. The jungle would always hum and buzz with the sounds of life. He felt the trees growing and the vines twisting and the insects crawling and flying. With the sixteen men of first platoon in front of him he, didn't worry much about trip wires or booby traps or punji pits, because someone else would have hit them. But he concentrated on snipers or an ambush on the sides of the column. He might not have been the one cutting the trail, but in the bush, Nick always walked point.

Within minutes of entering the jungle the men began sweating profusely, and their fatigues were soon soaked through. There would often come a point when they would sweat themselves dry and become totally dehydrated. Then the white salt stains would appear where the pack straps cut across their shoulders. This is when the heat stroke would set in. At first, you got dizzy, and your head felt like it would explode. Then the delirium would come and simple actions became near impossible. The brain would begin to boil, and then you would faint. Without water, salt tabs, and rest, you would die.

It had been nearly three hours now, and the pace was still way too fast for Nick's liking. The jive-talking point man who took Nick's place was withering under the weight of his hundred-pound pack and swung his machete blindly. He was past exhaustion and no longer paying attention to his surroundings. He began mumbling to himself incoherently. The men behind him could hear him cursing quietly at first. But as the morning wore on he unconsciously became louder and more careless. Sergeant Guerrero, sensing what was wrong, made his way forward along the beleaguered column. He was within fifteen meters of him when the single shot pierced the heavily laden jungle air. Back down the line Nick winced at the sound. "That was a carbine," he whispered to himself.

Quickly looking around, he saw that every man, like him, had instinctively dropped and was kneeling in the thick foliage. The fear and dread was obvious in their eyes, for they all carried M-16s and they knew that only the VC carried carbines. They heard first platoon returning fire. Then came the warning shout, "Fire in the hole!" followed immediately by the explosion of the grenade.

Nick easily visualized the scene up on point. The FNG had missed the spider hole and the sniper had popped up and nailed his ass. The slack men would run up to fire into the bush and the dirt and lift up the camouflaged cover to the tunnel and throw in a grenade. By that time the VC would have scrambled down into the safety of his burrow like a rat, leaving first platoon with another sad story to tell.

Sergeant Murphy stood up. "Hold in place men! Keep your eyes and ears open! If there's one, there could be others!" Then he squatted back down and faced off into the greenery. There was a muffled crackling of the radio on Hernandez's back. "This is three-six Mike, over." Sergeant Murphy's face was as red as his hair, and the sweat poured off his face as he held the dripping handset. There was a long silence as he listened to the lieutenant's voice on the other end. Then finally, "Yes sir! Fuck it, sir! That's all, just fuck it! Three-six Mike, out." Nick watched his sergeant's freckled face turn slowly toward him. They locked eyes. "Nick. You get your fucking ass up to the point! When you get there, you help carry the body out! And I don't EVER want to hear about your bad feelings again! Do you understand me, soldier?"

Nick hung his head, nodded, then rose up slowly. Holding his M-16 at port arms he paused in the stillness. What had just happened was no shock to him. But the fact that he had seen it coming, was. There was a pattern developing now, and it was very unsettling. He looked up sheepishly from beneath his helmet at the fury in the sergeant's bloodshot eyes. He wanted to cry. He wanted to ask forgiveness. He wanted the others to understand. But even he did not understand. Talking now would be futile. Crying was out of the question. He turned dejectedly and ambled up past first platoon, looking only at the ground. He could feel their condemnation, he didn't need to see it too. Straining under the weight of his pack, he stepped over and around them. Some were muttering insults and obscenities. Others just stared at him in awe. This was to become another one of many incidents that would fuel his growing reputation as some sort of psychic. And with it he would become a pariah in the platoon.

When he reached the point he found several grunts fanned out in a defensive perimeter around the fallen man who had so recently made them laugh and forget, just for a moment, the seriousness of it all. Nick dropped his pack, knelt down and cradled the man in his arms...

A cool breeze lifted up off the slope of the mountain. His brown and weathered hand lifted the blood-red wine to his lips, then set the glass down in the dark volcanic soil at his feet. He scooped up a handful and let it run through his fingers. Squatting in the field, like a Vietnamese, the old man held his graying head in his hands. Tears slid silently down his ruddy cheeks. It had become a ritual of sorts, these sunset memorial services, when he would talk with the ghosts. And there were many. Like countless times before, he sat with one eye smiling contentedly into the peaceful end of a beautiful day, but with the other intently rooted in the ghoulish horrors of his past. After a while, he reached down and took the glass and held it like a mother with a baby, or like a soldier with a fallen friend. And he said...

"I have talked to you and seen your face every single day for over forty years, but I still cannot recall your name. I know it is somewhere amongst the sixty-thousand others. I suppose if I really tried, I could find you. I could research the after-action reports. I could go on-line. I could go to the reunions. Or, I can keep you where you are... in my heart.

"I am the reason you died. You are the reason I live. There have been so many times when I thought I couldn't take it anymore. It would be so easy to put the barrel in my mouth again and squeeze off the last one. But then I remember you and your ultimate sacrifice. You lost your life so that I could keep mine. How could I commit such blasphemy? And so I go on. You have given me another day. A day to cherish, not to squander. A day to do not only what I would do, but what you would have done. So I will go on living, and I will live each day for you, my brother, though I will never know your name. I only wish that you could be here to share this sunset so that I could tell you. I've carried this pack a long time, and it's growing heavy."

Replaying the tape in his mind once again, Nick sat and watched the sun begin to sink into the sea. Startled, he heard it before he saw it. Having lived on the island for so long, he knew every species of bird that made Maui its home. There were mynahs, cardinals, majiros, cat birds, pheasants, and even golden plover, just to name a few, but never, absolutely never, had he seen a pure white dove before. He turned around quickly because the unique fluttering of its wings sounded so different as it landed nearby. And there it was, a living, breathing, universal symbol of peace. To Nick's astonishment it ambled across the soil directly toward him and stopped only a meter away. Without hesitation the soft and beautiful bird calmly nestled down at Nick's side and cocked its head to look up at him. Nick's jaw dropped. He could only stare, dumbfounded, at the exquisite creature that had just literally appeared out of thin air. Suddenly he felt the warmth in his heart. It grew and it spread throughout his body and it flushed his face in the golden sunlight. When his chicken skin finally faded, a blanket of tranquility enfolded him. Then Nick and the dove slowly turned and gazed contentedly out at the horizon, to a different place and time, together.

THE END

STUART NICHOLLS

EPILOGUE

The fairy-tale love affair between Hang and Nick continued for twenty-one years, with many travels to the U.S. mainland, Asia, and Europe. At home, each day began with coffee, breathtaking vistas, and feeding the white dove "Birdie" by hand. They worked their carnation farm in blissful harmony. Sunsets were spent with glasses of red wine and Nick serenading Hang on his guitar.

He began writing his memoirs in the hopes that their story would be inspirational to others seeking inner peace and happiness. Hang would help by correcting his poor grammar and sharing her feelings about their many adventures.

From the beginning, Nick's goal was to learn acceptance, forgiveness, and unconditional love. Though he traveled far and wide, seeking to learn these lessons, he needed to look no further than the angelic Hang who, by her example, lived those qualities everyday.

The ex-point man continued to cut a trail through paradise, exposing and avoiding the pitfalls of life that were potential threats. Nick was obsessed with creating and maintaining a perfect life, and he acknowledged that he was overly protective of his "Little Minh." But in the end, there was something that he could not shield her from. Tragically, just as Nick began writing the final chapter, God took over and wrote it for him. Hang died suddenly of a massive stroke with no warning on May 10, 2012, at the age of 59.

Many of us travel Thunder Road, whether it be in Tennessee, Vietnam, or somewhere between our ears. Its path may be fraught with booby traps, mines, ambushes, or full-on battles. But there are also detours, intersections, and shoulders upon which we may lay down our heads and cry... or make a stand and fight. It might take us deep into hell, or it can bring us home... if we let it.

GLOSSARY

'Aina	Hawaiian word for "land"
AK-47	Automatic assault-rifle used by the North Vietnamese Army and Viet Cong
AIT	Advanced Infantry Training
AO	Area of Operation
ARVN	Army of the Republic of Vietnam – South Vietnamese Army (U.S. ally)
Ba Muoi Ba	Vietnamese for 33- Beer brand name
Big Red One	Describes the insignia for the First Infantry Division
BEQ	Bachelor Enlisted Quarters
BOQ	Bachelor Officer Quarters
Chicken Skin	Hawaiian slang for "goose bumps"
Con Lai	Vietnamese for "child of mixed race"
CP	Command Post
DEROS	Date Eligible for Return from Overseas – end of a GIs tour of duty
Dinky Dau	Dien Cai Dau – Vietnamese for "crazy"
DMZ	Demilitarized Zone
FNG	Fucking New Guy
HCMC	Ho Chi Minh City – New name for Saigon after April 30, 1975
Huu Nghi	Vietnamese for "friendship"
Hoa Binh	Vietnamese for "peace"
IOM	International Organization for Migration – A United Nations agency
Iron Triangle	Viet Cong stronghold between Ben Cat, Ben Suc and Phu Loi (North of Saigon on Highway 13 aka Thunder Road)
IV number	Immigration Voucher number
LT	Lieutenant
LZ	Landing Zone for helicopters during combat assaults
MACV	Military Assistance Command Vietnam
NCOIC	Non-Commissioned Officer in Charge
NDP	Nighttime Defensive Perimeter

NVA	North Vietnamese Army – enemy of the U.S. and ARVN forces
ODP	Orderly Departure Program – another United Nations agency
Pupus	Hawaiian for "appetizers"
PSP	Perforated Steel Plates
REMF	Rear Echelon Mother Fucker – non combat troop
ROK	Republic of Korea
RPG	Rocket Propelled Grenade
RTO	Radio Transmitter Operator
Shaka	Hawaiian hand signal meaning "hang loose"
SOP	Standard Operating Procedure
Strack	Explicitly following military dress code
VVM	Vietnam Veterans of Maui club

Made in the USA
Lexington, KY
27 January 2013